A Race of Devils

a novel

Ken Schultz

Roberts Ross Publishing

A Race of Devils
by Ken Schultz

ISBN: 978-0-9822015-9-6 (paperback)
Library of Congress Control Number: 2010931675

Roberts Ross Publishing
Englewood, Colorado
Los Angeles, California
(877) 700-0616
www.RobertsRossPublishing.com

Book design by NZ Graphics

To my mother's great grandchildren.

ACKNOWLEDGMENTS

First and foremost, I am indebted to the Holy Spirit and His ever-present grace, which revealed itself not only in illuminations of the mind and inspirations of the will but also in the form of family and friends too numerous to thank. Really, it is by divine solicitude alone that this book was written.

My wife, Pat, and my children, Harry and Lynn, emboldened me with their love, as did the hero of my youth, my mom, Catherine Schultz. The same could be said of my first editors and siblings, Cathy Venskus and Amy Milnes, and my cousin, Theresa Foy Digeronimo. I am greatly indebted to all my business partners, especially Dick Monfort and John Alderman, who sustained me during the writing of this book. Professionally, my book coach from Boulder, Max Regan, and my publisher, Dr. Patricia Ross, forced me to tame the wild horse inside my head (to some extent) and are no small reason that the ambition of a lifetime was fulfilled. Finally, I bow to my confessor, Monsignor Peter Quang Nguyen, for leading me to the realization that our only reason for being is to give glory to God.

To those family and friends not specifically mentioned, please accept my undying gratitude; I have been blessed to know you and love you. Again, I thank God for your presence in my life.

Ken Schultz
May 23, 2010

"Beware of false prophets, who come to you in sheep's clothing,
but underneath are ravenous wolves. By their fruits
you will know them."
~ Matthew 7:15-16

"How sharper than a serpent's tooth it is to have
a thankless child."
~ King Lear (Act I, Scene IV)

Part One

Prologue

Monday, July 21, 2042 (9:34 A.M. MDT)
The Byron R. White Federal Courthouse, Denver, CO

The young priest had just finished hearing the confession of one of the female hostages. He was sitting in the gallery of an empty courtroom at the south end of the Tenth Circuit Court building. With her head bowed, she knelt ten feet away saying her penance. While he waited to escort her back to the other end of the building, he studied the lofty ceiling and noticed that, on the frieze high above the judge's bench, was an inscription: "Reason is the soul of all law." The irony was inescapable. *And folly is the soul of all anarchy,* he thought.

The seizure of the courthouse by Deacon Carroll and his rebel band—among them, the priest—was now in its twelfth day. The Carrollites were trying to force an emergency Supreme Court ruling in an "uplifted animal" case scheduled to be heard that fall. It involved the extension of full legal rights to a hairless chimp called Arthur that had been engineered with near-human intelligence, an evolution of the law, both civil and natural, that Christians fiercely opposed. The priest committed himself to the courthouse seizure— soon to be tagged *The Deacon Carroll Affair*—on the condition that it would be an act of *peaceful* disobedience. Sadly, until it started, he was oblivious to the Deacon's plan to use deadly force and take hostages.

After the woman finished her prayers, he took a minute to get acquainted with her. "You recited the Act of Contrition flawlessly," he said. "I take it you went to Catholic school?"

"Yes," she replied, sitting down beside him. "All my life." With a grin, she added, "You could say that I had God beaten into me."

"Me, too!" the husky cleric laughed.

Since a Catholic education makes storytellers of all, she told him how she climbed onto a window sill in the fourth grade and threatened to jump out if the teacher didn't stop saying that, unless she stopped talking in class, she was going to hell.

The priest countered with one of his own. "We had an algebra teacher, an old nun," he said. "Mostly blind and hard of hearing. The kids called her Twinkie." He shook his head in disgust. "I think back to what a beautiful person she was, but we were so rotten. Every time she'd write an equation on the blackboard, we'd inch our desks forward until, half way through the class, she'd turn around to find us right on top of her. Then, we'd reverse field and slide in the opposite direction. By the time the bell sounded, we'd all be bunched up in the back of the room thirty feet away."

The woman laughed. "She never caught on?"

"Oh, she knew. But what could she do? Everyone was in on it!" Sheepishly, he said, "No wonder I stunk at math."

She said, "We didn't have any nuns in our school, but I had a biology teacher. Boy, was he lame! One day we put poison ivy in his—"

There was a muffled pop, far off.

Then, another one, this time closer.

Then a hundred at once.

The moment the priest dreaded had come.

His first thought was to assemble the rest of the hostages and get them up to the third floor, as was the plan. However, when he and the woman ran into the hallway, one of the Deacon's men, the one guarding the 18th Street entrance, pointed to a spiral staircase straight ahead and hollered, "Get upstairs. *Now!*"

There wasn't time to argue. Like rolls on a snare drum, a loud fusillade of automatic weapons fire peppered the building from every direction. Windows shattered in a hail of bullets near the front entrance. The priest thought: *I hope the others stick to the plan and get upstairs.*

Grabbing his penitent's trembling hand, he coaxed her toward the staircase. She was almost too petrified to move, and they only made it to the landing between the second and third floors when a figure appeared from above—an American Ranger, dressed in black. He said nothing as he lowered his weapon. The priest threw up his hands. When he did, the woman broke and ran. A single, reverberating shot knocked her headlong onto the landing. The priest went to help her, but it was too late. Within seconds, she died in his arms, her face frozen in fear.

The Ranger stepped menacingly toward him on the stairs, but before he could fire again, more soldiers came flooding down. One of them slipped in the blood accumulating on the landing, straining his back. "Keep moving!" the shooter yelled. Then he shouldered his M-19 and knelt as if to assist his victim. Horrified, the priest stared into the man's pale, lupine eyes as the soldiers bounded past.

* * * * *

The priest was Reverend Peter Bernard, S.J. The woman was a widowed legal secretary named Rita Scanlon. The soldier who shot her was the commander of the Ranger battalion sent to retake the courthouse and wrest the nearly two dozen hostages from the grasp of Deacon Carroll: Colonel Anson Collier.

It took the soldiers less than ten minutes to complete the recovery operation. All the surviving rebels were herded into the same courtroom on the first floor where Mrs. Scanlon made her last confession. One by one, over the course of an hour, they were dragged off until Father Bernard was the only one left.

An officer wearing the star of a brigadier entered. He stood imperiously over the kneeling priest, hands on his hips. A dozen of his men looked on.

"Not exactly the place you'd expect to find a holy joe," he quipped.

Bernard raised his head, but made no reply. There were tears in his lucid brown eyes.

In a loud voice, the general continued, "It may interest you to know that the Deacon is dead. I guess that leaves you to answer for this fiasco."

Again, there was no response. Bernard just lowered his head.

Circling around him, the officer took his measure. He knew from the intelligence photo that Bernard was black, but his size was striking. Even on his knees, with his hands pinned behind him, he looked huge—six-eight, maybe three hundred pounds. He had the features of a Shakespearean actor or a Nubian prince. He certainly didn't look like a priest, especially with his clerics soaked in blood. Even his collar was smeared red.

His curiosity satisfied, the officer turned to the guards and said, "All right, they're ready. Let's get him out of here."

They detached the clip that bound Bernard's hands and feet in back and reconnected it in front. Standing him up, they marched him down the hall over crunching glass. When they emerged from the courthouse into the morning sun, a throng of reporters and curiosity seekers were waiting.

The scene exploded in a torrent of questions and whirring cameras. But the voices of the reporters were quickly drowned out by the curses and insults showered on the big priest by the crowd.

"What's the matter, Father? You were expecting a few altar boys?"

"They'll turn you out in stir, bitch!"

Although the guards labored to shield him, Father Bernard was jostled as he passed though the huge, Ionic columns and descended the marble steps toward a police van parked on the sidewalk.

Suddenly, a man burst through the cordon. He struck the big priest with a rock and opened a nasty cut above his ear. The soldiers quickly subdued the attacker, pushed the bleeding prisoner into the van and slammed the door.

Among the many eyes glaring in at him as the marshals prepared to depart were those of Sonny Collier, the man who shot Mrs. Scanlon in the stairwell. These were eyes, as the Russians say, "with teeth," and the memory of them haunted the Jesuit to the end of his days.

One

Saturday, July 2, 2061 (10:26 P.M. EDT)
New York, New York

"Harbor command, this is Unit Six, over."

From the Coast Guard station at Fort Wadsworth, the dispatcher answered, "Copy, Unit Six."

The pilot hollered, "We got a cowboy down in the channel. Speed in excess of thirty knots. Over."

"Roger, Unit Six. Maintain air surveillance. Surface units responding."

Minutes before, a sleek, black hovercraft had charged out of the Arthur Kill into the Ambrose Channel. Gliding over the water's sparkling surface, the big Wavejammer veered through a hodgepodge of ships and boats gathered in New York Harbor for a much-ballyhooed *Age of Sail* celebration. Tracing the same course that Verrazano took centuries earlier, it wasn't long before the boat reached the storied bridge that bore his name.

The Coast Guard gave chase from stations on Sandy Hook and Staten Island. But the launch accelerated to forty knots and moved swiftly into the Upper Bay before the cutters could intercept it.

The chase threatened to ruin a tightly-coordinated July Fourth extravaganza that would go down as the most memorable ever in the metropolitan area. During the day, the tall ships had paraded through the harbor, among them the recently overhauled *Constitution*, on active duty again for the first time since 2016. Toward evening, the stealth frigate *William J. Clinton* emerged from the terminal at Port Johnson and made a short run past Bay Ridge while fifteen, unmanned War Eagles buzzed around it like a flock of deadly gulls. Later, it anchored just south of Governors Island. Now, millions of revelers bobbing in boats or crowding the shoreline watched the dramatic climax of the day's festivities on a dark and cloudless sky.

The advertisements proclaimed:

"PYRO-LASERS: The Hottest Show Since God Divided the Dark!"

The soundtrack to this electrifying display, *The 1812 Overture*, thundered across the water in synchronous precision with the fireworks and images flashing in the sky. This night, however, the normally vivid images were marred by a steady wind, and many of those trying to watch the show found the added distraction of the pursuit helicopters to be more of a nuisance than the hovercraft.

Unit Six reported, "Harbor command, he cut his engines in mid-channel."

Rotating slowly to starboard, the Wavejammer descended to the surface in a blast of cool, salted mist. Nine hundred yards aft, Lady Liberty proudly thrust her new methane-fired torch into the night. At its mooring on Ellis Island, Old Ironsides dozed gently. Lording over all, at the confluence of the Hudson and East Rivers, stood the luminous towers of lower Manhattan.

The near-deafening fireworks drowned out the shouts of protest coming from the ragtag flotilla lining the channel, but the crew of the skiff ignored them. Clothed fully in black, in a nimble, no-nonsense manner that smacked of a pit crew at Indy, they busied themselves with what looked like the boat's fusion-mite engine. Whatever they were doing, their drill was so tightly orchestrated that the useless shouting soon died down. The onlookers grew curious.

Could these people be connected with the show?

As the Coast Guard cutters drew alongside the mysterious intruders, the eyes of most people were returning to the skies. Whatever the Wavejammer's role, it couldn't compare with the spellbinding sights and sounds that were bombarding the senses from on-high and from every point on the compass.

Simulated artillery shots boomed across the water from Craven Point and Battery Park. Peeling church bells rang out from transmitters on both Liberty and Governors Island. Suddenly, as *Opus 49* reached a crescendo, each of the three Wavejammer crewmen turned from their labors, bowed their heads, and, in an Olympian salute, raised a fisted right arm at the Guardsmen who were boarding their vessel. Seconds later, the thermonuclear device secured to the deck of their boat exploded.

* * * * *

The ensuing furnace of heat and light replicated, in miniature, the awesome power that divided light from dark at the universal dawn.

A blinding fireball—a tiny sun—ten thousand degrees and traveling at the speed of light, ignited flammable structures in every direction for ten miles. Then, shock waves, emanating from ground zero at supersonic speed, flattened skyscrapers, buildings, and other structures over half that distance. Forty-foot tidal waves swamped the low-lying areas. Showers of boiling rain, radiated soil, burning cinders, and hot ash soon began to fall. Another thousand fires were ignited by broken gas pipes, downed transmission lines, and exploded refineries.

Almost nothing within two or three miles was spared the violent energy of the star born that night. Battery Park, Wall Street, the Brooklyn Bridge, Red Hook, and Bayonne were all devastated. With them, museums, courthouses, shipyards, playgrounds, and office buildings. Cars, aircraft, ferries, homes. Men, women, children, and pets. Everything. The atoms that once comprised lower Manhattan,

Brooklyn, and northern New Jersey—those bustling temples to the human spirit—were soon drifting out to sea in a gritty, brown cloud that rose to twenty-five thousand feet.

Depending on local terrain and construction quality, the bomb laid waste, in seemingly random fashion, to many of the cities and towns within eight miles of ground zero. The shock waves pulverized all but the most rugged structures. Those barbequing, swimming, lighting firecrackers, sitting in traffic, drinking beer, watching concerts, and chasing fireflies died instantly from the heat flash or got severely burned. Many others were blinded by the intense light.

Outside eight miles, in cities like Babylon, Paterson, and Asbury Park, the damage and death were also extensive. Many of those living in these areas who were not killed, burned, or blinded were hightailing it to safety. Even in areas a hundred miles removed, where there was not much damage or loss of life, chaos reigned. Airplanes crashed, either from crews being flash-blinded or from the awesome wind shear. Cars and trucks were strewn like confetti about the streets and highways by the electromagnetic pulse. Flooding caused by the tidal surge was extensive in the salt marshes along the coast, and thousands living on the adjacent lowlands drowned as a result. A hot, choking ash snowed down on the unfortunate survivors, and the gagging smell of burned flesh permeated the air. Panicked refugees fleeing into and out of these regions soon became party to the kind of human disaster more commonly seen in places like Somalia, Cambodia and the Punjab.

So it was that the thread which suspended the sword of Damocles over the United States was cut at the foot of Freedom's shrine.

Two

As pyro-lasers were flashing above New York, four men and a woman sat around a campfire on the banks of the Blackfoot River. The Nez Perce had once led Meriwether Lewis to this place on his journey home, calling it "the road to the buffalo." These were the waters that haunted Norman Maclean. The campsite was on the Bennett spread near the Scapegoat Wilderness, below the town of Lincoln.

The bulls and browns were hungry that day, so the whole party was tired, happy and no less hungry than the trout, which were served, pan-fried, with red potatoes and sourdough dumplings, as the sun retired. After everyone had their fill, the fire was stoked, the whiskey was poured, and the oldest man, tall and angular, started telling war stories. *His* war stories.

The third one drew the most interest. "It got Hollywood fast," he recounted, knocking the ash from his cigar against a log protruding from the fire. "The crazy bastards were everywhere. Martinez and Crowder were wounded and Irish was bleeding to death. Sixty of us were still holding them off on the perimeter, while the corpsman worked on Irish."

He paused for a second, saying plaintively, "I can still hear the boy's screams to this day." Then, even more somberly, he added, "Five men, including three officers, were dead."

The old man was James Freeman, the former President of the United States. With the exception of the outfitter, Miles Garvin, the rest of his listeners had heard the story before. But, that night, the firelight, the pine scent, and the sound of the river combined to give it added potency.

"I remember thinking how important it was to not be taken alive," he said, in a voice as clear and forceful as the river. "Hundreds of times, in the days leading up to the capture of de LaSalle, the media ran that tape of the twenty-two Marines buried alive outside Port-au-Prince. You know—the one with the rebels shoveling dirt into the faces of all the soldiers tied together in a ditch?"

Garvin nodded eagerly.

"Well, the nonstop coverage turned de LaSalle's men rabid. To them, it was a vindication of their methods. We knew if we were taken alive, there'd be no exchange of prisoners. Most likely, they'd hack us to pieces like the Afghani or the Chiricahua used to."

Lena Walker smiled at Garvin's fascination. No matter how many times the General told it, she never tired of hearing about her father's exploits during the West Indian Revolt of 2035. He was a lieutenant colonel then, the leader of an airborne unit sent to Haiti to capture the rebel leader Auguste de LaSalle. The mission was successful but proved more dangerous than anticipated.

"For twelve hours, we beat back their attempts to rescue him." The clenched fist of the avuncular Freeman gave some hint to the level of desperation. "Sometimes, the fighting was hand-to-hand."

Lena noted that he omitted the part where he saved the life of "Irish" by dragging him to safety under heavy fire from where he lay wounded in mid-block. This bit of heroics, which earned Freeman the Silver Star, was a staple. But the little flourish about the Afghani and the Chiricahuas was a first.

He must have picked that up at the last reunion, she thought.

That his story mesmerized Miles Garvin was understandable.

It was a one of her father's best yarns. But tonight he was really bringing it.

"The men were advised to consider the alternative to capture. Again, we weren't going to surrender. Not that day. Not ever."

An ember popped and landed on Garvin's boot. He fanned it away quickly, then returned his eyes to the General.

"By dawn, our ammunition was so low we fired in single shots. As the last of it was distributed, we heard the sound of the choppers. In fifteen minutes, we were headed home with de LaSalle and six of his henchmen. The death count was five hundred Haitians. Estimates had the wounded at twice that number. Out of the four platoons we sent in, only the five men I mentioned were killed. All of our wounded survived, including Irish."

The wide-eyed Garvin asked, "What happened to de LaSalle?"

"Oh, he was convicted of crimes against humanity at the Hague."

With a flourish, the old man added, "It's funny—his men called him 'El Avispas.' 'The Wasp.' Well, he was so scared that he wet his pants on the way back to Gitmo." He shook his head deliberately. "That ended the rebellion. Since then, Haiti's been at peace."

This the old man said with a sigh. Then, slapping his knees with his hands, he rose stiffly to his feet. He stretched out his arms, yawning, then throwing a glance in the direction of his daughter, he winked.

She got up and gave him a hug. Affectionately, she said, "Goodnight, Teddy. Reveille at 0600."

The gaze of Miles Garvin was still riveted on him. It wasn't every day that a man from Missoula was regaled with war stories by a former President of the United States!

He was charmed for the same reasons as most of his countrymen. To start with, there was Freeman's physical stature. Miles figured he was six-three and more than two hundred pounds. Just as impressive were his features: the coat-hanger shoulders, muscular build, swarthy complexion, and sonorous voice. He had the look of an outdoorsman that belied his age. Only his silver hair, shuffling gait, and early bedtimes gave any hint of his seventy-two years. Because of his soldierly bearing, people seemed predisposed to accept his authority, and there was a time not too long ago when he was the most commanding figure on the planet.

But self-assurance wasn't this man's most endearing trait. What people loved most about him was his physical courage. It was legendary. And infectious. Normally, when a group of Easterners ventured into western Montana, it was Gavin's job to put *them* at ease. Tonight, in the presence of The Lion, it was he who felt safe, not only from the vagaries of the wilderness but of the planet itself.

* * * * *

The sound of Freeman's snoring, combined with the rushing wind and water, soon produced a weird harmony of man and nature.

Although it was getting late, Miles Garvin decided to drive up to Lincoln for some supplies he needed. Bob Fisher, the lead man in the ex-President's Secret Service detail, was scouting the perimeter of the camp. Lena stayed by the fire to talk with Jack Clancey, Freeman's former press secretary. Clancey poked the fire with a stick, while Lena poured them some coffee.

"I haven't seen him that fired up in a long time," she said, shaking her head.

"No, he gets crabbier every time I call," Clancey muttered, stabbing at the fire a bit more forcefully.

She waved her hand, saying, "Well, he *hates* retirement. And he's never—"

Whatever she wanted to say wasn't coming easily. Her eyes seemed fixated on the treetops.

"—he's never really come to grips with what happened."

"The Bird Watch?"

She nodded ruefully. "He knows he blew it."

With the surety of an eyewitness, Clancey recalled, "No, all he had to do was keep his pants zipped, and he would have smoked Gonzales in the primaries."

Lena handed him a black coffee in a white, metal cup, saying, "He changed so much after my mother died. Not to me, of course, but . . . oh, what's the difference?"

The former press secretary studied Lena's face in the light of the fire. The golden aura, reflecting on her dark, European features, gave her a physical allure that induced one to stop and admire. Like her mother, she was slender but not tall, with tomboy hair and hazel eyes. Her face had a graceful symmetry with no flaws to distract the casual admirer. And her smile! Jack considered it her finest asset. Combined with a husky voice and spitfire personality, it made her irresistible. He would have stared longer, but it made him uncomfortable.

"Does he ever talk about it?" he asked.

"Never. How could he? He's too ashamed. Turning the White House into a bordello! Hundreds of reporters lining the fences or perched on the nearby rooftops, tracking the movement of all things female through the North Portico. Women prostituting themselves for a night in his bed. He was such a tomcat!"

Pulling a camp chair over to where Clancey was seated, she added, "And there was certainly no shortage of tabbies."

"A far cry from the days of Calvin Coolidge," Clancey said.

It had happened during Freeman's first and last full term and was triggered by the death of his wife, Sarah. Rather than press his grief with quiet dignity, he embarked on a notorious campaign of sexual conquest. The Lincoln Bedroom became something akin to a hutch at the Chicken Ranch. An amorous romp with Big Jim guaranteed instant notoriety to any budding celebrity or publicity hound, and his nightly escapades soon became grist for the supermarket tabloids, the society pages, and the bloggers. It got so grotesque that, in 2055, at the ripe age of sixty-six, an entertainment magazine voted him "the sexiest man alive."

"What was he thinking?" quizzed Lena.

"Obviously, he wasn't thinking," said Jack, rubbing his forehead. "What a circus that was. I can't believe it took so long for the press to skewer him. But, like Mom used to say, 'no harm done until someone loses an eye.'"

The party hierarchy was outraged by Freeman's antics since his indiscretions left them vulnerable in the upcoming election. It was red meat to the left, but Church groups, women's organizations and school officials were also calling for him to step down. By the time the Iowa caucuses rolled around, the drumbeats thundered loudly to replace him on the ticket with Tito Gonzales. Although his administration scored some notable achievements in the area of public safety and tax reform, it was the unofficial scoring he did on the second floor of the White House that eventually drove him off the ticket.

When he lost the major primaries to Gonzales in February of '56, the media, like the party, finally turned on him. He was quickly given a handle that rhymed with lame duck but was decidedly less flattering.

Clancey threw another shaft of split pine in the fire. Sparks popped and floated sideways. They listened as the wind, and the snoring shook the tents. The chill became more pronounced. The great stars Altair and Vega—the Eagle and the Vulture—were poised to enter the Arctic twilight that spills into the lower forty-eight on summer evenings.

Sipping her coffee, Lena asked, "Has he said anything to you about his health?"

Jack knew better than to soft-pedal a question from a member of the Freeman clan. Physically, Clancey had the hardy traits of the black Irish. His dark, wavy hair, heavy beard, and strong jaw gave the impression of a much taller man. Wiry and fit, he moved with the jaunty assurance of a welterweight. And although he rarely lost control of his emotions, his ready-to-rumble disposition was always close to the surface. One could never be too sure that he wouldn't use his hands to settle a difference of opinion, and that's the way he liked it. But however strong-willed he was, compared to the Freeman alpha, he was a hopeless beta.

He replied, "Last month he said his heart medication isn't really working. His angina's gotten worse."

"I know about that. It's something else. I tried to draw it out of him today, but he wouldn't open up. Something tells me it's serious."

This was the first time Jack and Lena had discussed the General at any length or in any depth, and each was surprised at the transparency of the other.

"What makes you think he—"

Clancey was cut short by Agent Fisher, who burst out from behind the General's tent with a horrified look on his face. He gasped, "A bomb just exploded in New York! The whole city . . . it's gone!"

To Jack and Lena, it was an alarming display for a man so guarded as Fisher.

Clancey looked at him like he was crazy. "What do you mean, gone?"

"It exploded during a fireworks display," stammered the agent. "The bomb, I mean." He took a deep breath, composed himself and said, "The whole area's been devastated. Millions are dead."

Visibly frightened, Lena asked, "Is it war?"

The agent shook his head no. "We're on red-alert. They think it was a terrorist attack."

For five decades, WMD attacks on the United States were regularly predicted, and the probability of one mounted with each passing year. There were two orange alerts during Freeman's presidency, but nothing had happened. Now, the greatest fear of the past twenty presidents had been realized.

"What do we do?" Jack said.

"My orders are to sit tight . . . at least, until I get further orders. Our movements will be restricted anyway." Then, pointing to the surrounding wilderness, Fisher said, "Besides, this may be the safest place in the country right now."

Jack grabbed his teletran off the cooking table and turned it on. The three of them stared in disbelief at the gruesome scenes that were already flashing across the net. A reporter opined, "This is the worst disaster in our nation's history."

With that, Fisher said, "We better wake the General."

Clancey grabbed him by the wrist as he turned to go. "Wait a minute, Bob. We really need to think about this." Looking at Lena, he touched his chest and explained, "His heart. He might react badly."

Had Freeman been a sitting president, it was the agent's duty to notify him immediately of such trouble. However, in the heat of the moment, Fisher couldn't remember if the same was true of a *former* president.

Clancey knew it wouldn't do to keep the news from Freeman for long. Although there were no major crises during his term in office, before he came to power, he earned a reputation for being at his best when things were at their worst. As a soldier, he was said to possess the same "four o'clock courage" that a historian once attributed to Ulysses S. Grant. That is, you could wake him at four in the morning and tell him the enemy was turning his flank, and he would remain completely composed. However, Clancey honestly feared that the strain on the old man's heart might be too much.

While Fisher moved away to take a call from the Billings field office, Clancey and Lena stood by the fire watching the teletran with morbid fascination as the scenes of panic and devastation multiplied. Gently, Lena asked him, "Are your parents still in New Jersey?"

"No, they're down in Florida."

He punched up their number, but the circuits were all busy.

The network's probably fried, he thought. Then, he suggested, "Maybe you should wake your father, Lena. That way we can—"

Before he could finish, the tent flap whipped open. Out stumbled Freeman. Though rumpled and drowsy, he had sensed something was wrong.

Fisher told him about the bomb. He only nodded, then went over and put his arm around his daughter. When she lifted her eyes to him, he pulled her tight. Clancey handed him the teletran.

The old man watched for a few minutes. His determined expression never changed until he heard the words, "*Millions feared dead or wounded,*" at which he shook his head in disbelief.

Turning to Fisher, he queried, "What're your people telling you?"

"It's bad, sir. It was a big bomb. Two to five megatons."

"Terrorists?"

"That's what they think, but no one is sure."

"What about us? What do we do?"

"All air and space traffic has been grounded, so we're not going anywhere."

Freemen thought for a second while he surveyed the camp. The absence of anger in him was telling; he was as cool as a stone at the bottom of a river.

"The real danger now is from a follow-on attack," he said. "Maybe chemical or biological. Remember what happened in Jerusalem?"

His reference was to the 2045 attack on Jerusalem that triggered the War of Retribution. A medium-yield bomb was exploded near the Wailing Wall, and within days, ricin gas was released in Tel Aviv and Haifa. This second attack was only minimally effective, but had it been executed properly, it would have been a mortal blow to the State of Israel.

"Where's Miles?"

Fisher answered, "He went up to Lincoln. He'll be back soon."

"Bob, I have to get back to Washington. Can you arrange it?"

"Sir, I'll try, but my orders are to—"

He raised his index finger to indicate that a call was coming in. "Minuteman One?"

After a moment, his eyes widened and he said, "It's for you, sir. Air Force One. *The President.*"

Freeman grabbed his headset.

"Tito!" he shouted.

"Hello, Jim. I suppose you've heard?"

"Yeah, but the details are sketchy."

"It's unbelievable, Jim. I'll brief you later, though. Right now, I have a question for you. It's my intention to invoke war powers and declare martial law in that area. I need someone I can trust to take command. Will you do it?"

Only one answer could be expected.

"Sir, it'd be an honor."

"Thanks, Jim. I had a feeling you'd say that. I have an order in hand restoring you to your former rank. There'll be some carping over in Hell's Bottom, but I'll handle that. I'm making arrangements to have you meet me wherever I am in the morning—West Virginia or Shreveport. I really don't know how long I'll be up here, yet."

Then, as an afterthought, he added, "I know this isn't how you planned to spend your retirement, Jim, but I need you. I'm sending a plane to get you. When you get on board, I'll have someone there to brief you."

"Thank you, sir. May I ask where we should meet it?"

"I'm not sure. Where are you?"

"East of Missoula."

"Then I'll have them meet you there. We'll communicate the final arrangements through the Secret Service."

The President paused momentarily, then said, "I have to go, Jim. Thanks again. *Godspeed.*"

"Thank you, sir, I want you to—"

The transmission ended before he could finish.

Godspeed? Such a blessing was wasted on Freeman. *If there is a God*, he thought, *why is it that, just when his love and mercy are most suspect, people start showering him with praise and thanks*? In his mind, God, if he did exist, was a cruel and arbitrary tyrant. Any earthly ruler of similar bent, still in possession of his head, would certainly deserve his contempt, not his worship.

Coincidently, Lena's thoughts were fixed on the same object. The presidential summons reminded her of an old barracks saw: *No one loves God or soldiers until they need them.*

In the darkening sky, the Eagle and the Vulture continued their ascent.

Three

Saturday, July 2 (10:28 P.M. EDT)
Upper Darby, Pennsylvania

From a steeper angle, these stars also cast their light on Peter Bernard—at least, on the roof of the restaurant off the West Chester Pike where he stopped to eat on his way to Baltimore.

Seated in the bar area at an elevated table, he was halfway into a meatloaf sandwich, thinking about how much better it was than the oily, green-and-gold variety they served in prison, when he drew a long hair out of it with his teeth. As he turned in disgust to signal the waitress, on the wall in front of him, the initial reports of the bombing burst onto the VuScreen. Between these odious events, his appetite disappeared. All he could do was sip his coffee as the barrage of frenetic news stories—and the queasy feeling in his stomach—got worse.

There were only a handful of people in the bar, and nothing that was said was said privately. The bartender, a fat man with black, horn-rimmed glasses, who seemed to be lost in amazement as he turned up the sound, surmised, "It must have been like this during *The War of the Worlds.*"

A white-whiskered coot at the end of the bar shot back, "I tell ya, it's the goddamn Chinese!"

Peter ignored them. *Prison chatter,* he thought.

Ten days prior, he had been released from the super-max federal penitentiary in Ellison, Colorado where he'd done a five-year bit. It had nothing to do with the two years he got for his involvement with Deacon Carroll. This more recent conviction was on a charge of sedition—inciting rebellion against the state—that sprang from the notorious Spark-Park Bombing in 2055.

The bombing occurred at a baby factory owned by the Neugenesis Corporation in Phoenix that produced genetically-engineered babies to customer specification. Bernard organized a peaceful protest against the company, and for three hours the demonstration proceeded without incident. Then a bomb exploded inside the building, killing twenty-three people, including two cops.

The priest was charged with a host of crimes, but there was no tangible evidence connecting him to the blast. So the Justice Department manufactured a charge of sedition against him—a tactic recently resurrected from America's colonial days. The prosecution was led by the woman now serving as the Attorney General of the United States, Angela DeKalb. She saw to it personally that the "Crimson Collar," as pundits commonly referred to Bernard, was duly punished, if not for his actions, then for his beliefs.

Sitting in the diner that evening, with his doctorate in American history and a fistful of parole papers, the priest had a better appreciation than most for how the New York bombing would affect the country. Undoubtedly, it would further erode the government's commitment to maintaining a balance between personal liberty and public safety and lead to even more draconian security measures than those that led to his show trial five years before.

Footage of a gigantic wave hitting an amusement pier appeared on the VuScreen. Only then did it occur to Peter that his family back in New Jersey might be in harm's way. Anxiously, he tried calling them—several times, without success.

"All circuits are currently busy."

Since his parents were dead, Diane and Phil Armstrong were all Peter had in the way of immediate family. His father died when he was an infant and his mother just before he entered college. Diane was his sister, whom he had introduced to Phil, his old college roommate, at the St. Patrick's Day parade in New York one year. Phil was a moderately wealthy stock trader who owned a summer home in Seaside Park. That's where, in an early summer idle, Peter had celebrated his return to "life on the bricks." Now the priest was on his way down to Baltimore to meet with his new superior and, although he had never mastered the nuances of an air-drive vehicle, Phil lent him his new Avatar for the trip. Needless to say, he was well-served on the initial leg of the journey by the car's intuitive, anti-collision system.

"*I'm standing on the New Jersey ramp to the Ben Franklin Bridge*," a newswoman reported. "*As you can see the traffic is already at a standstill, and the tollbooths aren't even open. The bridge authorities have informed us that the worst is yet to come. Already the parks in Center City are teeming with refugees.*"

These were troubling scenes for a man trained to look for God in all things. But then it occurred to him: *Maybe it's him who's looking for me!*

The waitress came to refill his coffee. "How far is it back to the bridge?" he asked, pointing at the television.

Without looking at him or the screen, she replied curtly, "About three miles." It was obvious she didn't want to be there as she angrily punched the particulars of his meal into her Checkmate, printed out a receipt and moved on.

Peter looked out the front window to assess the traffic situation on the Pike. It wasn't very congested, yet. Having just spent the day sightseeing in downtown Philadelphia, he now contemplated a return.

Although this decision might have seemed quirky to some, it wouldn't have surprised anyone who really knew him. He had a reputation for quirkiness. Back in his university days, he rarely matched his socks, had a penchant for white shoes, and smothered most of his food in fried onions and mustard. Once, he wore the same white shirt for an entire week, as evidenced by the ink stain on the pocket. One year, before spring break, he dumped an entire bag of dog chow on his back porch and left the sliding glass door wide-open so his schnauzer could eat while he was gone. That was the year he stranded Phil Armstrong in Fort Lauderdale for two days. Although, with age, his idiosyncrasies became less pronounced, he was still anything but boring. And what remained of these peculiarities after he became a Jesuit measured poorly this man who had devoted his life to the service of God and country.

* * * * *

If the essence of a person can be distilled into one adjective, the best fit for Peter Bernard was "high-minded." From an early age, he had been fascinated with American history and, as an African-American scholar, on the residual impact of slavery after the Civil War. He wrote his doctoral thesis at Notre Dame on the country's first brush with terrorism, the Ku Klux Klan. Two years later, in 2038, he became a Professed Priest of the Society of Jesus, eagerly serving the second year of his novitiate in the slums of Kingston, Jamaica, succoring the poor, sick and dying with the Missionaries of Charity. Three years later, he volunteered to join in the relief of earthquake-ravaged San Bernardino. Despite these pastoral and humanitarian efforts, however—and true to his formation as a Jesuit—the Reverend Doctor Bernard was always more soldier than shepherd, more Jeremiah than John. His love for God, and his fellow man, was always more grounded in the mind than the heart.

It was his native idealism that gave rise to Father Bernard's crusade against the commercial eugenics industry. While teaching at Loyola University, he came to regard this business—a loosely-regulated and exceedingly-popular method of sexless, on-demand, laboratory conception—as an evil akin to slavery and abortion. After his ordination, he began writing a series of essays in defense of God's creative monopoly. These gradually gained the attention and acclaim of the Church hierarchy. Even the Holy Father had commended his work,

dubbing him, "the Pen Writing in the Wilderness." The leaders of
other faiths—the Evangelicals, in particular—joined not only his
fight against the eugenics complex but also his forays against the
de-Christianization efforts of the Humanist elite.

Not even the prison term he served for his involvement with
Deacon Carroll could deter him. On his release, Bernard intensified
his attacks on the bio-engineers and began taking them to the streets.
Prior to that time, the abominations of these gene-splicers were
invariably met by the authorities with a wink and a nod, but the
protests he led to stop the reckless manufacture—and attendant
scrapping—of "designer babies" eventually led to greater oversight
of the industry, however feeble it proved to be. Since the rapid growth
of commercial eugenics was due largely to the legal protections afforded
to it by the Humanists—both in government and out—Bernard's
attacks against them became more frequent and intense.

Mounting a frontal assault on "the invisible hand of Humanism"
was, to say the least, a daunting task though. The power and influence
of these crafty puppet-masters far exceeded their numbers, and their
victory in the hundred year struggle with Christianity for the heart
and soul of America was virtually assured. Indeed, the Christian lines
had shrunk to the point of near-collapse; to Peter Bernard, that only
made them more defensible. Tirelessly, he prayed and worked for a
reversal of fortunes, holding to the tenets of his faith and modeling
his protests on the nonviolent tactics of Martin Luther King. And
just as Dr. King's activities won for him the undying hatred of the
white supremacists, Bernard's won the contempt of the secular
Humanists.

Two years before his conviction in the Spark Park Bombing, in a
scholarly, Catholic journal, he wrote a much-celebrated article, "The
Tarring and Feathering of God," in which he argued:

> Since the middle of the last century, the government, especially
> the court system, has been removing the ethical laces in the

nation's shoes. In one decision after another, in the name of "privacy rights," a person's inalienable right to the pursuit of happiness, however sordid or debauched, has been upheld. At the same time, the Creator of that inalienable right has been tarred and feathered and run out of town on a rail . . . As a consequence, instead of ensuring the separation of church and state, a union of the two has been formed, a union in which atheistic humanism has been declared the de facto *religion of the state.*

Further on, he explained:

The base stock of all culture—that stew of politics, law, science, education, art, entertainment, business, media, charities, and family—is religious belief. In America, for more than three hundred years, that belief and, thus, the culture, were flavored by Christianity. At one time, our country could rightfully have been called the King James version of democracy.

But, during the twentieth century, a neo-Pagan cult emerged in Europe and America whose high priests and priestesses declared God dead and elevated man (in the words of Protagoras) to "the measure of all things." The votaries of this long-gathering revival of Greek humanism—that began during the Renaissance and led to the Enlightenment—quickly installed Reason on heaven's empty throne. "They exchanged the truth of God for a lie and revered and worshiped the creature rather than the creator." *(Romans 1:25).*

At the end of the article, he described the looming danger to mankind:

Almost unseen, the Humanists have imposed on the West a "dictatorship of relativism." They have indoctrinated us with the foolish but popular notion that there are no objective, moral truths. This deceit was succinctly summarized by George Bernard Shaw: "The golden rule is that there is no golden rule." *A hippie might add, "If it feels good, do it!" However, Truth, like nature, abhors a vacuum, and Order demands that someone define it.*

So, imagine this scenario. A faction emerges from the black hole of relativism that is intent on providing the definition, a totalitarian bloc whose will to power (to borrow from Nietzsche) is unstoppable and triumphant. These Overmen may even be genetically-programmed to that end. On seizing power, they usher in a dictatorship that makes the rule of the Humanists seem quaint. Gradually, they manipulate the definitions of Truth and Justice and Goodness and Beauty—those given to us by God in nature and in Revelation—to serve their demonic purposes. Then, like Kurtz, the Utopian-turned-despot in Conrad's tale, they lure us deeper and deeper into the heart of darkness until the day finally comes when the same verdict is leveled on us that he leveled on the savages he was sent to save: "Exterminate the brutes."

Americans once held to the belief that God's Word is the truth and that the truth sets us free. But the Humanists contend that, "God is dead." If he is, the inescapable conclusion is that so is the truth and with it freedom and, quite possibly, humanity itself.

Naturally, the Humanists, dominant in government and in every other social institution, were incensed by this article and, in response, spared nothing to crush him—first, by slander and harassment, then, by engineering his conviction in the Spark-Park Bombing. Their vicious *ad hominem* attacks continued long after the door to his cell slammed shut. He served his sentence in a facility, Ellison, where a sudden death at the hands of racist inmates was a constant threat. All of his appeals were denied and his parole hearings postponed.

That he eventually developed something of a persecution complex was understandable: *he was being persecuted!*

It had the desired effect, too. During the Spark-Park Bombing trial, Bernard declared that "the only thing still liberal about America was its tolerance of child manufacture, sexual deviance, aberrant marriages, capital punishment, unfettered abortion, and stealth euthanasia." Though he only saw conditions worsen while he was at Ellison, all the injustices he suffered finally shattered his innate idealism, leaving him cold and indifferent to the struggle between Christian and Humanist. Now, as he watched the reports of the bombing that evening, the culture war had about as much appeal to him as the thick, lengthy hair he just extracted from his meatloaf sandwich.

* * * * *

His immediate reaction to the bombing was both selfish and not. Five years in prison had left him spiritually withered, and he was painfully aware of it. Only rarely did he say daily Mass anymore, or read from his breviary, and he gave away the last rosary he owned years ago. With an eye to recapturing the joy and fulfillment he experienced during his novitiate, he thought: *Some of those refugees congregating down in Center City will need the services of a priest. It'll be like Kingston or San Bernardino.* In charity, he sought the renewal of hope and with it, faith. *That'll refill my tanks,* he assured himself.

So, with visions of Teresa of Calcutta and Damien of Molokai, he paid his tab, left the restaurant and headed back downtown to give, in the spirit of Ignatius, greater glory to God.

On foot.

Frustrated by his inability to drive his brother-in-law's skittish Avatar, he parked it in the lot behind the restaurant.

Four

Instead of Missoula, General Freeman's party took a chopper from Wolf Creek to Malmstrom AFB where they had been instructed to meet the plane the President was sending.

Lena Walker sat in the jump seat behind the pilots. In a voice inaudible to her, Freeman asked Jack Clancey, "Are you ready to go back to work?"

Looking at his old boss in disbelief, then staring straight ahead, Clancey thought: *Things are moving way too fast!*

But, before he went completely blank, he quickly considered his options. Although he had serious misgivings about going anywhere near New York, two things worked against him. The first was that he was a hopeless adrenaline junkie. The second was that he couldn't refuse the old man. Figuring the safest place to be in the weeks ahead, even in the northeast, would be at Freeman's side, he also calculated it would afford him some leverage in providing for the safety of his parents.

He asked, "If I refuse, how long before you have me taken out and shot?"

"Shortly after we land."

"Then I'm in."

When they boarded the plane, after another quick call from the President, Freeman decided to get some sleep. Jack and Lena sat up watching the calamitous scenes from back east. Then, Clancey's hand-held device went black.

Lena surmised, "They're probably having technical trouble."

"Maybe," said Jack, "but it's more likely that the government shut them down—under the terms of the Tranquility Act."

Lena replied, "Well this is certainly worse than the attack on Los Humanos."

In the first half of the twenty-first century, there had been a running battle between the government and the press concerning the latter's role in matters of national security and public safety. Then, in response to the media's hysterical reaction to the Los Humanos small pox attack, Congress passed the Common Defense and Tranquility Act. Essentially, it prohibited the publication or transmission of any militarily-sensitive or panic-inducing information during times of national emergency.

"That was the most blatant example of yellow journalism since Pulitzer and Hearst," recalled Jack.

"I remember. Some of the stories were just so grisly," said Lena. "I wonder how many fatalities might have been avoided if the Act was in force back then."

"It sure did a job on the right to free speech," Jack said. "The country was ill-served. People were so mad that, once the smallpox epidemic was snuffed out, a lot of them thought that the press should be, too."

"What year was that?"

"2041."

With admiration, Lena said, "More than once I've heard you say the press got what it deserved."

"Well, the problem was—and still is—that the press has no governing code of ethics, no internal oversight. Had it been more discerning in editing its product both during and after the attack, the Act would have died in committee. But, the old saying 'if it bleeds, it leads' took precedence over everything else, including civic duty." He furthered that, "Unfortunately, the news business is like any other—higher motives rarely translate into higher profits."

"Wasn't foreign ownership of news organizations part of the problem, too?"

"Yes, by calling the patriotism of the press into question. At the time of the attack, most Americans already thought of the press as a fifth column—an agent of foreign interests. While we were wrestling with a national catastrophe, our adversaries were gaining valuable intelligence, as well as daily readings into our collective morale, simply by listening to their teletrans. At best, the 'yellow dogs' were giving aid and comfort to the enemy. At worst, their inflammatory reporting during national emergencies was causing a clear and present danger, like shouting 'Fire!' in a movie theater."

Lena was concerned about the difficult assignment her father had taken on, so she changed the subject, asking, "What do you think, Jack? Has Teddy gotten himself into a no-win situation?"

Clancey answered cautiously. "Given his age, it won't be easy. But his experience in Jerusalem will help."

"What about his health?"

From the moment Freeman accepted the President's call to arms, Jack Clancey knew his motivation for doing so transcended mere duty. The old man was determined to restore his tarnished image. And, at his age, he might not get another chance. Most likely, he accepted the commission *because* his health was failing, but Clancey couldn't tell Lena that.

As it turned out, he didn't need to. Before he could answer, she had already made the connection. "He's going out in a blaze of glory, isn't he?"

It wasn't Clancey's habit to discuss the inner workings of Freeman's mind with anyone, especially the man's daughter.

"I don't think it's that," he said, "I think—"

"Oh, Jack, don't patronize me," she shot back, waving her hand in disgust. "Please. You know as well as I do that he's desperate to redeem himself." Earnestly, she turned to him in her seat. "He's all I have, though. This little adventure could cost him his life. It's so absurd! We have to find some way to change his mind, if not for his sake, then for mine."

"Well, if it makes you feel better, I'll do everything in my power to steer things in that direction."

She said with surprise, "Wait a minute . . . what do you mean? Are you going with him?"

"Yes," he replied, craning his neck in frustration over the widening inquiry. "He asked me to handle press matters."

"When was that?"

"On the way to Malmstrom"

Lena fumed. Since the president's call her father hadn't given one thought to *her* needs and safety, although that wasn't out of character for him. Whenever the guns sounded, he marched. These continual desertions were her mother's lifelong lament. Only, this time, he was abandoning *her.* So she decided to do some marching of her own.

"Well, I'm going with you."

Jack fumbled for a response. "There's no way. He'll never agree to it. It's too dangerous. Not with the threat of radiation poisoning." He looked at her tenderly. "As much as you fear losing him, Lena, he has an equal fear of losing you."

"Either way," she said, "the survivor ends up alone."

Five

Convening a meeting of his Cabinet, President Gonzales asked for a moment of silence. As he bowed his head, he was haunted by the gruesome, low-level aerial photos of the carnage he had been examining. A naked, old woman, with skin raw and red. A staggering, hairless dog. A screaming child, burned black, writhing in pain. Liquefied streets and smoking buildings. Tornados of whirling dust and debris. Flaming winds of hurricane strength.

Directly across from the Commander-in-Chief was the empty chair of Vice-President Roberts, who was home in Alabama recovering from back surgery. The chair of the Secretary of Defense, Elliot Thompson, was also empty. He was en route from Hawaii. All others, except for his legal counsel, were present. The staffers, whose ranks were winnowed by vacations and no-shows, sat against the walls.

The President began, "You've all seen footage of the devastation caused by the bomb. I've asked Dick Sloan to brief us in detail. Let me warn you that what you are about to hear is very unsettling."

"Thank you, Mr. President," said the scholarly Sloan, who was serving his first term as National Security Advisor. His appearance was uncharacteristically drawn and haggard. "To begin with, we haven't been able to identify the perpetrators. No one has claimed responsibility for the attack and, in all likelihood, no one will. Our enemies have denied any complicity in it. The threat board at the

Pentagon confirms that no country capable of mounting a nuclear attack has thrown so much as a pebble in our direction. Our forces are deployed at DEFCON TWO, but our guns are trained at everything and nothing. The possibility of a follow-on attack, either chemical or biological, is high."

He caught his breath, then added, "Based on what the Pentagon and the Department of Public Safety have told us, we're almost certain this was an act of terror, but, at this point, all we have is the list of usual suspects. So retaliation is impossible."

Taking a sip of water, he said. "It was a medium-yield bomb. We haven't determined the exact signature, but it was a plutonium device, somewhere in the neighborhood of two or three megatons." His even tone and expressionless mien concealed his anxiety, and everybody in the room knew it. "The blast and its thermal effects were lessened because it was detonated at ground level . . . over water. However, the shock waves and radioactivity generated in a ground-burst are greatly amplified." With down-turned eyes, his voice cracked as he said, "We estimate there could be as many as five million casualties."

Some of his listeners shifted anxiously in their high-backed, leather chairs as he spoke. The rest were too stunned to move. Everyone knew the significance of the word "casualties."

Sloan had taken to the skies with the President on Air Force One minutes after the bombing. Together they had spent the night monitoring incoming reports and planning a response. At about four in the morning, they received clearance to land at the presidential crisis center in West Virginia, where the cabinet was already assembling.

With a look of exhaustion, Sloan leafed through his notes, thus allowing the imperious Jacob Morgan, Secretary of State, to break in.

"Mr. President, production and storage of the materials used to make this kind of bomb were outlawed by treaty fifteen years ago.

The cost of building one from scratch is prohibitive. Doesn't that argue for the involvement of a nation already in possession of one?"

"It may be that a foreign nation sold the bomb, or parts of it, to a domestic terror group, Jacob."

"But, with our detection systems, how was it smuggled into the country?" asked the Secretary of Transportation. "It's inconceivable."

"Not anymore," replied the Commander-in-Chief, glumly.

Dick Sloan jumped back in. "It's impossible to say at this juncture how or where the bomb was procured, but the odds are that a foreign government isn't involved. It may be a loose nuke or a broken arrow—a bomb stolen from our own arsenal. We don't know."

Unwilling to venture anything that might sound foolish or insensitive, the somber Cabinet sat quietly.

Sloan finished his report. "As I mentioned before, the devastation is mind-boggling. The loss of life—"

The words caught in his throat. Even Milton or Dante couldn't adequately describe the hellscape created by the bomb.

Accordingly, the President took over. "Whoever detonated this thing figured it would obliterate or contaminate an unprecedented amount of territory," he said. "Not even the destruction of Jerusalem compares to this. However, there's a chance most of the country will be spared from contamination. The wind's still blowing out of the northwest, so the fallout's being driven out to sea. The long-range forecast is favorable. High pressure over Canada with northwest winds. I need not tell you how critical it is for the wind to continue from that direction. It's also critical that we have good weather for a few days, but I'll let Dick explain why."

After a sip of water, Sloan resumed his analysis. "As soon as the surface winds have calmed, the Air Force will begin spraying a chemical compound called E-Rad in concentric circles around ground zero. For those of you who aren't familiar with it, it's a mixture of inert chemical and biological agents. The active agent is an isotope, Protonium 223. Protonium bonds with the radioactive particles produced by the blast and accelerates their decay. The biological agents consume the residue. Dangerous emissions are thereby reduced. It worked beyond expectations in Jerusalem and, although it won't be of much to help those already exposed, it will eventually cut the level of surface radiation by some 90 percent. Estimates are that an initial scrubbing may only take a few days. A little of this stuff goes a long way."

He stopped to blow his nose and said while he did, "Since the biological agents in E-Rad work best in moist conditions, the importance of rain-making in the coming weeks can't be overstated. In the short term, though, fair weather will allow us to spray around the clock."

Talk turned to restoration of the power grid, the Internet, and satellite communications. Transportation systems needed to be rerouted, particularly bullet trains and air traffic. Water storage and treatment facilities would require special attention to mitigate the impact of continuous runoff, as well as radioactive contamination. Manufacturers of artificial skin, bone marrow, burn salve, cancer drugs, and optical microchips would need government assistance to ramp up production right away.

The President said, "The cost of these actions will put an enormous strain on the Treasury. A financial meltdown is all but certain. The Japanese and Hong Kong markets open tonight and the future's market is already signaling a panic. When the electronic Bourse reopens we should see a sell off in Treasuries and stocks unrivaled in our history." With resignation, he concluded, "A full-blown depression is not only possible but probable. By Tuesday, you may not be able to get twenty bucks from a cash machine."

Each Cabinet member wrestled inwardly with this dizzying array of problems, struggling to assess the impact on his or her area of responsibility. However, all of them were interested in the answer to one question in particular, and the Interior Secretary finally asked it.

"Mr. President, we're all tasked with the responsibility of reacting to problems that arise *beyond* the pale of the explosion, but who'll handle the problems created *within* it?"

"That job will go to the military," explained Gonzales. "At the suggestion of the Attorney General, we've created a special military district to administer the area in question. It'll incorporate all the territory south of—" He stopped, deferring to the Attorney General.

"Maybe it's best to let Angela brief you."

"Certainly, Mr. President."

Angela DeKalb, a forty-six-year-old Serbian beauty with dark, flowing hair, got up and pointed a remote control device at the wall behind her. Instantly, a huge map depicting the northeastern United States appeared. There was a red triangle situated on it.

"The district will look like this," she said calmly, retracing the lines of the triangle with a laser pointer. "The northern boundary will run due east from Binghamton, and continue along the Massachusetts-Connecticut border, then drop south from Newport to Cape Charles, Virginia. From there, it'll run back to Binghamton along the Susquehanna."

She paused to gauge the reaction of the cabinet. There was none, so she continued.

"Everything within these borders will be quarantined. All movement into and out of the cordon will be restricted. The military will be granted jurisdiction over all civilian operations. Formally, it'll be called the Mid-Atlantic Military District. The Atlantic Cordon, for short. Once order is restored, control will be turned back to the state and local authorities."

Turning to the President, the wheezingly fat Jacob Morgan said, "Sir, I hope I'm not being too presumptuous, but who will command this Cordon?"

The President never hesitated. "Those duties will be assumed by Jim Freeman. I signed the order restoring him to four-star rank this morning, and he'll assume the duties of military governor immediately."

The meeting ended soon afterwards. Before he left for Foggy Bottom, Jacob Morgan accosted Dick Sloan. "What's the rationale behind the appointment of Freeman?" he asked.

"Angela said he's the obvious choice. According to her, he strikes a perfect balance between the civilian bureaucracy and the military."

"Has she forgotten how he cheapened the presidency? Hell, everyone knows he was past his prime a decade ago. Defense will be livid."

With some degree of irritation, Sloan replied, "Look, Jacob, regardless of his shortcomings, no one can question his military credentials. And he's still an icon. The President's hoping his appointment will soothe people's fears and inspire some confidence. The move should play well on Main Street. Or whatever's left of it, anyway."

Also irritated, the Secretary of State responded, "Well, I can tell you this: it didn't play with us! It's a mistake, Dick. He may fly into battle with the Valkyries, but in the fish market of politics, he's a pigeon."

Six

Sunday, July 3 (7:14 A.M. EDT)
Presidential Bunker, West Virginia

Soon after the President declared a state of emergency in his address to the nation, following a brief stop in Omaha, the jet carrying James Freeman's party landed in West Virginia.

Before they disembarked, the General told Lena and Jack, "Orders are to make you as comfortable as possible. My meetings could take a few hours. I'll see you afterwards."

It puzzled Jack why he wasn't invited to attend.

From the tarmac, Freeman was whisked into the crisis center. Though his clothes still smelled like pine smoke, during the stop in Omaha, he rested, showered, and shaved, so he looked relatively fresh and alert. By comparison, after ten hours of mind-bending tension, the others in the room appeared tired and disheveled.

Tito Gonzales arrived just before Freeman. As the General shook his hand, he said, "I expected to meet you in Shreveport, sir."

Gonzales explained, "So far the wind's been favorable, Jim. I hope to return to Washington after the meeting."

The President took his place at the head of a conference table shaped like the state of Michigan, only bigger. There were two dozen civilian and military advisors seated around it. He directed Freeman to sit next to him.

Staffers scurried around the table, delivering a flurry of reports to their respective bosses. Electronic maps circled the room. Hundreds of tiny red lights blinked information about hot zones, crisis points, and troop dispositions. And, for the first time since the Los Humanos smallpox attack, all of them were located inside America's borders.

The President said a few words about the gravity of the situation, then turned things over to the Chairman of the Joint Chiefs, Admiral Towne.

Towne, who was almost as tall and gray as Freeman, looked even more imposing. But he spoke in a demeaning, high-pitched whine. After some opening remarks, he announced, "Because all the evidence points to a case of domestic terrorism . . . that no foreign power was directly involved, the DEFCON level has been lowered from TWO to THREE."

He added, "A follow-on attack is still possible but not likely to come from abroad. We're ready to engage any internal threat, but without hard intel, it'll be like chasing a chicken in a blindfold."

This observation put the ball squarely in the hands of Avery Milliken, the Director of Public Safety, or, as it was commonly known, the DPS. His agency, a division of the Justice Department, was responsible for domestic intelligence. Created in the '20s and formerly known as Homeland Security, the DPS was an amalgam of such agencies as the FBI, DEA, ATF, and Border Patrol. When Milliken failed to make an appearance at the President's earlier Cabinet meeting because of problems related to sealing the borders, he was "strongly advised" to attend this one. If the bombing was a case of domestic terrorism, he had the most to answer for it.

Small and silent, his outsized features, balding pate, and pock-marked face gave him an almost sinister visage. However, Milliken was more aloof than sinister. He had few friends in or out of government. His only confidante in the Cabinet was Angela DeKalb. Even the President was put off by him. He was just too curt and humorless.

But he was an excellent administrator with a noteworthy record of success. Many considered him to be the best cop in the country.

As the Los Angeles—now Los *Humanos*—section chief, he apprehended the al Jinn terrorists who perpetrated the smallpox attack at
the summer Olympics. This collar eventually propelled him into the
top spot at DPS. It was the signal achievement of his life. The previous night's bombing accounted for the signal failure.

Addressing the group, he stammered, "Let me begin by saying . . .
well, I concur with Admiral Towne's assessment. But . . . I mean . . .
in addition, by process of elimination, we think the ongoing threat
is internal rather than external." Milliken coughed hard, wiped his
brow with a hanky and said, "I can also tell you that there've been
no intercepts suggesting that a follow-on attack is imminent. No
human intelligence, either." This was as close as he would come
to an admission of failure.

Tito Gonzales was about to take his hide off but thought better.
It wouldn't accomplish anything. It was too early to begin assigning
blame. Since, ultimately, it would rest with him, anyway, any rush to
judgment would only accelerate *his* appearance in the dock. And
besides, he had more pressing things to attend to than dressing down
subordinates.

"Let's discuss our priorities," said Gonzales. "As I see it, aside
from determining who's responsible for the bombing, we have three.
*To gain control of the evacuation. To deliver relief to the victims. And
to restore law and order.* As you are aware, I have asked Jim Freeman
to assume command of the Cordon." He glanced at the General and
said, "Jim, I know you haven't had much time to study the situation,
or consider these priorities, but have you any initial thoughts?"

"Yes, sir. Thank you."

The old general paused and looked around the table. He didn't
stand.

"It's been a few years since I've seen most of you. If only it were
under less sobering circumstances," he said.

Only Nicholas Risden, the Army Chief-of-Staff, caught this double *entendre* because most of the men who once pulled a cork with the General were either retired or dead.

"I'm humbled by the President's confidence in my abilities," he said, "and, wholly dependent on your support for my success. I hope you will be generous with it in the days ahead." With deference to Gonzales, he said, "Mr. President, if I may, I'd like to address the three objectives you listed?"

The President nodded for him to proceed. Freeman got up and directed a pointer toward the far wall where a map of the Cordon— one similar in all respects to that which Angela DeKalb used earlier– was queued up. Moving toward it, he referenced several pages of handwritten notes as he spoke.

"A quick study of the terrain reveals that gaining control of the water crossings is critical. Then we can attend to the land routes."

Arching the pointer from the lower Delaware to the Tappan Zee Bridge, then down through Yonkers and across Nassau County, he said, "Obviously, managing things in this area will be our greatest challenge. It could take as many as three divisions. However, until we can secure the perimeter and reduce the congestion caused by the flight of the refugees, delivering any meaningful aid to the victims trapped closer to ground zero will be impossible. Field hospitals must be set up on the perimeter to treat the wounded or triage them to larger facilities. So, we will need to commandeer hotels, resorts, and universities. Local hospitals should be emptied of all but the most critical cases. Doctors, surgeons, and nurses, regardless of specialty, should be pressed into service from the surrounding states. Burn specialists must be recruited, if necessary, from foreign countries."

As he spoke, many in the room grew sullen and cross. The brass, especially Admiral Towne, was livid over the president's decision to appoint Freeman governor of the Cordon. They saw it as a cheap political stunt. Most of the elements of the plan he was proposing were already being acted on. Now, whatever credit due would surely accrue to him. To boot, Freeman's on-the-fly assessment, absent any hard data, staff work, or consultation with the Joint Chiefs, was nothing short of audacious. However, out of respect for his résumé, no one uttered a word.

That Freeman was incorporating most of the Pentagon's planned response into his analysis came as a relief to the President, though. For his part, Tito Gonzales was indifferent to the brass's resentment. As a former governor, he was never comfortable with the level of power and influence wielded by the military establishment in Washington. If the Pentagon saw his selection of Freeman as a cheap trick, so be it. The declaration of martial law was serious business. He wasn't about to surrender control of it to the cowboys at Disneyland East.

However, the reason Freeman's assessment so closely mirrored the strategy preferred by the Joint Chiefs was simple. Originally, *he devised it.* Where the Pentagon's planners needed to examine the record to find parallels to the current crisis, Freeman simply searched his memory.

Known as the Jigsaw Strategy, it was the same blueprint he used after Jerusalem was bombed in '45. Although its tactical and logistical elements were difficult to execute, in terms of strategy, it was elegantly simple. The name derived from the first stage of the plan, which was to outline or border the problem area as one would a jigsaw puzzle. Then, based on received intelligence, those areas within the border that were easiest to access and restore were returned to normal. After the low-hanging fruit was picked, the full weight of operations would shift to the area closest to the blast. Although the reclamation process would defy solution at first, eventually, the math would get easier, and even the most vexing problems would be solved. That would signal the end game—the point at which control of the Cordon would be returned to the civilian authorities. In terms of concentration, perseverance, flexibility, patience and discipline it really was like a complex jigsaw puzzle, only the pieces were human lives and fortunes.

Freeman finished his review of the President's first objective and moved to the second.

Returning to the map, he explained, "Once the number of refugees dwindles down, we can redirect the relief effort to the area closest to ground zero. But that will also depend on the abatement of surface radiation to a safe level. Until then, we'll airdrop supplies of food, water and medicine from bases throughout the country."

Admiral Towne interrupted him. "General, excuse me. If we wait for the radiation level to drop *before* we begin extending relief to the areas hardest-hit, it will only serve to compound the number of fatalities. Shouldn't we begin to address the needs of the people in those areas immediately?"

"Admiral, our only viable option is an airdrop. Our medical resources will be taxed to the limit providing relief on the perimeter. We have to help the refugees moving toward us before we can redirect our efforts to the interior. Besides, that's where we'll find most of the treatable sick and wounded anyway. Sadly, there is little hope for those victims who are unable to flee. Other than palliative care, there's probably not much we can do for them. The Israelis called it 'rational triage.' It sounds heartless, but it's the only way to ensure the survival of the greatest number of victims."

Straightening his back and shuffling some papers, the admiral huffed, "I guess I don't see it that way."

Freeman studied Towne for a moment. *Is he posturing? Trying to make himself look more cautious or compassionate than I am?*

When the admiral confirmed this suspicion with a contemptuous look, Freeman changed tactics. He asked, "Admiral, if a ship is sinking should the captain's priority be to save those in the crew who are doomed? Or those with a chance to survive?"

The room went still. Only the machines spoke as the admiral's face flushed with rage. He couldn't answer without exposing the frivolity of his comment. Looking to the Commander-in-Chief for support, he found none. Gonzales just stared back at him.

The brush-back worked. Towne, insulted and embarrassed, vowed that, if the General wanted to play rough, he'd accommodate him. But not today.

"Go on, Mr. Pres . . . er, General," he barked.

Without a qualm, Freeman addressed the President's third objective.

"Now, regarding the restoration of order, things could get dicey unless our troops are able to begin peace-keeping operations ASAP. This puts a premium on quick execution of the first two objectives. As the Director of DPS said, it also argues for a generous deployment of troops. In the meantime, we'll coordinate our efforts with local law enforcement agencies in the region. Most will be rendered ineffective by death or desertion. This will be particularly true as we move closer to the epicenter. It may be years before local authority is reestablished there."

To accentuate the gravity of his next remark, Freeman pointed his finger in the air. "Don't be surprised," he warned, "if all this requires the use of deadly force. Lawbreakers must know from the outset that it is not our intent to prosecute them *but to eradicate them!* In that sense, it won't be a traditional peace-keeping effort. But reacting to any criminal activity with zero-tolerance will go a long way toward suppressing both the number and proportion of incidents."

Freeman scanned the assembly to assess the impact of these words. Admiral Towne looked like he was about to pop. Rather than poison the water between them any further, the General ended mechanically, "The President's goals are attainable but not without a full measure of teamwork, ingenuity, and resolve from all parties involved. Again, I'm honored to lead this effort and promise to do everything in my power to work myself out of a job in short order." With that, he sat down.

A reassured President smiled for the first time in hours. "Thank you, General."

It was a gratifying display of political acumen by a man rarely credited with having any, and a solid performance by an old soldier thirteen years removed from duty using only handwritten notes. Most of those present were forced to concede what some already knew: General Freeman was one of the most capable leaders of his generation. Although he was still dressed in woodland attire and smelled like a campfire, in aspect, timbre, and deportment, he appeared more presidential than the President. Nevertheless, his analysis failed to quell the resentment over his appointment with those thinking rank.

"Are there any questions for General Freeman before we move on?" asked Gonzales.

Dryly, Admiral Towne asked, "Where will you locate your headquarters?"

"In Philadelphia," Freeman replied. "Depending on the number of divisions allotted to me and the speed with which they arrive, I intend to deploy them clockwise from that city until we reach the southern shore of Long Island."

Ensconced in the safety of the presidential bunker, not many of Freeman's detractors would have thought to establish a base of operations so close to the front. The threat of radioactive fallout, even in Philadelphia, was still very real. To some, this instinctive double-quick to the sound of the guns seemed foolhardy.

Apart from the President, there was at least one other man in the room who was favorably disposed toward Freeman. That man was Nick Risden. Freeman and Risden were old acquaintances. The Army Chief of Staff served under Freeman during the war. Although he was transferred out of the Middle East before the effort to rebuild Jerusalem began, he knew that Freeman was the optimal choice for command of the Atlantic Cordon.

He may be a hotdog, thought Risden, *but there's no questioning his ability. Or his loyalty.*

Once, after a night of bar-hopping on Beale Street, Freeman and

Risden had gone into a diner as the sun came up. After a full helping of hot cherry pie, Risden took ill and vomited over the counter into the décolletage of a waitress who was flirting with Freeman. The woman got hysterical, so Freeman threw down a fifty, grabbed his bewildered mate, and bolted.

Ever since, a debate over the nutritional value of cherry pie would commence whenever they met. Listeners knew it was an inside joke, but neither man ever revealed its origin. Risden was particularly grateful for his superior's silence. Freeman could have entertained lots of people at his expense over the years, but he wasn't one to take advantage of a man. Especially, a fellow grunt.

General Risden also knew that most of the resources Freeman required would be drawn from his command. He wanted to help, but his options were limited. His best divisions were deployed over-seas. And, except for one, there were none that could respond overnight—or even in a week. The question was, would his old mentor be satisfied with the one?

"General Freeman," he said, "you mentioned it may take as many as three divisions. We're spread pretty thin at this point. If we commit a reinforced division now, can we supplement it in time with Guard units and still get the job done?"

"General, I think . . . eventually, yes. But so much of our long-term success depends on how quickly we gain control of the evacuation and relief effort. If, as they say, we get there first with the most, it will lighten our load later on."

"What do you propose, then?" he said, feeling the old man out.

The General leaned forward and looked to the far end of the conference table.

"I notice that Travis Hawkins is here, today. Is that because you've decided to mobilize the 301st Infantry?"

"*It is,*" Admiral Towne growled angrily. "Have you got a problem with that?"

"Not at all!" Freeman countered. "That's like having *two* divisions.

I can't think of a better outfit to throw into the breach than the Three-O-One."

Freeman's reaction was sincere. He knew the 301st was held in reserve for just such an emergency, but it was also one of the most celebrated units in the army. In addition, Travis Hawkins was an excellent officer.

All eyes now turned to him as Risden asked, "General Hawkins, how soon can you get started?"

The ever-volatile Hawkins, no stranger to the sound of the guns himself, never blinked.

"We'll be on the ground in twelve hours, sir."

There was a stir in the room.

"And," he added with a nod to the former President, "it's a privilege to be serving under General Freeman again."

Roo Hawkins was no bootlicker. A former college athlete like Freeman, he loomed taller and more muscular than most people but, like Milliken, was silent to the point of humorlessness. A quiet storm. Since he seldom confided his feelings to anyone, those who knew him usually took whatever he said at face value. However, in this instance, he lied. No one was more resentful than he was at being passed over for command of the Cordon.

As the commander of the 301st, when he was summoned from Ft. Belvoir that morning, he assumed he had been tapped to oversee the new military district. During the night, a friendly source inside the Pentagon told him that his name was at the top of Towne's list. Anticipating the call to duty, he gave orders for his division to mobilize.

Then, on the drive to Arlington, he heard about the President's appointment of Freeman. Already angered at being passed over for the top spot, now his division was going to be placed under Freeman's command. It was typical Army BOHICA.

* * * * *

When the meeting adjourned, Hawkins approached Freeman.

"General, do you have any immediate orders?"

The General smiled and spoke frankly.

"I'm told that you had designs on this appointment, Travis?"

Hawkins stared at him but said nothing.

Freeman continued. "Look. I understand your disappointment. But it's reassuring to have your division on board. I came here today with you in mind."

The younger man reacted without emotion. Lying again, he said, "I'm fine with the arrangement, sir." Quickly-and curtly-he repeated, "Have you any immediate orders?"

With a smile, Freeman moved over to the map outlining the Cordon's boundaries. Waving the laser, he lent a little more detail to the points he made previously, then said, "Don't put your command at any undue risk. This is going to take time, and it's going to be hot. The last thing we need is a high rate of attrition among the men. They're not likely to get much reinforcement, or help from local law enforcement in the weeks ahead, so don't push them too hard."

Hawkins, feeling the sting of events, merely replied, "Is that all, sir?"

"That is all," the General replied. "Good luck, Travis."

"Thank you, sir."

The younger man saluted and left.

Freeman was aware that what little credibility he left office with was a gift from Travis Hawkins. After losing to Tito Gonzales in the primaries, people started comparing him to such failures as Buchanan and Harding. But, days before the September convention, a Ranger regiment commanded by Hawkins routed an army of Muslim separatists in the Philippine jungle. Under other circumstances, Hawkins might have gained lasting distinction. But there were charges of atrocities that, though unproven, forever sullied his victory. So all the glory fell to Freeman, who did little or nothing to vindicate Hawkins.

Now, Freeman was stealing Hawkins' thunder again, albeit inadvertently. That the younger man was able to subdue his resentment was a credit to his character. That the older one was so blind to it was a charge against his.

* * * * *

Before President Gonzales returned to the White House, he pulled Freeman aside.

"I appreciate the way you handled yourself today, Jim. I only ask that you keep your good eye on Hawkins. There's no doubt as to his professional capabilities, but I have serious reservations about him personally. From what I hear, he's a loose cannon. I won't put up with any thuggery. There's no telling what he might do under conditions of martial law."

The General was reassuring. "Sir, I don't anticipate any problems with Travis. He's got a racy motor, but he's a good soldier. I understand your concern, though. We'll use only what force is necessary to bring the situation under control."

"Thanks, Jim. I don't need to tell you how important it is to restore the Cordon to civilian control as soon as possible. I'll take you up on that pledge you made to work yourself out of a job in short order."

"Sir, I expect to spend Christmas on the ocean course on Kiawah Island."

Seven

Sunday, July 3, 2061 (9:01 A.M. EDT)
Presidential Bunker, West Virginia

By the time Freeman entered the temporary quarters assigned to Jack Clancey, he had become a testament to Army logistics. Gone were the flannels, khakis, and hiking boots. In their place was a dark-green, Class A uniform, a service cap with a gold-braided visor, and a pair of glossy, black oxfords. Although the ribbons he had amassed during his long, distinguished career were yet to be added, he wore the same four stars on his epaulets as he did when he retired from the army.

To Clancey, he not only looked different; he *was* different. His whole persona had changed. He was back to being *The General*. The eyes were filled with newfound determination. A flood of adrenaline erased the stoop of age. The thick silver hair, weathered hands and crow's feet now signaled experience, not decline. In the net, he looked and acted as if he had gained two inches and ten years.

The former press secretary was so impressed by the transformation that he opined in a low but jocular voice, "Aren't you the cat's ass!"

Although this backhand compliment brought a slight grin, Freeman otherwise ignored it, asking, "Is Lena here?"

"She's down the hall. Catching up on some sleep . . . I think."

"Has she said anything about my leaving for Philadelphia?"

"Uh . . . she's not really happy with it."

Freeman winced. With obvious frustration, he groaned, "I was hoping you'd find a way to smooth it over."

"I'm sorry, General, but you know how she gets once her mind is made up."

"What do you mean—her mind is made up? What about?"

"About going with us."

"Dammit, Jack! The least you could have done is disabuse her of that notion."

Nothing's changed, thought Jack. Freeman's habit of offloading the blame on him whenever things went wrong was still alive and well. Also intact was the speed with which their relationship could morph from buddy-buddy to superior-subordinate. But their years together gave Clancey an innate understanding of when to talk and when to shut up. And now it was time to shut up.

Fortunately, Freeman's anger was fleeting. Angling for a solution to the problem, his thoughts were interrupted by a knock at the door. Before Clancey could open it, Lena burst in, her hardened visage betrayed by a half-bitten lower lip. "What time are *we* leaving?" she asked. The pronoun told all.

Noting the determination in her voice, her father answered, "Lena, we have to talk. Could you excuse us, Jack?"

Clancey got lost.

Not wanting to appear insensitive at first, Freeman just took her in his arms and held her without a word. She stiffened. After a few seconds, he raised his hands and cupped her head, kissing her softly on the forehead. Then, he motioned to a nearby loveseat saying, "Please, sit down."

Parked beside her, he stroked her hand and said, "It breaks my heart to say this, Lena, but I can't take you with me. One of Bob Fisher's men is going to stay with you in Shady Grove until we can find someone—"

"That won't be necessary," she insisted, rising quickly. "I'm going to Philadelphia, whether you take me or not."

He stood, too, saying, "Honey, please . . . there's no way I can *protect* you there."

She cried, "And how am I supposed to protect *you*?"

Freeman, looking old again, couldn't respond.

Tearfully, she pleaded, "You *have* to let me go. I can look after you, take care of you. I know your health isn't good. Besides, since I sold the gallery, there's nothing to keep me here. I need you. You're all I have."

"You're all I have, too," he said sadly. It startled her when he abruptly added, "*That's why you're not going.*"

Disconcerted, she wandered round in a circle, then stopped and stared at her feet, wiping her eyes and balling her fists. After about a minute, she said contemptuously, "So, you're gonna do to me what you did to Mom?"

Initially, Freeman was too shocked to answer. Bristling, he went over to where she was standing, towered ominously over her and replied, "What did you say?"

With no trace of fear or remorse, she coldly repeated, "*You're gonna abandon me just like you did Mom?*"

In the heat of the moment, Lena's long-suppressed resentment over his treatment of her mother popped to the surface like a cork. She could no more hold it back than she could an onrushing train.

* * * * *

In 2027, Jim Freeman's wife, Sarah, was abducted and raped by al Jinn terrorists while on a business trip to London. Although Scotland Yard rescued her in less than two hours, the media frenzy that ensued greatly compounded the tragedy. Had the press displayed even a modicum of grace in reporting the event, or eventually just backed off, things might have turned out better for the Freeman family. But it wasn't to be.

The abduction was triggered by then-Captain Freeman's military success. A revolt in Saudi Arabia left its oil complex badly damaged.

He was sent there to coordinate the defense of the civilian contractors trying to effect repairs. During his tour, hundreds of rebels were either apprehended or killed. As a result, a radical imam issued a *fatwah* against him. Since he didn't care to die in a Riyadh alleyway at the hands of some hooded assassin before he had tucked his daughter into bed a few more times, he transferred back to the States at the earliest opportunity. The al Jinn, the exceedingly vicious faction of Saudi rebels responsible for the Los Humanos smallpox attack, instead took their revenge against his wife while she was visiting her father in Europe.

By virtue of his storied football career at West Point, James Freeman was a national property long before he took the field in Saudi Arabia. So, when the spouse of this national hero became the target of terror, it sparked the righteous indignation—and lurid fascination—of the entire country. And it wasn't just the tabloids that made hay with it. The mainstream media was equally crass. For months, the story dominated the news. And, years later, reporters were still sifting through the garbage of their suburban Washington home to find another angle on it.

After the rape, "Teddy" dutifully nursed his wife back to health. But the media poured over the details of Sarah's travail with such heartless repetition that he could never put it behind him. Eventually, the universal knowledge of her defilement at the hands of the terrorists became an embarrassment to him. His desire for her was poisoned, and he began to treat her like tainted merchandise. Their bed grew cold. Absorbed in self-pity, this gallant warrior was anything but in coming to the aid of the person who loved and needed him most.

Conversely, Sarah never abandoned him. All during his ascent to power, she stood by him, ignoring the growing whispers of his infidelity. Nor did she stop loving him. Despite the frosty bed, she stubbornly refused to end their union or allow it to become a marriage of convenience. Her love for the man was so sublime that it transcended the ebb of human passion. It even transcended his enormous conceit. Due to the sheer force of her will, and his reluctance to oppose it, their marriage lasted thirty-six years, most of it in a spiritual and sexual vacuum. She found the strength to go on by immersing herself in the solicitude of her father and daughter and by prayerfully returning to her Jewish roots. In a magazine interview, she even forgave the men who brutalized her; this was her answer to the pain and mortification they caused her.

Only when she died suddenly a few months after Freeman was reelected did he begin to realize the magnitude of his crime. Outside of his marriage, and the child it produced, he wasn't much more than a career mercenary. And, to those who knew them, between the two, Sarah Freeman was the better soldier. Her life was one of those obscure, heroic struggles that, in the words of Victor Hugo, "no flourish of triumph salutes."

With her husband blinded by vanity, the only real witness to her victory over cruelty, hatred, and loneliness was Lena Freeman, who never forgot her father's less-than-knightly behavior.

* * * * *

"*You're gonna abandon me just like you did Mom?*"

It was the first time Lena let on that she was aware of her father's spinelessness. His outrage sank almost as fast as it surfaced. He knew a coward when he saw one, even when he was standing before the mirror. Now it was apparent that his daughter did, too.

Other than humble acceptance of her judgment, his only recourse was to fight back. And his only option in that regard was to question *her* fidelity.

He groused, "This assignment will probably be the toughest of my career, and you send me off by questioning my honor! Why can't you understand my predicament? I'd love nothing better than to stay here with you. But I've been called to duty. I can't—"

She interposed, "It's always that way with you, isn't it? I mean, when it comes to duty, honor, and *country,* you always give your inspired best. What prevents you from doing the same for your *family?*"

Checked by the force of the question, the old man broke off his defense and retreated back to the loveseat, docile and numb.

Divining his pain, Lena knelt down before him, took his big, leathery hands in hers, and kissed them.

"Daddy," she said, "I'm sorry to hurt you. I love you so much, but I've never been this frightened." She gazed at him through another flood of tears. One spattered onto the back of his hand. "I know you're worried about me, but you don't seem to understand: *I'm worried about you, too!* I want to share whatever dangers there are in Philadelphia with you. Or any place else for that matter. Please don't deny me this. *I beg you.* Take me with you."

The old general wore a look of resignation. Oblivious to the depth of his daughter's angst, and still smarting from the sting of her accusations, he said with icy resolve, "I can't. I'm sorry."

Without another word, she rushed out the door, if for no other reason than to get as far away from him as possible.

In the adjoining room, Clancey listened to the entire argument in disbelief. Never in his long association with Freeman had he heard *anyone* speak to him so bluntly. Emboldened by Lena's grit, he went into the living room.

"General," he said, "can I make a suggestion?"

Sensing that Clancey was about to complicate matters, Freeman replied, "Don't do it, Jack."

"Don't do what?"

"Don't get yourself in the middle of this thing. It's a no-win deal."

Despite the red blotches forming on Freeman's cheeks, a sure sign that his bird-like patience was exhausted, Clancey pressed on.

"Sir, you're probably right, but I feel compelled to say something."

Angrily, the General barked, "Man, where do you get your balls big enough to think that—"

Then, suddenly, he backed off. In deference to Clancey's years of service, he yielded. "All right, what is it?"

"Sir, my duties in Philadelphia will be limited. I spent the whole afternoon thinking about it. As I see it—"

Freeman raised his hand. "You can stop right there, Jack. You're not going."

"Huh?"

"The Chiefs want a uniform to handle the media. I jumped the gun when I asked you to come along. I'm sorry, but it's out of my hands."

Eight

Sunday, July 3 (9:30 A.M. EDT)
The Department of Justice, Washington, D.C.

When Attorney General DeKalb met with her staff, they were none too happy about being called downtown. Before the meeting one griped, "Didn't the President warn us against taking unnecessary risks? We should be home with our families until the danger passes."

But, despite the possibility of a wind shift and the outbreak of rioting in the capital, the AG insisted. After all, her plate was full. The crime of the century had just been committed. The whole country was fast devolving into a state of anarchy. And, like the President, she was already suffering manpower shortages caused by vacationers and no-shows.

Anyone would have forgiven her if, like her staff, she was nervous or short-tempered that morning. But, according to habit, she sat at the head of the mahogany table with her porcelain hands laid one atop the other as cool as a tigress.

The head of the criminal division, Steve Nunn was wrapping up an overview on the current state of affairs.

"The President's directive to shoot on sight any looters or troublemakers is having the intended effect. Although the riots in Houston and St. Louis are still out of control, order is being restored in other cities. The harassment of emergency service personnel is still a problem, though."

DeKalb asked, "Have we announced that all rioters will be tried at the federal level under the terms of the Anarchy Act?"

"Yes," he replied. "Twenty minutes ago."

It was a favorite tactic of *agents provocateur* to incite riots at times and in places when the government's attention was diverted to some other emergency. Feeling it was treasonous to destabilize the social order during such times, Congress passed the Anarchy Act of 2050. Essentially, it gave the president unilateral authority to suspend the right of assembly for ninety days. It was one of the highlights— or, depending on one's politics, lowlights—of James Freeman's administration.

"Good," said DeKalb. "It's my intention to ask that the President also suspend the writ of *habeas corpus.* If he does, we'll coordinate with the DPS to round up every suspected anarchist, terrorist, and enemy agent in the country. Putting them behind bars will help us determine who's responsible for last night's attack and lay waste to the schemes of anyone seeking to capitalize on it."

Habeas corpus is a sacred writ of common law dating back to the Middle Ages. It guards against illegal imprisonment. It is an order written by a judge directing a custodial authority to present an arrested person to the court. In terms of civil liberties, it is among the most basic. The Constitution guarantees that it cannot be suspended, unless, during a rebellion or invasion, the public safety requires it. The most notable suspension in the past was during the Civil War, when Lincoln shelved it for four years, during which time the wholesale and arbitrary arrests of Confederate sympathizers and his political enemies were rampant. Thousands of people were imprisoned without ever facing their accusers or being informed of the charges against them.

If there were any objections to DeKalb's plan, none were raised. Her staff was just too green. After President Gonzales was reelected in November, the AG cleaned house at Justice. Steve Nunn, the only holdover, was retained at the insistence of Gonzales himself.

* * * * *

Early in his career at Justice, Nunn had occasion to work with Angela DeKalb on a few special projects. As a result, he probably knew DeKalb better, professionally speaking, than any man alive. But these past collaborations also caused Nunn's wife, Teri, to become jealous of her. She always suspected them of having had an affair. To ease these suspicions, while they were vacationing in Bermuda two weeks before the bombing, he talked about his relationship with his boss one day as they sat in beach chairs at the water's edge.

"Honestly," he said as he popped open a beer, "I've worked with her for eleven years, and I still can't figure her out."

Teri asked, "Where's she from?" It bothered her that his eyes were hidden behind a pair of Ray-Bans.

"Well, she was adopted. Her father was a big-shot investment banker down in Boca Raton who was always away on business and never home. Word is he agreed to adopt a baby as a concession to his wife, who was an emotional train wreck. Apparently, she would have made a good dog trainer. Angela's childhood was an endless stream of beauty pageants, voice lessons, dance recitals, and cotillions. When she wasn't being shown, she was sitting in church. So, lots of pageantry but not a lot of love. I think it left some scars."

Angela's hostility toward her domineering mother led to the darkest episode of her life. In the eighth grade, she started "cutting" to relieve the emotional pain of being treated like a dancing poodle. Mostly, the cuts were to her legs. Before the razors found her wrists, though, her father intervened. He took her to a psychiatrist who, for a substantial wad of cash, agreed not to document her therapy sessions.

The doctor diagnosed the problem immediately. Angela had a dissociative disorder. So, on his recommendation, mother and daughter were disassociated. The latter was enrolled at Alden-Forrest, the prestigious girls' boarding school in Maryland. There, free of her obsessive mother, she blossomed.

Churning the sand with his feet, Nunn explained, "Someone told me that the mother OD'd on barbiturates when Angela was fifteen and that her father more or less blamed her for it. But he gave her the best as far as an education goes. She became the valedictorian at Alden-Forrest, then duplicated that feat four years later at Stanford."

"I thought she went to Harvard?"

"That was law school. Her father died two months before she graduated in '36, so she found herself, at the tender age of twenty-four, rich and triumphant, but alone. Six months later, while going through her father's papers, she learned that's how she entered the world—alone."

"So she didn't know she was adopted?" Teri asked as a wave washed over her feet and swirled beneath her chair.

"No," said her husband, rising to move her beach bag back from where they sat.

"So how did you meet her?"

Sitting down again, Nunn recalled, "The first time was through a mutual friend. She was clerking for Wanda Williams at the Supreme Court. Then, we both started at Justice the same year. So I've watched her for a long time and, I must say, despite her secular bias, she's a brilliant prosecutor."

"What do you mean, 'secular bias?' Her atheism?"

"Yeah, she's an avowed secularist, a director of the Humanist Guild. She believes that the free use of intellect is the only path to individual or collective salvation. At least, that's how she put it once in a magazine interview." From the same interview, Nunn had gathered most of what he knew about his boss's childhood.

"But I thought the Humanists believe that all ethics are situational—that everything is a function of self-interest and necessity."

Taking a pull on his beer, Nunn wiped his mouth with the back of his hand and said, "That's right."

"Then why did Gonzales appoint her? What good is a prosecutor who thinks all ethics are situational?"

The only answer Teri's husband could come up with was, "Because she's brilliant. A constitutional scholar. Even a candidate for the Supreme Court. As I understand it, that was the primary consideration, along with her youth."

And young she was. After handling several high-profile prosecutions in the criminal division, when Arthur Simpson won the presidency in '48, he appointed her solicitor general at the tender age of thirty-six. She rewarded him by winning many of the cases she argued before the Supreme Court. Then, two years later, there occurred an assassination attempt on Simpson that left him mentally diminished; James Freeman assumed the presidency.

Dissatisfied with the lukewarm treatment of a few noted anarchists, Freeman ordered his Attorney General to put DeKalb in charge of the criminal division. That's where she was when Tito Gonzales tapped her for the AG position in 2056. Her ascent made her a veritable celebrity. It also made her many enemies at Justice, most of whom she wasn't able to dispatch until her second term.

"Is it true what they say about her and Freeman?" asked Teri, rubbing some sunscreen on her shoulders. "Did he really promote her after a night in bed?"

There was a saying at the Justice Department that "the air has ears." For a man in Steve Nunn's position, it went double. Even on the beach in Bermuda. So, he answered carefully.

Raising his voice a little, he asserted, "Those rumors have never been substantiated. Actually, the only thing that's really certain is that Angela DeKalb is one of the most talented women in America."

And, due to her tireless efforts to separate church and state in all matters of social significance, DeKalb also became the nation's most visible proponent of the Humanist Revolution. Christians often denounced her as "the Devil's Advocate." And, for Peter Bernard, whom she prosecuted in the Spark Park bombing, the nickname was painfully accurate.

Nine

Sunday, July 3 (10:47 A.M. EDT)
The White House, Washington, D.C.

With clearance from both the Secret Service and the Pentagon, the President returned to Washington. He spent his first hour there down in the Situation Room—or Sit Room—listening to a stream of gloomy CRITIC reports. Then, on receiving word from the weather service that the wind would continue out of the northwest for some time, he went upstairs for his meeting with Angela DeKalb, determined to conduct the duties *of* his office *in* his office.

When Angela entered, he was standing by the door to the Rose Garden, ramrod straight with his hands clasped behind his back. It was the kind of thoughtful pose that might grace the cover of a magazine had he been more photogenic.

Tito Gonzales wasn't very tall. Nor was he very trim. Molded in body and spirit by Hispanic blood, and hardened in the *barrios* of Oakland, he was the antithesis of the ruling-class patricians who had preceded him in the People's House for three centuries.

Notwithstanding his plebeian features, he was a very capable man. His road to the presidency, which included multiple terms as both the mayor of Sacramento and governor of California, was marked by political acumen, executive competence, good fortune, and pluck. He was not a man to be taken lightly, despite his lack of a commanding presence. Proof of this could be found in the truncated careers of many opponents. A master of the political arts, he had a homespun, mayoral style reminiscent of Reagan or Obama.

Without turning around, he said, "Good morning, Angela."

"Good morning, Mr. President."

He gestured for her to sit, then folded his arms. "We're waiting for Katie Holman. Is Avery coming?"

"Yes, sir."

Without making eye contact, he asked perfunctorily, "How's it going over there?"

"We're a little short-staffed, sir, but the wheels are turning."

Gonzales never moved. Angela wasn't sure if he was even listening. Something seemed to distract him.

Actually, his eyes were glued to a pennant stuck in the middle of the Rose Garden. It was a memento given to him by the Oakland Athletics, after their World Series victory the previous fall. He ordered it placed out on the grassy quad after returning from West Virginia. Flapping zestfully to the southeast, it gave him visual confirmation of the more sophisticated meteorological reports he was receiving.

But there was something else that reassured him as he stood there watching. A flock of birds was pecking hungrily at the recently watered lawn. *Canaries in a coal mine*, he thought. The ravenous appetite of these creatures boded well for the wingless.

That the leader of the free world was using a pennant and birds to inform his decisions in an age of technological wizardry was an irony not lost on him.

His matronly chief-of-staff, Katie Holman, entered the room at the same time as Avery Milliken. Holman politely nodded to DeKalb, then sat on the couch across from her. The Director of Public Safety sat beside his boss. The President finally turned away from the window, picked up the Washington Ledger laying on his desk—the New York Times was conspicuously absent—and joined them, sitting next to Holman.

He held the paper out with arms extended. A sixty-font headline screamed:

ARMAGEDDON

The President waggled it, saying, "This is our first order of business—putting an end to this crap! File a cease-and-desist immediately. How dare they incite matters like this?"

"Sir," responded Angela, "I already took the liberty of doing so."

"Good!" He flung the paper on the floor, saying, "I won't stand for this kind of crap. The sooner we make an example of these people the better."

Since Gonzales rarely used bad language, his stress was evident. Immediately, he shifted gears.

"Do we have any leads?" he asked Milliken.

"Just one, Mr. President. Surveillance satellites and Coast Guard officials confirm that there was a high-speed chase in the Ambrose Channel just before the explosion last night. The subject of the chase was a Wavejammer K-11, one of those high-powered hovercrafts you see in boat races. We have reports that a similar model was stolen from a boatyard at the Jersey shore in April. So far, we haven't been able to confirm it, but there's a possible link between the two incidents. An investigative team is headed for New Jersey as we speak. We're also studying the satellite photos and Coast Guard dispatches for clues."

"But no leads on *who* might be responsible?"

"No, sir. No one has claimed responsibility—yet. It could be any one of a number of groups. We're focusing right now on the most obvious ones. The Harpies. The Army of God. And, of course, al Jinn."

Katie Holman listened as the President, Milliken and DeKalb speculated about potential suspects. Though she was indifferent to Milliken, she had an intense dislike for Angela DeKalb. Her feelings were visceral, not rational. Every fiber of her being told her that DeKalb was not to be trusted, an opportunist whose naked ambition was as shameful as it was bereft of ethical bounds. Holman never doubted the rumors that the AG slept her way to the top at Justice.

Although her opinion was more the product of a gut-level aversion than jealousy, had the opposite been true, anyone would have forgiven Holman. Angela DeKalb had "the same thing" as the strumpet in the old blues song: she could make a preacher lay his Bible down.

Her name was a fitting testament to her beauty. Regardless of her forty-six years, most men still found Angela irresistible. She could have pursued a career in Hollywood as easily as in Washington. A confident, regal air defined her movements. She spoke in clear, unaccented tones. Because she rarely smiled, she often seemed emotionally detached, although she was usually well mannered.

Her face was telegenic: sea-green eyes, high cheekbones and full, inviting lips, set against a fair complexion and black hair. If that wasn't enough to make a man turn his head, then her other tangibles were. She had the figure of a starlet, rich in womanly curves and untouchable mysteries. However businesslike the tailoring of her outfits, framed by such a body and scented by the most expensive perfumes, they only served to underscore her siren appeal. This velvet glove of sensuality, when coupled with the mailed fist of her intellect, gave her a power over people that she used to great advantage.

Unfortunately, the construct of her motives, as well as her methods, fell well short of her angelic form.

In a side-by-side comparison with Angela, Katie Holman could charitably be called dowdy. Her frumpy, fashion-resistant wardrobe was the butt of many jokes, most of which were self-directed. She was a thickset woman with a vibrant, healthy face, a coif of sandy brown hair, and warm, pleasant features. She wasn't a grand thinker but a doer, adept at recruiting the best talent, organizing them into an effective team, recognizing opportunities, eliminating obstacles, and fulfilling the directives of her boss. Quick to laugh and slow to anger, her outgoing personality won Gonzales many friends on

Capitol Hill. She was a shrewd negotiator, alert to danger, and full of creative, if offbeat, ideas.

In the navy, her shipmates tagged her with the nickname "Boomer" because her voice was quite loud. When Tito Gonzales adopted it as a pet name for her, it stuck with her for the balance of her career.

After reviewing a list of bombing suspects with Gonzales and Milliken, DeKalb steered the discussion toward the suspension of *habeus corpus.*

The President stroked his brow.

"Angela, I'm really not comfortable with suspending the writ," he said. "This is no time to put the Constitution in a drawer."

"Sir, I realize that you swore to faithfully execute the law, but what good will that do if we lose control of the country? In order to defend the Constitution, we have to defend the government. The nation is teetering on total anarchy. Our enemies walk freely among us plotting further terror. The last thing we need is a repeat of what happened during the smallpox attack. Once civil order is lost, we will pay hell restoring it. Right now, maintaining the due process of law should *not* be our primary concern. It's more important to ensure the survival of the government than a host of rights that can be reinstated later on. Abraham Lincoln was clear about it. He said that a limb may be amputated to save a life, but a life ought never to be sacrificed to save a limb."

"There's no way we can accomplish the same objective under the aegis of the Anarchy and Tranquility Acts?" asked Katie.

"It would take too much time to secure the arrest warrants. In addition, I can't assure that, when Tuesday comes, the federal courts will even be operating. Suspending the writ is the only way to strike a swift and decisive blow. It will allow us to cast a wider net, nab the most dangerous threats and buy time to sort through our catch."

Holman asked, "And what if a lot of innocent fish are caught in your net?"

"It's worth the risk." Turning back to Gonzales, Angela stated, "Not only will it give us a leg up in apprehending those responsible for last night's attack, it may also preempt any additional attacks."

This element of DeKalb's strategy had particular appeal to the President. Determined as he was to apprehend the criminals responsible for the attack, he also wanted to ferret out any other would-be plotters. "It sounds to me like you're advocating the same approach the military favors, a wholesale declaration of martial law."

"Mr. President, I would strongly urge you *not* to do that. We made the right decision to institute it in the territory most affected by the bomb. It's a war zone. However, the same argument cannot be made at the national level. Leave the military out of it. The Supreme Court, and the history books, will condone your need to suspend the writ in a time of national emergency. However, you will be judged harshly if you cede the wholesale administration of justice to the military. The courts may not be operating by Tuesday, but they will be in short order."

Katie Holman, who was with Gonzales in California during the smallpox attack and knew firsthand how bad things could get, was nonetheless leery of DeKalb's plan. "Wouldn't it make sense to get the approval of Congress first? "

Without so much as a look in the chief-of-staff's direction, DeKalb sniffed, "Although that would be politically expedient, it would tip our hand. The plan is to initiate a massive dragnet, using the element of surprise. Once we've picked up the most dangerous suspects, we can announce the suspension and ask for Congressional approval." She waved her hand gracefully as she said, "I can't image how they could withhold their blessing, given the current state of affairs."

President Gonzales was warming to the logic of it. Despite the political firestorm it might create, it was strategically sound. He asked Milliken's opinion.

"Mr. President, I agree with the Attorney General wholeheartedly."

Gonzales wasn't surprised, although Milliken appeared to be more confident than usual.

DeKalb added, "I'm quite certain we can defend our actions in court, Mr. President."

"If we issue a suspension edict, how soon thereafter will the dragnet begin?"

Angela resisted the urge to smile. The horse was almost in the barn. But, to avoid the impression that she was slapping him on the ass, with a nod she deferred to the Director of Public Safety for the answer.

He said, "It will take us about two hours to get started, sir."

"Two hours?!"

"Yes, sir. We already have a list of suspects." Waving the one he had in his hand, he added, "This is only a third of them. Without the need for warrants, most will be in custody within a few hours."

While Gonzales examined the list, DeKalb interjected, "Mr. President, it's critical that the suspension edict is handed down *after* the dragnet is complete, not the other way around."

"Why?" asked Katie, fulfilling her duty to ask dumb questions.

This time, put out by her interruptions and the doubts they raised, the AG turned condescendingly toward Holman. "It's the only way to maintain the element of surprise," she snapped. Then, to Gonzales, she added in a more conciliatory tone, "I can't stress that enough. We can't telegraph our move. It'll drive all the bomb throwers into the woodwork."

Pushing the barn door back open, Katie Holman said to her boss, "Not to minimize the need for decisive action, but, acting without some forewarning of the suspension, or the sanction of the Congressional leadership, is not something I would advise."

DeKalb countered adamantly, "We must act, *then* suspend." Leaning toward the President, she offered, "In the meantime, you could meet with the leadership to arrange a vote. You might request the authority to deport any suspicious foreign nationals, as well."

The President was squarely on the horns of a dilemma. Both of his advisors were right. To act boldly meant initiating the dragnet before he announced suspension or received Congressional approval. This might cost him politically, but it could also preempt a follow-on attack and strike a fatal blow to the enemy within. To act cautiously meant reversing the tactical order: seeking Congressional approval, announcing the suspension, and then initiating the dragnet. This approach might be more tenable politically and legally, but an excellent opportunity to capture the perpetrators of the bombing and ensure against future attacks would go begging.

He reflected, "Let's talk about the downside of all this. What are the political implications of suspending first and legitimizing our actions later?"

Angela said, "Mr. President, there will be the usual fuss about civil liberties. In suspending the privilege of the writ, you will be accused of denying due process. Or not having probable cause. Your opponents will harp about the right to counsel. The right to bail. The absence of indictment by a grand jury. The right to a speedy and public trial. The right to confront hostile witnesses or secure favorable testimony. Illegal search and seizure. Cruel and unusual punishment." She paused and smiled. "Should I go on, sir?" she asked.

"No, I get the idea."

Intent on slamming the barn door, DeKalb said, "Mr. President, though suspension of the writ will result in some innocent people being arrested and detained without due process for a short period, once the courts are back in operation and the suspension is lifted, we'll be back to business as usual. You have my word on that. Once we have the most dangerous suspects in custody, we'll secure the warrants required to hold and prosecute them. What matters most now, though, is what I said before: we *must* ensure the survival of the government. And that demands that we use the element of surprise."

Gonzales studied the face of his chief law enforcement officer carefully, scanning her eyes for any sign of doubt. There was none. Then he looked at Milliken, who seemed to relish the thought of turning loose the hounds. Finally, he looked at Boomer Holman.

In her mind the survival of the government was hardly at issue, but she kept silent, staring back at him stone-faced. It was not a look of disagreement but a time-honored signal that the decision was in his hands.

Lincoln's analogy stuck in his mind: *Risk a limb to save a life.* The situation called for boldness.

And, with that, the barn door closed.

Gonzales addressed DeKalb and Milliken as one. "You may initiate the dragnet. I trust that you will work quickly, though, and minimize the time between its execution and our announcement."

With a look of consternation, he said, "Your plan is a good one, Angela, but you're putting us on a treacherous course. A lot can go wrong. Don't let it."

"Thank you, sir," said DeKalb. "I know I speak for both of us in saying we appreciate your confidence."

Milliken nodded in agreement. "We'll get it right, sir."

Her position lost, Katie Holman jockeyed for the last word. "Sir, if I might ask—" She stopped herself.

"What is it?" the President demanded.

Holman knew she was on dangerous ground. His decision was final. She didn't want to appear as though she was second-guessing him.

"Is it your intention to seek immediate approval for suspension of the writ?" she asked.

"It is."

"Then, sir, I would simply remind everyone that our efficiency in executing the plan should not come at the price of effectiveness."

"What are you saying?" asked DeKalb, with more than a touch of venom.

"I'm saying that it would do us no good to win the battle and lose the war. If we use excessive force in pursuit of these suspects, we'll be conceding the ethical high ground in our arguments before Congress and the court of public opinion. We mustn't do anything that would turn the body politic—or 'the history books'—against us. With respect to Mr. Lincoln, a life can be saved by the amputation of a limb, but it can also be lost."

Then, in desperation, she turned to her boss and added, "Maybe we should run it by Michel first."

The President remained silent. Michel Paggiano was his chief counsel. He was en route to Washington from Cuba, where he was vacationing with his family. Although Boomer's suggestion was patently disrespectful to the AG, her idea to run the plan by Paggiano was a good one. But there just wasn't time.

Angela DeKalb was mad enough to spit. She stared coldly at Holman.

But before they could lock horns again, Gonzales repeated, "No, unless something else comes to light, we'll move forward as planned."

Angela stood up, thanked him, then bowed slightly in the direction of Katie Holman, saying, "And *thank you* for all your insights, *Boomer.*"

With that, she excused herself. As she left the room, Milliken followed like an obedient pup.

When they were gone, the President got up and walked back to the window. After a short time, he said, "Katie, did you really have to get into it with her like that?"

"Sir, that woman is a disaster waiting to happen. I'll concede that she has a decent plan, but—"

"But what?"

"—but it will backfire unless we get Congressional support. That's a fact."

A smile came across the President's face, "You never were one to mince words, Katie."

"No, sir, I guess not."

She watched him for a minute, thinking about the decision. "You know," she said, almost whimsically, "when I was a kid back in California, I read a book about the Hell's Angels. There was a part in it where the author described how the gang would ride their bikes down to Santa Cruz on the Coast Highway at night . . . skirting the cliff walls at a hundred miles an hour in search of 'the edge.' It was a given among the Angels that the only members who *truly* knew where the edge was *were those who'd gone over it!* In a sense, that's what we're doing. In choosing between basic liberties and the need for security, we're skirting the edge of moral certainty at a hundred miles an hour."

She paused momentarily, then concluded, "I just don't think it should be left to Angela DeKalb to find out where the edge is."

Ten

On the weirdest day of Peter Bernard's life, the first he spent at Ellison, the guards implanted an RFID bolus in his shoulder. Convicts called it a *bird dog*, or simply, a *dog*. It served to monitor his whereabouts in the prison whenever he was not in his cell. When he was released in June, the tracking code was transferred to the parole authorities. Now, a faceless watcher in Kansas City monitored every move he made by satellite.

The watcher's report would read: *He requested and received an assignment to the provincial office in Baltimore, where his former mentor at Loyola is the superior. But, for some reason, on his way there, he ditched his brother-in-law's car outside Philadelphia, then hiked back downtown.*

* * * * *

When the Jesuit arrived at the ballfields adjacent to the reservoir in Fairmont Park, he found a mass of refugees camped there for the night. After changing into his clerics at a nearby hydrostation, for almost ten hours, he ministered to all, Catholic and non-Catholic alike. Most people asked for nothing more than a simple blessing; others, confession. It surprised him how few asked for the Eucharist. Because he had no wafers to consecrate, he could not honor such a request anyway. But it still struck him how, in times of uncertainty,

Catholics valued the forgiveness of their sins over the physical communion with God.

Peter had just finished praying with a family from Staten Island when a young girl came up and stood anxiously beside him. He put his hand on her head. "What is it, dear?"

With a slightly Hispanic accent, she said, "Father, my papa's dying."

"Take me to him," he replied.

The man was a young Mexican named Jorge Alvarez, and he didn't appear to be much older than his daughter, whose name was Amelia. She told the priest that they lived near a refinery in Elizabeth. When the bomb exploded, it set off secondary explosions in the storage tanks. Her father was burned, mainly on the legs, trying to stop their home from catching fire. How the family got to Fairmont Park the priest had no idea, but he assumed that the man's Spanish-speaking wife drove them there.

He quickly anointed the man, saying: "*By the Sacred mysteries of man's redemption may almighty God remit to you all penalties of the present life and the life to come; may he open to you the gates of Paradise and lead you to joy everlasting. Amen.*"

Within minutes, the man was dead. Embracing his wife and child, Peter did his best to console them. It was difficult to know if this anointing had been a routine passport to eternal peace for the unlucky Alvarez or a last ditch appeal to God's infinite mercy. As Peter got up to go, the wife started wailing hysterically and fell across her dead husband's body, kissing him and re-anointing him with her tears. Amelia, crying softly, watched the big priest go with eyes so sad that it made him choke. He spent the next few hours mechanically moving from family to family, person to person, his heart heavier than a bucket of lead.

At dawn, the park began to empty out. Hearing that Franklin Square was still full of people, many more seriously wounded, Peter shouldered the orange backpack that he borrowed from the trunk of his brother-in-law's car and moved east. On the way, he changed back into his civvies in some overgrown bushes next to an old boathouse.

The hours he spent on the iron pile at Ellison with his *vatos* hadn't prepared him for an airless, sleep-deprived hike through the inner city wearing a heavy pack on a midsummer day, even if it was only a mile. Exhausted, he inquired as to the location of the nearest Catholic church. A black kid told him, "Seis blocks. That way." He pointed north.

Compared to Center City, the neighborhood surrounding St. Francis of Assisi Parish was sedate. Other than a few broken windows, there was no sign of the pandemonium affecting the more heavily-traveled routes. As Peter approached, a few holdovers from the twelve o'clock Mass came out through the large, wooden doors. A rush of cool air enveloped him. Although reticent to go in dressed in baggies and a tee shirt, he did so anyway.

Except for an elderly charwoman tidying up the altar area and a few locals getting right with God, the church was empty. Peter took a seat halfway down the center aisle and set his backpack in the pew beside him.

He couldn't kneel. He couldn't pray. It was so refreshing that all he could do was sit in the comfort of the cool, dark church with his eyes closed. His legs were cramped and sore, so he did something that he wouldn't dare do under normal circumstances. He stretched out in the pew, laid his head on the pack, and went to sleep.

Eleven

"**B**egorra! Now there's a sight you don't see every day," the little priest said to the disgusted charwoman. Though it wasn't his intent, the sound woke the bearded black giant with the close-cropped, salt-and-pepper hair.

Peter was only asleep for a few minutes when the charwoman took exception to his irreverent snoring and called the pastor. Half-dazed and slightly embarrassed, he sat up, draping his arms over the pew in front of him. After a lengthy yawn, he said, "I'm sorry, Father."

"It's all right, son. Not to worry."

The scandalized charwoman stormed off.

"God bless you, Mrs. Hahn," cried the little man. His accent had the same lilt of laughter that makes the angels sing.

"There now," he said as he turned back to Peter, extending his hand, "I'm Luke Monaghan. And who might you be?"

During his walk into town from Upper Darby, Bernard had a premonition that he would *somehow* be implicated in the bombing, especially if Angela DeKalb had anything to do with it. After all, thanks to her, he just spent five years in the stony lonesome for a crime he didn't commit. Like an animal that senses an impending quake, his instincts told him to run. Although he didn't, he still thought it best to conceal his identity. But he was never a good liar, either. So he answered, "I might be a priest . . . like you. My name is Father Peter."

There was a disconnect between his response and his appearance, but the old priest took it in stride. "Very well, then. Father Peter it is."

They shook hands.

"Father, I came down to see if I could be of any assistance to the refugees. I was on my way to Independence Square, but I thought I might clean up first." In the middle of another yawn, he explained, "I didn't get any sleep last night."

Although Monaghan usually chased away the skells who camped out in his church, he was glad in this case that he had made an exception. "Please make yourself at home, Peter. May I call you Peter?"

"Certainly," replied the younger priest.

"Good," he said. "I'm not a formal man."

Father Luke, though white-haired and frail, was an amiable imp with a smile that radiated goodwill. Acting like an old acquaintance, he told him, "You're welcome to freshen up in the rectory."

"That sounds great. Thanks." Grabbing his pack, Peter stood up. He was at least a foot taller than Monaghan.

"You may not be thankin' me all that much once you see what I've got," warned the little Irishman. "The air conditioner is dead, so it's pretty toasty over there."

A native of Cork, Luke Monaghan came to America as a teenager and entered the Order of Friars. In 2046, he was named the pastor of this Hispanic mission church in the heart of Philadelphia. Although he was past normal retirement age, he had convinced his superiors to forego closing it for financial reasons and to let him stay on. He wasn't just the pastor. He was the only priest.

Upstairs in the rectory, Peter showered. As he was dressing, Monaghan called from the foot of the stairs, "I'm making a snack for us. Join me out in the garden when you're ready."

"Thanks. I'll be right down."

The heat upstairs was stifling, so Peter didn't tarry any longer than was necessary. When he came down, Monaghan was in the kitchen, retrieving a couple green apples from an ancient, like-colored refrigerator. Peter noticed that there were only two or three items in the fridge, one being an open container of baking soda. The bare shelves, relic appliance, broken AC, and dusty aspect of the rectory in general spoke of the Franciscan's Spartan existence.

"Can I help with anything?" he asked as he entered.

Kneeling in front of the fridge, Monaghan looked up with a start, saying, "Land sakes, man! What happened?"

Not only was Peter dressed in his clerics, his hair and beard were gone.

Stroking his cheek, Peter explained, "A concession to the heat."

Rising, his host exclaimed, "I know it's hot up there, but heavens! I'll call the repairman tomorrow."

The older man handed the younger a tray of apples, crackers and cheese, picked up a pitcher of tea, and led him out to a patio between the church and rectory. On it stood a dripping-wet, wrought-iron table and three chairs. An alleyway led out to the street, but the buildings muffled the sound of the traffic. As if on cue, the sun ducked behind the high-pitched roof of the church as they came out and a veil of merciful shade descended on them.

"I hosed down the furniture to cool it off," said Monaghan. "It'll be dry soon enough."

Adjacent to the patio was a grotto surrounded by a small but bountiful garden. In the grotto was a statue of the Blessed Mother and before it, a kneeler. With seeming indifference to the heat, a multitude flowers rioted around it. As Peter set the tray of food on the table, he caught the scent of the roses. Stooping to take a whiff of them, he suddenly got light-headed and almost fell over.

The diminutive Irishman moved quickly to steady him, then guided him over to one of the chairs, which not only was hot but almost buckled under the weight of his frame. He soaked a cloth napkin with iced tea, wrung it out, folded it and pressed it against Peter's forehead.

The big priest unbuttoned his shirt and took a deep breath.

Monaghan figured Peter was suffering from heat stroke, but, actually, he was just exhausted. And the last time he had eaten was the night before when he found the hair in his sandwich. As the old man touched the cool napkin to his guest's forehead, he squatted down to look into his eyes. He didn't have to squat very far; Peter was almost as tall sitting down as he was standing up.

"There," he said, in a calm and soothing voice, "That's better. Now you've got some color back in your cheeks."

Peter couldn't help laughing. "You got a good eye, Father."

Satisfied that his visitor was sufficiently recovered, the spry old priest hurried back to the kitchen. He returned with a plastic bag full of ice which he handed to Bernard. "Here, this way you won't get all wet."

Peter traded the napkin for the ice pack. For a time, he sat silently, rubbing his head and neck with it.

"Sorry, Father. I'm really tired. This heat's doing a number on me. It's been a long time since I—" He stopped short of revealing any clue to his identity.

"Peter," the kindly, old man said, picking the paint off his chair with eyes cast down, "I know who you are."

"You do?!"

"Yes," Monaghan said. "I knew it was you as soon as you said, 'My name is Father Peter.' You're not a man who's easily forgotten." Then, quickly, he raised his glass and said, "And I'm honored to have you as my guest."

"Thank you," Peter said. "I guess you know, then, that I was only released from prison a few weeks ago?"

"No, I didn't."

Peter shook his head. In a dejected, almost teary voice, he said, "I can't shake the feeling that it won't be long before I'll be heading back there, either."

Having just met him, the elderly pastor couldn't tell if he was being melodramatic or just kidding. "Why?" he asked.

The big man told him about his fear of landing on the government's list of bombing suspects.

"Why would the government suspect you?"

"Because I'm a convicted felon in a case related to a bombing. And, having just been paroled, if the computers don't put me at or near the top of the suspect list, then General DeKalb will."

The little priest, unsure who this general was, stuffed an apple wedge in his mouth and once again asked, "Why?"

Peter was impressed how the old man kept using this simple modifier to peel his onion. But Luke Monaghan's sympathetic ear and simple hospitality were therapeutic. The big priest marveled at how quickly he came to trust him with his most intimate secrets.

After telling him of how the Devil's Advocate prosecuted him in the Spark Park bombing, he concluded, "I spent five years in a box for exercising my free-speech rights. At my trial, when I quoted Scripture, her toadies labeled it 'hate-speak.' Not only was her prosecution of me unjust—it was criminal!"

Monaghan kept snacking, so Peter kept talking.

"You're probably not aware that when the Church was stripped of its not-for-profit status in *Ogden vs. The Archdiocese of New York*, DeKalb was clerking for Wanda Williams, the justice who wrote the majority opinion. Essentially, she helped to construct the prevailing argument."

"No, I wasn't," Monaghan admitted. Although he wasn't conversant in legal matters, no churchman could forget the Court's decision to eliminate the deductibility of contributions and the exemption from property tax that religious organizations enjoyed.

"She's a menace," Peter insisted, "and, unless she and her Humanist allies are stopped, their campaign to de-Christianize this country will do for America what Robespierre did for France."

"*Guillotine* justice?"

"Exactly! Christians have already been silenced and ostracized.

Can the next Great Persecution be far off? It's not like it hasn't happened before. History reeks with instances where the law, applied in a moral vacuum, has been used as an instrument of oppression and terror. Blacks know it. Jews know it. So do women and indigenous people. *Certainly the Irish have felt the lash!*"

It wasn't often that Monaghan had an opportunity to discuss matters of church and state with someone of Peter Bernard's stature, so he was enjoying himself. And the big priest's reference to his homeland only drew him deeper into the conversation. He said, "These Humanists—it's hard to put a finger on them. It's easy to see why they're called 'the invisible hand.' How would you depict them?"

"Well, I find it helps to contrast them with us Christians because, ultimately, we're both fighting for the same prize: the soul of humanity. Except our tactics are diametrically opposed. We adore God. They adore man. We stand for faith and reason. They stand for reason. We believe that man's true purpose is to serve God and attain salvation. They believe it is to foster laws and science. We bow to Absolute Truth. They hold that all truth is relative. We believe in the power of God's grace. They, in the power of self-actualization. We recognize all men as children of God. They don't."

With a hint of frustration, Peter asked, "But if we aren't all children of God, then whose children are we?"

The Irishman smiled. "It's a good question."

He refilled their glasses, saying, "It does seem like they're winning the battle, though. For souls, I mean."

"Oh, especially the souls of the *intelligentsia*," said Peter. "The Western elite is dominated by Humanist thought. They control the universities, the laboratories, the courts, the theaters, the board rooms, the schools, and, most important, the media." Shaking a clenched fist and squinting slightly, he added, "They have a stranglehold on the one commodity that is essential to gaining and holding power: *Information.*"

Sometimes, it is more important to ask the right question than to give the right answer, and Luke Monaghan was an expert in that regard. "I think I understand what you're saying," he said, "but, getting back to Angela DeKalb. One thing still puzzles me. On one hand, you fear her power over you. Yet, you say she's a menace that must be stopped." He looked imploringly at his guest as he asked, "Are you in retreat or on the attack?"

Rotating the glass of tea in his hands, the Jesuit felt cornered. His initial impulse was to pontificate, to insist that he would never retreat, or that it wasn't the right time to attack. But his host would see through it. So, he answered honestly. "Father," he said, "I confess . . . I've lost my resolve."

"Then take courage in the Lord, my friend."

Peter shifted nervously. "But resolve isn't just courage. There's judgment, too. And good judgment tells me that to continue fighting is useless. Especially if the inevitable outcome is another prison term. Or worse."

Monaghan's image of Bernard, once as distant and one-dimensional as the photo on a book jacket, was gaining perspective. Clearly, he wasn't the Crimson Collar—the traitor born of the media—but a tragic, almost heroic, figure, wracked by human failings. His struggles on behalf of the weak and vulnerable had left him similarly disposed. He was proof of the adage that the best of men are men at best. The little Franciscan's heart went out to him, although he wasn't about to feel sorry for him. Or let him feel sorry for himself.

"Father Peter, what makes you think this fight is yours to win or lose?"

"It's not! I know that. But I used to be arrogant enough to think God wanted me sounding the trumpet. Not anymore, though. What little ministry I did in prison helped me to see that the real work of a priest has nothing to do with politics. Now, whenever I see men like you, happily tending their flocks, I'm drawn in that direction. Like I said, I'm tired of fighting. And, what's more, I'm tired of losing."

The little priest chuckled. "Yeats said that out of the argument with others comes politics, out of the argument with ourselves, poetry."

The Jesuit's eyes beamed with recognition. Standing up, he cried, "That's it! I'm too busy fighting with myself to fight anyone else." With a thump on the chest, he protested, "I want to find the poetry in *me*. I want my life to be my own."

Father Luke popped another apple slice into his mouth and, chewing it slowly, waved a paring knife—and the white-skinned, blue-veined hand that held it—in the direction of his guest, saying, "But—that can't be."

Taking his seat again, Peter unconsciously appropriated the old man's pet modifier. "Why?"

The Franciscan pointed to the gold ring on the big man's left hand. "Because, you took a vow."

Then, blaming his eighty-five-year-old bladder, the Irishman abruptly excused himself and went back to the rectory.

When he returned, he brought with him another pitcher of tea, and as he freshened their drinks, Peter said, "You know, you'd think that, after so many years of discernment, I'd have reached a better understanding of my vocation. But I was always idealistic. A man on a mission. Then, suddenly, I was holding a dead woman in my arms. That had a chilling effect on me. All my visions of glory, not to mention the better part of my reputation, died in that stairwell with her."

"Ah, yes, Deacon Carroll. They called it the blackest episode for Catholics since Nero's fire. Just how did you get mixed up in that stink?"

"Oh, it all started when a Colorado company created a genetically-modified chimpanzee with the ability to sequence the alphabet on a computer. The company filed a procreative liberty suit to have it declared an American citizen with full civil rights. It was appealed all the way to the Supreme Court. George Carroll was fearful that the bio-engineers would prevail. We all were. So we seized the courthouse in Denver demanding the case be heard in an emergency session." He lowered his head and, with a sigh, said, "It was such a stupid move."

"Where did you get the guns?"

"I was told the seizure would be peaceful—an exercise in civil disobedience. So I didn't know about the guns. But Carroll smuggled them onto the roof in boxes supposedly containing new air-conditioning units. The attack was timed to coincide with the delivery of the boxes. Then, he took the hostages, and everything turned to crap. After the first night, he said I could leave, but I was concerned for the prisoners. I tried to negotiate an end to the standoff, but . . . well, you know what happened. Mrs. Scanlon was killed and the Deacon along with her, so I took the fall."

"I remember. A soldier killed her, right?"

"In cold blood."

"Didn't he say that his weapon discharged accidently?"

"And I'm the Prince of Wales."

Monaghan stifled a laugh. "He won the Medal of Honor or something, didn't he?"

"Not for that!"

"No, I mean, before that?"

"He did. And that's what put me away. People were forced to decide between a subversive priest and a war hero. I never had a chance. So I pled guilty to conspiracy and criminal trespass."

"I forget his name?"

"Anson Collier. The leader of the Pathfinders."

"Really?" said Monaghan. Then, it suddenly hit him. "Oh, sure. *Sonny* Collier."

For a while, the little Franciscan said nothing. Then, he recalled, "You were a history professor, right?"

"Yes, at Loyola."

"So you must have some strong opinions about the Pathfinders, considering that Collier's their leader?"

Indeed, he did. "They're a political phenomenon," he said, "and like the Know-Nothings or the Klan, committed to white supremacy. But it doesn't stop there. They also think that our democracy is a lesson in mediocrity, that the solution to our problems is *less* suffrage, not more."

"My understanding is that they're also obsessed with secrecy. Like the *Cosa Nostra*."

"That's true. The more talkative ones can usually be found floating face-down on a riverbank or disemboweled in the bottom of a dumpster."

The old priest said, "I also read somewhere that they want to overhaul the Constitution?"

"That's right. Restoration of the electoral college in presidential elections. Senators elected by legislatures. Popular election of representatives only."

"And no one could vote or hold office without a high school diploma?"

"And fifteen years of citizenship."

Monaghan said, "You probably know they want to make English mandatory, too."

"Yes," said Peter. "Actually, most of the changes they're proposing are very popular with whites, especially those who are feeling disenfranchised by the black-and-brown majority."

Monaghan seemed perplexed. "What majority?"

"Well, if you factor in the white congressmen aligned with them, the so-called *Simpaticos*, the traditional minorities of African, Hispanic and Asian now have a decided majority in the House of Representatives. But control of the House isn't the only issue. The justices at the Supreme Court are also decidedly pro-color. And, when Tito Gonzales won election to the presidency, many whites saw that as the final straw. Really, it's not unlike the four score and five years leading up to the Civil War."

"What are you saying? That another civil war is imminent? That whites will somehow secede?"

"It's not beyond the realm of possibility. Today, social institutions have replaced the states in vying for power with the federal government—even the institutions within the government itself. For instance, if the military or the DPS decide that 'secession' from the established order is preferable to conceding any more power to the black-and-brown majority, it might trigger another civil war." Peter thought for a moment, then added, "This time, though, if there is bloodshed, Americans of all stripes will die."

Monaghan studied his guest intently. "So then, as you see it, racism is as alive today as it was in the 1860s. Or 1960s."

"It may not be as overt or intense as it once was, but the *belief* in racial inequality is only slightly less prevalent today than it was six hundred years ago when it displaced religious intolerance as the perfection of human hatred."

The Jesuit leaned back, put his big hands on his freshly-shaven head, and, with a distant look, surmised, "And it'll probably stay that way until men of all colors are subjected to a new form of racism—one contrived from the beliefs of genetically-superior humans. The so-called *transhuman race*."

Having just read a magazine article about the creation of a hermaphrodite with the reproductive organs of both sexes that was designed to populate deep-space colonies, Monaghan said, "Everyone marvels at these prodigies with IQs of 220, the eight-foot athletes, and the musicians with six fingers on each hand, but all I see are tragic monsters, unloved, and doomed to roam the frozen wastes apart from humanity."

Also channeling the words of Victor Frankenstein, Peter said, "What I see is a race of devils, one that will make our very existence a condition 'precarious and full of terror.' But it won't be the monsters roaming the frozen wastes, unloved. It'll be us!"

Twelve

Sunday, July 3, 2061 (6:20 P.M. EDT)
The Scharon Building, Philadelphia

It took Travis Hawkins four hours to secure a headquarters for General Freeman. One call to a former Academy classmate, a partner in a commercial real estate brokerage, was all it took.

The top floors of the Scharon Building, vacated by a bankrupt hedge fund the previous summer, were available for immediate use. It was an ideal location, strategically placed on the perimeter of the Cordon. It had plenty of open space and came partially furnished. Its access points and communication links were easy to guard. A five star hotel, the Armitage, was next door. And most important, there was a heliport on the roof.

Hawkins wasted no time in securing it, and when Freeman arrived that evening, a company of men from the 301st Infantry was already deployed throughout the building. A platoon of specialists with anti-aircraft weapons was monitoring the airspace as Freeman's AJ-95 SkyShark touched down—a redundant measure, since a half-dozen unmanned War Eagles, with their laser tracking and delivery systems, were circling overhead.

Freeman, Bob Fisher and another Secret Service agent named Art Reynolds climbed out of the helicopter. A ruling on the status of the former President's Secret Service protection was still pending, but his security team had already been halved.

Two of Travis Hawkins' subordinates, one short and squat, the other tall and lanky, walked forward, saluting.

"General," the shorter, older one hollered over the roar of the engines, "I'm Colonel Phillip Essing. This is Major Jeffery Robbins. General Hawkins has assigned us to your staff. Unless you object, I'm to serve as your executive officer. Major Robbins will be your adjutant. At your whim, of course."

Under normal circumstances Freeman would have filled these positions with men of his own choosing. However, having just returned to the army after a thirteen-year hiatus, he was not only without staff, he didn't know who to pick in assembling one. Hawkins calculated correctly that, if Freeman was to hit the ground running, at bare minimum, he would need an XO and an adjutant.

Returning Essing's salute, as the rotors decelerated, Freeman shouted, "At ease, Colonel. Pleasure to meet you." The two men differed in height by more than a foot. They shook hands.

Freeman shook the hand of the younger, taller officer whose height left them virtually eye-to-eye. "Pleasure to meet you, too, Major." Noticing that both men were unsure of his traveling companions, the General said, "These are Agents Fisher and Reynolds from the Secret Service."

Again, a round of handshakes.

A detail of soldiers was moving their baggage into the building when Colonel Essing said, "Care for a quick tour of the facilities, sir?"

"Not right now, Colonel. I'm sure it'll do. Just let the General pick his office, and give me the one next to it."

A look of consternation came over Essing's perspiring face. "Sir, I believe it's General Hawkins' intent to establish his divisional headquarters at a different site. He didn't have time to discuss it with you before he left this morning, but he feels strongly that a presence further to the northeast is necessary. Most likely in Newburgh or Bridgeport. Or somewhere out on the Island."

"Did he give any reason?" inquired Freeman.

Cautiously Essing replied, "I don't mean to speak for him, sir, but I know he wants to create an alternative system of command-and-control in the event something catastrophic happens here. Since our ultimate objective is to deploy in a clockwise fashion across the Cordon, putting the divisional HQ further to the northeast will also help to alleviate any logistical problems we encounter as we move in that direction."

The General delayed his response. The Cordon was small enough that redundancy wasn't a priority. On the other hand, the argument about locating in the path of the planned deployment was sound.

Shortly after parting with Hawkins at the Pentagon, Nick Risden told Freeman how resentful the younger man was at being passed over for command of Cordon. If he approved Hawkins' decision to locate the divisional headquarters in a spot removed from his own, it might ease that resentment by giving him greater autonomy. In light of the President's admonition, though, it would also make a close monitoring of his activities more difficult. Freeman decided not to take issue with Hawkins on it but resolved to keep him on a short leash.

"Very well, Colonel," Freeman said. "I'll take it up with General Hawkins. In the meantime, I'd like to get a look at things from the air before it gets dark. So, let me change into some fatigues, use the bathroom, and I'll be back. Keep the bird warm." Then he followed Major Robbins inside.

* * * * *

When the General returned, he was wearing lightweight, urban-camos and a boonie hat. On his hip was a 9mm, semiautomatic Glock. He had a black carrying case slung over his shoulder.

"Colonel Essing," he asked, "have any living arrangements been made for me yet?"

"Yes, sir. Next door. You'll be staying at the Armitage—in the presidential suite. The Secret Service has the rooms adjoining yours."

This was welcome news to the General, having once before enjoyed the luxuries of the Armitage during the '52 presidential campaign. "Good," he replied. "Let's get rolling then."

With the exception of Agent Reynolds, who was off casing the hotel, his party boarded the SkyShark again and took off.

Freeman directed the pilot, "Follow the Delaware south. I want to assess the situation on the bridges down there."

The time was 1915 hours, and the glitter cast by the sinking sun on the river belied the tragedy unfolding below. Colonel Essing distributed pencil dosimeters and film badges. These would detect even the slightest exposure to radiation.

The General opened the black carrying case and pulled out a small but sophisticated, camera/transmitter. He gave the device to Robbins, shouting, "I know it's not part of your job description, but see if you can figure out how to work this thing. President's orders. He wants to see what I see."

They flew over the demolished Chester-Bridgeport crossing where ferries were working around the clock to keep pace with the flight of the refugees. Minutes later, they were alongside the Delaware Memorial Bridge at the southern end of the New Jersey Turnpike.

Hovering above the east bank, they descended to a height level with the crown of the bridge. Then, using their field glasses which were linked to the onboard monitors, they watched as the news reports they were seeing became flesh-and-blood realities.

"Holy Toledo!" marveled the General.

A snarl of machines and humanity jammed the southbound approach. Traffic was backed up on the turnpike at least ten miles. Even the new magneto-foils, with a maximum elevation of twenty-two inches, were prevented by the guardrails from escaping the morass. Abandoned vehicles were turned on their sides to open clogged lanes. Others were burning, the smoke intermittently restricting the view from the air.

Unbelievable! he thought.

The bridge was a dual span of near identical construction. Four lanes went south, four north. On the southbound approach, a few of the more desperate and resourceful drivers were using any means available to cross into the northbound lanes. Soldiers from the 301st were doing their best to stop them. That part of the span was already crowded with refugees crossing on foot after leaving their vehicles behind. Below the anchorage, hundreds were slogging through the meadowlands toward the river to wash radioactive particulate from their skin and clothing.

After a few minutes, Freeman yelled to the pilot, "Spin around. I want to see the other side."

The chopper did a one-eighty. When it did, Major Robbins was afforded a panoramic view of the sun reflecting off the stately trusses and towers of the bridge. Traffic was unusually heavy on the river below as boats sped toward Delaware Bay. Ferries and other small craft were advancing slowly toward Wilmington from the river towns in New Jersey. Like their fellow sufferers on the opposite side, hundreds of people on the Delaware shore were bathing on the docks of the exclusive Pigeon Point Yacht Basin.

The General surveyed the situation on the eastern bank, then hollered, "Fly over to the Wilmington side."

There, the presence of the 301st was more evident. Almost a full battalion was deployed along the causeways and cloverleafs. The soldiers struggled to maintain order and to clear the massive pile up at the apex of the southbound span. Two twin-prop Sky-Mules with electro-mag pickups were removing the disabled or abandoned vehicles that clogged the roadway. Several tow trucks assisted them at ground level. The Sky-Mules worked slowly, carefully negotiating the bridge's four hundred foot towers and its network of cables. Their loads were being dumped directly into the river.

Above the drone of the engines, the General asked Colonel Essing, "What's the radiation level?"

"The readings on the Ben Franklin and Walt Whitman bridges were at fifty rads, sir. I don't know what it is here, but it can't be much higher. That's compared to thirteen thousand at ground zero, though. Fortunately, the wind is preventing the movement of fallout in this direction."

"Have the men received the necessary inoculations and thyroid block?" asked Freeman.

"Yes, sir. Before we left Virginia."

"What about body armor?"

"The whole division is equipped with Geller A4s. We'll need them once we start moving toward ground zero, but right now, battle dress will suffice."

"All right then," shouted the General, "set me down."

"Excuse me, sir?"

"I want to get a look at things on the ground."

Had he stuck a gun in his mouth his party couldn't have been more surprised. Or perplexed.

"Sir, with all due respect," shouted Essing, "there's considerable danger down there. It's not advisable to land. We can't guarantee your safety."

"I couldn't agree more, sir," chimed Fisher, who was sitting in front of the General next to Essing.

Freeman looked at both men knowingly and smiled. "I appreciate your concern, gentlemen, but when I accepted this assignment, I knew I'd have to take some risks. So put me down."

The pilot found a clearing in one of the cloverleafs and landed the chopper in it. As soon as it touched down, Freeman threw open the starboard door and jumped out with the others in tow. They jogged through the wind-whipped grass to one of the exit ramps. As they entered the southbound causeway, the magnitude of the calamity hit them full-force.

Dozens of people moved toward them, some hastened by fright, some languid with pain or exhaustion, most clustered in groups. The ones with no apparent injuries were moving fastest, although mostly everyone bore some visible effects of the blast. At minimum, cuts and scratches. Others had burns or slings or crutches. The clothing of some was spattered with dried blood or partially shredded, revealing makeshift bandages. Many were filthy and covered with dust. Some were partially undressed, nursing raw flash burns on their arms and faces. One man sat listlessly on the curb, his hair and eyebrows singed off and suffering from what appeared to be a garish sunburn. Another limped toward the General, arms akimbo, as if allowing them to drop would be too painful. As he went past, Freeman noticed that his burned flesh looked slimy—and smelled horrible.

A man ran wildly down the causeway, pushing and shoving those in his path. In stark contrast, a few angels lent succor to the weak and infirm, who lay on the sidewalks with heads bowed, or on the pavement with glazed eyes, praying for death. Hunger and thirst, not to mention the heat, added greatly to the general misery.

Having just read DeSegur's account of the retreat from Moscow, Freeman was haunted by the ghosts of Napoleon's camp followers, wandering the banks of the half-frozen Berezina River in terror, agonizing over how best to die. Only the Cossacks were missing from this reprise.

Pushing through the hapless throng, and the stench of rotting flesh, the General finally reached the top of the bridge. There, soldiers from the 301st labored to untangle the pile up. Nimbly avoiding the bridge supports, one of the Sky-Mules was lifting a disabled RV from the middle of the swarm. Turning toward them, an officer recognized Colonel Essing and saluted. When he saw Freeman, his eyes widened, his back went stiff, and he again saluted smartly.

"Sir," he blurted out. "Colonel Thomas Meyers, First Battalion, Second Brigade, *sir!*"

"Pleased to meet you, Colonel," replied the General, returning his salute. "How do you report?"

"Well, sir, the accident happened at around 1800 hours. When traffic began backing up, the magnetos in many of the idling vehicles crapped out. I'm told they were weakened by the EMP. Anyway, people just started abandoning their cars. We're close to clearing it though. The trick will be to maintain some semblance of order once traffic starts moving."

"Would it help to establish a line of vehicles in all four lanes to pace things?"

It was a simple suggestion but one that Meyers hadn't considered, absorbed as he was with breaking the logjam.

"That's a great idea, sir! I'll get on it."

The General nodded, then, removing his boonie hat and sunglasses, motioned to Fisher and Robbins. "Follow me," he ordered, as he waded into the fracas on the Jersey side of the bridge.

Neither man was bold enough to stop him. Robbins was glued to the camera's viewfinder. Fisher, drawing his gun, did his best to shield his charge.

As they negotiated the phalanx of autos and trucks, an amazing transformation took place. Freeman's face was instantly recognized by the horde. Word of his presence spread rapidly. It was the Lion of Jaffa, come to deliver them.

One fat guy, standing on the hood of his car, yelled, "Hey, General, whadder you doin' here?"

"We rented a place in Ocean City!" he hollered back.

Many in the crowd laughed or smiled at this allusion to the normal bumper-to-bumper congestion found along the shore routes on summer weekends.

The General's irreverent humor was like a sedative. As this timeless figure moved through the crowd shouting orders and encouragements, a relative calm descended. Brawling men and shouting women were pacified, even crying children. Cameras on the scene, including the one held by Major Robbins, recorded it for the ten o'clock news. And posterity.

"Never in a million years," swore Fisher.

Angered at Freeman's decision to land in the first place, the General's indifference to danger astonished him. The Silver Star on display in his trophy case at home suddenly took on greater significance. Here was a side of the former President that Fisher had never seen, in that he had never watched him respond to the kind of crisis that lays bare the soul and reveals one's true measure. Nonetheless, he was still angry. Nor could he shake the feeling it was a courage bred of recklessness.

Ever the beneficiary of good luck and good timing, not more than half an hour passed between Freeman's appearance on the bridge and the resumption of movement. Those closest to him knew that, compared to the Sky-Mules and the 301st Infantry, Freeman's contribution to the whole effort was, at best, corollary. But that was not how the people on the bridge described it.

Nor was it the way the networks spun it later that evening. The hour-long footage Robbins shot was transmitted directly to the Sit Room at the White House where President Gonzales, sensing its power to boost the nation's morale, ordered it released to the media.

Thirteen

Sunday, July 3, 2061 (9:14 P.M. EDT)
Franklin Square, Philadelphia

"**C**an we put down there?"

It was almost dark by the time Freeman returned to Philadelphia, and instead of landing atop the Scharon Building, he directed the pilot to a clearing by the Ben Franklin Bridge. Although traffic on the bridge was flowing smoothly, in the park nearby, the aid stations were jammed with refugees.

The General brought hope to these tormented souls as well, moving among them, inspiring them with confidence and awe. He sympathetically inspected the wounds of a middle-aged man, stooped to tie the shoelace of a frightened boy, hugged an expectant mother, and held up a bulky water container while an old woman drank.

"Keep your spirits up," he implored them. "Don't be frightened."

Through it all, Robbins stayed glued to his hand-held camera like a teenager to a teletran.

During this encore performance, the General came across a huge, black priest ministering to a dying man in one of the Red Cross tents. He was on his knees, and in his hand was a gold crucifix. Their eyes met, and a spark of recognition flashed between them. Freeman knew the man, but he couldn't recall how or when. As he moved around to get a better look at his face, the priest turned away, lowering his ear to the victim's lips. Embarrassed at having intruded on such an intimate moment, Freeman moved away.

Fifteen minutes later, when he returned to satisfy his curiosity, the patient's body was covered by a sheet, and the priest was gone.

The grueling pace and emotional demands of the day finally caught up with the silver-haired warhorse. His legs were aching from fatigue, his belly from hunger. Wearily, he said to Fisher and Robbins, "Let's head back to the hotel."

On landing in Franklin Square, the General sent Colonel Essing north to inspect the bridges near Trenton. Thus deprived of transport, the three men had to walk from the park to the Armitage. Though only three blocks, Fisher was beside himself the entire way.

Near the Graff House, where Thomas Jefferson wrote the Declaration of Independence, they passed a furniture store that, days before, promoted a blowout mattress sale with live sex acts in the block-long display windows. These were now shattered; the bed frames were empty. Refugees slept on the pilfered mattresses out on the Mall, a few hundred yards from the Liberty Bell.

Robbins commented, "Have you ever seen so much broken glass?"

It was spattered about in all its forms, from knifelike shards to tiny crystals. In the rising glow of the streetlights, it twinkled and glistened like some theme park illusion. By the time they reached the Armitage, it was imbedded in the tread of their boots.

Having failed to recognize the august presence before him, the bell captain asked Freeman's party, "Would you gentlemen be so kind as to remove your shoes before entering?"

The management had reason to be concerned about what the guests tracked through the huge, brass doors. The lobby floor was made of Vermont marble and was covered in places by costly Persian rugs.

The hotel was a magnificent structure. Massive, marble columns imported from quarries in Sicily rose majestically to the vaulted ceiling from which two rows of crystal chandeliers hung. A wide staircase leading up to the banquet halls on the mezzanine dominated the room. On the walls, the Founding Fathers and a bevy of unsmiling

Philadelphians peered out of gilt-framed oils. Elegant furnishings of leather and cherry were clustered everywhere, and fresh-cut flowers still adorned the dozens of elegant vases that dotted the room. The quiet, dignified mood of the patrons stood in stark contrast to the frenzied rabble out in the street, as it might have in the hostelries of St. Petersburg on the eve of the October Revolution.

A diminutive man with pince-nez glasses scurried up to pay tribute. It was the hotel manager, a man named Sanger. Agent Reynolds followed him, a look of disgust on his face. Sanger apologized for the inconvenience of having to remove their shoes, an apology the General graciously accepted.

"As you can imagine, Mr. President, things have been hectic around here since last night. The hotel is half-vacant. Most of our patrons were scared off by the bombing. But we're very honored that you've chosen us to serve you."

The bookish manager went on, confidently reassuring Freeman that the Armitage was the perfect choice for an extended stay. He cited the luxuries of the presidential suite, the hotel's French chef, the full-service spa and the Olympic pool.

When he was finished hawking these amenities, he said, "We stand ready to serve your every need."

"Thank you, Mr. Sanger," the General replied. "I hope you won't consider it too much of a burden, then, if I *request* that you make immediate arrangements with the Red Cross to move the most seriously wounded refugees lying down in Franklin Square *here*. I trust you understand the urgency of this request and how great a service it will be to our nation. I further trust that you will do all in your power to provide for their safety and comfort when they arrive. Your firm should generate an enormous amount of good-will as a result of this *unforced* act of compassion, and I commend you for it in advance."

As the color ebbed from the startled manager's face, Art Reynolds, who was standing behind him, smiled broadly. After haggling over the details of the General's stay for the past three hours, his opinion of the little man wasn't good. Watching him squirm to the General's subtle injunction was a tonic. His smile spoke volumes.

The General gritted his teeth to avoid laughing at the manager's drooping reaction to his "request."

When Sanger stumbled away, the affable Reynolds turned to him and said, "If you don't mind my saying so, sir, that was great stuff! That little—" Suddenly fearing that Freeman might find his informal tone disrespectful, the agent checked himself.

But the old man's response quickly allayed that fear.

"Well, thank you, Arthur," he replied. Then, with feigned concern, he whispered, "It was the least I could do once I heard about all the vacancies."

All of them laughed for the first time that day.

As they crossed the lobby in their stocking feet to the elevator bank, one of Essing's young lieutenants approached.

"This came for you about an hour ago, sir."

He handed Freeman an envelope marked "Confidential."

Freeman stopped beneath a large painting of Franklin and his kite and pulled out his reading glasses.

> *Bridgeport, Connecticut*
> *2130 hrs*

General Freeman:

Colonel Essing has informed me of your concerns about establishing redundant command. Although it is my considered judgment that Bridgeport would offer many deployment advantages, I will go no further than to make temporary arrangements for division HQ until I hear from you.

The situation is fluid, chaotic, and dangerous to the north and east of NYC. Local law enforcement and rescue units, though swamped, are performing admirably. Two NY Guard units have been summoned by the Governor to the Tappan Zee, but other crossings are, as yet, unsecured. The Thruway and the LIE are bottlenecked. Rail service is down. Need more Guard units ASAP.

Colonel Essing also informed me about your "reconnaissance"' at the Delaware Bridge. Your inspired leadership is reminiscent of the war. I salute your compassion and courage.

Respectfully,
Gen. T. Hawkins

The subordinate tone of the letter came as a relief to Freeman.

He told Major Robbins, "Notify General Hawkins that he may proceed with establishing his headquarters in Bridgeport."

A crowd of reporters was beginning to congregate around them. Agent Fisher gently nudged the old man toward the elevators.

In a whisper, Freeman also instructed Robbins, "Tell Colonel Essing I want to meet with General Hawkins and the rest of his staff at 0900."

With that, Fisher all but pushed him into the elevator.

Silently the General and his two Secret Service agents ascended to the penthouse. It was 10:13 P.M. Eastern Daylight Time. Twenty-four hours had passed since the bomb exploded in New York Harbor. All were now bone-weary from the sleepless night, the strained emotions, the demands of travel, the breakneck pace, and the gravity of the moment.

Then, suddenly, as the doors opened to the penthouse, the General collapsed.

Fourteen

By the time Steve Nunn broke from his work to survey Pennsylvania Avenue, it was dark outside. Like most people in key government positions, he had not slept since the bombing. It was, by far, the most grueling day of his life.

As head of the criminal division, he was responsible for carrying out the dragnet President Gonzales sanctioned that morning. The initial results were very encouraging. Many of the most dangerous subversives were already in custody, but that didn't make Nunn any less tired.

The success of the sweep didn't surprise him. Planning for it had been in the works ever since Angela DeKalb assumed office. At her behest, developing a coordinated response to a crisis like this one had become the highest priority of his division. For the better part of four years, she peered over his shoulder while the plan was developed. Code-named Operation Cockroach, it wasn't long before the planners in his department took to calling it *la Cucaracha*. It was a two-stage operation designed to emasculate the nation's domestic adversaries if it ever came under attack or experienced a civil emergency.

The first stage involved the systematic monitoring of anyone deemed to be an enemy of the state. Prior to passage of the Anarchy Act, this type of surveillance was illegal. Even under its terms, some of the tactics employed in *la Cucaracha* were questionable.

Thousands of unsuspecting suspects had been placed under routine surveillance during the past eighteen months.

The second stage of Cockroach began nine hours ago. It required close coordination with the DPS and entailed a massive dragnet conducted by thousands of law enforcement officials across the country. Of the fifteen thousand names on the enemies list, over four thousand were already under arrest.

If only we'd implemented it sooner, he thought.

The traffic down on Pennsylvania Avenue was light, even for a Sunday evening.

It can't even rightfully be called traffic.

There was a knock on the door.

"Come in," he yelled.

It was Angela DeKalb.

"Where's Doris?" she asked, referring to his secretary.

"Oh, I let her go home."

Nunn could count on one hand the number of visits Angela made to his office in the past, so this meant something.

Never one to chitchat, the AG asked, "What's the latest on the investigation?"

"The DPS has some information on the skiff. I think they called it a Windjammer."

"A Wavejammer," she corrected.

"Yes, the one that was being pursued by the Coast Guard just before the explosion."

Angela nodded but said nothing, his cue to continue.

"Well, it *was* the same one that was stolen from the boatyard in Toms River last April. The owner of the marina was able to identify the registration numbers from a satellite photograph."

"Good."

Rifling through some papers on his desk, Nunn cited another critical finding. "They did some time-lapse analysis of the satellite photos. It confirmed that the final location of the Wavejammer was at the epicenter of the blast. It's the first solid piece of evidence we have, but it's far from conclusive."

"Sounds awfully conclusive to me. Any thoughts on who might have done it?"

"None. Apparently, the launch set out from a makeshift boathouse near Perth Amboy. It's still too early to examine the records at the county complex, but we just got word that there's a hot site in Baltimore. That should tell us who owns the property along the Arthur Kill."

"The Arthur Kill?"

"It's the river channel that runs between Staten Island and New Jersey." Then, anxious to relay some good news, he said, "The early returns on Cockroach are really impressive."

"That's why I'm here," she replied. "I wanted to commend you in person."

Another break with tradition. A compliment from DeKalb was as rare as the truth. However, she immediately conditioned it.

"We need to keep the heat on, though. All night. When people start firing up their teletrans tomorrow our secret will be out. Anyone who's eluded us so far will head for cover. Essentially, we have another six hours of prime fishing."

"Are you afraid the details of the plan will leak?"

"No," she said, "not really. But if they do, we'll issue cease-and-desist orders to buy more time. But the element of surprise will be gone. There's already been a considerable amount of speculation on the net. So far, no one has put two and two together. They're calling it a logical response to the bombing."

Steve listened patiently, even though DeKalb was only repeating what he had been telling himself all day. Angela relished her role as the mastermind of Operation Cockroach, and in the interest of survival, he wasn't about to shoulder her out.

"That reminds me," she said. "How well do you know Stewart Addison?"

"From the Bureau of Prisons?"

"Yes."

"Not well. Why?"

"Two reasons. I wanted someone to act as a liaison between General Freeman's staff and us. But I also want whoever it is to be familiar with prison ops. So, he came to mind."

"Prison ops?"

"Yes, we'll have to transfer some of the prisoners housed inside the Cordon to other locations. Having Addison on the General's staff would help to expedite the process."

"That makes sense," replied Nunn.

Actually, Nunn thought Addison was a jerk, one of those effeminate andros who acted disdainfully toward everyone and everything. Nothing about him could be mistaken for honor or integrity. The man was a weasel. He couldn't imagine what Angela saw in him. *Unless,* he thought, *she just wants to keep tabs on Freeman.*

Angela looked at her watch. "I have to go. I'm late for a meeting with Legislative Affairs. There's a powwow with the congressional leadership tomorrow to discuss suspension of the writ."

Then, as she was about to exit, she stopped suddenly and asked, "By the way, who owned the stolen boat?"

"The boat?"

"Yes," she said, impatiently, "the Wavejammer."

"Oh, it's here somewhere," Steve said. He leafed through some papers until he found the DPS report. "The guy's name is Phillip Armstrong."

Fifteen

Monday, July 4 (5:15 A.M. EDT)
The Armitage Hotel, Philadelphia

"General Freeman?" Bob Fisher shook him tentatively.

The old man blinked and rolled over with a grunt.

"Sir, your orders were to be up by 0500. It's a little past that, now."

Again, the old soldier grunted, although this time with an iota of consciousness.

Agent Reynolds and Major Robbins stood beside Fisher. All were relieved to see Freeman stir. When he passed out the night before, the two agents carried him to his bed with the help of the guards posted at the penthouse door. Then, they called in the regimental surgeon. He diagnosed the problem as mild exhaustion. After he left, Fisher and Reynolds took turns watching their charge and catnapping through the night.

The red-haired Major tried a different tack. "Sir, would you like some coffee?"

The old man extended his arm, and Fisher pulled him into a sitting position. All he had on was a pair of skivvies. Rubbing his eyes with his palms, he accepted the cup from Robbins and took a sip. The temperature of the brew was perfect.

"Thanks, Major," the General said. "I hope you'll forgive me . . . I can't remember your name."

"It's Robbins, sir, Jeff Robbins."

"Robbins. Of course. Were you able to set up a meeting with General Hawkins?"

"Yes, sir. He'll be here at 0830 hours."

Yawning, Freeman set the cup on the end table. As he sat hunched over on the bed with his hands tucked between his legs, the fog began to lift.

Robbins asked, "Would you like some breakfast, sir?"

He thought for a minute, then said weakly, "A Denver omelet would be great."

As the young Major turned to go, Freeman said, "I'd like to get another reading of the situation from the air today, Major. Give me thirty minutes."

"Roger that, sir. I'll notify the pilots."

Fisher groaned inwardly, but he was relieved to see the General stand. The old man yawned, stretched lazily, then sneezed so hard it pressed out a fart.

Fisher and Reynolds both bit down on a laugh.

The General asked, "What happened last night?"

Fisher answered, "You collapsed in the elevator. The doctor said it was exhaustion. So he implanted an endorphin battery in your neck." Mirthfully, he added, "You might get in thirty-six today, General."

Freeman nodded and cracked, "I might even carry my own bag."

He ran his knotty fingers around his neck, feeling for the battery. His hair shot out in every direction, and his shoulders were bent. When he picked up his coffee and headed off to the bathroom, Fisher noticed that the movement made him wince.

But, in the dry heat of the sauna, Freeman made a quick recovery. Although his performance on the bridge the night before brought back memories of his triumphal landing in Tel Aviv at the outset of the war, it also signaled the enormity of the task ahead.

Small victories, he decided. *That's all I can hope for.*

He imagined an approach similar to the Fabian strategy of George Washington. He didn't need to win; he simply couldn't lose.

But, like Washington, will I be denied the men and matériel I need?

Regardless, he knew from his experience in Jerusalem that, even if he had all the king's horses as well as his men, it would take many years to put this Humpty together again.

His thoughts turned to his daughter Lena, specifically, to their quarrel on the previous day.

She's so stubborn. Like her mother. You can't win with her.

Anyone who knew Freeman well and was privy to these thoughts would have burst out laughing. Nobody was more stubborn or argumentative than James A. Freeman. Nobody.

But in his mind, leaving her behind was the lesser of two evils. *There's no way I could let her come with me. This is a war zone! Maybe in a couple of days.* He brightened. *That's it!* He would call and tell her to come up in a couple of days, when things were more settled.

There was a knock on the sauna door.

"Everything okay in there, General?"

It was Fisher.

"Yeah, Bob, I'm fine. But, could you do me a favor? Call down to Shady Grove. I want to talk to Lena."

The response was delayed.

Finally, Fisher cracked the door and said, "Sir, she left last night for Atlanta."

"Atlanta?!"

"Yes, sir. Apparently, she drove down with Jack Clancey. That's where he lives now."

Sixteen

After Clancey got ditched by Freeman, he decided to rent a car and head down to Georgia. Lena, feeling no less ditched, asked to go along. Willing to share the threat of fallout at her father's side, she had no desire to sit at home and wait passively for it to find her there. Besides, Jack Clancey was the closest thing she had to a brother. She felt safe with him.

So after a few hours sleep and a quick snack, they left her house in Shady Grove in her Centurion Airdrive and headed south. It was after one in the morning when they left and, because Jack had a Tuesday meeting in Augusta with his editor at *Veriquest*, they took the less scenic route.

At a rest stop outside Florence, Jack went inside to get coffee. A headline from *USA Yesterday* immediately grabbed his attention:

ALL HAIL THE LION!

Returning to the car he said, "Check this out," as he tossed the paper over to Lena. On the front page was a close-up of her father holding a young girl in his arms, pointing to some object in the distance with assurance. His intervention on the bridge was the big story. The text of the President's address to the nation was below the fold.

While Jack recharged the hydrogen tank, Lena read the article. When he got back in, she commented, "God, this reporter was impressed. Listen to these descriptions: 'commanding, authoritative, decisive.'"

"It must do the old boy good to know his name is on the lips of people all over the world again," quipped Jack, as he pulled out of the station. Quickly, he added, "And this time with approval."

Lena laughed. "Did you know he cooked all that 'Lion' business up from a book he read as a kid?"

"Oh? How's that?" said Jack, turning onto I-95.

"Well, after the Old City of Jerusalem was bombed and the Arabs attacked, he landed with the American Expeditionary Force." She thought for a moment, then corrected herself. "No, I guess the AEF arrived in Tel Aviv a few days before he did. He came ashore on September first near the ancient port of Jaffa on a helicopter from the aircraft carrier *Jimmy Carter.*"

Still perusing the paper, she recalled, "The welcoming ceremony was arranged by the Israeli government, but it was Teddy who suggested having one. I'll give him credit. He knew the powerful symbolism of landing there. The critics called it a cheap rip-off of MacArthur or Patton, but it was actually a cheap rip-off of Richard the Lionheart."

"What do you mean?"

"Well, here's how he told it. Nine hundred years before Teddy's arrival in Jaffa, Richard of England leapt from his red galley and splashed ashore in the waist-deep surf, wearing only a mail shirt and a steel cap, firing his crossbow. His Crusaders were grossly outnumbered by the army of Saladin, which was encamped there on the beach. Hundreds of Christians were trapped in the citadel nearby. Somehow, Richard's knights won the day, and the Christians were delivered." She stopped for a second, then added, "I guess Teddy figured his arrival was no less auspicious than Richard's."

"Sometimes it's hard to fathom just how calculating that old man is," said Jack.

She said, "He took me there after the war . . . I think just to crow about it. He was really proud of the fact that, not only was his crusade bigger, it was also more successful."

"But who came up with 'the Lion of Jaffa' thing?"

"Really," she laughed, "that's the genius of it! A swarm of Israelis was on-hand to greet him when the helicopter landed. And, although there were a quarter of a million Americans who helped save them from certain annihilation, that's not how it went down. They were absolutely wild with joy—like those Christians trapped in the citadel. And Teddy never fired a shot. He just stood in the back of a scout car, waving to the adoring crowds that lined the streets."

With a mouthful of coffee cake, Jack asked, "So he figured that, eventually, someone would equate his arrival with Richard's?"

She nodded. "The next day, the headline in *Haaretz* read something like 'The Return of the Lion.' Now, every time he hears his name mentioned in the same breath as Richard's, his head gets bigger than a beach ball."

Folding the paper, she said, with eyes as sad as her voice, "But this thing? I know it's an attempt to bottle the same lighting, but it's not worth it. Like you said, he's a schemer. Under the guise of duty, honor, and country, he's looking to gain some measure of personal redemption and salvage his wounded pride. Only, I'm afraid it won't work this time."

Jack could only shake his head. He, too, was less than optimistic about Freeman's quest for crowning glory. "He's a different man from the one I knew. Much more impatient. And contentious. Like he's more interested in winning an argument than a friend. And he's more forgetful, too. Hell, the other day, he couldn't even remember that I had moved down to Atlanta."

"Just out of curiosity, how did you two meet?" Lena asked, throwing the paper in the back seat.

"It was at a cocktail party back in the '40s. I was in the advertising business, selling canned news stories to the networks for business clients. When we met, he was Army chief-of-staff. It's funny, too. Even though he was fifteen years my senior, we got along great—because we're both from Jersey."

Jack pulled into the high speed lane and engaged the anti-collision system, remembering, "When he agreed to be Art Simpson's running mate in '48, he asked me to be his press secretary. So I joined the campaign and, after we won, I sold my business and hooked up with him permanently."

"Is it really true that Simpson only chose him for his marquee value?"

Picking crumbs from the coffee cake off his lap, and popping them into his mouth between occasional glances at the road, Jack replied, "That's my take. Beyond the ceremonial duties associated with the vice-presidency, Simpson never trusted him with anything important." Jack chuckled as he said, "Man, we had a great time that first year: foreign junkets, state funerals, lavish vacations. Lots of laughs on the rubber-chicken circuit." Then, becoming serious, he said, "That all changed on May 10, 2050, though."

On that day, Arthur Simpson was shot at the dedication of a cold fusion plant near Sacramento. Although he survived, he suffered extensive brain damage. Five days later, Freeman was sworn into office. Clancey served as White House press secretary until the end of his presidency.

* * * * *

As they approached the outskirts of Columbia, South Carolina, Lena commented, "This is where I was born."

"Really," said Jack. "I didn't know that."

"Yep. In 2019, a few months after my father was reassigned to Fort Jackson."

"Was that when he was at NATO?"

"Uh, huh. Mom said he hated the politics in Brussels. And, he was afraid of being ground off in a desk job overseas. His first love was commanding troops, and he wanted to rejoin the 82nd Airborne, but the only thing available at the time was a company command with the infantry training group down here."

"I bet that made Sarah happy."

"Oh, man, she hated it. Can you imagine a wealthy, Dutch Jewess, the daughter of a London art dealer, arriving with trunk loads of Left Bank *peintures* to the mildewed bathrooms, whining spouses and bird-sized mosquitoes of a pineland Army base?"

Clancey chuckled. "From what I remember of her, no. That's why she moved to D.C., right?"

"Yes, after my grandparents were killed in a car accident. Teddy went up to liquidate the estate, and my mother fell in love with Princeton. It reminded her of London and her days at Wellesley. So one night, after dinner, she made it known that she had hidden her tears long enough. She was done playing the role of the stoic army wife and wasn't coming back here. Or to any other post for that matter."

"I remember hearing that when he asked her if she wanted a divorce, she answered, 'No, I want a discharge!'"

"Yup."

"That was the first of many separations, huh?"

Lena nodded. "It didn't last long, though. The brass wasn't about to send the kid who made 'The Catch' to oblivion in the Arabian desert or the jungles of Columbia. They wanted to showcase him in their dealings with the White House and up on Capitol Hill. So his transfer came through in six months. I think that's when he was as- signed to the State Department as special liaison for asynchronous warfare."

"I know you told me once, but why do you always call him Teddy?"

"That's what folks called him in high school. His baseball coach said he looked like Ted Williams."

Jack recalled, "He told me he threw a no-hitter in his senior year."

"April 9, 2007, to be exact. His eighteenth birthday. To hear him tell it, he was the second-coming of Cy Young, but Mom was always quick to confirm his boasts." Pausing momentarily, she added, "Believe it or not, she said that at one time he actually thought of becoming a minister."

"Get out!"

"Honest. Grandpa Charles was a professor of religious studies at Princeton Theological Seminary. He and Grandma took my father to services at the cathedral on campus every Sunday. Since he was an only child, my grandfather spent every waking hour pounding the Bible into him. At first Teddy loved it. Then he entered high school, and sports and girls quickly disabused him of any ministerial dreams. He became indifferent to religion, and by the time he graduated from West Point, he was downright hostile toward it."

Lena's earlier mention of "The Catch" spurred Jack to say, "Did you know that Academy plebes are asked, '*Who made The Catch?*' And, if they answer 'Willie Mays,' they have to walk hours?"

"No, I didn't, but I'm not surprised. He's like Blanchard and Davis up there! I don't know how many times the Knights lost to Navy before his touchdown ended the drought, but it was a lot. That was his first taste of glory." Retrieving the newspaper from the back seat, she looked at it for a second, tapped the photo of him holding the little girl and said, "I think a lot of his exhibitionism stems from that day."

As a junior at West Point, Freeman caught a desperation pass that beat the Middies. A picture of it even made the cover of *Sports Illustrated*. As a result, a place of honor in the illustrious lore of the Academy was granted to him. And he distinguished himself in all respects there. His intelligence, conditioning, and final rank foreshadowed the making of a great war fighter. He left the Corps with the undying admiration of the entire brigade.

"And if his father had anything to do with it, it would have never happened."

"No, I guess Grandpa hated football. That's why Teddy never played in high school."

"Your father told me that old 'Bishop Charles' would quote Biblical injunctions against it."

"Mom said Dad never forgave the Bishop for that, always calling him a 'peace queer.' Heck, that's why he enrolled at West Point—to spite him! When he made the football team his freshman year, he sent back the Bible his father gave him as a boy with an inscription in red ink: 'A double-minded man is unstable in his ways.'"

And with that, Jack Clancey learned the root of the former President's anti-Christian politics.

Seventeen

Monday, July 4 (8:06 A.M. EDT)
Franklin Square, Philadelphia

"The Mass is ended. Let us go in peace to love and to serve the Lord," said the celebrant.

"Amen," responded the congregation, which consisted of a thousand sick and anxious refugees. They were gathered around an altar—a folding table covered by a picnic blanket—in the southwest corner of the leafy park. To the east the sun was rising, and with it, a ray of hope.

"And God bless America," added Father Peter Bernard, his voice cracking with grief for his little flock.

For most of the previous afternoon Peter had taken advantage of Father Luke's hospitality. The old Franciscan even heard his confession. But toward evening, the needs of the old Irishman's parishioners began to mount, and he excused himself. After a two-hour nap in the sweltering rectory, Peter hiked downtown to ply his trade. A few hours later, when he saw James Freeman staring down at him while he anointed a dying man, he almost panicked. Thinking his old nemesis had recognized him, he quickly returned to St. Francis.

After a fitful night of sleep, it dawned on him that, even if Freeman did finger him, it didn't matter. He had done nothing wrong. So that morning he returned to Franklin Square with two bags of communion wafers to say Mass. When it was over, he judged it the most exhilarating experience of his life.

Back at St. Francis, Luke Monaghan had just finished the eight o'clock Mass. Peter waited while the old Irishman chatted with a few parishioners on the front steps.

When Monaghan said goodbye to the last of them, he turned to Peter and asked, "How'd it go?"

"Better than I might have hoped."

"Good," said Monaghan, in his lyrical way. "Very good."

Peter admitted, "I was really nervous. I don't know if I've ever preached to a crowd that big."

"I bet it was a corker," Luke said, reaching high to pat the younger man on the shoulder.

They walked toward the sacristy. "I don't know," Peter said, fumbling with his Mass kit. "I talked about Washington's prayer at Valley Forge. Another desperate hour in our history."

"Is that so," said the older priest? "I'm not familiar with it. You say it was a prayer?"

"Yes, well, there are questions as to how and when he offered it, but it's always inspired me."

"What did he say?"

"That religion and morality are critical to our political success. That any man who subverts them can never claim to be a patriot. That we will never be happy as a nation without emulating God's justice, mercy, and love. Things like that."

"Hmm," the Irishman sighed, clasping his hands behind his back.

In the sacristy, Monaghan removed and stored his vestments, tidied up, then inquired, "Would you care for some breakfast?"

"Sure."

Over a bowl of cereal in the rectory, Peter said, "I've decided to move on, Luke."

Monaghan noticed that he appeared nervous and distracted.

"Oh? Might I ask where to?"

"Baltimore. I have to report to my superior."

"Well, that's fine, so long as you know you're welcome to stay here as long as you'd like."

"I know, Father. You've been like a brother. I'll never forget all you've done for me."

Peter finished his cereal and put his dishes in the sink. "I'll go up and get my things. By the way, you don't happen to have a smaller pack than the one I'm using, do you?"

Monaghan thought it an odd request but answered, "Matter of fact, I do."

Rummaging through the hall closet, he pulled out one of those rucksacks popular with schoolchildren and suicide bombers—a dark green one.

"I found this under a pew last year."

"Thanks."

Peter took it and went upstairs. There, he did something that would forever alter his fate.

Though he tried to dismiss his encounter with President Freeman the night before, with each passing minute, the rabbit in him grew. He went into the bathroom, locked the door, and took off his shirt. Opening his shaving kit, he pulled out a pocketknife. Feeling at the bump on his right shoulder, he made two small incisions in the shape of an X directly over the spot where the bolus was implanted. Then, like a teenager dispatching a pimple, he squeezed the flesh between the tips of his forefingers and like his cell mate predicted it would, the bird-dog popped out.

Tony Two Palms would be proud, he thought.

As he raised the bloody chip to the light for inspection, it slipped from his hand, bounced into the sink, and disappeared down the drain. Since there was no possibility of retrieving it without a plumber, he opened the faucets full-bore and attempted to flush it into the Gulf Stream.

Then he pressed a wad of toilet paper on the cut to stop the bleeding, covered it with a band aid from the medicine chest, and returned to the bedroom.

Stripping off his pants, he folded his clerics and put them and a few other items in the rucksack Monaghan gave him. Then, he donned a pair of cargo shorts and a tee shirt, stored his dirty laundry in the big, orange backpack, leaned it against the wall in the corner of the room, and headed back downstairs.

Monaghan was waiting for him by the landing near the front door. Over his shoulder was a dish towel.

Peter said, "I wonder if I could ask another favor? I left some clothes in my backpack upstairs. Could you keep them for me?"

"On the condition that you come back for them someday."

"It's a deal."

The older priest knew something was wrong. He asked, "What's bothering you, Peter?"

He kept mum about removing his "dog," but told the old Franciscan of his encounter with James Freeman the previous night.

Monaghan listened intently. When Peter was finished, he squinted a little and said, "Remember yesterday—when I asked you if you were on the attack or in retreat?"

Peter nodded.

"Well, you never really answered my question."

It took awhile for Peter to respond.

"Honestly, Father . . . I don't know."

Tenderly, Monaghan said, "Come, walk with me."

He grabbed a book off one of the shelves in his den and led the younger man back over to the church. There, he directed him to the front pew. It was still cool and dark inside. A few people were scattered about, apparently with the idea of isolating themselves from each other.

The two priests sat quietly for a few minutes.

Monaghan knew that his friend's inner trial wasn't between attacking and retreating. His dilemma involved a choice of a different kind.

Leaning close, he said in a hushed but resolute tone, "Listen, Peter, a good person like you, a person who renounces evil, still has a choice to make. It's like the rich young man who asked Jesus what good he must do to gain eternal life. Jesus tells him to keep the commandments. The young man responds that he does but still feels lacking. Do you remember what Christ said? 'If you wish to be *perfect,* go, sell what you have and give to the poor. Then come, follow me.' We know the young man went away sadly because he had many possessions."

"But," Peter asserted, "I've already made the choice between—"

Raising a bony, white finger, Monaghan stopped him. "Please. Hear me out. Christ was addressing the question of holiness. Sainthood. Beatitude. And that kind of perfection isn't simply a matter of doing what's right or good. Or of keeping the commandments. It's the subjugation of our entire being to God's will."

Squeezing the book in his hands, he said, "I'm not telling you anything you don't know, Peter. Just look upon this as a gentle reminder. Obviously, total submission to God's will is a tall order. Most people are frightened off by the finality of it. Like the rich young man, they cannot abide the loss of power, glory and wealth. The glamour of sin is too great. And as hard as attaining perfection on an individual basis is, to your Humanist adversaries I would say that, on a collective basis, *it's absolutely impossible.* Why, even the Church looks to the Second Coming to realize its perfection."

His mein grew sad as he said, "But, Peter, in truth, you have the same problem as the Humanists. You're resisting God's will. You don't reject him outright like they do. You just don't trust him enough to abandon your earthly desires and surrender to him mind, body and soul. You're still in thrall to the things of this world. You're still trying to run by the power of your own lights." Then, with a wry chortle, he added, "That's the irony of it, though. You're free to do so. Because what pleasure can God derive from our love and obedience if it isn't given freely?"

Monaghan suddenly grew animated, waving one hand and clutching the book with the other.

"Who knows? The day may come when you abandon the fight against secularism for what I call the pick-and-shovel work of salvation, like serving in a foreign mission or teaching in a classroom. Heavens! You might even leave the priesthood. My point is that, whatever you do, you must ask yourself one question: *Is it God's will?* Remember, even Christ deferred to his Father in Gethsemane."

Then, he finally handed the book to Peter. It was a leather-bound edition of *Paradise Lost*. "This may help you to discern his plan for you. Read it, and you'll see what I mean. And try not to think about the fact that it was written by a Protestant."

It was so richly appointed that Peter was reluctant to accept it. Shaking his head, he raised his hand and closed his eyes, saying, "I can't."

"Please," the old pastor insisted, as he closed his young protégé's hands around it. "I want you to have it. All I ask is that you remember me in your prayers."

With a shrug, Peter replied, "Luke, I don't know what to say, except thanks."

With that, they moved to the side door. As they shook hands, Peter said, "You know, I really do appreciate your help. I only pray that if the Lord wants me to continue the fight against humanism, well, that . . . eventually, I don't wind up like them."

The old Irishman shook his head empathically. With a twinkle, he said, "No, Peter, these secularists—they're high-powered intellectuals. You'll *never* be like them."

Eighteen

General Freeman's first staff meeting went off without a hitch, due largely to the administrative talents of Colonel Essing. Most of the meeting was spent discussing the need to accelerate the radiation abatement effort.

Throughout the meeting, the only person who never entered the discussion was the "liaison" from Justice, Stewart Addison. He sat at the end of the table furthest from the General, occupying the only chair, the one he rolled over from Freeman's desk. Everyone else stood.

Shifting frequently, as if discomforted, he exuded an air of impatience, even irritation at the length and depth of the meeting. Each time an additional photo or map was introduced for analysis, he grimaced as if to say, "Not again!" Despite the gravity of the situation, he fussed over his clothing and fingernails, seemingly oblivious to the proceedings.

It was apparent that Addison spent a considerable amount of time each day primping himself. His grooming and wardrobe were impeccable. Tall, pale, and slightly overweight, he took great care to conceal his small town Midwestern roots. He wore an olive green, double-breasted Italian suit. This was set against a long, richly-patterned silk tie of violet and gold. His wavy hair was platinum-dyed and combed into a Flatbush Avenue duck-tail at the base of his neck. Barely visible behind droopy lids were light gray eyes, so light as to appear silver. At forty-one, his skin was nipped-and-tucked to perfection. A treasury of exotic jewelry and rings adorned his wrists and fingers. Absent his paunch, he was on the outside what most people wished they were on the inside: flawless.

Ostensibly, he was assigned to the General's staff to oversee the needs of the federal courts and prison population within the boundaries of the Cordon. But in reality, he was a mole, the personal agent of Angela DeKalb, planted there to protect her interests.

When DeKalb recommended that the President appoint James Freeman as governor of the Cordon, she knew that under the law, his power would be arbitrary and absolute. With that in mind, she wasn't about to risk all by giving Freeman *carte blanche* in matters of lasting legal significance. She intended to keep her fingers in the pie, and she had the President's blessing in that regard.

After two hours of concentrated deliberation, the meeting was about to end. Most of those present took note of Addison's aloofness.

The General was particularly put out. That Addison was a spy was obvious. The question was whether or not he had any other practical value. "Mr. Addison, are there any matters of concern to the Justice Department at this point?" he asked.

Addison's response was calculated to rankle. With an exasperated sigh, he uncrossed his legs and rose out of his chair, pushing away from it with a pained expression. It left everyone with the impression that standing to address them was more trouble than it was worth. When he spoke, it was with the kind of teeth-clenched, jaw-jutting formality of a Boston Brahmin.

"Since I've only just arrived, it may take a day or two for me to fully assess the ongoing threat to our prison population. I can assure you, General, that once I have, I will make our wishes known."

"Please do," said Freeman, with mock concern.

It was all he could do to keep from ripping into the man. Of all the pompous, pretentious nose-pickers he had the misfortune of meeting during his years in government, this one had to rank near the top.

"*Please* do," he repeated.

Nineteen

Monday, July 4 (10:33 A.M. EDT)
The Department of Justice, Washington, D.C.

Steve Nunn thought it was a mistake. He didn't like surrendering the element of surprise in an investigation. To announce or to leak even minor findings went against his grain. It was beyond him now, though.

Angela DeKalb smiled as she made her way to the podium. She wore a light gray suit and heels, the perfect contrast to her long, raven hair, which was gathered discreetly in back. Tall and alluring, without a word she commanded the silence of the room. She spoke softly but clearly.

"This morning, I am pleased to report that, since the bombing two nights ago, the government has arrested or detained more than eight thousand individuals. All are suspected of treasonous or seditious activities."

The number caught the reporters by surprise. She knew it would so, ever the tactician, she paused for a moment to allow for effect. Then she laid out the government's twofold objective: to trap the perpetrators of the attack and to prevent the possibility of a follow-on. Since the President announced the temporary suspension of *habeas corpus* earlier that morning, she buttressed the "life-and-limb" rationale he gave for doing it. Then she addressed some specifics about the attack itself, including the particulars on the Wavejammer theft.

She finished her prepared remarks by saying, "So far, there is no clear indication as to who perpetrated the bombing, nor is there a group claiming responsibility."

She stopped, scanned the room, and pointed to a questioner in the first row.

It was Alice Silverman from UPC. "You say that there's been no claim of responsibility, but did the bomb have a signature? Was it one of the ones stolen from the Russian arsenal in '49?"

"The exact signature of the bomb hasn't been determined, but early indications suggest it's not Russian. One conclusion can be drawn from the nature of the attack, however. The people who did this were well funded, well organized, and obviously, very secretive. Otherwise, they couldn't have pulled it off. The sheer logistics of such an enterprise eliminates most of the little fish from consideration."

The next question: "Yesterday, John Chambers, the publisher of the *Washington Ledger* was arrested on charges of sedition. Can you please elaborate?"

"Under the terms of the Tranquility Act, the government can move to suppress news organizations for inflammatory reporting during times of national emergency. The reason Mr. Chambers was arrested was for just such a violation. Yesterday's headline in his paper, implying that the end of the world is at hand, was deemed highly inflammatory and as such, a threat to public safety. Mr. Chambers has been released on bond, but make no mistake. Our intent is to prosecute any news organization that violates even so much as the spirit of the Act during this crisis."

Her words had a sobering effect, but one feisty news hound asked, "Can you tell us if anyone *in this room* is at risk?"

A vexing smile came over the Attorney General's face. A few reporters chuckled however timidly.

"No," she assured them, "so far, the media has reacted as one would expect. At this stage of the crisis, some overreaction is understandable. Let me remind you, however, especially those whose message is primarily visual, the type of footage that was broadcast at the outset will not be permitted as time goes on. Nor will some of the more explicit published reports we've read in the past two days. Referring to her notes, she said, "Keep in mind that, under the Tranquility Act, *any film, picture, image, drawing, text, or word that compromises our common defense or domestic tranquility* is expressly forbidden in times of crisis."

She put particular emphasis on her next comment, staring down at the reporters and holding her right index finger high. "Be fore-warned. If your intent is to toy with the already-fragile mindset of the American public, incite further turmoil, or advantage our enemies, we *will* bring an action against you."

A chill descended on the room. The sight of the press frozen in silence attested to the oppressive power of the Act. Still, there were a few reporters willing to take chances. One was Turk Findley from the *Los Humanos Examiner.* "You said that the couple from New Jersey is cooperating in the investigation. Are they suspects, too?"

"No."

"Who stole the boat?" cried someone from the back of the room.

That the press would ask such a question was as natural as flowers in spring, but she found this one particularly irritating.

"If we knew that," she snapped, "we'd be attending to far more important matters right now. Of that, I can assure you."

A woman from the Global News Network was next. "Martial law has been declared in the states impacted by the bomb. It's my understanding that, under martial law, the civil rights of the population within the district are suspended. Is that true?"

"Yes. It is."

"And that the civil courts cannot subsequently review the decisions of the military authority or question any abuse of its powers?"

"For the most part, that is correct."

"Then is it fair to say that General Freeman's powers are dictatorial?"

Shaking her head decisively, she said, "No. Until the courts can resume normal operations, the General is responsible for the administration of justice within the Cordon. He has a wide degree of latitude, but he *is* answerable to the President for his actions, as well as his superiors at the Pentagon. There will be considerable congressional oversight. The Department of Justice also has a liaison on his staff who will ensure close coordination between my office and his. Checks and balances do exist, so to characterize his power as dictatorial is neither fair nor accurate."

"Last question," she said, pointing to a reporter from the *Miami Herald*.

"Hypothetically speaking, then," the woman asked, "if a person disobeys an order from a police or military official and is shot dead, there will be no investigation or inquiry into the shooting?"

"If that person is engaged in a criminal act, inciting a disturbance, or threatening resistance to the civilian or military authorities, then that's true—there probably won't be. The Atlantic Cordon is a war zone. If there are violations of the Geneva Convention, such as unprovoked atrocities against the civilian population or prisoners, justice will be meted out but only insofar as it applies to the rules of war."

What little patience the AG had for the media was wearing thin so, with a perfunctory smile and polite nod, she excused herself.

A hurricane of unrequited questions blew her out of the room, masking the awed response of the Fourth Estate to the suspension of *habeas corpus* and the launch of Operation Cockroach. It was testimony to how far the press had fallen from its once-vaunted role in the world's greatest democracy. The infamous scribblers so detested by George Washington and the majority of his successors had been thoroughly silenced by the oppressive terms of the Tranquility Act.

Twenty

Monday, July 4 (11:04 A.M. EDT)
The Scharon Building, Philadelphia

"Peter Bernard! That's who it was!"

"Who?" inquired Major Robbins.

"The man I saw last night in Franklin Square."

The General was eating a turkey sandwich in his office, watching a rerun of the DeKalb press conference. Conspicuously missing from it was any mention of the "persons of interest" list he heard was forthcoming. While munching on the sandwich—which tasted more like baloney than turkey—he swiveled around in his chair and looked out on the river, the bridges, and the waterfront.

Robbins said, "If you don't mind my asking, sir, who's Peter Bernard?"

"The Crimson Collar," Freeman answered, swiveling back to face him.

The gangly adjutant looked perplexed.

Freeman liked the kid and didn't want to leave him behind. "Don't they teach history anymore, Robbins? You've never heard of the Deacon Carroll Affair?"

"No, sir."

"Well, of all the things that happened in my life, that was certainly one of the strangest."

He gave the Major a full account of the incident, including the charges made by Bernard against Sonny Collier.

Finishing, he said, "I'll never forget how out of place he looked. The priest, that is." He lowered his eyes and added, "Later on, when I was president, Ms. DeKalb prosecuted him in the Spark Park bombing." Taking another bite of his sandwich, he calculated, "He must have completed his sentence." The image of Bernard ministering to the man in the Red Cross tent prompted him to say, "Funny, he seems like a decent guy. I guess he just can't get out of his own way."

"You mentioned Colonel Collier? Is that *the* Colonel Collier?" asked the young aide while collating some papers.

"The very same."

"Why did he shoot the woman?"

"I don't know. He said his weapon misfired. I ordered him not to go in with his men, but not only did he go in, he was so far out in front of them that, with the exception of the priest, no one else saw what happened in the stairwell."

Robbins asked, "How did he win the Medal of Honor?"

"I can't remember all the details. It was during the Cuban Reclamation, when Gitmo came under attack. An amphibious assault was launched from South Florida. The objective was to seize Havana. Collier was with the 82nd at the time. They dropped into the southern mountains to block any relief effort. He almost single-handedly wiped out two companies of Venezuelans who had his men trapped in a ravine. How they got there I'll never know, but old Sonny sure made up for it."

"He must have been quite a soldier," assumed the affable Robbins.

"He was, but he was a lousy officer. By the time he joined the 77th, he'd become something of a martinet. He drove his men almost as hard as he did the enemy. Very bright, but never showed any feeling toward them. It became a source of friction between us. Then he made the mistake of putting a move on my daughter at a regimental dinner!"

The old soldier shook his head and laughed. Noticing that his adjutant was no less captivated by this yarn than Miles Garvin was by the one he told out on the Blackfoot, he kept going, albeit more seriously.

"The rift really widened after we retook the courthouse. I mean, he disobeyed a direct order. I tried to look the other way, but the brass wouldn't have it. They were under a lot of pressure from Washington to call an inquiry because a Catholic priest was insisting that Collier shot the woman in cold blood."

Robbins, who might have made a good cop, asked, "Did he?"

"I really don't know. I asked him once. It was in the officer's club down at Fort Benning during the Georgia-Florida game. He wanted me to get with his attorney and go over my testimony before the hearing. But I didn't want it to look as if I'd been coached."

* * * * *

Actually, Freeman was half-lit when they talked, but he assured Collier that he intended to downplay his entry into the building as a misinterpretation of orders.

"Don't worry, Sonny," he said reassuringly, "this will be easier than fishing with dynamite."

Collier had no reason to doubt him. From the outset, he felt that Jim Freeman was his strongest witness.

And that's how Freeman testified when he took the stand. He also stated that, to the best of his knowledge, the shooting was accidental.

But, during the cross, he was grilled about the order he gave Collier to avoid any *direct* participation in the fighting. The success of Collier's defense hinged on this weasel word. How Freeman interpreted it was crucial. But ill-prepared and surprisingly muddled, he flubbed it badly, coming across like a teenager trying to explain how a bag of pot got under his mattress.

Actually, what made his testimony implausible was its truthfulness. After listening to excerpts from the battle record, he was forced to acknowledge that it was absurd to think his order was misinterpreted and admitted that Collier's presence in the stairwell could only be construed as participating *directly*.

Quick to capitalize on this opening, the prosecutor hammered on it mercilessly, casting aspersions on Collier's motives for doing what he did. Ultimately, Sonny's defense was successful in arguing that his weapon discharged accidentally, so he was exonerated in the death of Rita Scanlon. But the prosecutor's relentless assault on his character left the panel members with the impression that he was headstrong, impetuous, and, to some degree, malicious. As a result, the only Medal of Honor recipient from the Cuban Reclamation was reprimanded for insubordination.

It was tantamount to dismissal. With his file compromised, the stars so many predicted for him went begging. He was doomed to a colonelcy for the balance of his enlistment. As a result, Collier left the service a few months later.

That ended the military career of one of the army's great legends. And, ultimately, it was the indifference and inconstancy of his former commanding officer that Anson Collier would forever hold to account for his downfall.

That is, apart from the Crimson Collar.

* * * * *

The General skimmed over these less-than-flattering details of the court-martial, though, saying, "He got a fair trial. Of that I'm sure. But whether he shot her intentionally, I really don't know."

"The Pathfinders sure love him," offered Robbins.

"Oh, yeah," said Freeman, wiping a blob of mayonnaise off his trousers. "Until he arrived, they were operating on the political fringe, but their ranks increased pretty steadily after that. He's made hay with discontented whites. But the Pathfinders are very protective of their membership lists, so it's hard to figure out who actually belongs. Any attempts they made to gain power via the electorate proved futile, though. Oh, they won some elections at the state level, but they never gained any meaningful clout in Washington."

The General was unaware that once Anson Collier realized it would take a hundred years to gain the Congressional pluralities necessary to spark a *peaceful,* second American revolution—and that it could only be done by flying into the teeth of an ever-strengthening black-and-brown majority—he determined that the power his Pathfinders sought could only come from the barrel of a gun.

Seemingly spellbound by Freeman's oral history, Robbins inquired, "When did Collier take over?"

"Oh, I think during the war. In the mid '40s."

"So he didn't fight in the War of Retribution?"

"Noooo! After the reprimand, he retired. Just before I went to CentCom."

As he finished his turkoney sandwich, crumbling the crusts up in the wrapping paper, Freeman waxed philosophical. "You know, I served with hundreds of officers and non-coms in my career and, overwhelmingly, they deported themselves well. There were a few exceptions—men who used their authority to selfish or sadistic ends." Rising from his desk, he wiped his mouth and turned to look out the window, saying, "And, of that group, Collier was the most noteworthy. If anyone was capable of shooting a defenseless woman in the back, as Bernard contended, it was Sonny."

Twenty-One

Monday, July 4 (11:26 A.M. EDT)
Center City, Philadelphia

When Peter Bernard took leave of Luke Monaghan, he doubled back toward Franklin Square. As he did, he pondered Monaghan's allusion to Christ in Gethsemane.

That story always intrigued me, he thought. *The Jesus who walked on water, silenced the wind, raised the dead, and forgave his killers was surely a manifestation of the Divine. But the Jesus of Gethsemane! So wracked by doubt and fear on the eve of his death that his sweat fell like blood—that was a man.*

Then, distracted by the passing of a police cruiser, he immediately began to doubt the wisdom of cutting out his dog.

What was I thinking? I'm acting like a paranoid kook.

It was too late to undo it now, though. He reasoned: *I could say it got infected. It happens all the time.* But that would require a call to Kansas City.

At the corner of 12th and Noble, he spotted a digital tickertape circling the exterior of a radio station. Across the screen, in red letters, crawled the following message:

> **"JUSTICE DEPT NAMES FATHER PETER BERNARD A PERSON OF INTEREST IN NY BOMBING."**

The shock was electrical, similar to what one might feel if they stuck a butter knife in a wall socket.

"So much for Independence Day," he groaned aloud, as he stumbled toward a sheltered bus stop.

He sat on a bench in the rising heat trying to recover his wits. Presently, the message cycled again. This time it was preceded by:

"STOLEN WAVEJAMMER IDENTIFIED BY NJ COUPLE AS BOMB DELIVERY VEHICLE."

However dazed he may have been, Peter could still add two and two.

While down in Seaside, his brother-in-law told him about the theft of his custom Wavejammer. Over the Easter holiday, he took it to a local marina to have it prepped for the summer. A few days later, the marina called to say it was stolen. Phil Armstrong was haggling on the phone with the insurance company the whole time Peter was staying with them.

But there's no way he's in on it!

He wasn't even sure if the Wavejammer in question was Phil's.

But why else would they name me a person of interest?

Then, there was the unfortunate run-in with President Freeman the previous evening.

If he didn't recognize me then, he will now.

Between that encounter and the fact that his dog was now flitting through the sewers of Philadelphia, it wouldn't take long for the government to zero in on his whereabouts. He was reminded of something his cell mate at Ellison used to say: "It's hard to hit a moving target." Now, the words of Tony Two Palms took on a new meaning.

Tony Vitelli's nickname, in mob parlance, was an allusion to his manhood, although—and Peter was eternally grateful for this—he was an avowed hetero. And by baptism, a Catholic. He was the best cellie Bernard could have had. *Nobody* crossed him. If you were a passenger in his car, it spared you the usual vagaries of prison life: rapes, thefts, shakedowns, tune ups, and mud checks. And because Peter was not only black but a priest, within a month he would have been hit in the neck by the Aryan Brotherhood or the European Kindred had it not been for Two Palms.

So Peter not only trusted Vitelli's advice, he acted on it. Within minutes, he moved past the spot where he said Mass that morning. Nervously, he walked toward the Ben Franklin Bridge thinking that, any minute, the soldiers would grab him.

Negotiating the flood of refugees, by the time he reached the center of the near-empty eastbound span, the sun was almost directly overhead. There he stopped to rest. His heart was still racing, but the steady breeze provided some much needed relief.

Far below, the waters of the Delaware flowed toward the Atlantic. The briny smell of banks and shorelines permeated the air. Down on the river, the boats looked like bugs darting across a pond, their wakes rippling in chevrons behind them. Above him, the gulls dipped and floated and screeched derisively, as if reveling in his misery.

From this lofty perch, Peter noticed the huge, vertical cables rising ominously around him. Having spent the last five years in a cage, his reaction to this sight was understandable.

There's no way I'm going back.

So he shouldered his pack and descended the bridge into New Jersey.

One can be certain that Caesar crossed his Rubicon with far less trepidation.

Part Two

Twenty-Two

General Freeman was inspecting a field hospital on Long Island when reports of a hostage situation in the vicinity caught his attention.

"Where is it?" he asked.

"About two blocks from here," Major Robbins replied.

"Let's go!"

Having notified the Gonzales administration of his decision to waive Secret Service protection, Agents Fisher and Reynolds were no longer with him.

Robbins argued, "It's not safe, General."

Freeman snapped back, "When I want your opinion, Major, I'll ask for it."

In the week following the bombing, the mood of the country turned ugly. It was estimated that between five and six million people were either dead or missing in the environs of New York. Almost everyone could name a friend or relative among them. The loss gave way to sadness, despondence, anxiety, and fear, but, by far, the prevailing emotion was anger. Like Hotspur, the American people were wasp-stung and impatient. The cries for vengeance mounted.

The collapse of the financial markets only heightened this choler. Half the nation's personal and public wealth was wiped out by the time the markets reopened on July 6. It was conservatively estimated that thirty-three million people would lose their jobs.

As fortunes plummeted and tempers flared, the probability of
a bloodletting grew. Once the government identified the actual
perpetrators of the bombing, a hail of retribution was sure to fall on
anyone and everyone associated with them. Surprisingly, even
though Peter Bernard was one of two dozen named as persons of
interest, there was no immediate retaliation against the Catholic
Church.

Wild theories and accusations circulated. The media fed this
speculation with wanton disregard for the truth. Or the Tranquility
Act. Driven by these fictions, vigilante groups began to act on their
prejudices.

With each passing day, the level of criminal activity in the Cordon
escalated. Lawbreakers were lured to the unguarded billions in wealth
like bees to nectar. Street thugs, syndicate hoods, escaped cons, and
other assorted jackals slunk into the Cordon to feed on the entrails
of the once-mighty Gotham. The threat of death seemed to heighten
their appetite for lucre.

Manhattan Island is a natural saddle of stone. Most of the skyscrapers are built on the downtown swell and the midtown cantle.
The structures located in the former were decimated by the blast, as
were any located in what might be called the seat. But those in the
cantle north of 34th Street, though severely damaged and often
decapitated, were still standing. These lonely spires attracted the bulk
of the thieves.

A dozen banks were robbed on Tuesday, and three times that
number on Wednesday. In addition, many museums were hit, including the Met, the Guggenheim, and the Whitney. The great basilicas,
synagogues, and mosques were sacked. Posh hotels and executive
offices were emptied of valuables. Not even police stations or armories
were safe; several had already been emptied of guns and ammunition.

Amid this lawlessness, hundreds of thousands still needed treatment, evacuation, or burial. Of the living, thousands were flash-blind.
Many of the able-bodied refused to evacuate, determined to guard what

remained of their worldly possessions even if it meant exposure to radiation. Against the advice of the government and in response to the favorable winds a steady stream of displaced persons were returning to their homes for the same reason. This reverse migration played havoc with General Freeman's ability to seal the perimeter.

Then, just when it seemed his burden couldn't get any heavier, a group called the Greenshirts, the paramilitary wing of the Pathfinder Party, sought to capitalize on all the chaos, anger, and doubt by launching an *intifada* within the Atlantic Cordon.

It was within the context of these complications that Freeman and Robbins, together with an escort of troopers the Major rounded up, arrived at the scene of the hostage-taking.

"What happened, Lieutenant?" Freeman asked the officer in charge as they crouched behind an overturned sports car.

"Sir, my platoon was assigned to guard the hospital. We heard a volley of shots fired from this direction, so we came to investigate. When we did, this guy started shooting. We have the building surrounded, so he's not going anywhere. But he's got a hostage. A young woman."

"Has anyone been hurt?"

The overmatched first lieutenant answered, "No, sir."

"Has he made any demands?"

"Yes, sir," the officer replied, sardonically. "He wants to talk to Charlie Selkirk, the center fielder for the Mets."

"Anything else?"

"Sir, he keeps ranting about his mother . . . that she's some kind of alien life form. He's a real fruitcake."

"Can we get someone in position to take him out?"

"Sir, I thought we might be able to coax him out without any bloodshed."

Red blotches erupted on Freeman's face as he barked, "Did your unit *not get* my order about zero-tolerance, Lieutenant?"

"We did, sir, but this man—he's not all there. And we don't know where the woman is, either."

"Lieutenant, I want you to tell your men—"

Suddenly, the man appeared in the entryway with a shotgun. Furtively, he looked around, then yelled, "I'll let the girl go, but, first, someone has to bring me some chocolate cream pi—"

A shot rang out, and he fell headlong onto the sidewalk.

Returning his Glock to its holster, Freeman declared, "That's how we define zero-tolerance, Lieutenant."

Twenty-Three

After Jack Clancey met with his editor in Augusta, he and Lena stayed in town and slept round the clock. The next day, Lena dropped him off in Atlanta and continued on to Columbus to visit her Aunt Tootie. She learned of the shooting up in Valley Stream when she stopped for coffee at a bistro in East Point. The VuScreen on the wall above her showed footage of the incident, filmed by Major Robbins, and released by the Pentagon at the insistence of Admiral Towne. It nearly tipped Lena over. Joseph Conrad said that action is consolatory, but her father's certainly didn't console her. Over the final hundred miles, her anxiety mounted; the shooting was the first thing she and her aunt talked about once she was settled in. Sitting at the big, oak table in the out-of-date kitchen watching Tootie make spaghetti, Lena voiced her concerns about it.

Her aunt nonchalantly remarked, "He always was a crack shot, you know. Walter so envied his eye."

This, too, was small comfort to Lena. "You don't think it'll make trouble for him?"

"Heavens, no. The President warned us that all rioters and looters would be shot on sight."

"Not by the *former* President, though!"

Tootie Thomas laughed. She was old-school. Her husband, Walter Thomas, was the garrison commander at Ft. Benning when Jim

Freeman was with the 77th Rangers. At seventy-five, she'd seen everything. The only thing that surprised her about the shooting, given all the reports of criminal activity in the Cordon, was that it didn't happen sooner.

Sitting beside her, the old woman told Lena, "Honey, these are drastic times that call for drastic measures. No one's going to fault your father for what he did."

"That's not what's bothering me."

"Then what is?"

"The whole thing!" she cried, bursting into tears. "He's obsessed with redeeming himself. It's a damn fool move, and I, for one, think he's bound to fail."

Her aunt reached over and hugged her, stroking her hair while she sobbed on her shoulder. For a minute, neither woman said a word.

Tootie knew that by a "damn fool move" Lena meant her father's decision to accept a command in the first place. Softly, she posited, "He was recalled by the President, dear. How could he refuse?"

With tears streaming down her cheeks, Lena told her aunt about the argument she had with her father, how she accused him of abandoning her just like her mother.

The wife of the late General Thomas remembered it well. After Sarah was raped, Freeman requested an assignment to the 75th Ranger Regiment at Fort Benning. Strings were pulled, and even though he was nearing forty, he re-qualified in the Airborne and Ranger schools. It was an eye-popping feat for a man his age. When a sister regiment, the 77th, was formed, he accepted command of the First Battalion.

It was with elements of this unit that he distinguished himself in Port-au-Prince, capturing de LaSalle, and winning the Silver Star. He was promoted to command of the 77th Regiment in '39. In that capacity, he ended the siege of the federal courthouse in Denver three years later. He left his beloved Rangers shortly thereafter.

The winds of war were blowing in the Holy Land again. Another old friend, Billy Estridge was made head of CentCom. He requested that Freeman be assigned as his deputy. When Estridge died just before Jerusalem was bombed, Freeman was elevated to command the Middle Eastern theater. He remained throughout the war until '46 when he returned to Washington to become Army Chief-of-Staff.

So Tootie Thomas was quite familiar with the abandonment Lena described and how Jim Freeman parlayed his wife's refusal to live on an army base into a virtual divorce.

"He was never there for me as a kid," Lena wept, "and now I'm afraid he won't be there *at all!*"

Tootie asked gently, "Then what are you doing here, child?"

Twenty-Four

Friday, July 8 (8:58 A.M. EDT)
The Scharon Building, Philadelphia

"And, Major," Freeman yelled, "see if you can get . . . oh, never mind."

He was about to have his aide call Lena to see if she was ready to talk but thought better of it.

It's my problem.

They hadn't talked since their argument on Sunday. Now she was giving him the silent treatment. Three times he had left messages asking her to call him back, all to no avail. Nor did it go very well when he called Clancey to find out why she followed him down to Atlanta.

"Jim, that's between you and Lena," Clancey said.

"Where do you get off calling me Jim?" Freeman growled.

That shortened up the conversation considerably.

Freeman's personal challenges were nothing compared to the professional, however. The state of emergency had been lifted for the rest of the country, but the Atlantic Cordon was still in dreadful shape. And, the previous night, his command was dealt a major setback. Now, he was waiting to brief the President on a revised plan of action that he and General Hawkins formulated that morning.

Major Robbins' high-strung voice came over the intercom. "Sir, the White House. Line one."

Rather than hit the conference button, the General picked up the receiver. "Good morning, Mr. President."

"Hello, Jim. Anything more to report?"

"Just what we know already. A company from the First Battalion, Third Brigade was ambushed on the Hutchinson River Parkway around 0100. They were escorting a shipment of body armor to the brigade depot in White Plains. Forty-one men were killed; one hundred and twenty-nine wounded. Apparently, they were heavily outnumbered. The attackers drove them off and captured two thousand suits. What disturbs me most, though, was the nature of the attack."

"How so?"

"Because, it had all the earmarks of a paramilitary operation. The attackers wore camouflage and used standard military hand signals. Many were young, but the leaders were older men. The initial reports say that some of our boys were executed. It was a *very* well planned strike. And they were well-armed. Most were carrying either Tavors or TL-25s. What's more, this isn't the kind of loot your garden variety hood is looking to swipe. Until now, that's what we've been dealing with. But if this is a terrorist organization, or a faction like the Greenshirts, we'll pay the devil rooting them out. Those taser-lasers are a serious force multiplier."

"Weren't they used in the robbery of the Met?" Gonzales asked.

All too casually, Freeman replied, "You got it."

"So, is there a connection between the two?"

"Too early to say. But imagine the kind of firepower a few Monets or Picassos would buy on the black market."

It was a chilling prospect. As the President silently considered the diabolical brilliance of it, Freeman threw in another sobering thought.

"Tito, whoever made off with that body armor—they aren't planning on leaving anytime soon. And, it appears they knew *in advance* the contents of the cargo and the route of the convoy. At best, we have a security breach in our ranks. At worst, a spy. If it was the Greenshirts—"

The President interrupted him. "That's the second time you mentioned the Greenshirts. Why's that? Is that who attacked us?"

"I think so. All the evidence points to them."

"Why are they doing it?"

"That's a great question. As you know, they've been preaching revolution for years. Maybe they're trying to gain a toehold in the Cordon to use it as a base of operations. Possession of that body armor would certainly benefit them in that regard."

"How do you propose to deal with them?"

"Obviously, we have to devote more manpower to policing operations. However, at this point, it's all we can do to maintain the relief effort. As I see it, there are only two options. I can request more troops, but I know that our resources are strained. Strengthening me will only weaken someone else. Besides, any additional troops will be slow to arrive."

"What's the other option?"

"To drastically reduce the size of the Cordon."

"Explain."

"Well, sir, currently, the Cordon consists of approximately twenty thousand square miles and thousands of municipalities. Many of those municipalities have already resumed normal operations. Or will in the near future. My plan is to reduce the size of the territory under martial law. It's an opportunity afforded to me by the diminished threat from radiation. The new district would include six counties in north Jersey, the five city boroughs, Westchester, Rockland, and Nassau counties in New York, and Fairfield County in Connecticut. So my staff would be dealing with the bureaucracies of three states instead of seven. The reduction in size would greatly simplify my job. And shrinking the perimeter by half will double my equivalent manpower. With my troops poised on the edge of no man's land—"

"Please, Jim, don't use that term," implored the President. "I'd like to think it won't come to that."

"I understand, sir. Anyway, once the troops are repositioned, it will allow me to get started on the heavy lifting. That means leapfrogging some areas that are still pretty unsettled, but I'll gain valuable time and space in this fight."

"It'll also serve as a down payment on our promise to return the Cordon to civilian control at the earliest possible date," said Gonzales.

The General smiled. "I knew the political dividends wouldn't be lost on you, Mr. President."

"On the other hand, something tells me that redirecting our resources toward the restoration of order will bring allegations that the relief effort is being short-changed."

The General thought: *Admiral Towne.*

He answered, "As the size of the Cordon is decreased, we'll concentrate the abatement efforts nearer to the center. That will enhance my range of action on both fronts. I'll be in a position to extend relief and recovery where it's needed most and, at the same time, challenge the activities of these criminals."

The President took a moment to contemplate the proposed change, then said, "I'm concerned that we're moving too fast, that we're leaving too much unfinished business."

"I understand, Tito, but I have no choice. If I don't react to what's happening now, my ability to extend relief to the interior will be impossible without a substantial increase in manpower. *I need to attack!* Waiting for these jokers to come to me is a recipe for disaster."

"Say you've convinced me. What's the first step?"

Freeman breathed a sigh. "All elements of the 301st Infantry will redeploy to the periphery of the redrawn Cordon immediately. In the former territories, incoming Guard units can assist the Red Cross and FEMA under the purview of the respective governors. In effect, martial law would be lifted in all but the realigned territory."

President Gonzales conceded, "It's hard to argue with the logic of it. I'm inclined to go along, but I'd like to talk it over with Angela

DeKalb and a few of the others first. I don't suppose you've talked to Admiral Towne or General Risden, yet?"

"I ran it by Nick. He's the one who recommended shortening our internal lines. He thinks it's the only solution to the manpower shortage. With his support, I don't anticipate any objections from Towne."

"All right, then, you have my permission to go forward with the realignment. But I reserve the right to ask that you stand down if my advisors find any serious fault with it."

"How soon can I expect a final decision, sir? I don't mean to sound pushy, but I really need to get cracking before the rain starts."

"I'll call you in two hours."

"Fair enough. I'll wait to hear from you before we roll."

On hanging up, Freeman mused, *No mention of the shooting. If he's not put off by it, no one else should be.*

Twenty-Five

Friday, July 8 (9:23 A.M. EDT)
The Department of Justice, Washington, D.C.

Anticipating a call from Philadelphia, Angela DeKalb sat in her office reading field reports from around the country. Operation Cockroach was now in its final stages. Eleven thousand suspects were in custody. Although there were detractors—politicians, journalists, the plaintiff's bar, and of course, the American Federation of Civil Liberties—for the most part, the nation was hailing its success. If legislation extending the suspension of *habeas corpus* until the end of the year was passed, she would be in position to extinguish any internal threat to the country for years to come. Tito Gonzales won the presidency on his promise to maintain the law-and-order policy of Jim Freeman. So, it was conceivable that DeKalb's hardline stance in response to the bombing might help her to capture the same prize.

But the primaries were still months away. Her immediate problem, other than determining who was truly responsible for the bombing, was space. The prisons and jails teemed with detainees. Thousands of others were camped in the yards of state and federal penitentiaries. A number of temporary facilities were under construction to house these prisoners, but most of them would take weeks to complete.

The Marshals Service was transferring the population of the new prison in Mahwah, New Jersey to facilities outside the Cordon. When they finished, they would begin refilling it with the most odious suspects arrested in the dragnet. Since Mahwah was under the purview of James Freeman as military governor of the Atlantic Cordon, a prisoner could be held there *indefinitely* under the terms of martial law. Even if Congress limited the suspension of *habeas corpus* to a few months, it wouldn't apply to prisoners at Mahwah or Danbury or any other federal prison within the Cordon.

The Marshals Service had already assured her that the Mahwah transfers would be completed by the middle of next week. Then, the process would be repeated at Danbury. Her only constraint was the lack of manpower and transport.

The phone rang. She pushed the conferencing key, and Stewart Addison's blurry face appeared on the VuScreen in her office. Ever since the blast, electronic transmissions from inside the Cordon were hit-and-miss.

"Good morning, Stewart," she said.

Brusquely, he replied, "We have a problem."

"What?"

"I just learned that General Freeman recommended a reduction in the size of the territory under martial law, and that the President approved it. The proposed realignment would put many of our medium security facilities outside his jurisdiction as military governor."

"But why?"

"Because hostilities have worsened in the interior. He claims there aren't enough men to conduct relief operations and maintain order at the same time. That's why he proposed shrinking the Cordon to half its size."

"Did you mention that the transfer plan depends on moving our prisoners to facilities *inside* the Cordon?"

"No. You told me not to tip our hand."

"You couldn't take General Freeman aside and tell him in confidence?"

"I do what I'm told," he said flatly.

Masking her anger, Angela replied, "I'll get back to you."

She dialed the President direct and was surprised to be put through immediately. His meeting with Dick Sloan was just ending.

"Good morning, Mr. President. This is Angela DeKalb."

"Angela. I was about to call you."

Feigning ignorance, she asked, "Why's that?"

"Well, we're considering a request by General Freeman to reduce the size of the Cordon." He described the General's fifteen-county strategy and tacked on, "I wanted your input."

Angela responded carefully. Since the President wasn't aware of her prisoner relocation plan, she was forced to conceal her objections. She also knew that lifting martial law in a sizable portion of the Cordon and returning it to state and local control was a development that, under any conditions, warranted the wholehearted support of the Justice Department.

Accordingly, she lied. "Sir, my immediate reaction is favorable. Apart from the political advantages, it would certainly help in gaining Congressional support for the suspension of *habeas corpus*. In addition, it will check the growing violence. The only question I have concerns the courts. I'm not familiar with the General's 'county' theory. I only know that, in hindsight, it was a mistake to draw up the borders of the Cordon the way we did."

"Why do you say that?"

"Because, had we known then that the threat of fallout would be minimal, we'd have given greater consideration to the needs of the polities within it. General Freeman's right. There are many municipalities within the Cordon where the police and the courts are still functioning. Our decision to create the military district by drawing a triangle between points A, B and C may have been worthwhile militarily, but it wasn't a political necessity."

"So what are you suggesting?" Gonzales was perturbed. The triangle was her idea. Now she was using pronouns like *we* and *our* to share the responsibility for it.

"We should take our time regarding this realignment. Arbitrarily focusing on certain counties will only compound our original mistake.

This time we should do it right."

There it was, again. "*Our* original mistake" and "we should do it right." Irritation forced the President into rigidity.

"Time is a luxury I don't have, Madam General. Besides, General Freeman has given greater consideration to the problem than you think."

Wisely, Angela relented. She was tempted to inform Gonzales of the prisoner transfer plan, thus explaining why she wanted to act cautiously in realigning the Cordon. But her intent was to handle the transfers as an administrative matter within her department, then brief him *ex post facto*. Ostensibly, that would insulate him from any fallout should it go wrong, or become politically untenable. But for some reason Gonzales was in a surly mood, so she decided against it.

"Sir, I mean no disrespect to either you or General Freeman. Apparently, you've made your decision. Whatever it is, I'm whole-heartedly behind it."

"Thank you, Angela," the President said. "You're right. I have made my decision. I'm going to honor General Freeman's request. I suggest you contact him later today to ensure a smooth transfer of power to the civilian authorities in those areas affected. Please let me know if there's anything I can do to make that job easier."

The only person that could make Angela DeKalb's job easier was the General himself, and she decided to meet with him in person without further delay. Trusting the job to a squirrel like Addison was out of the question.

Twenty-Six

Monday-Friday, July 4-8
Between Philadelphia and Newark

On leaving Philadelphia, Peter Bernard's primary objective was to avoid detection and buy time. He had convinced himself that the real culprits in the bombing would soon be caught, thus absolving him of any complicity.

In a doughnut shop near Camden, he heard a news report that became the basis of his flight plan. The newscaster was interviewing a cop, who said, "Due to the electromagnetic pulse of the blast, most of the satellite and ground-based surveillance devices we use to monitor people's movements have been rendered useless, particularly those closest to ground zero." Peter deduced from this statement that his best option was to move north and east. Granted, the danger from radiation was still high, but Luke Monaghan told him that the government had a plan to abate it.

It's the only drawback I can see to heading in that direction.

It was a drawback he had grossly underestimated, but that was understandable. Even on a normal day, it is difficult for a six-foot-seven inch black man to blend with his surroundings. And, for one evading the law, it was next to impossible.

Knowing that Newark was predominantly a black city, Peter calculated: *If I can make it there, I may be able to hide in plain sight. And if the reports I'm hearing are true, all the confusion should provide ample cover.*

With these considerations in mind, he set off. But, first, he made a quick stop in Maple Shade to buy a few supplies at a sporting goods store. Wandering up and down the aisles, he was sure that everyone in the place was on to him. The shelves were thoroughly picked over, but he found what he needed: a map, a baseball cap—which he donned immediately—a palm-sized flashlight, bug spray, water, energy bars and, most important, toilet paper. At the checkout counter, he lowered the baseball cap over his eyes and avoided looking into the security cameras.

To make his journey less stressful, he mapped out a rural route. Moving by night, he avoided the main thoroughfares, resolving to walk the entire distance, if necessary. Hiking eighty miles on foot would be difficult and time-consuming, but it was better than sitting in a cell. Besides, the adventure of it appealed to him. He reckoned: *If I get lost, I'll follow the drinking gourd.*

This allusion to the Big Dipper was ironic. His route was one of those that his ancestors traveled to escape bounty hunters on the Underground Railway. Now he was spurred by the same fear that kept them moving northward. And he paid the same price: the loss of all that went before. Like those distant fugitives, what lay ahead for him was impossible to imagine, but it promised to be dangerous and difficult. At another time, these parallels might have fascinated a man lettered in American history, especially a black man. But Peter Bernard was preoccupied by the same idea that consumed his predecessors: *Freedom.*

During his journey, the priest took care to disengage from the world around him, virtually ignoring those traveling in the opposite direction. He talked to no one, avoiding all contact with the unruly hoard. Near Moorestown, he spied a weeping family squatting on the curb, the youngest of whom held a rosary in her hand. Though obviously Catholic, and even more obviously in distress, he skirted them.

At Hainesport, a desperate, old man screamed from the center of the street: "Help me! My daughter's dying! Help me, please! Someone!"

Peter responded by redoubling his pace.

The tragic circumstances of these refugees certainly aroused feelings of pathos in him and, during these moments, he wrestled inwardly with his conscience. But desperation always blocked him from relieving his shame with action. Most times, when he felt the urge to emulate Mother Teresa or Father Damien, he turned off the road to find an empty building or an alternate route, rationalizing his conduct by recalling the mind-numbing despair of the concrete and concertina wire.

"I'm not going back," he kept repeating. "I've paid my debt."

On occasion, he was forced to change course or hide out. Except for a short ride in the bed of a farmer's truck, he traveled entirely on foot. With only a few hundred dollars of gate money in his pocket, he became very frugal. Food and water were luxuries to be conserved, so he was continually pestered by hunger and thirst. And bugs. His clothes were soon salt-stained even though he washed at every opportunity. Next to his Mass kit, which he never used, the toilet paper became his most prized possession. And it surprised him how quickly his sneakers wore out.

The trek took six days. His slow pace was attributable to the many directional changes he was forced to make, but there were other reasons as well. One was the beauty of south central New Jersey. The big priest was smitten by it. Despite the oppressive heat, a few dozen bug bites, a snarling Doberman, miles of poison ivy, the discharge of a farmer's shotgun, an ill-disposed skunk, and a maddening case of diarrhea, Peter was in no hurry to leave the counties of Burlington and Monmouth. He marveled at the ample forests, clear-running streams, and grazing horses in such a densely-populated state. After five years behind bars, this footloose ramble through the remnants of a simpler time was sweet release. He had little desire to see it end. Each dawn when he completed his movements he read from *Paradise Lost.*

The book so absorbed him that, one day, he didn't sleep at all. That morning, he camped on the shore of a wooded lake outside Freehold. The place was deserted so, he stripped down and took a swim in the cedar-colored waters. After washing his clothes, he breakfasted on some raspberries and plums that he found in back of a deserted roadside stand. Then he resumed his place in the book, where Raphael recounts to Adam the details of Lucifer's fall. Possibly it was the Eden-like setting that locked him into the passage. Whatever the reason, by noontime he was itching to write something of his own.

Other than a few personal letters, he wrote nothing at Ellison, assuming that nothing he wrote would pass the censors. A small tablet of paper and a pen survived the downsizing of his kit back in Philadelphia and after a few false starts he got in a groove.

It's amazing how fast the words come back after so long a hiatus, he thought.

Propped against the bough of a massive tree, for the balance of the day he worked on the draft of a letter he would send to the press in the event of his arrest. Several times he stopped to cool off in the waters of the lake, or to chase off the chattering jays, but other than that he wrote steadily until nightfall. The following day, he edited and recopied his letter.

That night he resumed his hike. During the next forty-eight hours, with each passing mile, his odyssey became more furtive and careworn. The rural charms of South Jersey, the bucolic farms and hamlets that previously slowed his progress, were gradually displaced by the encroachments of suburbia and, eventually, urbia. In response, he quickened his step.

He didn't buy any newspapers or angle for the latest news, either. The sense of purpose that filled him after the Mass in Franklin

Square was gone, snuffed out by the sight of his name crossing that ticker on the radio station. His prayers also diminished, and what few he said were mostly self-serving. There was no longer any demonstration of concern for others in them. Or the truth.

The big priest was coming unmoored. In reaction to the injustice he had suffered over the years—and currently suffered from—by the time he arrived in Newark, all his attention was focused on himself. Having walked the waters of faith his entire life, Bernard was now sinking in waves of self-pity.

Twenty-Seven

Lena Walker drove back to Shady Grove on Friday. She stopped in Atlanta at Jack Clancey's request. There, he announced he was going with her.

"My editor at *Veriquest* wants me to do a piece on your father for the August edition."

"What kind of piece?"

"Oh, just an insider's view of the situation, maybe using his relationship with Sonny Collier or the shooting as a *leitmotif.*"

Still upset over the incident, Lena begged, "Please, Jack, don't. At least . . . not the part about him shooting that man."

He shrugged. "Have you talked to him yet?"

"Not yet. The next time I talk to him, it'll be in person."

"I know how you feel. When he called the other night, I wanted to belt him." Then he smiled. "I can't help rooting for the old coot, though."

Looking away, seemingly disgusted with herself, Lena replied, "Me, too."

The same attributes that made people cheer Jim Freeman also made them hiss. His greatest strengths, to excess, were his most visible weaknesses. He was so confident that it often became arrogance. His gritty determination could easily turn to obstinacy, his worldliness to lust, his industry to greed. His simple faith in others made him gullible. So, too, there were times in the past when his greatest asset, courage, spurred him to act rashly.

But there was nothing to admire in his vanity. At least, that's the conclusion Jack Clancey came to after a week of mulling it over.

Judging it best to leave Lena alone with her thoughts, as they pulled onto I-85, Jack recalled: *Since I've known him he's been more of a peacock than lion!* Then he cut to the heart of it. *At seventy-two, he's too old, too sick, and too vain to achieve what he wants most—erasing the embarrassment of a mediocre presidency.*

He didn't share this judgment with Lena, even though he knew that, as she sat next to him with her eyes closed and her arms folded, she was thinking the same thing.

Twenty-Eight

Friday, July 8 (9:02 P.M. EDT)
The White House

The *Archdiocese of Newark!?!*

"That's what they found," said the President, wiping his brow with a wide-open palm.

Katie Holman looked at her boss, stupefied.

"It's a joke, right?"

"It's no joke, Katie."

"Has anyone talked to the bishop?"

"No. The DPS is still pursuing other leads. It's all very premature, but there's no doubt as to the ownership of the property."

"Incredible!" Holman muttered.

She was sitting on the sofa in the Oval Office across from the President. On his lap was a two-page report from the Department of Public Safety. The crux of it was that the July 2 attack was launched from a boathouse near Elizabeth on property owned by the Archdiocese of Newark.

Tito Gonzales and his chief-of-staff sat staring at each other, turning the implications of this latest development over in their minds.

"Sir, I don't need to tell you, if this information isn't handled properly, it could have an *extremely* negative—"

"I know," interrupted Gonzales. He echoed more solemnly, "I know."

"I thought the boathouse was owned by an oil company."

"That was eight years ago. Since then, the property's changed hands three times."

He turned to the second page of the report. It read like a title policy.

"It was quit-claimed to the Archdiocese on December 28, 2059. The grantor was a company called Pilot Investments."

"Who signed for Pilot?" Holman asked.

"I don't know. I don't have a copy of the deed, just a summary of the ownership changes."

He tossed the report over to Holman.

The chief-of-staff reviewed it briefly, then put it down beside her.

"Mr. President, I can't help but think it's a hoax. A set-up or something. The Church may have been duped into leasing the boathouse to some nasties but to be directly involved in the plot? It doesn't pass the smell test."

"According to the DPS, the lease was never recorded."

"But lots of leases aren't recorded. Heck, a lot of them are only verbal."

The President motioned for her to follow him outside. With two Secret Service agents in tow, he stepped onto the porch leading out to the Rose Garden. Facing the South Lawn, he put an unlit cigar in his mouth and spoke in a whisper.

"This priest they're looking for—what do you know about him?"

"Peter Bernard?"

He nodded.

Holman looked at the ground and, without so much as moving her lips, muttered, "During your last term as governor, he was convicted in the Spark Park bombing down in Phoenix—for sedition, not the bombing. Before that, he was with Deacon Carroll. Why? Do they still think he did it?"

"His sister's husband owned the boat. It was reported stolen a few months before the bombing, but—"

Holman thought for a minute, then whispered sarcastically, "So, if the Church supplied the staging area and this priest or his brother-in-law supplied the delivery vehicle, who do they think supplied the bomb? The Pope?"

With the cigar centered firmly between his lips, he looked at her blandly and nodded again.

Seeing that he wasn't kidding, Katie choked back a wisecrack. Making no effort to moderate her voice, she laughed and said, "You realize that's utterly preposterous, of course? What *possible* motive could *he* have for bombing us?"

"I don't know. Please, Boomer, keep it down. I want as few people to know about this as possible."

He resumed in a hushed tone. "The DPS has obtained evidence that some key components were smuggled into Liberty Airport last year onShepherd One."

"*How?*"

"I don't know." Gonzales appeared flustered. "But, considering he has diplomatic immunity, it's not beyond the realm of possibility."

"Sir, with all due respect, casting the Vicar of Christ as an international arms smuggler *is* beyond the realm of possibility."

"But what if he didn't know about it? What if the conspiracy was hatched at a lower level?" Taking the cigar from his lips, he covered his mouth and said, "I admit, it's pretty farfetched to think that the Vatican would be mixed up in this, but it's a lot less farfetched *today* than it was yesterday."

Holman picked at the leaves on one of the diamond-shaped thyme bushes, saying, "I think it's more likely that, if there's evidence that components were smuggled into the country on Shepherd One, it's fabricated."

"I don't know."

"Sir, you always taught me that only fools do things that are contrary to their own self-interest. The Catholic Church is many things, but fools they aren't. The United States is their primary source of funds—"

She stopped short.

He finished, "—so anyone who might profit from cutting those funds off would be a natural suspect."

Holman's eyes never left the President's. Softly, she exclaimed, "This is a nightmare! The Church still has enormous clout. And, remember, the Hispanic vote put you here. If we even *hint* that Rome is under investigation, it will destroy the party's chances in the midterm elections and could spell defeat in '64."

"It'd be worse than that. If word leaks that the Church is under suspicion, it could set off a genocidal backlash in this country rivaling Darfur or Rwanda. It would probably destroy—" He was about to say something else but caught himself.

He was about to comment on how it would destroy his legacy, thought Holman.

The savvy chief-of-staff knew the President was troubled on more than just a political level. Born and raised a Catholic, as a man he grew apart from the Church. Like most pols, he had learned that there was an inverse relationship between adherence to moral principles and political success. They lived in an age in which fashion, not virtue, had become the pinnacle of human endeavor. Over the course of his career, Holman watched as her boss gradually renounced many of his deepest convictions to the inquisition of the Humanist elite. But Gonzales wasn't unique in that regard. The simple fact was that *any* Christian American, true to his or her creed, was simply unelectable. The same could be said of *anyone* who professed their faith in God. And, even though the electorate still included many such believers, representation of their interests at the highest levels of government was, at best, paltry, and that fact didn't bode well for the Catholics.

The President deduced, "The way I see it, there are three possibilities. First, the Church is totally *innocent* of any wrongdoing. Second, the Church is actually, in toto or in part, *responsible* for the crime. Third, as you suggested, they're being *set up*. Assuming that the first is true, the only plausible explanation for any evidence which points to them is the third. Right?"

"Right."

"So let's talk about who would want to set them up. Who are their biggest detractors?" He purposely avoided the word "enemies."

"No shortage there. Muslims. Jews. Any number of factions."

Gonzales shook his head. "In the past, at one time or another, yes. But not now. With the exception of an occasional dustup between them and the Muslims, the Vatican is at peace, even allied, with most other denominations."

The two of them mulled over the possibilities. Finally, Katie offered *sotto voce*, "The Humanists?"

He didn't respond, not even with a gesture.

So Holman added, again, quietly, "You know, if the Church *is* being set up to take the fall, then the real perpetrator ran the risk of infuriating the general public by attacking us. Who would take that risk? Like you said, it's suicidal."

On the basis of his conversation with General Freeman, the President speculated that it might be Sonny Collier. But he kept his suspicions to himself.

Instead, he sighed, "I wish I knew."

As he returned to his office, he warned, "Not a word of this to anyone. Okay?"

"Yes, sir."

"I can't stress enough—"

"Sir, I understand."

After summoning Dick Sloan again, who told him that the Chinese were sending a package of medical and financial relief, the President put down the receiver and rubbed his eyes.

First, the Pathfinders, and now the Catholic Church, he thought. *Who's next? The Girl Scouts?*

Twenty-Nine

The sign posted on the light pole indicated that busses would arrive at six, ten and two to shuttle any remaining refugees in the neighborhood of this inner-city crossing to Philadelphia. An aide worker coordinated the evacuation at the head of the block. Approximately two hundred people waited on line.

Addie Foster and her good friend, Rhonda Mizell, were standing halfway down the block in front of a hair salon. It was a good day to travel. A cool breeze made it feel more like a morning in June rather than July, and the effects of the bombing, though clearly evident in the dust and rubble, seemed less gloomy. On this day, the metallic smell was hardly noticeable. And there were no corpses anywhere.

Chewing on one of the candy bars that was airdropped onto the roof of her apartment building the previous day in a palette of medical supplies, Addie mentioned for the third time, "I sure hope Lennie doesn't forget we're coming."

"I told you, he only lives two miles from the bus station," Rhonda assured her. The line compressed as the first bus came into view from the west. She insisted, "He'll be there," as she slid forward a suitcase laden with her most prized possessions.

Central Avenue, a major artery, had been cleared of debris that week, but still the buses proceeded cautiously. The first one passed the Market Street intersection and stopped across from where the two women were standing. Another one pulled in behind it. There they waited, still and ominous. No one exited. Unsure of what to do, the refugees peered forward for a signal from the aide worker. When she started to cross over, many of them followed suit, despite a raised hand that told them to wait.

Addie also began crossing and Rhonda lifted her suitcase with both hands and started for the curb. Before she moved ten feet, she saw the windows of the bus click open. Through them poked the barrels of a half-dozen automatic weapons.

That was the last thing that either woman, or those seeking refuge with them, lived to see.

Thirty

Colonel Essing didn't know the exact time of the incident, but he knew where it took place.

"Newark."

General Freeman shook his head. With a trace of dejection, he asked, "How many dead?"

"About two hundred."

"And he's sure it was the Greenshirts?"

"No question. Our advance scouts found the king of hearts stuffed in the mouths of some of the victims—the death card they used on Thursday night. And the manager of the bus company said the men who hijacked the busses were wearing flash-green armbands."

Freeman couldn't hide his frustration. Banging his desk, he shouted, "What the hell is going on? What would motivate that lunatic to kill hundreds of innocent civilians?"

The portly Essing wondered what happened to the vaunted "four-in-the-morning" courage. For the past week the old man had grown increasingly short-tempered. Having steeled himself for another outburst, however, the XO simply replied, "I'm not sure, sir, but there is a clue. It appears that most of the victims were either black or Hispanic."

Freeman stopped pacing. "What are you saying—that the killings were racially motivated?"

"It's too early to say that with any certainty, but they may be."

"Colonel, were any whites killed?"

"Not to my knowledge, sir."

"Then, why wouldn't you say *most definitely* the attacks were racially motivated?"

"Sir, there are very few whites who live in that area, so why would we automatically assume that race was the motivation for the attack?"

Freeman looked at him gravely. "Because we know the attacker."

He went over to the conference table where several maps were strewn about. Finding one for downtown Newark, he grabbed the magnifying glass and studied it.

"You said it happened near city hall?"

"This area here," said the chief-of-staff, pointing to the spot.

"Well, that's not far from Branch Brook! Did Hawkins give you any indication what time the Second Brigade would get there?"

"The lead elements, within the hour, sir."

"Good. Tell him to take every precaution. If that's where Collier's operating, he might be tempted to take another shot at us. In fact, he's probably goading us into a fight. Make sure Michaels conducts a thorough recon of the area immediately. We don't need a repeat of Thursday night." Then, sternly, he warned, "It's incumbent on us to stop these killings. News of it will travel fast. It may trigger another spate of rioting. Or worse. We have to act quickly. Do I make myself clear?"

"Roger that, sir."

When Essing was gone, Freeman moved over to the maps spread out on the conference table. Figuring that the whole world would know of the massacre shortly, and that the outcry would be deafening, he knew the White House would come under increased pressure to nip Collier's insurgency in the bud.

What to do?

He gave the map a look and, before long, he hit on an idea. If the

Greenshirts were concentrating in Newark, it might afford him an opportunity to deliver a knockout blow.

General Hawkins was in the process of moving the Second Battalion of the Second Brigade (the 2/2) to Branch Brook Park in the northwest quadrant of the city. If two of its five companies wheeled to the south, then turned north, they might be able to pin the insurgents against the Passaic River, which wound through the city to the northeast. Setting the trap would require that they position another company between the park and the river to seal off any escape route. This hammer-and-anvil movement would spread the 2/2 awfully thin, but intelligence had it that there were only two thousand Greenshirts in the entire metropolitan area. With the 24th Armored Division due to arrive that night, a reinforced battalion could easily drive a few hundred of them into the river. Even if they were equipped with TL-25s. And, if the squadron of Cobras en route from Tucson arrived beforehand, that would improve the odds substantially.

We have to factor in the weather, though.

The entire Cordon had been scrubbed with E-Rad by the 923rd Special Aviation Wing that week. Secondary passes were made in the area closest to ground zero. Cloud-seeding operations were also concluded. So the rain required to release the ion-killers in the compound was coming. The "healing waters," as one writer dubbed them, were already dousing western Pennsylvania and New York. It was predicted that the Cordon would receive up to eight inches in the next two days. The forecast also called for thirty to forty mile-per-hour winds. This stormy complement to the fog of war would all but preclude the use of tactical air support.

The BattleKings from the 405th Artillery that Risden promised won't be available either; they're still en route from Texas.

Since both sides would be impeded by the deluge, Freeman was confident that the weather could only delay, not deny, the success of his plan.

He concluded: *No matter how you cut it, Collier is outgunned and outnumbered.*

The thought of it heartened him and diminished the anxiety caused by the massacre.

He reached for the phone. Tito Gonzales needed to hear it from him. When he was president, he always insisted on hearing bad news *immediately.* To his credit, Gonzales was no different.

But Freeman was loathe to make the call. It bothered him to be the continual bearer of bad news. He could only imagine the pressure Gonzales was under, never having been so challenged during his tenure. It seemed that every crisis *he* had to contend with—other than the assassination attempt that put him in office—was brought on by *him.*

Reluctantly, he punched the direct line to the Sit Room.

The responder informed him the President was in a meeting with the Attorney General, so, at Freeman's suggestion, she routed the call to Dick Sloan.

Sounding depressed, Sloan answered. "Good morning, General."

"Hi, Dick."

"What's up?"

"Well, I'm afraid I have some bad news."

"Oh?"

"There was an unfortunate incident in Newark this morning. According to our reports, a couple hundred civilians were massacred. I'm told the victims were mainly black and Hispanic, so it appears to have been racially-motivated. My suspicion is that it was done by Sonny Collier's men."

Considering the tenuous state of affairs throughout the nation and around the globe—that morning a missile was fired at an American cruiser in Cam Rahn Bay—to the National Security Advisor, this announcement came with all the subtlety of a blind side sack.

Unable to hide his alarm, Sloan choked out, "Why do you think it was Collier again?"

"They left the same calling card as the other night when they attacked my men out on the Hutch. The king of hearts."

Sloan was not only rocked; he was baffled.

"What's he up to, Jim? If his aim is to start a revolution, it's understandable that he'd target a military convoy carrying weapons and body armor. But why would he start killing civilians?"

"I don't know. To induce terror? Perhaps it goes even further than that."

He remembered how one of his professors at the Academy called racism the original sin of the American Genesis. Slavery. Segregation. Discrimination. It continually defined the course of the country's social and political history. Even the class warfare endemic to old Europe was fueled primarily by racial tensions in the United States. Sadly, after three hundred years, no redemption was in sight.

"Maybe he's looking to start a race war," Freeman offered.

"*A race war!* But why? That would put the kibosh on his political aspirations. It'd also frighten off the big Pathfinder money."

"Maybe he's trying to raise the stakes for the moderates in his own party, to push them off the fence. He's never been much of a political animal, you know." There was a slight pause, and he tacked on, "But he is an animal. That's why they call him the Rottweiler."

"Do you think he has designs of establishing a base for future operations in the Cordon?"

"No, I don't think so. He knows his tactics. He knows he can't hold any sizable territory for long. My guess is that he's lighting matches in a tinder-box. And, unless there's more tinder than we think, ultimately, he'll have no option but to cut and run. The only question is how much damage he does in the process."

In a dour tone, Sloan replied, "We need to put a bullet in this man, General."

"That's exactly what I intend to do. I have an entire brigade heading for Newark as we speak. Once they're established, we'll initiate operations against the Greenshirts in that area. And Collier is Bogey-One. If all goes well, the next time you see him, he'll be hanging upside-down from a meat-hook."

Freeman's bravado was small comfort to Sloan. There was a hint of panic in the NSA Director's voice as he said, "It's only a matter of time before word of the slaughter leaks. We'll need to address the media. How soon can you send us a report?"

"You'll have it within the hour . . . maybe two. There's only one thing I ask, Dick."

"What's that?"

"I don't want to hear any crap from Towne about working directly with you guys on this. I'm tired of him interfering with matters beyond his authority."

"Jim, that's a matter beyond *my* pay grade. Although I agree with you, you'll have to take it up with TG."

"You're right. Never mind."

"The President will be down any minute. He'll want to talk to you. Will you still be there?"

"I'll wait for his call."

* * * * *

Five minutes later, "TG" called back, his voice seemingly deeper than normal. "Jim, it's Tito."

"Good morning, Mr. President."

"It is?"

"No, I guess not. As Dick probably told you, we have a problem."

"Unfortunately, we have more than one."

"Why? What's going on?"

"First, tell me what happened up there."

Freeman repeated what he told Sloan and described the counter-measures he intended to take.

When he finished, Gonzales asked, "How soon can you put the plan into effect?"

"I'm hopeful that, by this time tomorrow, Collier's men will be swimming the Passaic."

"Good. I probably don't need to stress how important it is that we act immediately. If my own revulsion to Collier's death squad is any indication of how Hispanics or blacks will react in general, it won't be pretty. This could really aggravate a bad situation, so don't spare the ponies. *We need to make a statement.*"

"Speaking of ponies, Mr. President, we're still operating with a token force up here. Especially with the First Battalion cut up like it is. I feel like I'm going into this without my boots. Risden's doing all he can, but anything you can say or do to free up a few more Guard units would be greatly appreciated."

Freeman also repeated his objection to Admiral Towne's insistence that he channel all his communications through the Pentagon.

"I'll be meeting with Dick Thompson later this morning, and I'll address both those concerns."

"Thank you, sir."

"Anything else, Jim?"

"You said we had more than one problem?"

"Oh . . . yeah. One of our missile cruisers was fired on this morning down in Cam Rahn Bay. No damage, but . . . well, that's not even the worst of it."

Except for Katie Holman, Gonzales was not wont to share his most intimate thoughts with his subordinates. But, during the past week, he had taken solace in commiserating with his immediate predecessor. Also, he valued Freeman's opinion. Since he wanted to keep their conversation confidential, he moved into an unoccupied office. Then, in a hushed tone, he said, "I just got out of a meeting with Angela DeKalb and Avery Milliken. Apparently, she's convinced that, at some level, the Catholic Church had a hand in the bombing. So is Milliken."

"Because of Bernard?"

"Mainly, yes. If he's innocent, why is he running? As you know, he was convicted in the Spark Park Bombing, and even though his direct involvement in it was never proven, he still did time for sedition. It's probably just coincidental, but this whole thing started after he was released in June."

Freeman told Gonzales about seeing him in Franklin Square, adding, "If you remember, he also took the rap for Deacon Carroll."

The President went on to detail all he knew: the Armstrong's Wavejammer, the ownership of the boathouse, the air bill from Shepherd One.

"It's all so bizarre," he concluded. "But, in defense of the Church, most of the evidence is circumstantial."

"Have they determined a motive?"

"That's the rub. No one can tell me what possible reason they'd have for doing it."

"I don't know. Some of these priests are really radical."

"On social issues, yes. But not politically."

James Freeman was no apologist for the Vatican, but even he found the premise incredible. Offhandedly, he said as much. "Nah, even the Pope isn't dumb enough to *document* that he's dealing in nuclear arms."

The President chafed at this backhanded insult. Although he was no longer a *practicing* Catholic, he was still a Catholic. But, he let it slide.

He answered, "That's why I think they're being set up."

"By whom?"

"I have my suspicions."

Freeman took a flyer. "*Collier?*"

"So it crossed your mind, too?"

Pacing as he worked through his thoughts, the General responded with a full disclosure of *his* suspicions about that morning's massacre. His tone became more strident as he returned to the matter of the Church.

"Let's face it. He's secretive, diabolical, and ruthless. His organization has both the resources and manpower to develop and deliver a bomb and, I might add, the cheek to frame the Vatican for it. Maybe this insurgency is the follow-on attack we've been anticipating."

"I agree. But I can't help thinking it's so improbable, mainly because it's so contrary to his own interests, not to mention his party's."

"Mr. President, it's not improbable to think that Sonny Collier, or the goons that worship him, would do this."

The President sounded flustered. "That may be, but, unfortunately, we have no proof, even if the insurgency does imply a motive. All the evidence currently points to the Church, and my fear is that, if—no, *when*—it leaks that both Justice and the DPS have targeted them as the primary suspect, it will set off another round of violence, the likes of which we haven't seen since Los Humanos." With resignation, he predicted, "The truth simply can't withstand such accusations."

Gonzales' fear of reprisal against the Catholic Church was similar to the one Freeman had concerning the massacre. There was only one difference. The President was agonizing over religious strife, the General, racial. And, thanks to some big mouths and small minds in the Justice Department—and in newsrooms across America—both fronts exploded in an ordeal of fire and blood later that day.

Thirty-One

Saturday, July 9 (6:25 P.M. EDT)
South Orange, New Jersey

Saturday morning, the big priest arrived at the campus of Seton Hall University in South Orange where he snuck into one of the dormitories for a shower and a nap. Although the school was on summer break, the campus had been converted that week into a front-line hospital operation—a would-be MASH unit. With all the hubbub, no one asked him any questions. He slept all day in the basement of the building.

When he left the campus that evening, Bernard was tempted to ask the guard at the gate for directions into downtown Newark. But, still trying to avoid contact with anyone, he decided against it. Instead, he used his map to plot a course down South Orange Avenue through the Vailsburg section of Newark. If he *had* consulted the guard, he probably would have been advised not to take that route.

South Orange Avenue ran through the blighted West and South Wards, a pocket of extreme poverty. A haven for drug traffickers and murderers. A concrete jungle yet to be reclaimed by civilization. As such, until one reached the hospital district at its eastern terminus, it was a dark passage, even in the best of times—what some called "the Fourth World." Now, with the city in the grip of criminal anarchy, it was even more so. Unfortunately, this information didn't appear in the legend on Peter's map.

On his arrival in South Orange that morning, the day was cool and cloudless. Not so when he left. It was very muggy. Rain clouds billowed in the west. Surreal aberrations rose eerily from the heated asphalt. Horse flies pestered him. The postage stamp lawns, less than verdant before the blast, were stressed and blanketed with dust. Only the most wind- and heat-resistant flowers and shrubs were still alive. The denuded trees not only gave the sense of an early fall but lent a battlefield aspect to the landscape.

Not that anyone ever confused Newark with Amsterdam anyway, he allowed.

Other than the general dislocation and confusion attending the flight of the refugees, Peter saw almost no evidence of the bombing on his long trek from Philadelphia. Now, all that was changing.

In Vailsburg, the scenes grew increasingly dismal. Many of the buildings were burned out. Those with business concerns at street level were hit particularly hard. Only the storefronts with roll-down doors or sheeted with plywood were unmolested.

Homes fared little better. Several were in flames, but no one paid them any mind. Hundreds of gutted vehicles dotted the roadway like so many carcasses on the floor of a desert. Traffic signals were inoperable. There was no police or fire service, although the howl of sirens, some near, some far, never ceased. If a fire started, there was nothing to do but let it burn. If someone was attacked or injured, there was no rescuing them. For these reasons, the government was directing people to leave or avoid these precincts.

As Peter crossed under the rails of the Garden State Skyway into the West Ward, he was welcomed by a pair of moldy cemeteries on opposite sides of the street that were cluttered with broken boards and roofing shingles. The crosses jutting crookedly from the earth seemed to pass judgment on him. His doubts multiplied along with his fears.

The world he was entering reminded him of his novitiate service. There was both the physical devastation of the San Bernardino earthquake and the human despondence of the Kingston slums. Piles of garbage befouled his route. The rats feasting at them were plump and greasy; the dogs hungry and ill-tempered. Occasionally, a person or persons would dart anxiously from one corner to the next, or from one house to another. On one block, Peter saw a man hacking a ring off a cadaver's hand with a hunting knife. On another, a cluster of survivors huddled together offering comfort and companionship to each other like gorillas in an upland forest.

No one dared make eye contact with anyone else. Even the flash-blind averted their eyes at the sound of Peter's footsteps. Gunshots echoed in the distance. The choking smell of ionization—and the unburied dead—nauseated him, so he pressed a handkerchief to his nose to allay the stench. The unrelenting assault on the senses was enough to check the advance of a crusader.

Most of the victims the priest stepped over were the same unfortunates that, only a week before, he lost sleep to help. But he ignored them, nonetheless. He had his reasons. A low-flying, killer drone was passing overhead, which was one cause for concern. The aura of physical danger was another. But his biggest worry was that any loss of forward momentum would weaken his resolve and lead to retreat. His fear of being captured still outweighed any other.

With every block, the number of dead increased. Their skin was burned and withered and coated with dust. Peter assumed the burns were caused by radiation, and it scared him. On the trek north, he had convinced himself that Divine Grace would somehow spare him the blast's silent and lethal emanations. Now, he wasn't so sure, but he pressed on nonetheless.

"It's hard to hit a moving target," he somberly repeated.

Every so often, he noticed someone peering out at him from behind a curtain or door. These were the same hopeless faces he had seen in photographs of the mountain poor in Appalachia. Grimy, haggard, and sunken-eyed.

Stopping, he asked one of these stolid, black faces through a broken window, "Can you tell me the—"

But the face instantly recoiled behind the curtain without a word.

Down one side street, he saw the bloated body of a naked, white man stuffed halfway into a storm sewer. This was noteworthy because it was the first Caucasian he had seen since leaving Seton Hall. He didn't have time to dwell on it, though, because further down the same street he saw a cluster of not-so-friendly looking hoodies arguing outside a pawn shop. Careful not to draw their attention, he quickly moved on, only to hear gunshots ring out from that direction a moment later.

He started to run.

Fast.

Faster than his flagging spirit.

Towering thunder heads now hung overhead like an executioner's axe. A storm was imminent. The fugitive priest wasn't aware of its artificial cause but soon became intimate with its dreary effects. It steamed forward like an old, iron battleship, letting loose a barrage of lightning and thunder. Dust and litter, whipped into the air by dwarf tornadoes, blinded him momentarily. Giant raindrops plopped down, the wind strengthened to gale-force, and a fusillade of hailstones hit him with deafening fury. To escape these icy nettles, he ducked into the doorway of a dilapidated brownstone.

Refreshed by the cool air, he watched with fascination as the hail instantly transformed a July landscape into one more fitting to January. After an inch of slush accumulated, a violent rush of rain followed. Within minutes, there were ankle-deep rivulets of swirling ice and debris in the gutters. The litter that cavorted madly on the storm's approach was pasted, limp and lifeless, to the streets and sidewalks that, except for the shattered glass and burned-out cars, were empty. Finally, the unrelenting smell of death was checked.

Peter sat down, knowing he wasn't going anywhere for awhile. Pulling a stick of beef jerky out of his pack, he was about to take a bite when he heard a scratching sound on the other side of the door.

Probably a rat.

But, as he ate, the scratching grew more pronounced, more

desperate. Unable to ignore it any longer, he got up to investigate. The door was unlocked. Cracking it, he saw a tiny, wet nose sniffing frantically for air. He swung it open, and a little, black dog bolted out, running through his legs and down the stoop into the rain. It turned to examine him for a second, then took off.

The stink coming from inside the brownstone was overpowering. And unmistakable. But it raised in Peter a morbid curiosity.

Straight ahead were stairs leading to the upper units. On the right, the door to the ground-floor apartment was ajar. Covering his nose and mouth with his handkerchief, he opened it. An aegis of flies met him as he entered and, reflexively, he gagged: lying on a rug in the front room was the decomposed body of an old woman.

A halo of dry, blackened blood stained the rug around her head and a huge gash ran under her chin from one ear to the other, evidencing the cause of death. Her left arm and right leg were twisted beneath her, and the terror of her final moment was etched for all eternity in her yawning eyes and mouth.

The apartment was a shambles, indicating a robbery had taken place. Given the body's advanced state of decay, Peter surmised that it happened some time ago. The putrefaction was obviously accelerated by the heat. But it wasn't the smell that repulsed him so much as the swarm of maggots feasting on her neck wound.

Exiting, he grabbed his pack from the stoop and staggered into the street. The air, cleansed by the driving rain, smelled as fresh and sweet as the breath of God. He bent over like an exhausted athlete, clutching his knees while the rain pelted him. Then, he vomited.

A minute passed. Soaked and dizzy, he stumbled along until he reached an intersection a half-block away. A gray muck stuck to his leaky shoes. He leaned against the side of a building and heaved again.

Righting himself, he spotted a building with a shattered plate glass window. Approaching, he saw it was a laundromat. Stepping through the opening, he went in and sat against the back wall to collect himself.

"Good Lord!" he breathed.

It wasn't the first dead person he ever saw, but it was without question, the *deadest*. The awful funk clung to him. Accustomed as he was to the recent hot weather, and though the floor was still warm, Peter couldn't shake the sudden chill from the storm. He pined for a steaming cup of coffee. He always thought better with a cup in his hand and lacking something so basic made him wonder: *What am I doing here?*

An epiphany is defined as a flash of insight, or an event that causes one. Seeing the body of that dead woman was just that. It jarred Peter back to reality and forced him into what recovering alcoholics call a fearless moral inventory.

That he was at a dead-end was clear. To plunge any deeper into this "watery world of woe" or attempt to hide in this treeless jungle was pointless. Its shadows were not the safe haven he sought. In addition, the sight of that maggot-infested corpse disabused him of any hope that the shield of Providence would protect him from being poisoned or murdered. Death hung on every corner. It was in the very air. And that thought finally trumped his fear of being captured.

Peter was ashamed to think that, since learning he was a person of interest, had he been forced to choose between avoiding prison and remaining in the priesthood, he would have renounced his vows. His glorious visions of ministering to the sick and dying that led him back to Philadelphia on the night of the bombing now seemed so distant. In the past two hours alone, there were numerous opportunities to do God's work, and not once did he stop to give anyone so much as his blessing. To compare himself to such giants as Teresa and Damien was a travesty. He was nothing but a pretender. A selfish, sanctimonious fraud.

And a coward. What's worse, he was denying Christ as surely as his namesake did by the watch-fires of the dawn on the morning of the Crucifixion.

Thirty-Two

Saturday, July 9 (6:26 P.M. EDT)
The Scharon Building

Generals Freeman and Hawkins, together with their staffs, were working through the details of Freeman's plan to counter the Greenshirt insurgency, dubbed *Operation Clean Sweep.* Hawkins had only one objection to it: the time line.

"We need another day to do it right, sir. The Cobras arrive Monday."

"Travis, we don't have another day. Collier may be perpetrating other atrocities as we speak. I'm not even sure we should wait until daybreak!"

"But, if their strength and dispositions aren't what we think, without the full support of air and armored elements, the odds may favor them."

"That's a risk we'll have to take. The President insists that we make a statement."

"With all due respect to the President, sir—and you—political expedient makes for military disaster. If this thing turns into a fiasco because we rushed into it, the real cost will far exceed the price of waiting another day."

"General, your objection is noted, but we will advance as planned, relying on speed and surprise to compensate for the lack of air and artillery support." Then, addressing the entire group, Freeman cut to the chase. "We must position ourselves between Collier and the civilian population wherever necessary and without delay. If that puts our troops at greater risk, so be it. That's our job."

Roo Hawkins backed down. He knew they were out of both time and options, and the storm lashing at the windows of Freeman's office would corrupt whatever plan they devised as soon as the first shot was fired, anyway.

Incredibly, the news of that morning's slaughter had yet to reach the airwaves. But it was only a matter of minutes now, and if another massacre took place in the meantime, the question would rise: *Where was the Army?*

Much is said in jest, and Freeman concluded the meeting by saying, "Hollywood has it that King Leonidas said at Thermopylae, 'We can no longer defend the pass. So we will attack, and kill Xerxes.'"

Everyone understood his point. The best way to terminate Collier's insurrection was to terminate Collier.

At the conclusion of the meeting, Major Robbins handed Freeman a note to call Stewart Addison. It was urgent. The General fumed at how anything related to a fart-catcher like Addison could be urgent, but he made the call anyway.

"This is Stew," answered the liaison.

"Mr. Addison, it's General Freeman." His formality exposed his contempt.

"Yes, sir!" said Addison emphatically.

Freeman bristled at his insolence.

"Whadda you want?" he barked.

"Sir, I just received word that the Attorney General is en route to Philadelphia. She's arriving at seven-thirty and wants to know if you can meet her—possibly, over dinner. She knows it's short notice, but she's only in town for the night and has something urgent to discuss with you."

Freeman was curious to hear DeKalb's take on the Greenshirt massacre. He wondered if she would talk about the progress of the investigation, particularly as it related to the Catholic Church. He was also interested in something else.

"Tell Ms. DeKalb I'll meet her at my suite in the Armitage at eight o'clock."

"Yes, sir. Would you prefer a red or a white?"

"Excuse me?"

"Nothing, sir. I'll let her know."

Addison's impudence convinced Freeman that the first order of business when he met with DeKalb would be booting him.

On hanging up, he called Major Robbins, directing him to arrange dinner: rack of lamb, mint jelly, potatoes Lyonnaise, and mixed-green salad. The General also asked him to order a merlot.

"A '49 Phelps, if possible."

Thirty-Three

Before she left for Philadelphia, Angela DeKalb called Avery Milliken into her office.

"Talk to me about the Greenshirts," she said.

"What do you want to know?"

"Just give me what you've got."

"Well, they first appeared during the Red Spring of the '30s, a reaction to all the left-wing organizations that sprang up on college campuses. At the time, it was known as the Greenleaf Society."

Angela asked, "A poor man's ROTC, wasn't it?"

"Sort of. But it was fraternal, too. Very clandestine and mysterious initiation rites. Candidates were vetted carefully, some while they were still in high school. Also, they excluded Jews, blacks, and browns—and all but a handful of women."

"I remember reading that their mission was to restore the country to its former glory by hot blood and cold steel," Angela said.

"That's right. But the enthusiasm of the founding members wasn't sustainable. The social cost of a Greenleaf pin was just too high for the average college kid to pay—popularity being the working capital of youth. Nor was the Society able to command much allegiance from its alumni."

Angela declared through pursed lips, "But then, idealism and paychecks are rarely compatible."

The mole-eyed Milliken gave a high-strung laugh. "That's the truth! Anyway, by the late '40s, the Greenleaves were in decline. The legislation that outlawed paramilitary groups on college campuses really put a crimp in their activities and discussions with a bankruptcy attorney were under way when the cavalry arrived in the person of Anson Collier."

In 2046, Colonel Collier was named chairman of the Pathfinder Party. It always struck him how many of the party faithful were former Greenleaf members. Swimming in party cash, like the newly-appointed CEO of a high-growth company, he proposed a merger of the two organizations. The alliance would be mutually advantageous. The Party would gain fresh blood—a farm team, of sorts. The Greenleaves would secure access to Pathfinder capital and a *raison d'être*.

The merger was consummated and, as Collier predicted, the fascist underpinnings of the Pathfinders dovetailed perfectly with the reactionary agenda of the Society. The combination resulted in a whole that was greater than the sum of its parts.

Angela said, "But the Greenshirts have always operated *outside* the party, doing Collier's dirty work."

"Right," Milliken replied, "but everything they do requires his blessing."

The charismatic Collier directed his young charges against the people and policies he opposed. Crude insults, continual interruptions, and, invariably, fist fights were common occurrences at the rallies of his political rivals. Bothersome journalists arrived home from vacations to find snakes or rodents nesting in their homes. Many college professors were forced to defend themselves against charges of homosexuality, pedophilia, and infidelity. A judge was made to chew broken glass for a liberal ruling in a free speech case. Nothing was ever proven, but this last comeuppance was said to have been ordered by Collier himself.

"Was it Gonzales who conferred the 'Greenshirt' label on them after the riot in Haight-Ashbury?" asked Angela.

"No, that was the editor of the *Chronicle*."

Over spring break in '58, while the Great Bird Watch was taking place at the Freeman White House, a quarter of a million students—many of whom had nothing to do with the Greenleaf Society—gathered in Golden Gate Park to hear traditional American music and speeches filled with ultraconservative rhetoric. The featured speaker on the final night of this "festival" was Sonny Collier.

Although his delivery wasn't necessarily impassioned or fanatical, Collier's words so moved his disciples that, later in the evening, hundreds of them spilled out of the park onto the streets of Haight-Ashbury. Anyone who looked at them askance was bullied or beaten. No one was killed, and the property damage was limited to a few broken windows, but the Sunday morning papers and news shows were filled with allusions to *Kristallnacht* and Hitler's Brownshirts.

"I remember how Collier downplayed the whole affair as the workings of an exuberant few," said Angela.

Milliken responded, "He's also said, on more than one occasion, '*Suffer unto me the children.*'"

Collier's greatest triumph in merging the two organizations was the formidable private militia it gave rise to. Within a few years, this dedicated group was conducting training exercises that rivaled Ranger school or Quantico in difficulty. The ranks were also loaded with hundreds of disgruntled veterans.

Angela recalled, "In your report, you mentioned that the Pathfinders could mobilize a force of between ten and fifteen thousand effectives within two weeks. Is that still the case?"

"Yes," affirmed Milliken.

Three years before, the Department of Public Safety had published an exposé on Collier's invisible empire titled *The Pathfinder Threat*. It was a thorough analysis of the history and status of the party. It documented broad, grassroots support for their agenda among whites and detailed the considerable sums flowing into their coffers. The part dealing with the political ambitions and charismatic style of Sonny Collier always caught the interest of those reading about him for the first time. But the most alarming aspect of the report was its contention that the Pathfinders could put a sizable militia into the field within a fortnight.

On reading the report, one senator described Sonny Collier as "the greatest threat to the Republic since Jeff Davis." Calls for the suppression of the Pathfinders issued from the media, magazine editors, Hollywood stars, think-tanks, college presidents, union heads and both sides of the aisle in Congress. They were often characterized as a greater menace than the Communists of the 1930s. During the '58 presidential campaign, Tito Gonzales promised to crack down on them if reelected, and legislation was pending on Capitol Hill to outlaw the party.

Collier never really hid his desire to see the established order overthrown. At least temporarily. His goal was to suspend all federal elections for ten years, during which time he would rule arbitrarily like Solon the Athenian. This would provide enough time to retool the Constitution, the court system and the electoral process without subjecting the country to a period of anarchy. Once the changes he espoused were in place, a peaceful transfer of power back to a *pared-down* electorate could be effected. Most observers thought, however, that, for all his lofty rhetoric, if he ever gained power, his rule would be more like the brutal Sulla of Rome than Solon the Athenian.

It was significant that *The Pathfinder Threat* was issued by Avery Milliken's office rather than the Criminal Division of Justice under Angela DeKalb. Of all the leaders in government, the one who seemed least concerned about the mushrooming influence of the Pathfinders was DeKalb. She even went so far as to advise Gonzales against supporting legislation to outlaw them.

Thirty-Four

The Attorney General arrived that evening almost two hours late. Two DPS agents escorted her to Freeman's penthouse suite. He met them at the door.

"Madam General, welcome to the Cordon. It's a pleasure to see you again." His breath smelled faintly of hooch.

She offered her hand, which Freeman shook gently.

"Likewise, General. I'm sorry I'm late."

The door closed behind them. With the exception of Major Robbins, they were alone.

"Did you come straight from the airport?" he asked, escorting her to the living area.

"No, I had to meet with Stew Addison first," she said. "Just a routine update. I figured if he could brief me on the day's events, it would give us more time to discuss what I came to see you about."

The mention of Addison raised his suspicions, but the General buried them, saying, "I was just listening to the news reports about the massacre. They're saying it'll guarantee Congressional approval of the *habeas corpus* suspension."

"I'm hopeful. I still worry about the Court, but they won't be back till October."

Motioning for her to have a seat, as he hung up her raincoat, he asked, "How were things out at the airport?"

"I was surprised. Operations are close to normal."

"I've worked hard on that one. Traffic into Hartford has been restored to its pre-attack level, too. So things are progressing."

"I'm impressed with what you've accomplished so far."

"Thanks. It's proven to be quite a task." Moving to the bar, he said, "What'll you have?"

"Southern Comfort and soda, please."

As he mixed it, he observed, "I must say, Angela, I'm equally impressed by what you've accomplished. It may be raising some eyebrows, but you're doing the right thing."

"Thank you, although I had an inkling you'd approve. Most of what we're doing was your idea. Originally, that is. Had we only convinced—"

Major Robbins entered the room from the small study where he was completing the preparations for dinner. He nodded respectfully in the direction of the Attorney General, who returned it politely.

He said, "Excuse me, sir, but the arrangements are complete. Will you be needing me any more tonight?"

Without bothering to introduce the two of them, Freeman said, "No, Robbins, that is all." Then, approaching the redheaded Major, he turned his back to DeKalb and muttered, "Tell the guard we're not to be disturbed."

Alone again, Freeman walked over to the sofa, handed Angela the drink and sat down beside her. He left little room between them. This breech of etiquette signaled that his intentions weren't purely professional.

Leaning toward her with his drink extended and a pained look, he said, "Would you do me a favor and drop the formalities? It's tough getting used to all the 'sirs' again. As long as we're out of earshot from the rest of the humanity, would you just call me Jim?"

"Yes, Gen . . . er, Jim," she shrugged, clinking his glass. Then, looking around, she asked, "How secure is this room?"

The scent of her perfume was captivating, and Freeman struggled to maintain some sense of decorum.

"It's swept on a daily basis," he whispered, so closely she recoiled.

"Could you play some music, anyway?"

"Sure. What would you like to hear?"

"Anything will do. I like opera."

Reluctant to surrender his position, the General went over to the entertainment system on the wall and punched up the only opera he knew: *La Boheme.*

As he turned around, he saw Angela moving from the couch to an upholstered chair.

"We have work to do, Jim," she said officiously.

Freeman smiled. He remembered how adept she was in the game of cat-and-mouse. Pulling up a chair, he positioned himself directly in front of her.

"So what is it?" he asked.

She got to the point. "As you're probably aware, we now have fifteen thousand suspects in custody."

He sipped and nodded. "Yes, that little piss ant you sent keeps us apprised, as I'm sure he does you."

Angela ignored this remark, saying, "We still have more to go, but we're running out of space. As you know, we're emptying out the facility in Mahwah to make room for the most dangerous suspects. About four thousand in all." She leaned forward with her long legs crossed, her sylphlike arms draped over them. "I need your help, though."

A long time had passed since Freeman was last proximate to this beauty. Teased by memories of her ardent desire, her sexual prowess, and his utter exhaustion as he slipped from her bed, he found it hard to concentrate.

Reading him, Angela uncrossed her legs, sat up straight and tugged down on her navy blue skirt, as if to insist: *Now, Jim, behave.* But her sheer blouse, stiletto heels, and captivating perfume belied this show of protest.

Both Freeman and DeKalb were opportunistic, and neither suffered from any overarching sense of morality. The rumors about their night of lovemaking down in Palm Beach were true. However, the reason Freeman promoted her to the top spot in the Criminal Division wasn't due to some devil's bargain forged in the heat of passion. As he told his attorney general at the time, "She's a veritable Javert, and I want her loosed." Granted, if it afforded him a second or third helping of her earthy delights someday, then so much the better. Because both of them were discrete about their one-nighter on the Gold Coast, the rumors eventually waned.

Then, Sarah Freeman died. Following an abbreviated grieving period, Freeman again made overtures toward DeKalb. She was friendly but formal. It wasn't that she had any misgivings about seeing him so soon after his wife's death. She just didn't see how it could do her any good professionally.

Whenever they met at private functions he acted anything but presidential, more like a big, hard-licking, lop-eared hound. But she always held him at bay. This indulgent attitude toward him turned to disgust during the Bird Watch. When his term finally ended, and he no longer held any sway over her, she took to avoiding him altogether.

And there was nothing Freeman could do about it. Despite his high office, if he didn't honor Angela's wishes, she might reveal their secret, thus exposing him to abuse-of-power charges. Oddly, that he had committed adultery with her never bothered him. Forced to bow to this clever student of realpolitik, the aging Lion moved on, grudgingly, to other less difficult conquests.

But now she was back, seeking support for her latest intrigue. *Maybe it's time for that second helping*, he thought.

The General motioned for Angela to lean close. In the background, *O Soave Fanciulla* drowned out his boozy voice as he asked, "How may I be of service to you?"

She stated her purpose. "No more changes to the size of the Cordon."

Surprised, Freeman drew back. "Why?"

"Given your proposed realignment, because it's in Fairfield County, the prison at Danbury is still in the territory under your control. But if you keep reducing the size of Cordon, it won't be. You've already eliminated a number of facilities that might have been available to us. That will impair our ability to detain the greatest threats to our safety indefinitely."

Never one to coddle a criminal, Freeman saluted the logic of it.

"How does the President feel about your plan?"

"As it stands, I haven't discussed it with him."

"So, you're asking me to weigh in with my support before you take it to him?"

With eyes lowered, she nodded her head.

Leaning back, Freeman took a minute to think, occasionally tapping his fingers on the arm of his chair.

Finally, he said, "If I agree to forestall any further realignment—"

A knock at the door cut him short. Agitated, he went to answer it. *That red-haired dope knows I don't want to be disturbed!* As he opened it, he saw the guards giving the room-service cart a final check, while off to the side Robbins patted down the waiter.

"Oh, it's here?"

"Yes, sir," said Robbins. Then, having finished his inspection, he allowed the waiter to pass.

They moved to a table next to the windows in the dining area where the man arranged their meal. He removed the bottle of wine from the ice bucket to see if it met with the General's approval. Freeman asked him to show it to his guest.

Angela was amazed. "Yes, it's perfect."

He poured a taste into each of their glasses. Upon further approval, he filled the glasses, then excused himself.

Alone again, Angela took another sip and said, "How did you know that I prefer a merlot?"

Freeman cryptically replied, "You're not the only one who has sources, you know." Then, he added, "I might add that it's also a preferred vintage: 2049."

Angela was touched. Her pleasure only magnified her beauty.

"I'm flattered," she said. "But how did you know?"

Freeman came clean. "You mentioned it in your *Celebrity Confidential* interview. The only reason I remembered the vintage is because that's the year I became president."

"Well, again, I'm touched."

Freeman raised his glass to hers and toasted, "Here's to your continued success."

The meal began quietly. The long day left both of them with a powerful appetite. To the sound of the gentle music and the rain sheeting against the windows, Angela devoured her lamb. She nibbled at her salad and never touched the potatoes. Before Freeman was half-finished, she pushed her plate away.

They talked about the massacre in Newark for a while, then spent a little more time on Operation Cockroach. Eventually, the AG bought the discussion back to the realignment, saying, "Jim, about Danbury. I need to hear that you won't make any more changes to Cordon."

Chewing while he spoke, Freeman replied, "As you know, Angela, I was never one to pamper a crook. And I like the fact that your plan buys additional time to build the case against them. But I doubt that Gonzales will go along with it."

Angela said, "Frankly, he doesn't need to know."

Her brazen response gave Freeman a turn. Taking a dim view, he predicted, "You'll never pull it off."

Twisting nervously, she explained, "The transfers can be effected internally with an administrative order from the Bureau of Prisons, so it wouldn't require the President's direct authorization. Once the transfer is complete, I'll inform him of my actions."

"So, you're prepared to fall on your sword?"

"Of course."

Angela emptied her wine glass and touched her napkin gently to her lips. Then, moving again—this time inching her chair slightly closer to Freeman—she said, "We'll never have another chance like this again, Jim."

"No, probably not," he replied, with thoughts of something other than the dragnet racing round his head.

Pointing to the northeast, she continued, "If any good can come from this tragedy it's that we're now in a position to crush any ongoing threats in one fell swoop. We simply can't let this opportunity go begging."

That's the truth, thought Freeman. His biggest disappointment on leaving office, other than his libidinous behavior, was his inability to cripple the "ongoing threats" to America's safety. Even with DeKalb heading the Criminal Division, his administration was unable to flush out the swarm of rebels, anarchists, saboteurs, traitors, spies, assassins, and terrorists hiding under the rock called **Civil Libertie**s. Every attempt he made to roll it away was frustrated by legal pacifists who branded him a despot or otherwise impugned his motives. Unable to mount an attack, he was always haunted by Napoleon's warning that the inevitable outcome of defensive warfare is surrender.

However, now the situation was changed and Angela's reading of it, accurate. This was a pivotal moment. The fortunes of war now favored the hard-liners.

Freeman thought: *Gonzales was smart to seize the advantage and attack. If he continues to show the same resolve as DeKalb, he'll crush these threats forever.*

"All you're asking is that I forego any further realignment of the Cordon till some future date?" he asked.

"Also, I need some logistical support," Angela replied.

"How so?"

"The Marshals Service hasn't enough manpower to safely escort the prisoners from the airfields to the prisons. We need additional ground transportation and troops to supplement their numbers."

"How many troops do you think it will take?"

"I'd say a hundred. Probably just for a few days."

The General ate the last of his potatoes, refilled both their glasses with wine and drank his down in one throw. He set his glass on the table without a word. Rising somewhat unsteadily, he threw his napkin onto his plate and turned to look out the window.

The rain pounded against it as if to do him harm. Nine stories below, his wet, miserable countrymen crisscrossed Independence Mall in search of food, water, and shelter. Since he took command of the Cordon, the sight of it had burdened him. But not tonight. Numbed to the plight of this human driftwood by the serial horrors of the past week, including the massacre that morning, there was only one thing on his mind at the moment.

Angela watched him with growing concern. He still hadn't given his consent. She was a bit miffed, expecting him to be more enthusiastic. Addison had mentioned more than once how much the General resented his presence. *Maybe that's the problem,* she thought.

"Jim, are you angry that I had one of my people join your staff?"

"Not really," he said. "Although you may find that particular person tits up in that river out there any day now."

Her laughter changed the dynamic.

Freeman walked over to the entertainment system. "And another thing," he said, "is this the kind of music you play when you're trying to sweat a confession out of someone?"

Angela laughed again, this time, more politely.

Freeman punched up his favorite Sinatra song: *Autumn in New York.*

"Look, Jim, I'll make a deal with you," she said, elevating her voice to compete with the music. "I've been working on the details of this prisoner exchange since we began the dragnet last weekend. The reason I sent Addison to you is that he used to be in charge of the

Bureau of Prisons. Nobody is more qualified to coordinate the transfers than him. Once it's done, I'll serve you his head on a plate if that's what you want. Just tell me I can count on your support."

Her request sounded uncharacteristically desperate, even more so after Freeman dimmed the lights. He took off his dinner jacket and folded it over a chair. There would be no more talk of prison transfers. Or Stewart Addison.

The magic of Sinatra's voice and the lush orchestration of Billy May were suggestive of a more elegant time and place. Taking her hand, he helped her up, put his hands on her hips, and pulled her gently to him. Her body pressed firmly against him. He kissed her hair, her forehead, and her cheek. When their lips met, her mouth was already open. The kiss was long and breathless. When she broke it off, they remained locked together.

The old man would charge Hell itself to spend the balance of his days in these arms. Angela's emotional and intellectual maturity was as seductive to him as her great beauty.

But her attitude toward him had not changed. She had no time for romantic entanglements. Although he was handsome and aristocratic, that wasn't the attraction for her. Her interests were purely pragmatic.

She thought to soften him up by playing on his gratitude. Lifting her head from his shoulder, she declared, "I was the one who recommended you for this post, you know."

Since leaving Montana, Freeman wondered how the President came to choose him for command, though he hid well his surprise. He was appreciative but not overly so.

"I guess that makes us even, then. Doesn't it?"

"What do you mean?"

"Is your memory that bad?"

She protested, "I thought I covered that marker."

"Oh," he said, "if you're referring to that night in Palm Beach, I just felt sorry for you. You seemed so lonely."

His sarcasm left no doubt as to where the negotiations were headed. "You drive a hard bargain, General."

He pressed closer and whispered boozily, "Don't fight it. It's bigger than both of us."

* * * * *

Sex was a means to an end for Angela DeKalb and never a casual undertaking. Generally, she abstained from it, though not out of any puritanical notions. She enjoyed a good romp as much as the next girl, but her motivation for having one was rarely pleasure. And, though she was opportunistic in choosing who would share her bed, contrary to Capitol whispers, she was not promiscuous. As a rule, with the exception of state dinners, Kennedy Center events, and other elite gatherings, she took pains to avoid the Washington social scene. Regardless, for a woman who rose every morning at four o'clock, ran or exercised daily, worked in the limo to and from work, spent a minimum of ten hours a day and six days a week at her desk or traveling on government business, then went to bed every night at ten o'clock sharp, she was the subject of more salacious rumors than the women who swim out to meet troopships.

Actually, most of the whisperings came as a result of her personality, not her behavior. Angela was well-mannered, charming, and respectful. However, she wasn't gifted with those traits that beget lasting friendships: compassion, humility, generosity, patience, and a sense of humor. In a word, selflessness. Her considerable physical and mental gifts set her apart from others. So, too, the air of superiority she exuded. Headstrong and vindictive, anyone who extended a hand to her usually wound up empty-handed. The only thing she loved was the law. That was her Jupiter. A fearsome, solitary feline, she was the complement to Nietzsche's *Ubermensch*. An *Uberfrau*.

* * * * *

"Is there somewhere I can make ready?" she asked.

Freeman led her into the bedroom and pointed to the bath.

She emerged a few minutes later wearing a terrycloth robe and her stiletto heels. Freeman lay on the bed, gray and naked but covered to the waist by the top sheet. She came around to the side and stood over him.

Putting a finger to the corner of her mouth, she said, playfully, "Can you help me, Mr. General? I'd do *anything* to get my hands on a few hundred soldiers."

The farmer's daughter routine made Freeman snicker, "I got a soldier right here for ya!"

From the moment Angela decided to ask for Freeman's help in effecting the prisoner transfers, she knew instinctively that he would make her pay for it in flesh. So she devised a plan to make short work of the payoff. As he reached for her, she pulled from her pocket a vial of oil and sat next to him on the bed. Halfheartedly, she began coating his hairy torso with the lubricant, which smelled of jasmine. After the General was sufficiently prepped, she untied her robe, letting it fall to the floor, then kicked off her heels, and climbed on top of him. Rubbing some of it on herself, she began teasing him. Between the warmth of the oil and her sorcerous movements, the old man struggled to delay his response, but her wiles got the best of him.

Freeman's premature reaction led Angela to assume the festivities were over, so she quickly climbed off him and sat on the edge of the bed. Her assumption was premature in its own right, however.

When she bent down for her robe, Freeman thought: *Where's she going?* As she straightened up, he grabbed her arm and yanked her back onto the bed. She let out a cry, more startled than pained.

Suddenly, Freeman's demeanor turned ugly. Kicking and clawing, Angela tried to resist him but was grossly outweighed and couldn't escape his still-powerful arms. Vainly, she raked at his flesh, though never letting go more than a few yelps. Certain that further resistance would prove fruitless, and fearful that it might make him more violent, Angela relented. Even then, the oil made it difficult for the General to find his mark. But he did. In one frantic minute, ten years of pent up frustration was unleashed, then Freeman suddenly stopped, unsated and exhausted.

Angela lay pinned beneath him. Having paid his ask, she set her sights on the prize. When Freeman rolled off her, she suppressed her disgust and, ever the opportunist, lay next to him quietly to await his consent to her plan—not before she rearranged the sheet to provide a buffer between them, though.

The General's heart was about to explode, but he was pleased with the outcome of the negotiations. Not only had he extracted a premium for his support; he had also collected some interest on the AG's long-delinquent account. Having milked her of the concession he wanted most—the obligatory quid in the *quid pro quo*—he decided to close the deal. Besides, if he welshed now, there was no telling what Angela would do, given her reputation for vindictiveness.

He said, "I'll do what you ask under two conditions."

"And those are?" Angela asked curtly, unmasking her pique.

"First, Addison is gone once the transfer of prisoners is complete."

"And second?"

"I want your file on Anson Collier."

"Anson Collier?"

"That's right."

"Why? Because of this morning's attack?"

"I have my reasons," he said. "Is it a deal?"

Before he could lay down any further conditions, she said, "Okay." Then, jumping out of the bed, she grabbed her robe and shoes and ran into the bathroom.

As she did, he yelled out, "When can we expect the first shipment of prisoners?"

She yelled back, "Monday," and coldly slammed the door.

After dressing, she came out and stood at the foot of the bed, her brow knotted in anger. "By the way, Jim," she said, "this is one deal you'll not want to renege on." From a tiny recorder she held in her hands, she replayed the words: *"I got a soldier right here for ya."*

Then, without another word, she was gone.

Freeman got up, staggered into the bathroom, and dropped some nitro. He elected to take a quick shower on seeing his wilted body and tousled hair in the mirror. Soaping off the unmanly smell of the love oil, he replayed the evening in his mind. It was of no small concern to him that DeKalb possessed a decidedly more accurate record of it.

She must've hidden that thing in her robe, he concluded.

Since a sin committed against another sinner seems less sinful, he never gave a second thought to his deplorable behavior. Years had passed since the last time he was a sheet or two to the wind, and now it was time to sleep, not think. Eventually, the throbbing in his head and chest died down. As it did, he drifted off to the words of Old Blue Eyes:

"Those fingers in my hair / That sly, come-hither stare /
That strips my conscience bare / It's witchcraft."

Thirty-Five

When DeKalb left the penthouse, she headed for Stewart Addison's suite three floors below with her security detail. The plan was to brief him on the negotiations with Freeman before returning to Washington. She also needed a minute to regain her composure before she left for the airport.

He met her at the door dressed in a paisley, smoking jacket with an unlit Meerschaum in his mouth. Through clenched teeth, he asked, "How did it go?" The delay in her response made him think not well.

Actually, Angela was momentarily preoccupied with his affectations: the jacket, the pipe, the accent. He looked like the crazy neighbor in a TV sitcom.

"As well as could be expected," she finally replied, hanging her raincoat in the foyer closet. "Danbury is safe—for now. The General agreed to forestall any further realignment until we have things the way we want them."

Then, with a sigh, she asked, "Can I have a glass of wine?"

"Certainly."

Addison's three room suite was not so plush as the penthouse, but it was elegantly decorated and well furnished. An ample dining area and a small kitchen led to the main room. Set before a gas fireplace was a long sofa flanked by two upholstered chairs with a coffee table in the center. Angela plopped down, clutching a silk throw pillow at the end of the sofa. Then, laying it aside, she opened her purse and took out a sedative.

"Will he provide troop support?" inquired Addison, while pouring two glasses of cabernet from a stock of wines he kept above the wet bar.

Angela, unsettled by all the "haggling" with Freeman, knew at some point it was discussed but couldn't remember the exact details.

"Yes," she said, "that's part of the bargain."

Addison came up from behind the couch. Her perfume was always so tantalizing, but now he was confused. Before, when they met, it was something French, maybe a lavender. Now it was decidedly jasmine, a bouquet one might associate with a wahine from the South Pacific but not the Attorney General of the United States. It aroused him nonetheless. A host of primordial chemicals surged into his bloodstream as he handed the wine glass over her shoulder and caught sight of her ample cleavage.

He wondered: *Might this be the night?*

His boss put the pill in her mouth, took a sip of wine, then looked up at him quizzically as he lingered behind her. Instinctively, she shuttered her blouse with her free hand.

Moving slowly around the sofa, Addison watched her, sensing a touch of vulnerability. He sat facing her at the opposite end of the sofa with one leg pulled beneath him.

What's different about him? she thought.

His mein was more like a gambler with a straight flush than a sissified toady. As he bared his smoke-stained teeth in a crude smile, Angela averted her eyes, staring instead into the barely-flickering fireplace. Circling the rim of her glass with a ruby-tipped forefinger, without resuming eye contact, she said, "I trust you know how important the success of this transfer is to me, Stewart?"

"Oh? How so?" he replied, airily.

"Relocating our prisoners to facilities within the Cordon is crucial. With the worst of them under the purview of the military governor—"

He interrupted, "No, you misunderstood. I know *why* it's important. I'm curious as to *how* important."

"What do you mean?"

"Well, is so important that you'd be willing to, say—pay up for it?"

When he asked the question, Addison closed one eye and held his wine glass up to one of the recessed lights in the ceiling, as if to assess its clarity.

Angela almost laughed aloud. *Not again! What am I? A pin cushion?* The thought of a dalliance with Addison was not only outrageous; it was repugnant. She would as soon screw a lizard.

Addison leaned a bit closer and said, "You know, we're not all that different, you and I."

"How's that?"

Fumbling for the right word, he stuttered, "Well, what I mean is that . . . well, we're both so . . . *ambitious.*"

"So we're both ambitious," she spit. "I fail to see how that precludes any differences."

"Ambitious to the point of using whatever means necessary to promote our careers," he replied.

The AG was astonished by his impudence. "And by what means do *you* propose to advance *yours*?"

While Addison gave generous consideration to his reply, Angela placed her glass on the coffee table. She positioned herself at the edge of the sofa so she could make a run for the door, wondering what the outcome might have been had she done the same upstairs. Given the dime-store quality of Addison's services, there was no way she was paying up for them. The only reason she didn't leave immediately was that his uncharacteristic boldness pricked her curiosity.

Addison slid toward her. He moved to finger her hair, but Angela pushed him away, spilling his wine. Then she broke for the door.

Pulling her raincoat out of the closet, she growled, "I don't know what gave you the idea that seducing me would advance your career, Stewart, but I can assure you, all you did tonight was ruin your prospects."

Still seated on the sofa, the effeminate lackey dabbed at the stain on his pants and jacket with a cocktail napkin and answered smugly, "I think not."

"No? And why's that?" Angela had her coat on and stood defiantly in the doorway, hands on hips, her lips pursed.

"Because I wasn't foolish enough to think that my *manhood* could open those doors." With a pouting look, he got up to get a towel in the kitchen.

Angela stayed where she was, disconcerted by his behavior. "If there's something you want, did you ever think of asking for it?"

At the sink, an almost tearful Addison rubbed the stain on his jacket. "And, if I asked for the deputy attorney general's position as a reward for a successful transfer, would you even consider it?"

The post was vacated in June when Angela's second-in-command resigned for health reasons. That Addison felt qualified to fill it was laughable. But Angela said nothing.

"No," he said. "You would have promised to give it 'due consideration' then blown me off once it was convenient."

"Maybe for the deputy AG position but not some other post." She lied: "I've always thought you'd make a good U.S. attorney."

"Yeah, right."

Addison's usual monotone—the one that smacked of old, New England money—was gone. In its place was the unrefined twang of a bill collector's son from Des Moines.

"Look, Angela, I'm not kidding myself. I'm not well-liked or well-respected. And the Bureau of Prisons isn't exactly a rocket to the stars. Now you've got me spying on the most powerful man in the country. *For God's sake, he's the former president!* It's not exactly the kind of work that opens doors. And, like I said, in that regard I'm no different from you. We both want our cut of the Capitol swag. I know I can't get there on my own. I need an angel, someone to grubstake my career. Like Freeman did yours."

"What are you talking about?" The insult finally registered. Indignantly, she demanded, "What gives you the idea I didn't make it on my own?"

Without hesitation, Addison said, "Don't kid yourself, Angela. Everyone knows how you make your bones in Freeman's bed."

It was an outrage. Not because it was a lie, but because *no one* talked to her that way. She opened the door to leave, saying, "Stewart, in the unlikely event that someone in the department is inclined to throw you a going-away party, tell them it's time to route the memo."

But Addison held his ground, shouting desperately, "Before you go, you may be interested to know why I'm going all in."

So, thought Angela, *here it comes. The hole card.*

On opening the door, she noticed that the two DPS agents in her security detail were gone. Their unexplained absence puzzled her, but she decided to handle first things first.

Her hand never left the lever as she closed the door softly and said, "So, tell me. Why *are* you risking all?"

Despite rehearsing his lines many times over, Addison delivered them poorly. "I have information," he said, with a glance toward the ceiling. "I haven't confirmed the source. The gist of it . . . well, you know—"

"C'mon, Stewart! I don't have all night."

"You might not say that once you find out what it is."

"Then what is it?"

"First, I want you to know that, well, it's not my intent to blackmail you or anything."

Angela folded her arms like an exasperated mother waiting for a child to come clean on a fib. Tenderly, she said, "Stewart, please tell me you're having a nervous breakdown."

Addison stiffened. "I received this letter the other day. There are things in it which should be of concern—of great concern—to you."

"Such as?"

"Well, maybe you better read it."

He opened a cabinet and pulled out an envelope. Removing the contents, he walked to where she was standing, gave it to her and said, "Here, please, sit," motioning toward the living room.

"No, thank you," she said contemptuously, snatching the letter out of his hand. She stepped a little further into the room to avail herself of the light, pushing him back as she did.

The letter was printed on three pages. It appeared to be the original, not a photocopy.

July 6, 2061

Dear Mr. Addison:

I have it on good authority that you are a trusted ally of the Attorney General. Because any direct correspondence between her and me, if disclosed, could cause her substantial embarrassment, I thought it best to contact her through you. I trust you will keep confidential the contents of this letter.

Angela leafed to the end of the letter. It was signed by Anson Collier. She looked at Addison in amazement, but he was already back in the kitchen trying to remove the wine stains from his smoking jacket. So she continued reading.

The Attorney General was born in Miami, Florida on December 7, 2014. She was adopted by Alex and Joanne DeKalb of Boca Raton on December 29th the same year. Her adoption papers list Anna Semynkova as the birth-mother, her birth-father as unknown. Of this, she is aware. However, the details of her entry into this world may not be. Her mother, a Russian émigré, deserves most of the credit for her origins.

Anna Semynkova was a brilliant geneticist, schooled at the University of Moscow and the University of Pennsylvania. Her dissertation was titled "The Reproduction of Human Life in Protein Lixiviates." Soon after she received her doctorate from Penn, she went to work for Steiner Laboratories in Arlington, Virginia. Steiner was a privately-funded research lab engaged in recombinant DNA experiments. It was in the Steiner labs that the word "acid hatch" originated. Essentially, it was a process of spermless insemination. By marrying the reconstituted DNA of two donors in a solution of liquefied proteins, the scientists at Steiner were able to fertilize eggs using chemically-enhanced male chromatids, electrical stimulation, and micronutrients. Once fully-formed, but before the first subdivision, the zygote was then transplanted into the uterus where, with supplemental hormones, the natural process of childbirth took over.

Steiner achieved some notable success with its hatching process; six patents were issued. But, for each success, there were innumerable failures. It's estimated that more than 1,500 children were hatched between 2014 and 2022. Many were born with significant birth defects. In 2020, Ms. Semynkova was shot and killed by a man whose child was one of these defectives. The public outcry over this cutting-edge, but controversial research resulted in legislation banning it in 2022, the same year Steiner was acquired by Neugenesis Corp.

In her will, Ms. Semynkova bequeathed all her prodigious research to the University of Pennsylvania. The federal government confiscated it two years later but not before her personal journal was stolen. That journal, which tells the story of Ms. DeKalb's birth, is now in my possession.

It was during her first three years at Steiner that Ms. Semynkova did her finest work. It was inspired by her association with an elite group of intellectuals known as the Guardians. These people—fearful that democracy's leveling effects were causing America to lose its propensity for the creation of genius—were committed to rectifying the problem through applied science. That is, commercial eugenics. Most of the capital flowing into Steiner's coffers came from Guardian accounts.

In one experiment, known only to her but outlined in her journal, Ms. Semynkova combined her DNA with that of a man with whom she was having an affair. Twin zygotes were produced: one male, one female. Without her lover's knowledge, these were implanted in her uterus. Nine months later—and long after the affair ended—she gave birth to twins in a Miami hospital.

The firstborn was the female. Ms. Semynkova, who was convinced that an out-of-wedlock child would place unwanted demands on her career, put the girl up for adoption. That girl was Angela DeKalb.

The boy? He was adopted, too, by a family from Jacksonville. However, by the time he reached the age of four, he was taken from his abusive parents and made a ward of the state. He retained the name that his adoptive family gave him, though: Collier. Anson Collier.

Angela was aghast. Again, she looked at Addison, who was back sitting on the sofa, nervously gauging her reaction. Suddenly, she blanched and staggered sideways. Reaching for the door, she lost her balance and fell, and bashed her head on a stone planter in the entryway.

Addison jumped off the couch and ran to help. Cradling her head, he anxiously patted her cheek. "Angela? Angela?"

She mouthed something unintelligible.

"What?"

"—can't be," she mumbled.

Addison was tall but not very strong. Angela, on the other hand, was leggy and full. He struggled to lift her. After a few awkward attempts, he finally got her up to a sitting position.

It never occurred to him that his boss would react so badly to the contents of the letter. He expected her to claim it was a lie, or cite proof to the contrary. If Collier really was her brother, it would ruin her professionally, especially in the wake of that morning's massacre. On the other hand, the only way anyone would find out about it was if she didn't cooperate with his demand to become deputy AG. Or compensate him handsomely in some other way.

"Are you okay?" he asked.

"The letter," she stammered. "Where's the—" Spotting it on the floor nearby, she reached for it, woozily.

Addison steadied her. "I'll get it," he said, picking up the scattered pages.

Handing it over, he said, "I didn't realize it would come as such a shock to you. In fact, I thought you might know about it already."

DeKalb said nothing. The third page was on top. With difficulty, she reread the last few paragraphs.

The laser of truth melts timeworn conventions and treasured beliefs faster than April snow. Old probabilities are shattered as new possibilities are cast. Just so, Angela DeKalb's reality changed the instant she read Collier's letter. Try as she might to deny its authenticity, she knew instinctively that its contents were true. The tone of the letter was utterly confident, and, from what she knew of him, Collier was a serious man, not the kind given to frivolous speculations about his or anyone else's parentage.

Addison tried to get her to stand so she could move over to the couch.

"Why don't you come sit down, Angela?"

"No, please. Just give me a minute."

Flush with perspiration, she brushed back her hair. Her left ear was sticky and wet, and her fingers came away covered with blood. The sight of it returned her to her senses. She knew she had to play for time. While Addison went for a tissue, she said, "If I do what you ask . . . what is it you want?"

"I think I've made myself pretty clear on that point," he said, handing her the tissue.

"The deputy AG position?"

"That's right."

"And what guarantee do I have that you'll keep your mouth shut?" She slowly rose to her feet as she said it.

"You have only my word," he replied, supporting her.

That's rich! she thought. *The only thing this pervert lacks more than virility is integrity.* But she played along. Nodding as if his word was better than Galahad's, she said, "I'll have the paperwork drawn up in the morning."

Then, retrieving her purse and folding the letter into it, she added, "I suppose you've retained a copy of this for your records?"

"Several," he said. "So, should anything happen to me, the whole world will know about you and Collier within hours."

Angela paid no mind to this threat. She responded in clipped fashion, "Well then, I'll look forward to working with you."

She removed something that looked like an electronic key from her purse and turned to leave.

Addison grabbed her forearm as she did. He took her in his arms as she twisted violently away, saying, "This needn't be strictly business, Angela." Searching the small of her back with his left hand as he held her closely with his right, he pinned her sideways against the door. Initially, she battled to get free, but then, to his surprise, she went limp and turned passively toward him. Awkwardly, he pressed his lips to hers, probing a wall of clenched teeth with his saurian tongue. At the same time, he reached down and attempted to breach the folds of her raincoat. Suddenly, a knifing pain at the base of his neck sent him reeling. He collapsed on the floor, paralyzed and struggling to breathe.

The key-like device in Angela's hand was actually a Medusa—a needleless syringe of synthetic snake venom. It was non-lethal but very effective in immobilizing an attacker by deadening the central nervous system.

Looking down at him coldly, Angela placed the device back in her purse.

"You know, Stewart," she said, "if Sonny Collier is my brother, he won't take kindly to the way you treated me here tonight."

And the same might be said about Jim Freeman, she told herself as she opened the door and hurried out.

Thirty-Six

Outside, one of the DPS agents, a man named Dolan, was back. Spotting the bloody tissue, he asked, "What happened?"

"Oh, it's nothing, really," she said with a wave of her hand. "I bumped my head."

Dolan gave her a clean handkerchief as they walked to the elevator. "Are you sure?" he said.

She nodded. He seemed oddly out of breath, even nervous. "Where were you?" she demanded.

"There's been a change of plans. We've been getting reports all evening that the Greenshirts are active in the immediate area. As a precaution, we're going to exit you from rear of the building. The limo's waiting for us there."

"Where's Cartier?"

"He's with the limo."

"You left me."

"I'm sorry. Cartier went down to coordinate the change with Freeman's people. I stepped away for a second to find a bathroom. It's my fault."

When the elevator opened into the Armitage lobby, they were met by an army captain with a detail of soldiers wearing the patch of the 301st Infantry Division.

"Madam General," the officer said, "my orders are to escort you to the airport."

He was a tall man with boyish features, and his deportment was more that of a cadet first-sergeant than a captain in the regular army. His men stood behind him, eyes forward, ramrod straight. Angela was put out by all the changes but physically, mentally, and emotionally drained by the depredations of Freeman and Addison, her deference to Dolan and the young officer was automatic.

"All right, Captain. Lead the way."

Winding through the administrative offices behind the front desk, then down a hallway next to the kitchen, they came to a door that opened into an alley off Market Street. There, the limo was parked between two old H-7s armed with laser cannons.

Cartier, the other security man, was standing in the rain toward the back of the line. He had his back to her and appeared to be making arrangements with the soldiers. Dolan held the door to the limo open while DeKalb ducked in with a gentlemanly assist from the captain.

"I'll sit up front," Dolan announced as the door closed behind her.

She barely had time to get situated before they started moving. Although, at first, she was slightly disoriented by the change in itinerary, Angela's knowledge of downtown Philadelphia proved solid. With the Scharon Building on her left and the Mall on her right, she knew they were headed north on Sixth Street, in the opposite direction of the airport.

Is it a feign?

She attempted to lower the glass between her and Dolan to inquire if that was the plan, but the controls were dead. Scooting forward, she banged on the opaque glass. There was no response.

What the—?

When the convoy turned east onto the Ben Franklin Bridge, it hit her.

I'm being abducted!

Instinctively, she took a transceiver out of her purse and pushed 199 to send a distress signal, unaware of the onboard jammers.

Figuring she could make a run for it if the limo slowed down, she gave the door handle a pull. It was inoperable. So was the one on the other side. The windows were bullet-resistant, so there was no use trying to kick them out. There was nothing she could do but wait— either to be rescued or to learn what fate had in store.

Kidnapping public officials or corporate executives for ransom was a common occurrence, but no one in the Cabinet had ever been abducted. *Dolan's in on it,* she thought, *but what about Cartier?* If only to dissuade such actions in the future, she knew the government would spare no expense to hunt these people down and secure her release. *But who is Dolan working for? The General? His men met me at the elevator.*

Then, before she could give it any further consideration, the limo screeched to a halt a few miles into Jersey. Some urgent commands were shouted, then the door swung open. The captain poked his head in.

"Madam General," he said, "you'll make it easy on all of us if you'll come along quietly."

"First tell me where we're going," she said.

"I'm not at liberty to say, ma'am."

Stalling, she repeatedly hit 199 on her transceiver, but the captain noticed what she was doing and knocked it out of her hand. Then he grabbed her wrist and yanked her out of the limo. Another soldier got hold of her other arm.

She screamed for help, kicking them as she did, but it was useless. Other soldiers grabbed her legs as they pinned her face-down on the rain-soaked shoulder. She arched her neck to prevent her face from being ground into the dirt and gravel. As she did, she saw the body of Agent Cartier fall listlessly to the pavement from the bed of the trailing vehicle.

The men unzipped her skirt and pulled down her panties to bare her hip. The last thing she heard was, "Inject it here."

There was the prick of a needle, a warm rush, then, soft release.

Thirty-Seven

After sleeping for a few hours in the back of the laundromat, Peter Bernard awoke to the sound of the storm, howling in concert with the interminable sirens. Flashes of lighting exploded against the building across the street and ricocheted toward him, revealing puddles of wind-driven rain a few feet away. The pounding on the roof, punctuated by blasts of thunder, nearly deafened him. He sat against the wall, entranced by this spectacle of nature. It reminded him of the tempest hurled down by the Lord to prevent Jonah's escape to Tarshish.

I must have read that story a hundred times, he thought.

It was a story that hit home for him, having been branded a Jonah by friend and foe alike. But, until that moment, it was like an optical illusion to him. Previously, he had only fathomed half of it. Now he saw clearly the cryptic image that had always eluded him.

I'm not like Jonah because I'm a jinx. I'm like him because I'm running from God, too!

He recalled the story. Commissioned to preach against the wickedness of Nineveh, Jonah instead booked passage on a ship bound for the ends of the earth. When the Almighty summoned the wind and sea to arrest his flight, the sailors cast him overboard. He delivered his famous psalm of repentance from deep in the belly of "a great fish." Spewed out on the land, he dutifully set off for Nineveh to deliver God's judgment. His preaching was so successful that the

Ninevites and their king repented. By atoning for their sins, they were spared destruction.

This angered Jonah. It was the reason he fled in the first place: he knew God would show mercy toward Israel's enemies if they repented. While he sat angrily on a hill overlooking the city, praying to die, God brought forth a gourd to shade him from the sun's heat. The following day, he caused the gourd to wither. This give-and-take was intended to school Jonah of God's right to judge his creation as he saw fit and that no man has the right to begrudge his mercy toward others.

Peter thought: *That's what I've been doing for the last five years— sitting under my gourd, praying to die.* Resolved to lead a softer life on his release from prison, he decided: *Let the yolk of martyrdom pass to some other dumb ox.*

Thus, when the Lord, in his wisdom, tried to whip him back into the traces, he bolted. He was running, not from the wasp of injustice but from the inscrutable purposes of God.

And Newark was his Tarshish.

Thirty-Eight

Sunday, July 10 (12:55 A.M. EDT)
The Armitage Hotel

Colonel Essing and Major Robbins were ushered into the presidential suite by one of the sergeants on guard. The General was sprawled across the bed, naked.

Essing announced, "General, there's a problem."

Freeman didn't respond.

Gently, Robbins rocked him by the shoulder. "General?"

The old man stirred.

Essing repeated, "General, we have a problem."

"Wha—?"

"Sir, the Attorney General was abducted by some men posing as troopers from the 301st."

"Abducted?!" Freeman croaked, as he struggled to sit up. "When?"

"About an hour ago. We think it was Collier's men."

Freeman stood, wobbled, then collapsed back on the bed like an unstrung puppet. Essing and Robbins helped him back to his feet. Indignantly, he shook them off and looked around the room, disoriented.

"There's more, sir. Stewart Addison is dead."

"Huh?!"

"Yes, sir. He was found down in the alley below his room. From all the broken glass, it appears he either jumped or was thrown out the window."

Except for the report that preceded it, Freeman might have welcomed this news. Instead, his shoulders sagged. He shook his head, stunned by the sudden turn of events. Then, embarrassed by his nudity, he cut things short.

"I'll be ready in a minute. Wait outside."

The two men retired to the living room while Freeman staggered toward the bath. Minutes later, they heard a crash. Rushing into the bathroom, they saw the General sprawled on the floor, unconscious. "Get a doctor!" Essing ordered, and Robbins was off. Essing tried to revive the old man but couldn't. He felt his pulse; it was weak. But, his breathing, though boozy, was normal. The Colonel deduced that it wasn't a heart attack. When Robbins returned, they carried him back to bed.

"What's that smell?" Robbins whispered, wiping his hands on his pants. "The whole place smells like a freakin' cat house."

"I don't know," answered Essing, although he was sure it had something to do with Angela DeKalb.

He felt Freeman's pulse again. It was stronger now.

"See if you can find some smelling salts," the panting Essing told Robbins.

The same regimental surgeon who treated him for exhaustion the week before was on the scene in minutes. He quickly applied a rejuvenator to Freeman's neck, and within seconds the General blinked his eyes.

Weakly attempting to rise, he mumbled, "Where did they—I need to—"

"Easy, General," the doctor cautioned. "We'll get to all that. Let's take things one at a time. Can you tell me what happened?"

"I was washing . . . think I slipped."

The doctor shined a small light into his pupils, then examined his head for any contusions. His venerable patient winced when he touched the bump on the side of his head.

"You've got a nice little hummock there, General." Turning to Robbins, he said, "We're going to need an ice-pack."

Again, the Major was off, this time to the kitchen.

After analyzing Freeman's heartbeat with a handheld EKG, the doctor took a companion EEG monitor out of his case. He moved the electrode strip from the General's chest to his forehead. After the first reading, he took a second. Then, he reset the apparatus and took a third.

With a confounded look, he turned to Essing and said, "Could you leave us for a moment?"

The Colonel reluctantly complied, closing the bedroom door behind him.

Since it was Freeman's second blackout in the span of a week, the doctor asked Freemen point-blank, "Have you ever been diagnosed with a brain disorder, General?"

Freeman told him, "No, never. Why? Is something wrong?"

"Well, I'm getting a reading here that your brain waves are, uh, abnormal. It's probably insignificant, but it needs to be checked. It could be indicative of a more serious problem."

The doctor was downplaying his concern. He purposely avoided any use of the word stroke. But even if he did mention it, it would not have come as a shock to Freeman.

Three weeks before, he was diagnosed with a brain tumor.

Before he left to go fishing on the Big Blackfoot, he had been having intermittent problems doing simple math and remembering names and places. Although these anomalies escaped the notice of most people, including his Secret Service detail, he was worried about them.

At first he thought it was related to his heart problem. Then, he started having difficulty operating things as simple as a teletran. Rather than wait for his annual checkup at Bethesda, he sought out an eminent neurologist from Charleston who solved the mystery. A golf ball-sized tumor was pressing against the areas of his brain which regulate those functions. It wasn't life threatening. The tumor was probably benign, and there was a good chance that tumor-devouring robotic mice, or *tumites*, could pare it down. But, to prevent further damage, the tumites needed to be implanted immediately. The technology was still bleeding-edge—there was some risk associated with it—but there were a number of trials in which it had proven wildly successful.

The medical-privacy laws ensured that Freeman's condition was known only to his neurologist and, against his advice, Freeman postponed the operation. The fishing holiday was already in the works, and Freeman had not seen his daughter in more than a year, so the implants could wait.

"Are you sure it isn't because I hit my head?" he asked.

"It could be," replied the doctor, "but it needs to be checked out."

Freeman vowed, "I'll do it, doc. But, first, I've got a few problems to attend to." He removed the band from his forehead and started to rise, but the doctor restrained him.

"General, you need to rest. Whatever it is can wait. I'll give you a sedative, and we'll discuss it in the morning."

"Doctor, you don't understand. The Attorney General was kid-napped. Her assistant is lying dead in the street downstairs. And, in two hours, we're planning to launch a major offensive against the Greenshirts. If I had a head full of tumors, I wouldn't stay in this bed. Not even if the surgeon general ordered me!"

Startled, the doctor replied, "Who said anything about tumors?"

The old soldier scrambled for cover. "Well, um . . . isn't that what you're implying?"

"Not at all. I'm simply saying that the reason you blacked out may be more serious than it appears. We need to do some tests. In the meantime, it's imperative that you rest."

"No deal, doc. I'm not going to lay here while my whole command goes to hell in a bucket. Now, let me up or I'll have you arrested."

Thirty-Nine

Shortly thereafter, the General joined Colonel Essing and Major Robbins in the lobby. The building was sealed off and teams of investigators from the Department of Public Safety were assiduously combing the desk area and the manager's office for clues. Behind the yellow tape, hundreds of reporters buzzed.

Freeman pulled Essing aside and said, "Where's Addison?"

The colonel replied, "He's still lying out there where they found him, sir."

"Take me there."

The portly Essing led Freeman past the kitchen, out the delivery door, and into the alleyway. There, working in the pouring rain, was another team of investigators from the DPS. There were also a few detectives from the Philadelphia police department. Broken glass crunched under their feet as they moved. Freeman tried to find the room that Addison fell from, but the rain obscured his view. The body was covered by a black tarp.

He asked one of the detectives, "Can I see it?"

When the tarp was lifted, he saw that the "liaison" had landed on his back, in a disjointed position. His face was expressionless—eerily so, like he was truly at peace. His clothes were soaked, his platinum locks matted flat. Other than his twisted, right leg which jutted out from his body at a perfect right angle, he looked relatively unscathed. But Freeman assumed every bone in his body was broken.

"Any secondary wounds?" he asked the detective.

The reply came, "Only a welt at the base of his neck." Then, almost as an afterthought, the detective added, "But keep that to yourself . . . if you would, sir."

Freeman nodded. Looking up into the driving rain, he said to his aides, "Let's get back inside."

They went up to Addison's room. After a cursory inspection from the doorway—the investigators had sealed the room off—they were met by short, stocky man in an oversized trench coat holding a teletran.

"General, my name is Bentley. I'm with the DPS. Do you have time for a few questions?"

"Make it quick, Bentley."

The inspector was clipped. "Sir, when Ms. DeKalb left your suite last night, did she say anything about a change in her itinerary?"

"No. Nothing."

Bentley made an entry into the teletran, then resumed, "Did she seem to be . . . well, out of sorts or anything?"

The General answered obliquely, "Other than a little disappointment over some of the decisions I had to make, no."

"Sir, forgive me, but two of the troopers in your guard detail said she was visibly distressed."

"Well, I don't know anything about that. Maybe if your agents had done a better job protecting her, you could've asked her *directly.*"

Bentley immediately backed down. "Yes, sir. Thank you, sir," he stammered. "That's all I had."

Freeman, Essing, and Robbins then repaired to headquarters over in the Scharon Building.

Forty

Another call to the White House was on tap. Again, Freeman wondered when he would be able to convey some good news; hopefully, in a few hours, when the 301st launched *Clean Sweep*. Until then, he needed to inform Tito Gonzales of the latest catastrophe. Hopefully, he already knew about it.

The General was connected immediately with the President, who was down in the Sit Room. It was a difficult conversation. As Freeman guessed, he was already aware of the kidnapping. But the nature of his response took Freeman by surprise.

"How could you let it happen, Jim? I thought the Armitage was safe. Now, I come to find that Collier's goons marched right in and took the AG out from under your nose. What was she doing there in the first place?"

Normally, Freeman would have bristled at these remarks, but the mention of Collier precluded it.

"Sir, she came to see me about a problem we're having with prison security. As you know, she worked for me when I was in office, so maybe she also wanted to get reacquainted."

Immediately, he regretted the choice of words.

Gonzales snapped, "What do you mean 'reacquainted?'" He wasn't buying it. He, too, had heard the rumors.

"Just that," Freeman lied. "We had dinner while we discussed the situation, then we talked about old times—and recent developments, for a few hours. Mainly, the massacre yesterday morning."

"By any chance, did she make any accusations with regard to the Church?"

It was an odd question, seemingly out of context. Knowing from his previous conversation with the President that DeKalb was suspicious of Peter Bernard, Freeman figured he was probing for leaks. Happy to finally say something truthful, he replied, "No, sir. She never mentioned it."

Although Gonzales seemed relieved, he was still miffed. Almost rhetorically he asked, "Why the hell would she put herself at such risk just to discuss something as mundane as prison security?"

Again, Freeman lied. "I honestly don't know, Mr. President. But I can tell you this. I only received word of her coming late yesterday from Stew Addison. I had no part in making her travel arrangements or providing for her security. That was handled by the DPS. When she left, I assumed they had things under control. But I'll take the hickey for the lapse of security at the hotel. It's a problem because there are still a lot of sick and wounded refugees being housed there. Even so, how were her security arrangements breached so easily? And what about Addison? You know he's dead, right?"

"Yes. I'm told there's some question as to why."

"Want to know what I think?"

"Of course."

"I think he was working for Collier. Once Sonny had the AG, he dispatched his mole. I know he was too much of a coward to jump, so he must have been thrown from that window."

"But why would Collier want DeKalb?"

"I don't know."

Then, out of the blue, Gonzales asked, "Are *you* all right, Jim?"

"Sure. Why do you ask?"

"I heard you took a spill."

"Oh, that. No, I'm fine."

He wondered if the President had an ear on his staff. "I slipped on a towel or something, that's all."

"Are you still planning to initiate *Clean Sweep* at first light?"

"Yes, sir."

"Then I better let you get back to work. You've a busy day ahead. Please call me if there's any break in the investigation on that end. And let's talk again before you kick off in Newark."

"Absolutely, sir."

When Freeman hung up, he called Essing and Robbins into his office.

Essing was delayed briefly. On arriving, he informed the General, "They found the limo over in Jersey. The driver and one of the AG's bodyguards are dead."

Freeman looked at both men and said, "Let's talk about Stew Addison." He repeated his theory about Addison being a double agent and added, "My guess is that the security man who *wasn't* killed was also working for Collier."

Essing was the first to grasp the significance of his suspicions.

"Sir, if what you say is true, then he may have knowledge of our attack plan."

"That's the problem, Colonel."

"But Addison wasn't at yesterday's staff meeting," reminded Robbins.

"That's right," Freeman said, "but who's to say that there isn't another spook in our midst?"

For a short time, the three of them speculated on it, then called General Hawkins to inform him of DeKalb's abduction, Addison's death, and the possibility that the details of *Clean Sweep* may have been passed on to Collier. The decision was made to accelerate the start of the attack in an attempt to catch the Rottweiler off guard.

But it was too late.

Forty-One

"It's time," the priest declared—to no one.

For Peter Bernard, the long retreat was over. Whether his decision to turn and face his accusers came as a function of grace or sheer despair, he didn't know. But he once heard a historian define *folly* as acting in a manner contrary to one's self-interest, and to continue running now was, at least in a spiritual sense, the purest of follies.

Turning on his flashlight, he took out his map to study the inset of Newark. He ate an energy bar while pinpointing his next destination: the Cathedral Basilica of the Sacred Heart.

He told himself, "Before I get frogmarched into oblivion I want the archbishop to hear me out." Then he mumbled, "Assuming he'll care, that is." The priest reckoned that the logical place to connect with him was at the cathedral, which was a couple miles north of his present location.

Oblivious to how dangerous his situation had become—a goldfish was safer in a tank of piranhas—he strapped on his little, green rucksack and stepped into the driving rain.

It was being widely reported that he was in the Newark area. Initially, the DPS was alerted to his presence there by the security guards at Seton Hall and, later, the drone. Now, only the stormy weather stood between him and his captors.

That the law was closing in wasn't the only danger, though. Another loomed that would make capture seem like a blessing. The massacre that took place in Newark the previous morning occurred while Peter was sleeping in the dormitory at Seton Hall. As a result, he had no idea that Newark was fast becoming the focal point of a showdown between the United States Army and the killer of Rita Scanlon. Had he known that Sonny Collier's headquarters was less than two thousand meters from his current location, he would have abandoned immediately his plan of surrendering to the archbishop and turned himself in at the nearest police station. Not only was Collier close by, he also knew of Bernard's presence in Newark from the evening news reports. The previous afternoon he had challenged his troops to be on the lookout for him.

"A black whale," is the laughing description that Collier gave. "A six-and-a-half-foot black whale!" He even went so far as to place a $25,000 bounty on the Jesuit's head.

As Peter sloshed through the downpour toward central Newark, the city took on a different look. The buildings and improvements were newer. There was more landscaping however barren and wilted. It was a more modern neighborhood, much less threatening. That is, until he entered onto the scene of the carnage from the previous morning.

Though it was still dark, he noted the growing number of corpses on the streets and sidewalks. On closer inspection, he saw that most of them had been shot. And all of them were black. Or brown. Since none were in an advanced state of decay, he assumed the killings were recent.

On his approach to Market Street, he saw a bank of floodlights that illuminated the Central Avenue crossing like a softball field. A few dozen men were at work there. He slowed his pace and approached cautiously. Stopping a block short, he hid in the entryway of an underground parking facility to observe the proceedings. A huge fire burned in the middle of the street.

Small vehicles, like those used on farms and golf courses, were darting to and fro. Piled in their hoppers were the bodies of the dead. A team of workers dressed in hooded, turnout suits used meat-hooks to extract the cadavers from the carts and carry them to the fire. Watching over the workers were a squadron of armed guards.

The flames licked high into the night and, together with the floodlights, drove back the darkness. Though the wind and rain were no match for the slaughterhouse stench, the reek of burning asphalt provided some occasional relief. One worker tidied up the perimeter by throwing blackened limbs and other human miscellany into the center and the priest estimated that there were at least thirty bodies on the pyre in various stages of immolation. Among them were a pair of unfortunates named Addie Foster and Rhonda Mizell.

It was an appalling scene, and the most appalling thing about it was that, like the bodies he passed on his way to that point, without exception, the dead were people of color—his color.

Suddenly, one of the carts started down the street in his direction. He ducked back into the garage as it flew by, then peeked out again. It screeched to a halt in the middle of the block he had just passed. Three men got out. Two loaded the hopper while the other watched for snipers. Peter was horrified by how coldly they gaffed the bodies.

Chilled, he disappeared back into the garage, emerged on a parallel street, and ran the rest of the way to the cathedral, a pain knifing through his gut. On reaching it, he gasped for air as he circled the building. The site of a papal visit the previous summer, the Cathedral Basilica of the Sacred Heart was far more magnificent than he had imagined but anomalous to the setting: a veritable diamond in a crush of glass. The man who governed the Church's affairs from this episcopate was usually destined for some high-level post in the Vatican, and it was just such a heavyweight that Peter sought. But the entire complex was locked tight. There wasn't a soul around.

He came upon a building in the rear that looked like a residence. Vigorously, he rapped on the door. No one answered. He tried again, this time with even greater urgency. Still, no one answered. Frustrated, he found a hiding place in the bushes nearby that was partially sheltered from the rain. There he resolved to wait until morning, when, hopefully, the archbishop would arrive to say Mass.

As he drank the last of his water, his thoughts turned to the dreadful pyre. And the meat-hooks. This awful reverie didn't last long, though, because suddenly, the tedious pounding of rainfall on the gutters and windows was split by the muffled reports of not-too-distant gunfire.

Forty-Two

When Specialist Benny Molina enlisted, Newark wasn't one of the exotic hot-spots where he expected see action. "Williams told me this was a real bung hole, but it ain't so bad. Not like where I grew up, anyway."

"Where'd you grow up?" his companion, a big Pollack named Guntesky, asked.

"Gary, Indiana."

"Never been there," said Guntesky, adjusting his poncho to better protect against the torrent. "Geez, before I enlisted, I never left Allegheny County."

The two men were members of the 301st Infantry. Earlier in the day, their unit, the 2/2, relocated to Newark from Easton, Pennsylvania. The battalion was now encamped in Branch Brook Park, near the Newark-Bellevue line. Molina and Guntesky, as members of the Second Squad, Charlie, were pulling security at a position on the northeast corner of the park near Lake Street.

God, it's been a long day, thought Molina. *And now I gotta babysit this goober.*

The officers and men of the 2/2 were sleeping off the exhaustion of breaking camp, moving sixty miles, then re-encamping. Dozens of tents were situated along a five-hundred-yard, north-south line in the loop created by Christopher Columbus Drive. The battalion was in a defensible position, with its back to a tall fence that separated the park from an old rail bed and had fields of fire on its front and both flanks. Due to the recent ambush of the 1/3 out on the Hutchinson River Parkway, Colonel Nathan Bryce tripled the number of sentries. Despite a downpour that diminished the effectiveness of satellites, surveillance drones, and spider-cams, there was a general sense within the command that the troop was well-secured. Besides, they wouldn't be there long. Operations were due to commence against the insurgents at 0500.

"Romeo Five, this is Romeo One, over."

Molina activated the transmitter in his body armor. The watchers in the TOC truck were aware of his exact coordinates.

He responded, "Romeo One. This is Romeo Five."

"Romeo Five, sensors indicate a rise in thermals near your position. Approximately fifty yards to the northeast. Lieutenant Wallace is on his way. Over."

"Roger that. We're on it. Over."

"I did leave home once," Guntesky said innocently, ignoring the warning from Romeo One, "to visit my uncle in Kentu—"

"Sshhh!" Molina stuck his hand in Guntesky's face. Flipping his NVGs down and shouldering his M-6A, he stepped forward, peering intently at the row of homes bordering the park on Lake Street. Dogs barked nearby. With few exceptions, the houses were dark. The rain seemed to intensify. Sirens howled far in the distance.

His vision was blurred by condensation from his breathing— and the watering caused by the Tabasco he rubbed in his eyes to stay awake. A couple of squirrels bolted into the rain from the alley between two houses. At the corner of Elmwood Avenue, he spied the signature of something small on a front porch. *Probably a dog.* But, another thermal, human in form, suddenly appeared at a window on the second floor.

Molina dropped to one knee. As he did, Guntesky, who was looking the other way, tripped over him.

"Damn it, Jethro! You are the dumbest mo—"

Molina never finished his critique. A slug hit him in the neck, severing his carotid artery and smashing his windpipe. He slumped to the ground, gurgling, and, within seconds, passed into the sweet forever.

Guntesky joined him there an instant later.

There was no muzzle flash or ballistics crack from either shot. Whoever the snipers were, their marksmanship was superb. The bullets hit Molina and Guntesky in the neck and face, respectively, thus lending a cruel superficiality to their armor and helmets. In the time it would take to light a cigarette, this scene was repeated up and down the battalion's front until all the sentries lay dead or dying in the bosomy turf and ankle-deep puddles.

Then, like warriors sprung from dragon's teeth, out of the alleyways separating the homes on Lake Street, a line of fifty, black shadows, armed with the latest in automatic and laser weaponry, emerged in echelon and headed toward the southern end of the canton on the double-quick. They held their fire, descending steadily on the sleeping battalion. However, as they reached the outermost line of tents, they were met by sentries coming from the south side of the encampment.

Suddenly, the dreary, sodden night erupted into a cacophony of cracks, pops, and flashes. These last illuminated the relentless, silver tracers falling from the sky. A siren blared.

What happened next was a testimony to Napoleon's maxim that tents are unfavorable to health.

While the pickets were responding to the southern attack—but before the siren wailed—another two hundred men were penetrating the camp swiftly and silently from Heller Parkway on the north. This larger force consisted of five forty-man platoons. The first three raced toward the center of the encampment. A fourth concentrated on those tents closest to the point of attack. The fifth circled down Columbus Drive to support the diversionary force on the south.

The attackers were outnumbered four-to-one, so surprise was

critical. The plan was to first degrade the 2/2, then destroy it in detail. Another crucial factor was the depth of infiltration. If the second wave of attackers could link with the first at some point near the center of the camp, the numerical advantage of the defenders would be neutralized and the entire camp would come under attack at once.

These marauders worked with great tactical precision. Their drill was simple. At each tent, one man would slash the side wall with a Ka-Bar or a machete and another would toss in a stun grenade. Two more would run interference, mop up, or act as replacements, if necessary. Then, the process would repeat.

Each team needed to take out three or four tents. The stun grenades limited friendly-fire casualties. When these grenades exploded, it was at an earsplitting 175 decibels. A blinding flash was emitted. The attackers wore ear protection and were shielded from the light by the walls of the tent. But the unfortunates inside them were instantly rendered deaf and blind.

The plan was a bold one, and its near-perfect execution resulted in another slaughter. A few soldiers escaped by fleeing into the surrounding neighborhood. Some ran south toward the ballfields on the other side of Bloomfield Avenue. Others hid in the overgrowth along the lake shore or under footbridges.

But the core of the battalion was lost. An overwhelming number were shot in various stages of undress, at the flaps of their tents or inside them. Some were killed lying on cots or on the ground in sleeping bags. Dozens fell trapped against the base of the fence between the park and the old rail bed. The TOC truck was set on fire and its crew mowed down as it tried to escape the heat and fumes. Those few who rose to give battle were riddled with bullets, lacerated by lasers, bludgeoned, gutted or burned.

The Greenshirts lost only twenty-three men, but the 2/2 was decimated. The casualty list was horrific: 859 killed, eight wounded, one captured. Only 147 men and women survived, primarily those who escaped to the south. The one captured? The battalion commander, Colonel Bryce, who was found later that day about four blocks away, decapitated.

The world would never know what grand schemes, heroic deeds, or unrealized progeny died that night. Despite its modest scale, the Battle of Branch Brook Park would go down as one of the most ignominious defeats in American history. It had no more strategic significance than the actions at the Little Big Horn or Ft. Pillow, but it would serve to electrify the nation in the same way those butcherings did.

It would also confer a degree of infamy on the Second Battalion of the Second Brigade. From that day forward, no drum taps or bugle calls would sound for the 2/2, which soon became known as the Sleeping Sheepdogs of the 301st.

Forty-Three

On hearing the sound of gunfire and sirens, Peter was perplexed. *Should I stay or move on?*

This was probably not a good time to present himself as a target, moving or otherwise. Still nestled in the bushes beside Sacred Heart Cathedral, he decided to stay put.

The blare of the sirens stopped, but the shooting, attended by explosions and flashes of light, continued. For ten minutes, the clamor rose to a crescendo, then began to diminish. Over the next fifteen, it was interlaced with screams and shouts. Then the noise died down, only to be replaced again by the steady beating of the rain.

Suddenly, two men came dashing down the street in their underwear. Peter could hear their labored breathing as they passed by. Seconds later, another man, this one dressed in black body armor and toting a weapon, appeared. He stopped, took aim, and fired.

A bolt of blue lightning cut through the night, touched the fleeing men, and killed them instantly. The shooter went over to examine the bodies, then turned to go back. When he did, the thermal sensors in his NVGs detected a figure crouching in the bushes.

Knowing he had been spotted and convinced he was about to be torched, Peter rose with his arms held high and cried, "Don't shoot. I'm not armed."

The gunman was taken back by his abrupt surrender. Training his weapon, he walked slowly forward, studying the big man intently.

His instincts told him to fire, but there was something about this target that stayed his hand.

"Identify yourself," he commanded. His voice, transmitted through the mouthpiece, sounded as if he was talking into a megaphone.

Without hesitation, the priest responded, "I'm Father Peter Bernard."

Forty-Four

Sunday, July 10 (4:20 A.M. EDT)
The Scharon Building

General Freeman and his staff monitored the ambush by listening to the radio transmissions between tactical operations command–the TOC truck–and the Second Battalion's headquarters in West Orange. One by one, the colonel, captains, lieutenants and non-coms of the 2/2 were dispatched by the Greenshirts until the highest authority available to the battalion chief was a warrant officer inside the TOC. Then the transmissions stopped.

Freeman was livid. "What a charlie foxtrot!" he hollered. Turning to Robbins, he ordered, "Fire up the bird. We're going to West Orange."

Ever since the attack on the Hutch earlier in the week, the General had a nagging fear that Americans were about to start killing each other in earnest for the first time since Appomattox. Now that fear had been substantiated. There was no telling how widespread, sustained, or effective the Greenshirt insurgency would be, but this much was certain: if a second civil war was imminent, this time the rebels would be led by a man who was the polar opposite of the wise and noble Robert E. Lee. Sonny Collier was the cruelest and most ruthless man he knew. A veritable Cromwell.

Freeman, Essing, and Robbins put on their body armor in the General's office. It was still raining hard when they lifted off.

Two minutes into the bumpy flight, the General told his two aides, "Ever since Thursday night's attack, I've been accumulating a file on Sonny Collier." Then, above the roar of the engines, he read from it to give them a glimpse into the rise of the Pathfinder Party and its charismatic leader.

Setting the files on his lap, Freeman observed, "This idea of a second American Revolution—that's Collier. When he took over in '46, he really committed the party to that goal, and because of his vision, their membership has exploded."

Colonel Essing sat silently as his subordinate, Robbins, responded, "After we talked the other day, I read that the party acquired its penchant for violence and secrecy under Collier."

"That's right," confirmed Freeman, who was put off by Essing's lack of engagement. He leaned toward the red-haired Major, saying, "They always retained a modicum of respectability by supporting several candidates for national office, but Sonny stopped pouring cash into unwinnable elections years ago. Instead, he used the money to arm his disciples and build an extensive, clandestine training network."

Adjusting his headgear, Robbins posed a question that only a political neophyte could ask. "How were the Pathfinders able to organize and equip the Greenshirts without any challenge from the government?"

The unspoken delicacy of this question related to the fact that Collier's party gained much of its strength while Freeman was president. But the General wasn't alone in failing to divine his former subordinate's plan to seize power and radically overhaul the machinery of state. It was so ambitious and so audacious that very few people, inside the government or out, gave credence to the rumors that it was even possible, let alone forthcoming. *Coup d'état* is a concept foreign to American civics.

Instead of taking umbrage to the Major's artless question, however, the General revealed, "When I was president, the DPS infiltrated them. At the time, they concluded that, although the situation bore watching, it was relatively innocuous. Considering what's happened since, though, I think the possibility exists that even back then security at the DPS had been compromised."

Essing finally chimed in. "After what happened to the Attorney General and Mr. Addison, it appears to be more probable than possible. Like you said, sir, it seems like the work of a spy. How else could Collier pre-empt *Clean Sweep* with a strike of his own?"

The General nodded emphatically.

Then Robbins asked the one question that for days had eluded the rest of Freeman's staff. "Do you think Collier's responsible for the bombing, sir?"

This kid is a lot smarter than I thought, judged Freeman. Until then, only he and the President had voiced any suspicions about Collier. "I do," he said.

As they approached West Orange, the irrepressible Major said, "At a rally in Grant Park last year, Collier said that even though the odds for a successful revolution were long, any country where half the people were illiterate—or didn't know who George Washington was—was ripe for a change. Especially since, unlike the Greenshirts, Americans aren't willing to bleed in defense of their beliefs anymore."

Forty-Five

Peter Bernard knew nothing of the Greenshirt insurgency. The shadowy figure who captured him soon met up with about a dozen other hooded figures in black, rain-soaked armor. Although he couldn't see the expression on their faces, they all appeared jubilant at having nabbed him.

As they bound his hands with a plastic tie, Peter asked, "Are you guys bounty hunters?"

A buzz of metallic laughter ensued. Through his transmitter, the man who caught him sang out, "You could say that."

"Keep your mouth shut," they warned, as he was led into a train station. They descended the stairs and entered the darkened tube. Half the men were in front of him, the other half behind. It was no use trying to escape.

Though the big priest was saturated and shivering uncontrollably, the temperature in the tunnel was actually warmer than above ground. In addition, their movements were so steady that, sheltered from the wind and rain, his shaking soon died down.

Presently, they came upon an abandoned train which they passed in column. The man in front of Peter shined a flashlight into one of the cars. Pressed against the window was the profile of a half-rotted zombie in a Mets cap. Loudly, he quipped, "There's always next year, partner."

Another buzz of laughter echoed through the tunnel, sending a different kind of shudder through the priest.

The troop pressed on as he took their measure. Though they wore military armor, their deportment was slapdash and juvenile. They didn't wear insignias or carry standard weapons. The only thing that identified them as a purposeful group was their flash-green armbands. And, they continually questioned the directives of their leader, a tall man with a distinctive limp.

They must be bounty hunters because there's certainly nothing soldierly about them. That would explain their excitement at having taken me prisoner, too.

Strangely, the paranoia that bedeviled the priest since leaving Philadelphia was gone. He didn't know where these men were taking him or what he'd find when he got there, but his qualms now rested on these immediate concerns, not on avoiding arrest. At present, he was less concerned with the judgment of the earthly courts than the heavenly. He felt as Jonah must have felt on the road to Nineveh, and he prayed that his soul wouldn't faint.

Again.

Forty-Six

On learning that the commander of the Second Brigade, an officer by the name of Keith Michaels, was meeting General Hawkins at Branch Brook Park, the General ordered the pilots, "Forget West Orange. Head straight for the park."

Both Essing and Robbins were stunned. These were the kind of extemporaneous changes that always drove the Secret Service crazy. Caution dictated that Freeman wait at battalion headquarters for Hawkins and Michaels to return. Unfortunately, General Freeman was not a cautious soul. Essing couldn't believe that he would put himself at mortal risk just to walk the killing fields. The only protection on the scene was a company of soldiers from the 2/3. The whole lot of them might get annihilated.

When the helo flared and landed at the south end of the park, Hawkins and Michaels were already on the scene. Their alarm at seeing Freeman striding silently toward them in the dim morning light would have been evident on their faces if they weren't all wearing protective headgear.

Soon, Michaels was repeating for General Freeman the postmortem he had just given General Hawkins.

He was cut short halfway through it, however, when Hawkins lost control and laced into him. "What the hell were you thinking, Keith?"

Freeman raised his hand. Pulling Hawkins over to the side, he looked around and whispered through his mouthpiece, "Let's look to our deportment in front of the men, shall we, Travis?"

Hawkins, who had serious reservations about Freeman's presence in an unsecured location, nodded testily, then turned to Michaels and said, "Lead the way. We need to get this over with."

Although the pelting rain had extinguished most of the fires, smoke still rose ominously from one end of the bivouac to the other. All was in shambles. Tents, vehicles, and supplies were riddled with holes, blown apart, or burned. The grass was matted down or churned into mud, as after a football game. The air reeked of charred rubber and plastic—and flesh.

No one spoke as, slipping and sliding, they inspected the carnage. With the exception of Freeman and Hawkins, it was a bloodletting like none of them had ever seen. The dead were scattered over fifty acres. Some in contorted positions. Some beheaded. Some limbless. Some eviscerated. Some barefoot. Some in their underwear. Some already shrouded in zipper bags. Their bodies and the muddy ground on which they died were sullied by the ubiquitous mark of the Greenshirts: the king of hearts.

A line of corpses was arranged near the center of the camp. These were the rebel dead. With the exception of their headgear, they were still fully armored and, but for the flash-green, identification band on their right arms, could easily have passed for troopers from the 301st.

Standing over these bodies, Hawkins asked, "Is this the extent of their losses?"

"Yes, sir," replied Brigadier Michaels.

"And we're certain that Colonel Bryce was captured?" asked Freeman.

"Well, sir, he's missing. No one actually saw him taken prisoner."

"And what about the rest of his command?"

"Dead, sir. With the exception of a captain from Dog Company.

He took a bullet in the arm and was airlifted to the hospital a little while ago."

To the brigadier, Freeman said, "You mentioned earlier that they hit us on both flanks."

"Yes, sir," said Michaels. "Essentially, we were trapped in this position by the railroad fence at our backs. Most of the men were asleep. They slashed the tents, then tossed in flash-bangs. A lot of the men died in their bunks. The crossfire was vicious. They had automatic weapons, tasers, deer rifles, shotguns—you name it, they had it. Some of the fighting was hand-to-hand. The only avenue of escape was to the south. Thank God they weren't waiting for us there, too, or no one would have survived."

The General said, "Our advance detection systems were rendered ineffective by the weather?"

"Yes, sir, but we compensated by increasing the number of pickets. Collier's men took them out with sniper fire before they attacked."

"Even still," Freeman said, "how did they get so many men in position to attack without us seeing them?"

Michaels responded, "There's a subway station at the north end of the park. To the best of our knowledge, they closed in on our flank from there . . . from below ground."

For a man who knew that his career was over, Brigadier Michaels remained remarkably composed. Even stoic.

"Is that how they got away so quickly?"

"Some of them. One of the survivors said they broke into separate units and melted back into the neighborhoods, too."

This bit of information confirmed that the insurgents were attacking from the east, from the area most affected by the blast. Freeman wiped the raindrops from the audio dosimeter on his forearm. It would sound an alarm if the level of radiation exceeded 300 rads. But it read only 196.

He concluded that if the Greenshirts were basing their operations on the fringe of ground zero, they really weren't running much risk of being poisoned. It appeared as though the radiation abatement operations were having some unintended—and undesired—consequences.

Beneath the flap of a nearby tent Freeman spied the gruesome countenance of a trooper shot through the eye. His left arm was also severed. He walked over to examine the body. On closer inspection, he saw it was a girl.

The wound to her arm never bled, cauterized by the laser weapon that inflicted it—most likely a TL-25. The sundered limb lay beside her. Like the price tag on an item at a flea market, a death card was slotted through her fingers.

Picking the card up, the General studied it momentarily, then put it in his breast pocket.

Returning to the others, he asked, "Any estimates on how many of our men were executed?"

Michaels responded, "It's hard to say, sir." He pointed to the young woman and said, "But a bunch were shot through the eye like that."

"You said we took a few prisoners?"

"Yes, sir, but they were airlifted to headquarters before you arrived. You probably crossed paths with them on the way here."

Then, Freeman asked the question he was most eager to have answered.

"Any indication whether Collier was with them?"

"You mean *here* with them, sir?" asked Michaels.

"Yes. Among the attackers."

"No, sir. Why do you ask, General?"

"I'm just curious as to how bloodthirsty that fiend really is."

Forty-Seven

Nearly a half hour had passed when, to the great relief of everyone, the General decided he had seen enough. Hawkins informed him he was headed for the battalion's headquarters with Michaels, probably to finish his ass-chewing. So Freeman, Essing, and Robbins boarded the SkyShark for the return flight to Philadelphia.

As they lifted off, the General told the pilot, "I want to recon the front for a minute."

Essing came unnerved. Looking back from his seat directly in front of Freeman, he advised, "General, it's too great a risk. We don't know what kind of SAM capability these people have. I strongly advise against it."

Freeman waved him off with an air of invincibility, saying, "Colonel, when I want your—" He checked himself. The characteristic red blotches welled up on his cheeks as he blurted out, "I'm not going to let this man thrash me like a dog!"

Essing rejoined, "Better a living dog than a dead lion, General."

Freeman might easily have exploded at this comment. As it was he just looked at his executive officer and replied, "Your objection is noted, Phillip."

The old man's blood was up and, in that state, there was no stopping him. Throughout his career, he never passed up an opportunity to survey the front, regardless of the risk.

They flew over Sacred Heart Cathedral toward the Passaic River, then followed it south. The ceiling was only about three hundred feet and, in that early hour, visibility was poor. So the detour offered them little in the way of additional perspective. They couldn't even make out the extent of the damage further to the east.

They weren't in the air three minutes when they began retracing their route. Suddenly, the warning sensors sounded on the control panel.

The pilot shouted, "We're hot! Someone lit us up." Then, he screamed, "Bogie at nine!"

He immediately dropped the nose of the SkyShark to decrease its altitude and mitigate the angle of attack. But it was too late. Robbins watched from his side of the ship as a spiral of smoke emerged from the roof of a downtown building. It was almost level with them. In seconds, the missile struck the engines housed atop the fuselage. The explosion ripped through the roof, blew off the door, and filled the cabin with smoke. A chunk of the door also bit off the tail rotor.

Robbins and the copilot were killed instantly. Freeman and Essing, still belted into their seats, were knocked cold. Only the pilot was conscious. He struggled to right the chopper. The rotors were still turning, but the bird was spinning wildly, and falling fast.

At first, they appeared headed for the river, but they ended up crashing in a stand of trees lining the promenade in Riverview Park. The rotors clipped the treetops like a gigantic hedge trimmer before they were sheared off by the giant limbs. The tail section smashed diagonally into the bough of a stout maple and snapped off. This caused the nose of the craft to auger into the ground, smashing the cockpit and killing the pilot. The only thing now separating Colonel Essing from the unyielding earth was four feet of compacted metal and a precious smidgen of airspace. Behind him, General Freeman hung lifelessly, suspended in his harness like a teen on a thrill ride.

A detachment of Collier's Greenshirts was close by when the Shark went down. They reached the wreckage in minutes. Wary of the leaking fuel, they circled it slowly. The starboard door was blown off. There hung the mangled body of Major Robbins. The larboard door was also gone. Two men dangled there, as well, face down in their seats.

The squad leader, a heavyset man, chugged onto the scene. Ignoring the smell of fuel, he approached the wreckage to get a better look. He pulled the hood off the man in the rear seat on the larboard side and found his prize.

"Peterson! Martin! C'mon," he hollered. "Let's get him outta here!"

These words were barely out of his mouth when a Scorpion gunship appeared in the sky. It hovered for a moment, then spun around, positioning to use its guns without hitting the wreckage. While the chubby squad leader and a few of his men labored to free the former President, the sodden ground and trees nearby exploded in a hail of cannon fire. Those who weren't killed scattered for cover and responded with automatic weapons. But these volleys were ineffective. They merely ricocheted off the Scorpion's armor-plated belly.

The pilot then sped to the south, banked and zoomed back in from the reverse angle. Again, he peppered the insurgents, spewing death. He skillfully avoided hitting the wreckage with his cannons. Since there was less than half a platoon with him in the chopper, the pilot's goal was to eliminate as much of the insurgent force as possible before he attempted to land. Pinning them in place would also buy time for the ground force now speeding toward them from Branch Brook Park.

It was a good plan but not good enough. Heading toward him from the same direction as the one that took out the General's SkyShark was another UltraSAM. Before the Scorpion had time to take evasive action, the missile struck it amidships. Bursting into flames, it spiraled down into the river.

The Greenshirts wasted little time. Extracting Freeman from his harness, they quickly disappeared behind a curtain of rain. When the relief column arrived, all they found were dead rebels, those who died in the crash, and the dying Phillip Essing.

Forty-Eight

When the call came from Nick Risden, the President was on his fifth cup of coffee in the Sit Room. He had been there since one o'clock in the morning, after learning of Angela DeKalb's abduction. The endless barrage of depressing news that reached him that morning was now compounded by reports that Jim Freeman's chopper was down.

"Mr. President," said the Army Chief-of-Staff, "the news isn't good. General Freeman is missing."

Tito Gonzales was incredulous. "What do you mean *missing?*"

Risden was cool. "When the rescue party arrived at the scene of the crash, the only man they were able to save was Freeman's XO, Colonel Essing—and he died within minutes. The pilots and the General's aide were also killed."

"Was Freeman captured?"

"We're pretty sure. His harness wasn't torn. It was unbuckled."

Gonzales was generally slow to anger, but, on top of the news about the Attorney General, this really set him off.

"General," he said, "I don't care what it takes. *I want these clowns taken out!* I'm tired of doing business on the cheap. I want whatever troops we have dispatched to the Cordon *now.* Spare nothing. Send in the Joebots if you have to, but find Freeman and stop Collier. The only thing I won't abide is any further delays or excuses."

"Yes, sir," Risden said. "It would help if you had this conversation with Admiral Towne, sir."

"I'll call him as soon as we're done."

"Thank you, sir. And, sir, I might add that General Freeman is a close friend. Nobody wants to find him more than I do."

"Then get on it, General!"

"Yes, sir."

Risden's face disappeared from the wallscreen.

"Get me Milliken," Gonzales demanded.

Within seconds, Milliken's craggy face appeared on his VuScreen.

"What's the status, Avery?" His disdain for Milliken was growing exponentially.

"Mr. President, we know that around two o'clock the Attorney General was transferred to a small plane at an airstrip outside Burlington. We found the plane abandoned at an airfield in Bergen County. It landed illegally about an hour after takeoff, and when the assistant manager at the airport went to investigate, he was shot dead. Due to the early hour, there was only a skeleton staff on duty. Except for a janitor, everyone was killed."

"Who owned the plane?"

"It was registered to a paper company in Wisconsin. We're pursuing that lead."

Gonzales wanted to throttle him. "I spoke with Jim Freeman earlier. He's convinced that General DeKalb couldn't have been abducted without the complicity of your people."

"Sir, please try to suspend judgment on that. It's still too soon to draw any conclusions. Ever since General Freeman ordered the manager of the Armitage to open it up to wounded refugees, that place has been a security nightmare. And, keep in mind, one of my agents in the detail protecting Ms. DeKalb was found dead on the side of the road in Camden."

"And the other?"

"He's missing, sir, but he's one of my most trusted men. I'd be shocked if he was involved in this."

"Do we know who killed Addison?" There was no longer any doubt in the President's mind that Addison's death was somehow connected to the kidnapping.

Milliken paused momentarily, measuring his words. "The last person known to have visited Addison was the AG. She went there after leaving General Freeman's suite. She left shortly after midnight, which is when the abduction took place."

"Wait a minute. Are you saying that Angela DeKalb is a suspect in Addison's murder?"

"No, sir. But, unfortunately, at this time, she's the only person we can place at the scene of the crime."

"Avery," the President said slowly, "doesn't it stand to reason that, if the Attorney General was abducted shortly after she left Addison's room, she may have been a victim of the same treachery that resulted in his death?"

Tito Gonzales stared at the screen at the Director of Public Safety, thinking, *Public safety, my ass!*

His urge to fire the man was intense, but, again, the timing was wrong. Things were bad enough. Two of his principal subordinates were already lost. Letting Milliken go would only create another void.

Instead, he struggled to make sense of it all. No president since FDR had to confront the myriad of domestic problems he was facing. Tito Gonzales was a strong man, but, with the capture of Freeman, the abduction of the Attorney General, and two heinous slaughters, all in the span of twenty-four hours, the indomitable spirit that marked his rise from penury to power was flagging.

Part Three

Forty-Nine

"General, I apologize for the humble digs, but the Newark Armitage was full." The speaker was Anson Collier. "Had I known you were coming, I would have arranged for more suitable accommodations."

James Freeman lay on the floor in an empty, windowless room, having regained consciousness only minutes before. Attempting to rise, he fell back with a grimace, a stabbing pain in his shoulder, his left arm in a sling.

"Please, sir, don't exert yourself. My surgeon thinks your collarbone is broken. Probably caused by the safety harness when you crashed. Otherwise, you appear no worse for the wear. You need to rest, though. We'll be moving you to a more secure location soon."

"Where am I?" the old man groaned.

"Oh, we're still in Newark. I think they call this the Commonwealth Building."

Two hooded soldiers guarded the door as Collier removed his headgear and took a knee. Brushing his black, silver-streaked hair, he said buoyantly, "It's been awhile, Jim."

The General lay silent, refusing to answer, staring into his former subordinate's lucent blue eyes.

"I must say that this is a gratifying moment. Very fortuitous." Collier shook his head and smiled broadly, his teeth even and bright. "I never dreamed of meeting you in battle. But then you never were one to lead from the rear. Were you?"

He lit a small, rum-flavored cigarillo, politely exhaling in the opposite direction of the General. "I guess that's just one of many qualities I inherited from you."

Still the General said nothing, but his silence didn't stop the garrulous Collier.

"I'm sorry to report that the others in your party were killed. It's a miracle you weren't, too, judging by the crash site. You're a very lucky man. Unfortunately, we lost one of our most valuable assets when your Shark went down."

"What are you talking about?"

"Phillip Essing."

"Essing?"

"Yes, sir. It was he who kept us informed of your movements."

The General was stunned. "Who else is working for you?!"

"Oh, that can wait. It's a long list, and there *just* isn't time. But rest assured, our network is extensive."

Collier took relish in how the news of Essing deflated his captive. "Can I get you anything, sir?" he asked.

Freeman shook his head. Then, looking at Collier sadly, he asked, "Why, Sonny? What can you possibly gain from all this?"

"Call it a window of opportunity, Jim. The bombing provided us with a chance to make a statement." Jauntily, he added, "Better here than on the floor of the Senate, wouldn't you say?"

"Are you responsible for the bombing, too?"

"Oh, no!" For a moment, Sonny appeared baffled, then he quickly rejoined, "We're out to win adherents, not alienate them."

"Do you *really* think that by killing American soldiers you can win adherents to your . . . your cause?"

"It gives me no pleasure, if that's what you mean. But it was inevitable. Unfortunately, anything worthwhile gets paid for in blood. Call it the cost of a better future."

"And what kind of future is that?" the old man mumbled, grimacing from the pain in his shoulder.

"A future not unlike the past," Collier said brightly. "A return to a better time, when men of talent and virtue governed the affairs of state."

"Is that what you consider yourself? A man of talent and virtue?"

"At the risk of sounding presumptuous, yes."

This cocksure attitude aggravated Freeman, but he was too groggy to challenge his captor more forcefully.

Although self-assurance was Anson Collier's most visible quality, there was more to impress. At six-two, he was handsome and square-shouldered, with soul-piercing eyes, long, straight hair, and the kind of perennial tan commonly found on the beach at Malibu. Intelligent and colloquial, in mixed company he was the consummate gentleman—anything but the maniacal ideologue portrayed by the media. His affinity to men and women alike won him many allies, and those closest to him adored him.

But in Collier's case, the media had it right. His charming wit and manners masked the soul of a Turk. The shooting of Rita Scanlon was one proof. So were the mysterious deaths of those Pathfinders who dared to challenge or renounce his authority. Then came the people like Addie Foster and Rhonda Mizell whose bodies were scattered all over central Newark.

"I don't know a lot of talented and virtuous men who would kill defenseless people to further their designs," Freeman said in disgust.

With seeming embarrassment, Collier replied, "Yes . . . well . . . it ain't bean bag, you know. Revolutions aren't made with rose water"

The old man felt faint. He covered his eyes with his good arm and said, "Spoken like a true butcher."

But Collier was unfazed. "I'm under no illusions, Jim. I'll do whatever it takes to win power, even if it is, at times, painful. My best weapon is fear, and I intend to use it."

"Then you'll be tried as a war criminal *and* a traitor."

"Only if I lose."

"Which you surely will," Freeman said, wincing from the pain.

"Ah, c'mon," Sonny pleaded. "Let's give credit where credit is due. So far we're not doing too badly. We've already decimated two of your battalions. My hope is that, like you, your subordinates will continue to underestimate our resolve. And capabilities. It'll make our job a lot easier."

Freeman parried, "And what will you do once the 24th Armor arrives? When the weather clears and we start pounding your positions with air and artillery strikes?"

Collier looked quickly at his watch and said, "Sir, we have no positions! When the 24th arrives, we won't be here. Besides, now that we have you, no forward spotter can be certain he isn't lighting up a target where you're being held."

"Do you really think that will stop them?"

The Colonel eyed him coldly. "I *know* it'll stop them. Who wants to be responsible for killing the former president? What man would risk killing you in order to kill me?"

Immediately, Freeman thought of Travis Hawkins. He rejoined, "Now you're underestimating my subordinates."

"Maybe so, General, but having you here gives me great comfort. I'll admit I was concerned about taking the field against you. It wasn't the match up I wanted—sort of like throwing a punch at the most popular kid in school. Now that Roo Hawkins is in charge, though . . . well, let's just say he's a lot more to my liking."

"It may come as a surprise to you, but Hawkins would be no less inclined to flatten this building with me in it than—" He coughed suddenly, again wincing in pain.

His captor answered, "That may be, sir. But if he acts impetuously, it will be to our advantage."

"If *he* acts impetuously! That's precious!" Freeman gritted his teeth. "What do you call massacring those civilians yesterday? Wasn't that a tad impetuous?"

"Not if you look at it from my perspective. I was fishing and I knew you'd rise to the bait."

"Nevertheless, it won't stop Hawkins from doing what he has to."

"Again, I disagree. It's unlikely he'll do anything that would put your life in jeopardy. Any such move would require approval from on high, and I can't imagine Gonzales or Risden giving it."

With the executions of the past two mornings so fresh in his mind, Freeman's enmity for his former subordinate was growing. But because their world view was so similar, it was a slow process.

During his term in office, Freeman looked at the Pathfinders as a restorative of sorts and didn't think it necessary to bring them under the government's lash. He greatly admired Collier's vision and energy. Under different circumstances, he might have thrown in with him. He, too, was tired of watching greasy politicos whore endlessly for money and votes, pass ill-conceived and patently destructive legislation, then cede their deliberative responsibilities over to the courts. But, he had taken an oath to defend the United States, and that still meant something to him.

Collier took the same oath. And it still meant something to him, too, although he perceived it as an altogether different duty. In his mind, the only way to defend the country's future was to overhaul the Constitution and place greater limits on the democratic process. That such change must be wrought violently was, to him, a crime of virtue.

He looked down on Freeman and said, "You know, capturing you was never part of my plan. Talk about acting impetuously. Your decision to put yourself in harm's way while we were monitoring your every move—*that* was impetuous." Then, he added wistfully, "Like I said, I can't believe how fortune has smiled. And it goes beyond you."

"I gather that you're referring to Angela DeKalb?"

This caught Collier by surprise. "You think we grabbed her?"

"That's what the President thinks."

Sonny didn't deny it. Grudgingly, he admitted, "Not bad. I'm impressed. He deduced that rather quickly for a bean-eater. Although our uniforms were a dead giveaway, huh? Rest assured that Angela won't be harmed. She and I have a lot in common."

"Collier," the General said, quietly, "you're crazy to think that by holding either of us you can avoid retaliation. No one is so important that the entire nation would be put at risk to save them."

"No. That's where you're wrong. So wrong."

He stood up, ground the cigarillo out on the carpet with his boot and looked down at the old man. "America's curse is that it continually sacrifices the common good for the individual. A cop forgets to read a criminal his rights, and he walks. Some parent disciplines her child and gets sued. Two lesbians are put off by the traditional definition of marriage, so it's changed. I could go on *ad nauseam*, but my point is that what's best for the country *will* be sacrificed to protect you. And her! That much is certain. Otherwise, this whole neighborhood would have been leveled already."

Freeman nodded negatively. Stalling, he changed tack. "Don't you know that whatever support you have among your followers will dry up as soon as word of what happened this morning gets out? The Pathfinders may not care that you murdered hundreds of innocent blacks, but even they won't tolerate the killing of American soldiers."

"No, you're right," said Sonny, still grounding out his smoke. "It'll be a true test of our resolve. Granted, some people will be frightened off by the display of force. But an equal number who've never heard of us before will be inspired to action. Even if I'm killed, the white rage that gives rise to my leadership will survive. The only question is whether it'll be strong enough and deep enough to withstand a prolonged fight. If it is, Thursday's action on the Hutch and the one in the park this morning may someday be equated with Lexington Green and Concord Bridge."

A hooded Greenshirt came into the room. He motioned to Collier, who stepped aside momentarily to hear his report. Returning to Freeman, he asked, "How do you feel?"

Freeman again denied him the courtesy of an answer.

Collier overlooked this slight. "No matter. Let's hope you're fit to travel. Apparently, your men are concerned about you. One of your battalions is deploying a few blocks from here. We're moving out. But, before I go, I must ask that you please cooperate with my men. We have no desire to hurt you. You'll be afforded every comfort possible, but things could get low-budget for a while."

"And if I refuse?"

Sonny became animated. "Why would you want to miss this? The fun's just starting!"

As they left the building, the General's thoughts turned to Essing's treachery.

If a soldier of his caliber would change flags, how many more will? And what about Hawkins? He assigned Essing to me. Is he a Collier operative, too?

He thought not. Collier seemed eager to butt heads with Hawkins. If he was in cahoots with him, he probably wouldn't have revealed Essing's subterfuge.

Fifty

Lena Walker and Jack Clancey rose early that Sunday and drove to Philadelphia in the rain from Shady Grove. It was Lena's intent to surprise her father. She was also determined to stay on, so she packed all her things. Both she and Jack were anxious to reconcile with the old man.

Entering through the stately, brass doors of the Armitage, they found the lobby swarming with rain-drenched, musky-smelling reporters and elbowed their way to the reservation desk.

Although news of the General's capture had not yet hit the airwaves, the room hummed with talk of Angela DeKalb's abduction, Stewart Addison's death, and the preliminary reports of an ambush somewhere in Newark.

After they checked in, Lena went upstairs. Jack stopped to chat with Chuck Findley from the *Los Humanos Examiner*.

"How ya doin', Turk?"

"Good, Jack. What're you doing here?"

"Oh, I came up to do a piece on Freeman for next month's *VeriQuest*." Looking around, he commented, "It didn't take long for the crows to gather."

Findley explained, "Well, most of us were here for a press conference, then the whole thing happened with DeKalb." He pointed to one of the high-backed chairs in the lobby, saying, "Abbie Johnson from the Monitor was sitting right there when they took her out.

Then, as if that wasn't enough, a guy from the Justice Department turned himself into a human pancake by jumping out a window. Now there's talk of another civil war."

Jack asked, "What time did—"

Findley raised his hand to interrupt him and hit the home key on his vibrating teletran. He read the message, as the room began buzzing. After resetting the screen, he handed it to Clancey. The text read:

My fellow Americans:

Earlier this week, hundreds of Pathfinders—patriotic sons of the motherland—began a quest that will one day return America to its former glory. Today, they engaged federal troops sent to stop them in a predawn battle. The federal forces were soundly defeated.

After the battle, a gunship carrying General James Freeman was shot down. The former President survived the crash but sustained an injury to his shoulder. Otherwise, he is in good condition. He will come to no further harm and be treated in a manner respective of the rules of war—as I trust our soldiers will be if they are captured.

In addition, we apprehended the fugitive priest, Fr. Peter Bernard. After a brief interrogation, this coward confessed to his involvement in the bombing of New York. He also implicated the Catholic Church in the plot. Apparently, the conspiracy runs to the "top echelon" of cardinals in the Vatican. It is a most disturbing tale of treachery and intrigue. We will hold Bernard in our custody until such time as justice can be duly administered—according to the Pathfinder code.

Anson Collier
July 10, 2061

Fifty-One

After snaking through the tunnel for about four miles, the soldiers guarding Peter Bernard arrived at a station under renovation. There, another fifty soldiers, also wearing hoods and armor, waited for them.

The scene that first transpired when the man who captured Peter rejoined his comrades at the Branch Brook train station was repeated on a grander scale. This time, however, given the congratulatory welcome he received, one might have thought he had just came ashore after circumnavigating the globe in a rowboat!

Everyone seemed exultant, although their expressions were concealed by their hoods. They jostled and pawed at the Jesuit. Some insulted him; others threatened. It was getting quite rough when the limping leader pulled him out of the throng and led him over to the door of a public restroom. He opened it and shined the flashlight in. There, Peter saw a most astounding sight.

Sitting on a bed of wet, flattened cardboard, beside a row of cracked and broken urinals, was the former President of the United States.

Freeman was dressed in the same black armor as his captors, but he wore no hood. He looked up, squinting, mouth agape, like a leper coming out from his cave. His hair was disheveled; his arm in a sling. Peter couldn't decide if his imploring look suggested desperation or resignation, but it reminded him of the homeless men who often camped out on the benches in Chicago's Lincoln Park. Or, better yet, those propaganda photos of downed Air Force pilots. The deterioration in his condition since their chance meeting in the Red Cross tent was striking, even piteous. It amazed the priest how a man could decline so swiftly in the course of a week.

"Sit over there—next to him," ordered the leader. Then he limped out.

As the door closed behind him, the room got black. Before Peter's eyes could adjust, the General shifted nervously, determined to put as much distance as possible between him and his fellow captive. As he did, his free hand slipped across the wet floor, and he lost his balance, falling backwards.

Loudly, he cried, "Son of a —"

Two guards peeked in momentarily, shining their lights. Menacingly, one of them said, "Hey, Salt and Pepper. Pipe down!" The other laughed and, again, the door swung shut.

As Freeman struggled to right himself, Peter helped him back to a sitting position. Several dark and putrid-smelling minutes passed.

The General finally broke the ice in the universal manner. "Is it still raining?"

"Yes, sir."

The priest made light of the situation with an allusion to Noah's Ark. "It's likely there won't be enough pitch and gopherwood to go around."

But this throw sailed over Freeman's head into the stands. The last time Freeman opened a Bible was the year Bernard was born. He had no idea what the priest was talking about.

Actually, Peter didn't understand the purpose of the question. Freeman's intent wasn't to make conversation. Continued rain meant that the search for him would be hampered: no satellite recon, limited use of omnicams and spiders, reduced listening capability and heat signatures.

The stench of sewer gas filled the room, but it was a minor relief from the death musk that permeated everything outside. As Peter's eyes adjusted to the lurid setting, water splashed around them in Caucasian rhythm.

Freeman injected, "You're the Carrollite, aren't you?"

Peter replied, "I am."

Then, for another stretch, no words were exchanged as both men reflected silently on their shared experiences. It was the third time they had met. The first was that morning in Denver. The second, a week ago in Philadelphia.

And, even if the General was wearing a hood, Peter might have recognized him still. The ex-President played a pivotal role in the two most ill-fated incidents of his life. Driven by an understandable curiosity, he studied Freeman's career while in prison. His knowledge of it was good enough to write the book Jack Clancey was thinking about. It did little to diminish the resentment he felt toward his oppressor, however. And it wasn't merely because, either directly or indirectly, Freeman was responsible for the seven years he spent in stir. It went beyond that.

To the priest, James Freeman was the enemy of all that was sacred. When he was sworn into office after Arthur Simpson was shot, he refused to take the oath of office on a Bible. As president, he occasionally ridiculed Christians, especially Catholics. During his second term, he snubbed a request by the Pontiff to meet with him on a visit to Italy. As his solicitor general, Angela DeKalb had the words Laus Deo removed from the Washington Monument. A number of clergymen were arrested by her as subversives, the most noteworthy being him.

Like DeKalb, Freeman was a professed atheist who believed that all hope for a better world could be found in the pursuit of happiness, in the laws of man and science. Conversely, the Jesuit believed, in the words of Augustine, that only through faith would mankind someday realize the "the joy of hope." Now, sitting next to him in the dark, the priest found it difficult to separate his hatred for Freeman's sins with his hatred for the man himself.

Although the General played a leading role in the drama that was Peter Bernard, the reverse wasn't true. The Crimson Collar was only a bit player in Freeman's operatic rise to power.

Until he spied him two weeks ago in Franklin Square, Freeman had not thought of Bernard in years. He had no real knowledge of the man. To him, he was just a no-count fanatic. An anarchist. Having been so recently jogged, however, his memory of their past encounter in the courthouse was fresh. He recalled how odd it was to see a devil-catcher in that setting. And, in truth, it was very odd to see him in this one, too. So, for a second time, he broke the silence.

"Bernard, have you given any thought to another line of work?"

Swallowing hard on his bitterness, Peter replied, "Are you offering me a job?"

"I think not," said Freeman, with evident disdain.

"See? That's how it is for ex-cons."

Freeman brushed this editorial aside, "What're you doing here, anyway?"

"That's a good question."

At first, Peter didn't want to go into it, but what else was there to talk about? And he had to talk to someone. He was like a man sprung from a basement after eating chocolate and drinking coffee for a week.

"As you know, I'm wanted for questioning in the bombing. That night you saw me in Philadelphia—"

"Then it *was* you?"

"Yup. I figured you'd recognize me eventually, so after I was named a person of interest in the investigation, I split. I headed up here to get lost in all the confusion. I was in the process of turning myself in to the archbishop when I got captured." Again, he paused a second, wiping the moisture from his head, then asked, "Maybe you can tell me *by whom?*"

Wow! He doesn't know, thought Freeman.

Despite the pain in his shoulder and the cauliflower growing in his head, the insertion of Bernard into his daymare started the General thinking more clearly. Straining to see Bernard's black face in the blackened room, Freeman reflected on the chain of events in the Deacon Carroll Affair. *The seizure of the courthouse. The standoff. The interminable negotiations. The media circus. The recovery action. The dead hostage. Collier's court martial.* Now the three principals in that business would soon be reunited.

Maybe that's what Sonny meant when he said the fun's just starting.

He couldn't believe Bernard's terrible luck. If his peril were any less, Freeman might have laughed.

How do I tell him?

Before he could respond, though, Peter said, "I might ask what you're doing here, as well?"

It was easier to answer the second question than the first, so Freeman explained, "I was on a recon flight over Newark when we were shot down. The next thing I knew, Coll—"

He stopped short. "I was captured," he said.

"Who are these people, anyway? Are they bounty hunters?"

Just as Jack Clancey was agonizing at that moment to find a way to tell Lena Walker about her father's capture, Freeman fumbled over how best to tell the priest the hard truth of their predicament.

Finally, he said, "Listen, Bernard, I hate to hit you over the head with this, but you're in hot water. The man who's holding us is Sonny Collier." Before Bernard could reply, Freeman tacked on, "I'm sure you remember him. *He's the one behind the intifada.*"

Peter was at once alarmed and befuddled. As the weight of his misfortune sank in, he asked, incoherently, "What *intifada*?"

The naïveté in this response struck Freemen. "Where have you been? Under a rock?"

"Yeah. A *big* rock. And it's getting bigger."

Freeman then related the events of the past few days, including the Newark Massacre. "Apparently, he's taking advantage of all the confusion, too. I don't see where it will get him, though. He'll soon be annihilated himself."

Then, in a quiet voice, he advised, "But, in the meantime, if you can get away, do it. He's—"

"—got it in for me. I know," Peter supplied glumly. "My cell mate, Tony Vitelli, told me he let a contract on me while I was at Ellison."

"Vitelli! You mean Tony Two Palms?"

"The same."

Impressed, after a moment of silence, the General asked, "Did he really have that guy Coffey thrown into a vat of roofing tar?"

"He denies it."

The General quipped, "You must have made quite a pair." Then, returning to the subject at hand, he sighed, "I don't imagine it's any consolation to you, Bernard, but Collier has it in for me, too."

"Why you?"

Freeman related the story of Collier's court martial. This time it was even more sympathetic to his role in the drama than the version he told Major Robbins earlier that week. There were some details he forgot that Peter needed to supply, such as Rita Scanlon's name.

Bernard listened respectfully despite his familiarity with the details of the case. If his own case had gone to trial, his lawyer planned to cast Collier's role in the incident in the same light as the JAG prosecutor. The General's story did give Peter some valuable perspective on the relationship between the two officers. But if his reason for telling it was to warn him about the Rottweiler, he needn't have bothered. So vivid was the priest's memory of the fiendish Collier that he now feared for Freeman's life as well as his own.

"So he had all those people in Newark massacred?"

"Yeah. A few hundred of them. I tell you the man is a killer. This morning his Greenshirts slaughtered one of my battalions in Branch Brook Park."

Finally, Peter understood the uproar he heard while hiding in the bushes outside the cathedral. He told the General about it.

With a grunt, Freeman shifted his position and his time reference. "You know, it's been so long. Refresh me on what you say happened in Denver."

The priest told it as if it happened ten minutes ago.

"I had just heard Mrs. Scanlon's confession. We were chatting afterwards when your men attacked. My primary duty during the siege was to look after the needs of the hostages. From the negotiations with the government, I knew the Deacon wouldn't go without a fight, so I devised a plan to ensure the safety of the captives. There was an interior room on the third floor. One large enough to hold them all. I got Carroll's permission to take them there in the event of hostilities."

"But we came in from the roof," Freeman interjected.

"That's right. Mrs. Scanlon and I were on one end of the building, the rest of the hostages on the other. So she was the only one I could help when the attack began." He told of meeting Collier in the stairwell, the shooting, and the soldier who slipped in the puddling blood.

Peter raised his fist in the dark, insisting, "*His gun never misfired!* He murdered her, General—plain and simple. And, but for that injured soldier, he would have murdered me, too." Plaintively, he added, "There have been times when I wish he had."

Freeman was moved by the priest's tale but puzzled nonetheless.

"I never could figure you out, Bernard. I mean, *you're a priest!* When you're not preaching in church, you're supposed to spend time in hospitals and nursing homes. How is it that you're always in hot water?"

"Well, I know this will come as a surprise to you, but, contrary to everything that's been said about me, I really do love my country. Only, I love God more. When the government declared war on him, I couldn't sit by. I took a vow to defend the faith."

"So that justifies armed rebellion, criminal trespass, and the taking of innocent hostages?"

Uneasily, Peter said, "Sir, joining Deacon Carroll was the dumbest thing I ever did. I was young and foolish. There's no way to make light of my guilt." Then stridently, he declared, "But I never had *anything* to do with the Spark Park bombing."

That put Freeman on the defensive. Again, he moved away slightly. "If, by that, you mean, I was wrong to have you prosecuted, then I'll stand by what I did. Even if I thought you were innocent— which I didn't—my feelings were immaterial. You had a fair trial, and you were convicted. What more can be said?"

"That I was framed?"

"Oh, c'mon, that's bull."

"The hell it is! Last year, a DPS agent admitted writing the letter that implicated me in the bombing. And the police captain from Phoenix who testified against me now says he was pressured into perjuring himself by his superiors. I was set up by the Humanists— in particular, by the woman who ran the criminal division of Justice *for you!*"

Backpedaling, Freeman stammered, "If you mean Angela DeKalb, yes . . . but . . . I trusted her judgment."

In his heart, he knew that if anyone was capable of framing a man for a crime he didn't commit, it was the woman he'd bedded the night before. It was the memory of his less-than-stellar behavior toward her—not the priest's insistence on having been framed— that caused the old man to retreat even further. Stomach churning, he said, "Look, Bernard, I'm not a lawyer or a judge. As president, I had a duty to enforce the law. I had no knowledge of the things you say happened. If they did, well—"

He stopped short of an apology.

Peter was disappointed, but he was also encouraged to think that Freeman was entertaining the notion of his innocence. So he backed down. He needed Freeman. The former President, like that soldier on the stairway, might be his only salvation. Besides, maybe Freeman was being truthful when he said he had no knowledge of DeKalb's fabrications.

Through the darkness, Peter saw that Freeman was greatly distressed by the pain from his injury. "How did you hurt your shoulder, General?"

"It happened in the crash. Collier's doctor said it might be broken. And that's what it feels like, too."

"Where do you think they're taking us?"

As if the priest wasn't worried enough, Freeman announced, "I don't know, but if it's any closer to ground zero, you've got a problem— dressed like that."

He read the digital dosimeter on his sleeve. It bathed the room in a sultry, blue light.

"Even down here, I get a reading of 212. That's not bad, but it requires protection."

"Then why aren't you wearing your headgear?"

Sounding embarrassed, Freeman said, "Oh, I took it off before we got here." He picked it up and laid it in his lap. "I was having trouble breathing." In reality, the knot on his head from his morning fall made it too painful to wear.

Dodging the subject, he repeated, "The radiation's another reason you should try to get away if you can. The risk of your staying here is . . . well, you'd be better off if you were arrested. If you do escape and I get through this—*which I will*—I'll put in a good word for you. But you should try to get away."

This show of concern, however mechanical, moved the priest. He thought to himself: *Am I really any more worthy of redemption than this Ninevite?*

Fifty-Two

Lena Walker was miserable. When Jack Clancey told her about her father, she became distraught. Clancey did his best to soothe her fears, but initially she was unresponsive, sitting bowed in an armchair with her head in her hands.

Handing her a box of tissues, he pleaded, "You can't give up hope, Lena. He's still alive. Collier may be a whacko, but he's not stupid. There's no way he's going to harm your father."

Disjointedly, she sobbed, "I met him once."

"Who? Collier?"

She nodded. "At Fort Benning, twenty years ago." She paused, took a tissue from the box, then stated, "He put a move on me."

Intrigued, Clancey sat down next to her.

"Oh, it was all very innocent," she explained, growing more composed with each word. "The regiment was holding orientation for a bunch of civilian dignitaries. A black-tie dinner was planned. Dad begged us, my Mom and me, to come down for the week. She wasn't real keen on the idea, but I talked her into it. Anyway, the whole time we were there, Colonel Collier made a pest of himself, always trying to do for us and stuff like that. But, at the dinner, I sat next to him. He's really very personable. Even witty."

Looking up, she recalled, "During one dance, a slow one, he told me he was smitten by me. That's the word he used. *Smitten.* And I guess I was taken by him, too. He's really quite handsome, you know."

Jack felt a twinge.

"Well, as I said, it all ended innocently enough. But that's not how the scandal mongers saw it. I remember that we danced to *The Talk of the Town*. And boy, the next day, it was. The base was alive with speculation about the budding romance between the CO's daughter and the war hero. To hear tell of it, we were getting it on *right there on the dance floor!*"

"How did that go down with your father?"

"Oh, he was livid. He threatened to drum the guy in charge of the seating arrangements out of the regiment. When I left, I never saw or heard from the Colonel again. And, despite my father's embarrassment, I always laugh when I think back to that night." Her face once again grew solemn. "Of course, that was before Denver, before Collier got in trouble."

This mention of *The Deacon Carroll Affair* tickled Clancey's memory. He asked, "Wasn't it Father Bernard who accused him of killing that woman?"

"Yes, but you don't think he really confessed to the bombing like Collier said?"

"It doesn't matter whether he did or not," stated Jack. "He's guilty until proven innocent. And so is the Church."

Lena got up and walked over to the window. The rain was still coming down in sheets, flooding the streets below.

Determined to take the offensive, she turned to Clancey, saying, "Do you think it would help if I appealed to Colonel Collier personally?"

"I don't see what good it would do," cautioned Jack. "He might have some memories of his own of your evening together. And they might not be as rosy as yours."

If Lena wasn't mistaken, there was a touch of jealousy in his voice but, pressing on, she said, "Isn't it common procedure to try to soften the heart of a captor by establishing some personal bond between him and the family of the captive?" Her hazel eyes brimming with tears, she further pleaded, "And who better to arrange that than you?"

Clancey had doubts and, for a while, argued against it. But, finally, he gave in.

"I'll set up a taping with a local studio," he said, underestimating her urgency.

She persisted. "What about the reporters downstairs?"

"Surely you're not planning to use them?"

"Why not?"

"*Because they'll eat you alive!*"

"Not if you do *your* job!"

Again it struck the former press secretary how willful, like her father, she was. In the end, he was powerless against her. Reluctantly, he spent the rest of the day arranging and preparing for Lena's press conference.

Fifty-Three

The Attorney General awoke to the rattle of thunder on the window above her head. Hailstones peppered it like pea gravel. Though daylight peeked round the curtain, grayness masked the hour. Between the window and the curtain, a hollowed-out moth dangled from a web.

A breathing tube was taped into her mouth. Her clothes were soggy. Sore and foot-bound, with her hands tied in front of her, she shifted onto her side. As she did, the legs of the light, metal bed screeched on the concrete. She faced a stairway leading to the main floor of a house. A very old house. Muffled voices and footsteps sounded up above.

Blinking profusely, she surveyed the room's sparse furnishings. A chest of drawers with a cracked mirror. A postage-stamp of shag carpet. An old, red-leather ottoman. Two cheap velvet paintings, one of Elvis, the other of Emmett Kelly, hanging crookedly on the far wall. Overhead, a bare-bulb dangled from the joist. The air was cold and dank and, in addition to the usual basement odors of paint and mildew, smelled oddly of jasmine.

She tried to recall what had happened, but initially this retracement was stalled by the pounding in her head and neck. The ties binding her wrists cut her skin. She tasted blood, probably, a cut from the breathing tube. To make matters worse, she was thirsty. Very thirsty.

Resisting the urge to cough because it might gag her or alert those padding around upstairs, she gently cleared her throat and tried to raise some saliva.

It was the discordant scent of jasmine that returned her to full awareness. Flinching as she lowered her face toward her bosom, a quick sniff told her she was the source of it.

And, in that instant, like a baby-grand snapped from a cable ten stories high, her recollection of the past evening came crashing down.

She remembered how her abductors manhandled her and how she arched her neck to prevent her face from being ground into the pavement, then she recalled how her bodyguard fell lifelessly to the road from the trailing vehicle. Working backwards, she recalled the duplicity of Addison, then, Collier's letter. Finally, she came to Jim Freeman.

She had been raped.

And shaken down.

And shanghaied.

And, for the first time in memory, she was truly frightened. The whole night was so gauzy and revolting that, had it not been for her shackles and the smell of the love oil, she would have written it off as a nightmare.

Who took me? she wondered. *And why?*

That started her thinking about her shoulder bag. Not only was the recording of her compromise with—and by—Freeman in it. So was the letter from Sonny Collier. If either of them fell into the wrong hands, it could ruin her.

It doesn't matter. It's almost certain I won't leave here alive, anyway. Still, she thought, *it's not how I care to be remembered.*

From above, a sudden outbreak of shouting ensued. A disagreement of some kind. The door leading to the stairs swung open, and a man appeared. He descended only halfway, then turned and bellowed, "Turn on the damn light!"

Blinded at first, Angela's eyes adjusted as he took off his head-gear.

It was Anson Collier.

"Of all the stupid ideas, Jennings," he snapped at the man behind him. His shiny, wet body armor looked as if it was polished.

"She went into shock. We put the tube in so she didn't choke," his subordinate sputtered.

Collier dispensed with his gloves, sat next to her on the bed, and gently removed the tape that held the breathing device in place.

"I'm sorry, Madam General," he said in a comforting tone. Scowling, he cursed under his breath, "Conscripts!"

DeKalb was too unnerved to respond. Collier threw the plastic tube across the room. He drew a knife from the sheath on his belt and cut the plastic ties that bound her hands and feet. Then, he helped her to sit up.

"Some water?" she croaked.

One look from Collier, and Jennings was off.

Sonny and Angela were alone, sitting close. He stared at her shamelessly.

The front of her white, silk blouse was filthy and, on the collar, there was a large spot of dried blood. Except for her stockings, she was barefoot. Her hair was disheveled; he fought the urge to rearrange it. Its color was the same as his. At least, the same as his used to be. He admired her elegant features: the olive eyes, fulsome lips, and lusty figure. Her pale, glistening skin was a mystery, however, in that it wasn't swarthy like his. The only thing that put him off was the smell of her perfume. It smacked of a Havana B-girl. Otherwise, her beauty was Eve-like.

He noticed that her wrist was bleeding. Though the cut was only minor, he unzipped his armor and pulled a handkerchief out of his shirt pocket. Before he could touch it to her wrist, though, Angela snatched it away to wipe the blood from her lip.

Jennings returned with a canteen. Angela took a long pull from it, then lowered it with an emphatic sigh of relief. After gathering herself for a second, she said in a raspy voice, "I hope you have an explanation, Colonel."

Turning to Jennings, Collier said, "That's all. Get out. Shut the door behind you."

A pack of Greenshirts who had been watching from the stairs scurried off. While they did, Collier opened the curtain to let in some light in. Then he paced for a minute.

Angela studied his angular movements, while trying to summon up the contempt he deserved. But her curiosity was equal to his and would not abet any competing emotions. It also displaced her fears, which were lightened by his apologetic tone.

"I'm so sorry about all this, really. My men had orders to use kid gloves. Unfortunately, this is a citizen army. Orders are often misinterpreted."

But, instead of berating him, Angela simply asked, "The letter? Did you write it?"

Her "brother" never hesitated.

"Yes."

"Is it true?"

He gave an affirmative nod.

Angela laid back on the bed, more dizzy than devastated. Collier pulled the red leather ottoman over.

In a whisper, he revealed, "Only a few of my men know about that letter. If we must talk about it, let's do so quietly."

"Do you really think Addison will honor your request to keep it secret?"

"Yes."

"And what makes you so sure?"

"Because after you left him last night, Mr. Addison ended any speculation to the contrary."

"How do you know?"

"His body was found this morning in an alley behind the hotel."

"*He's dead?!*" Angela exclaimed, sitting back up.

Collier shrugged in a decidedly neutral manner; one side of his head almost touched his shoulder.

Seeing this, she remarked, "I'm not sure I understand."

"He fell from the window of his apartment," he answered, still studying her closely. "Not long after you left him."

"Was it a suicide?" she asked, though she knew that Addison was too infatuated with himself to even consider it.

"No. The authorities suspect foul-play."

His derisive tone led Angela to assume Collier knew Addison personally and that he knew more than he was letting on. But she postponed any further inquiry to address a more immediate need.

"I wonder, Colonel, is there a bathroom upstairs? I'd like to . . . wash up."

Collier smiled broadly. "Certainly," he said. "Please pardon my dreadful manners."

He led her up the stairs to a small commode on the first floor, then posted himself outside like a Beefeater. Angela took her time washing up, stopping only to ask for her shoulder bag.

When Collier inquired about it, Jennings answered, "Sorry, sir. That was left in the plane by accident."

Angela closed the door to the bathroom and looked despairingly into the mirror. Gone was the letter, the recorder, the tranquilizer gun, the signaling device—even her basic identification. All subsequent primping activity was slowed considerably by this sobering development. As she wiped away a tear, she concluded: *Soon the whole world will know.*

Fifty-Four

General Freeman checked his dosimeter: forty-six rads. Promptly, he pulled off his headgear and gently fingered the knots on his head with his free hand. Glancing nervously at the guards outside, he looked down at Peter Bernard, saying, "Do you wanna talk? Or just rest?"

It was strange question. He and the priest were locked in a conference room in the lower reaches of a swanky office building above the entrance to the Obama Tunnel. The charred sign out front identified it as the Baldwin Towers. Collier's engineers had provided part of the building with electricity by linking an auxiliary fusion generator to the power plant. Through a bank of interior windows, a few Greenshirts watched them from out in the hall. Freeman was sitting in a conference chair. Peter was laying on the floor, eyes closed and hands bound, his back sunk deep into the lush carpet.

They had just completed the long journey from Harrison Station, a grueling, daylong march. The boots and armor of the soldiers shielded them from the elements, but the priest wasn't so fortunate. His thin muslin clerics were soaked and covered with mud. His flapping sneakers afforded him no protection. In addition, he was tired and nauseous.

Peter attributed his nausea to the apprehension of meeting Collier. And, certainly, that was cause for distress. But, down in the tunnels, when General Freeman gingerly donned his headgear after checking his dosimeter, the big priest was forced to concede that fear was only partly responsible for his queasiness.

Conversely, Freeman's condition was a marked contrast to what it was when the journey began. The endorphin battery planted in his neck that morning must have kicked in during the trip. With each mile, as Bernard weakened, he became stronger, more alert.

Both men assumed that the Rottweiler would be waiting for them when they arrived at their destination, but he wasn't. Apparently, he was occupied with more pressing matters. This only served to heighten Peter's anxiety and made him wonder if Collier was toying with him. Thus, when Freeman asked whether he wanted to talk or rest, rather than punish himself with such thoughts, he opted to talk.

With eyes half-closed and words half-formed, he slurred, "Sure, General. Waddaya wanna talk about?"

When the answer came, it was stranger than the question.

"God."

Fifty-Five

From the basement of the White House, Tito Gonzales watched as the violence from the week before reignited: first, in reaction to the Newark Massacre, then to the Rottweiler's press release. Dozens of cities were burning, although there was a notable difference between these riots and those that preceded them. Then, the property burned and the people killed were in places like East Little Havana, Bayview, and Roxbury. Now, the bloodletting had spread to South Beach, Pacific Heights, and the North End. This time the American Dream was burning and with it a raft of churches, mostly Catholic.

The deepest fears of Tito Gonzales and James Freeman were being realized. In the course of twenty-four hours, the ethnic hatreds, religious enmities, economic frustrations, and inherent violence of the American people had exploded into a universe of fire and blood. Gonzales recalled Edmund Burke's adage that all men who are ruined are ruined on the side of their natural propensities.

The same is true of nations, he thought.

And no one understood that better than Sonny Collier, who, despite all his high-toned rhetoric and protestations to the contrary, started the country whirling down this vortex of racial and religious strife.

Fifty-Six

Sunday, July 10 (4:30 P.M. EDT)
The Baldwin Promenade, Weehawken, N. J.

Having reeled in Angela DeKalb, the Rottweiler headed back to his main headquarters, where his troop carrier pulled into a subterranean garage. At least a hundred Greenshirts were assembled there. As Collier exited the vehicle, they stood with their heads bowed. On their extended right arms they wore the ubiquitous, flash-green armband. On some, Angela noticed that an omega symbol had been added. This identified them as Collier's elite guard.

His party climbed the flight of stairs leading to the ground floor. There, all the windows of the charred lobby were blown out. Dust and glass covered the furnishings. Through her headgear, Angela saw the rise of Manhattan Island to the east. Drawn to the view, she emerged from the building into a large courtyard that was adjacent to a promenade running north and south. Confident in the body armor that Collier's men had scrounged up for her, she looked at him and pointed, as if to say, "May I go further?"

He waved his consent.

The metal fence that once prevented strollers from falling down the escarpment was mangled and melted. There were three concrete pavilions, two of which were blown down. Angela walked to the one that remained standing to survey the damage.

Collier walked with her, handing her a pair of binoculars. A courier's shout stopped him: he was needed in the command center. He told his men to watch DeKalb and went back inside.

The rain seemed to be letting up, so beneath the fast-scudding clouds Angela had an intermittent view of the opposite shore. It was a grey and ghastly sight, reminiscent of the Modernist deathscapes from World War I. One might have thought that a malefic titan, standing a mile over the city on the Brooklyn shore, had swung a colossal scythe from south to north. The downtown skyscrapers were sliced clean off and, across from where she stood, midtown Manhattan was left a rising stubble of jagged steel. Now, Battery Park melded as seamlessly into the water as it had when Henry Hudson first explored this River of Mountains. The Englishman wrote at the time that it was "as pleasant a land as one can tread upon." On seeing it this day, he would be inclined to replace the word *pleasant* with *devastated.*

The sight made Angela shudder. For ten minutes she peered through the binoculars, straining against the gale to see across the churning water. Only the eastern support of the Brooklyn Bridge was visible. As her eyes traveled over the flattened reach that was once the holy ground of capitalism, past the storied neighborhoods of Chinatown, Tribeca, Little Italy, Soho, Hell's Kitchen, and Greenwich Village, the swath ascended gradually until, in the area below Central Park, the tops of most buildings were still intact. The Empire State was a twisted Goliath, cleaved at the head by a force more prodigious than David. With its arty crown undone, the Chrysler Building was unrecognizable. Those buildings still standing on the humbled skyline seemed hopelessly out of plumb.

When Collier returned, she breathed, "It defies the imagination."

The guards backed away on Collier's command.

She asked, "Are we in danger of radiation poisoning, standing here like this?"

Collier tapped the dosimeter on his arm; it read 162. "Not too bad."

Angela studied his form carefully. *Could he really be her brother?*

She always relished her status as an only child and if, at this stage of her life, she was burdened by the pain of loneliness, she wouldn't have chosen a man like Sonny Collier to lighten it. Inwardly, Angela railed against the possibility of their common parentage, but her instincts kept insisting it was true.

"That letter you wrote," she said, "first of all, why did you send it to Addison?"

"As I said, I wanted to avoid any direct contact with you. For your sake."

"So you chose *Addison* as your confidante?"

"Frankly, Angela, the list of people who qualify as one of your confidantes is rather short. At the time, letting him deliver the letter seemed like the best approach. But I never thought he'd blackmail you."

"Then you know about that?"

He shook his head yes, saying, "We bugged his room."

Voicing her suspicions again, she asked, "Did you kill him?"

"Yes."

Rolls of thunder boomed to the west, signaling the approach of another squall. It was difficult for Angela to read Collier's emotions without seeing his face. He must have sensed it, because suddenly, he stripped off his headgear.

"Ah, that's better," he sighed, refreshed by the breeze.

He helped Angela remove hers, saying as he did, "I think it'll be okay. For a little bit."

She tossed her flattened hair and both drank in the saline air.

Looking at her as only a brother could, he said, "You know, I never had anyone that . . . I've been alone all my life. If I seem like I was raised by a pack of wolves, well, there's a reason. *I was!*"

If the moment called for a touch of pity, Sonny could find it only in himself. Planting his forearms on the railing that skirted the pavilion and staring across the white-capped river, he explained, "For the first fifteen years of my life, when I wasn't being shuffled from one abusive family to the next, I was a ward of the state. I was destined to become either an angel or an animal. Unlike you, there was no permanence for me. My abandonment was total. But I survived." The wind whipped his graying hair as he surveyed the desolation.

She eyed him dispassionately. "I still don't get why you gave the letter to Addison."

With a grin, he conceded, "I guess it can't hurt to tell you. He was working for me."

Dejectedly, Angela fell back and plopped down on one of the benches inside the pavilion. Sonny sat down beside her.

"Is that why you killed him?" she managed.

"Yes," he admitted, with no hint of remorse. "He'd outlived his usefulness. The man—if you could call him that—was the soul of duplicity. He was forever playing both ends against the middle. So, after you left his apartment last night, we did an experiment to see if he could find some middle ground between his room and the street."

Angela was less outraged than curious. "Who else is working for you?"

"You'd be surprised. We have *lots* of allies in the administration. But I'd rather not discuss that now." His face brightened as he said, "Let's talk about Anna Semynkova."

Angela masked her anxiety with a scornful look. "You don't expect me to believe all that, do you?"

"No, I don't. When I found out, I didn't either. But it's true, Angela. Every word of it. Well, except for one thing."

Angela stared at him in silence.

"I referred to our mother as Anna Semynkova so you wouldn't get confused. But, it's an assumed name. Her real name was Sonya Marynkova."

That explained one thing. After her father died, Angela spent endless nights searching for information on her real mother—with no success. If, on her birth certificate, her mother's name was an alias, she may as well have been looking for the phone number of a person in North Dakota with a directory from North Korea.

"Would you like to see her picture?" Sonny asked.

She nodded with a look like she was hitting on fifteen in blackjack.

He opened the breast pocket of his Geller T-suit and pulled out a 5x7 photograph, saying, "I found this last month on the Neugenesis website."

Any lingering doubt she had as to the authenticity of his claims went bust the instant he turned over this face card.

The same scowl that stared back at her from a thousand mirrors did so now from the photo. The likeness was uncanny. However, some of the physical differences between the two women were obscured by the black-and-white image.

Had Sonya Marynkova been standing before her, Angela would have seen that she was actually much shorter, with a figure much rounder. Her hair might have raised some doubt: it was short and henna-dyed, not long and black. Angela would surely have noticed that the woman's unsmiling face hid a mouthful of crooked teeth. And had they the opportunity to speak at any length, she would have noticed that, although Sonya's intellect was even sharper than hers, she wasn't nearly as poised or confident. But these traits are not deduced from a photograph. All Angela could see was the same thing Sonny saw—and that was her mother.

"Convinced?" Collier's demeanor was subdued, almost contrite. With his pure blue eyes, tousled hair, and winning smile, he was every inch the trusty scout. This, too, was convincing.

Angela said, "There was something in the letter about an organization?"

"The Guardians, yeah. It was one of those groups whose members had to have an IQ the size of Alaska. They fell into disrepute when their founder, a quintessential highbrow, murdered his whole family in a fit of rage."

"You said its charter was to increase the level of human genius through genetics?"

"Among other things. Essentially, they subscribed to the Humanist Manifesto. You know—atheism, relativism, the scientific method."

His tone was off-putting. Everyone knew Angela DeKalb was a *director emeritus* of the Humanist Guild. She countered, "You know, I could care less if the things I believe are offensive to you."

"No, not offensive—just trite." With an air of contempt, he smiled and shook his head. "You Humanists," he said, "you strip God of his wondrous power then use it like a line of case workers at the unemployment office. Today, instead of measuring man's glory against galaxies and eons, you measure it against meters and minutes. It almost makes me pine for the return of old Jehovah! You define nothing but the mediocre. You demand nothing but the average. You inspire nothing but the ordinary. By standing for everything, you stand for nothing. We live in a moral vacuum of your devise, yet your dominion over the lives of billions continues—unchallenged!" Deferring momentarily to a gust of wind, he shielded his face with his hand and said, "Until now, that is. That moral vacuum is about to be filled."

She sneered, "By you?"

"That's right," he declared, his voice as blustery as the air.

Intimidated though she was, Angela couldn't resist a further exploration of his motives. "And just what do you propose to do?"

"Let's just say that should the power of God fall to me, I'll have no qualms about using it."

"Is that how you imagine yourself—as God?" Pointing toward Manhattan, she added quickly, "And, if so, might this be an example of your holy wrath?"

He gave a wounded look. "Is that what you think?"

"Only politicians answer a question with a question, Colonel."

"Perish the thought," he replied. "I may be the son of the destruction himself, but I'm no politician." Then, as he again examined the ruins on the far shore, he parried her question with, "Word has it that the Catholics were in on it."

Angela replied, "Well, we're certainly not ruling anyone out. *Including you!*"

"Look, Angela," he conceded, "the last thing I want to do is fight. If I insulted you, I apologize. I was only trying to be playful, but . . . I know, sometimes I play too rough. I'm aware of how passionate you are about your beliefs. When I found out about our common maternity, I spent a lot of time reading about you, studying your career. It intrigues me how close your world view corresponds to Sonya's. Having never talked to her, or even known her, it seems that your views are almost identical to hers."

"What are you saying? That there's some kind of extra-genetic link between her and me?"

"Yes."

"But, that's absurd."

"You underestimate Sonya Marynkova," he warned. "Remember the goal of the Guardians was to increase the level of human intelligence through genetics. Or, using a computer analogy, to juice up our microprocessors. What if she found a way to upload the *operating system* as well?"

He let the words register for a moment, then asked, "Wouldn't that explain the world view shared by you and her?"

"Are you saying that she programmed my mind?"

"Yes."

"Oh, come on! How do you explain *your* views then?"

"That's easy. I'm more a product of nurture than nature."

"How's that?"

It was a mindless question, proffered to buy time while she wrestled with the ominous implications of Marynkova's work.

"I don't know. I'm not a sociologist. But I know it was our mother's intent to fashion our minds as well as our bodies."

"How?"

"Like I said, I don't know."

"No. I mean how do *you* know she was trying to do that?"

"From her journal."

Angela grew intent. "Can I see it?"

"Of course!"

One of the Omegas interrupted him, waving him urgently off to the side.

During this time-out, Angela tried to make sense of it all. Try as she might to dismiss Collier's story, Sonya's now rain-spattered photograph wouldn't allow it. And he seemed so sure of his facts. She decided to suspend further judgment until she saw the journal. In the meantime, she rationalized.

And if I was born as he says? How many murderers, liars, and thieves were conceived through the ages in an act of love?

True to her Humanist creed, she resolved that there was no moral dilemma in her condition. She had always believed that the mind and spirit die with the body. So, with no glory attending the end of her days, what did it matter if there was none at the beginning? The circumstances surrounding her birth were wholly irrelevant. Her devotion to progress was so strong, her love for law and science so great that, even if Collier was right, the definition of "humanness" would simply need to be modernized.

And the whole thing about being programmed by this woman? It's not possible. At least, it wasn't in those days.

That Sonya Marynkova could produce an embryo from strands of DNA was no great feat. Things like that were done every day in laboratories around the world. What was inconceivable was that she could actually hard-wire the brain. Speculation was rampant that, with the recent advances in genetic engineering, such breakthroughs were imminent.

But her experiments were performed more than forty years ago, when theories about mind-molding were still in their infancy. The nano-instruments she needed to apply the technology hadn't even been invented yet.

So Angela remained skeptical of Collier's claim that the dour puppeteer staring back at her from the photograph was capable of such a premature discovery.

Fifty-Seven

When Jim Freeman indicated that he wanted to talk about God, Peter rolled over on the floor, balanced himself on the palms of his shackled hands, and stood up. Sitting in a chair beside the General, he rubbed his eyes and asked, "In what respect?"

"In every respect." And, with that, Freeman went mute. Capitulation was so loathsome to him.

Peter asked tentatively, "Is it hard for you to talk about God, General?"

"No. It's not. But, for the first time in my life, it's hard for me to talk about me." He looked around nervously. "I know what you're thinking—that this is some kind of foxhole conversion. And, in a way, I guess it is. But it wasn't the Rottweiler's doing."

Freeman was treading lightly, feeling for the walls, as one does when moving through a darkened room.

From his experience with the inmates at Ellison, Peter Bernard knew that, in these initial moments of uncertainty, it was important to shut up. Transmissions of grace need little amplification.

Freeman again glanced painfully over his shoulder at the sentries standing in the hall. Turning back, he said softly, "Last month I was diagnosed with a brain tumor." Then, he added quickly, "It isn't life threatening, though. The doctor said it could be reduced with tumites—those little implants that eat tumors—and with radiation. But I postponed the start of treatments to go fishing with my daughter in

Montana. Then the bombing happened, and I got the call to assume command of the Cordon. So I still have this thing inside my head." He paused, then whispered, "This morning I blacked out, and I think that's what caused it. Either that or the wine I drank last night. Anyway, when I fell, I hit my head pretty hard. The regimental doctor said my brain waves weren't normal. I didn't tell him why, but it really scared me."

Peter nodded.

"The whole time I was in Montana, I couldn't stop thinking about it. I spent more time angling for a way to tell my daughter than I did for the fish. She was having such a good time. I didn't want to ruin it. But I wanted to talk with her about something else that's growing inside me, too."

He paused, searching for the words, his face etched with sadness. The coat-hanger shoulders drooped as he said, "I'm hounded by regrets, Father. Over the rupture with my dad. Over how cruelly I treated my wife. And for making such a hash of my presidency. But my biggest regret is the decision I made to turn on God for *my* failures. Most men will tell you that the dumbest things they ever did came after a fifth of whiskey, but mine stemmed from that decision."

He fell silent. Again, he appeared stymied.

Peter sensed it was a pivotal moment. It humbled him to witness this great man's catharsis, particularly since he was only hours removed from his own. He asked, "What caused you to turn on him . . . God, I mean?"

Freeman shook his head and smiled. "Would you believe, because my father wouldn't let me play football in high school?"

The priest wasn't surprised. He had heard enough confessions to know that, in retrospect, the motivation for many life-changing acts often seems trivial.

The General continued. "He was a professor of theology at Princeton Seminary. A good man but very strict. Very obstinate. 'Bishop Charles' we called him. Always took a hard line in matters of the faith and often used the Scriptures against me. That's what he did with football. He thought it was too violent and would quote the Bible to make his case—as if Jeremiah once watched a game in horror from a sky-box at Giants Stadium!" In anguish, he lowered his head and said to the carpet, "So we had a falling out. We rarely spoke after I left home. Years later, my CO convinced me that he was only being protective, but I still couldn't find it in my heart to forgive him. Talk about being obstinate! As things turned out, I made him look wimpy."

The old man sighed, "Anyway, I became convinced that religion was the root of all evil. As a cadet at the Academy, I visited the hole where the World Trade Center once stood. It offended me how the terrorists praised Allah afterwards and how the television evangelists claimed it was the Lord's retribution for the sins of our nation. Then, al Jinn raped my wife. After that, it was *total* war. I marched against God with drums beating and flags waving." He hesitated, then said, "But you know that, don't you?"

Peter nodded, saying, "What I didn't realize, until now, is that you're really not an atheist."

"What do you mean?"

"I mean, you may not be religious, but at least you're willing to concede that God *exists.*"

"That's fair." The General coughed hard, then groaned from the pain it caused him.

Anxiously, Peter made a motion for him to go on.

"Anyway, it seemed that, as the years passed, more fuel was added to the fire. Down in Haiti, de LaSalle started executing our soldiers, calling himself the Divine Avenger. Afterwards came Deacon Carroll—and you." Freeman looked sadly at his fellow captive and, with a touch of agony, added, "If that wasn't enough, then war broke out in the Middle East."

With another downward glance, he said, "It got so bad that wherever and whenever I spotted God, I attacked. For thirty years.

And not once during that time did I ever consider retreat." Wearily, he admitted, "Until now."

"Why?"

Looking up, he croaked, "Because I've lost the desire to fight. I'm tired of getting my ass kicked! I realize now that there's no hope of victory. I can't dictate the peace. It only comes with surrender." Exasperated, he gushed, "Like the Bishop used to say, 'His will be done.'"

To Peter, it amounted to a punch in the stomach. The only thing stranger than finding himself in the belly of a great fish was to find that he wasn't in there alone. The priest marveled at how this man, so different from him in so many ways, could be experiencing an epiphany so similar to his own.

Fighting back the urge to tell his story, he asked, "What brought you to that conclusion?"

"The tumor. Hearing that word is like hearing the first cut of the gravedigger's shovel. And, even if the doctor assures you that your condition isn't fatal, it still gets your attention. When I was younger, killing and dying were the products of my trade—and I saw plenty of it. For obvious reasons, I tried not to think about it too much. But not anymore."

His eyes grew moist.

"Earlier this week, I killed a man. It was the first time I fired a weapon in anger since Port-au-Prince. It caused quite a sensation, too. As always, they called me a hero. But there was nothing heroic about it. True, he was holding a woman hostage and tying up criti-cal resources, but it wasn't kill-or-be-killed. We could've used other means to subdue him. Hell, a rubber bullet would have sufficed! Only I wanted to make a statement about *zero-tolerance*. So, I shot him." He sat up straight and adjusted his sling, saying, "No matter how much I try to shrug it off, though, my conscience won't let me. It's just another link in a long chain of regrets. Now that I'm facing the prospect of my own mortality, I'm not ashamed to say that it has me worried."

"But, you've faced death before."

"That isn't what worries me."

"What does?"

Softly, he replied, "Hellfire."

Fifty-Eight

Sonny finished with the messenger and returned to where Angela was sitting, pacing anxiously in front of her.

"Something wrong, Colonel?" she asked stiffly.

"No, not at all. Actually, things are going better than planned. This thing's become an embarrassment of riches."

Angela knew it was a front. If he was indeed her brother, he certainly didn't have her cool demeanor. And, if what he wrote in the letter was true that he was only a few minutes younger than she was, he acted as if he was a generation removed.

Nonetheless, he cut a commanding figure and when he turned on his lights, one felt like a deer. His resonant voice and diamond-blue eyes could hold the attention of even the most careless listener. Although he was obviously headstrong and, at times menacing, he could be charming, too. Like her, he asked no quarter and he gave no quarter, and he appeared willing to accept the consequences. If he wasn't a born leader, he certainly was an irresistible one.

"So, when will you lay siege to Washington?" she asked.

He chuckled, "That may take some time, although we *have* invested Jersey City . . . or what's left of it!"

Angela laughed, too, this time without reserve.

"And for that you've risked all in what can only be regarded as the historic equivalent of Harper's Ferry?"

"Oh, my legacy will be greater than Potawatomie Brown's."

In disbelief, Angela rubbed her still-aching neck as her words took a sympathetic turn. "You know," she said, "I really don't object to many of the reforms you espouse. In fact, if it wasn't for the racism that colors them—and the violent way you seek to impose them—I might have supported you. But, changing the electoral process by use of force is entirely unacceptable."

It was a mistake. These were buttons one didn't want to push. He sat down beside her, insisting, "That's because your interests are best served by diffusing *political* power as widely as possible throughout the electorate, by making the masses think their votes actually count. But we both know it's a sham."

"Oh?"

"Regardless of what system of government a country chooses," he argued, "the elites will control it. And even the elite succumbs to the influence of the strongest, smartest and richest among them. That's the lesson of history—and of nature, as well."

With her head cocked haughtily, Angela inquired, "By the 'elite'— am I to assume you mean the Humanists?"

"I am. Surely, you don't deny that your power is supreme?"

"I'll admit that our ideology is powerful but only because it appeals to a higher sensibility."

Sonny's mood darkened again. With growing ardor, he said, "No, it's powerful because, while the masses brawl for power at both ends of Pennsylvania Avenue, you people secretly control that part of our government which lies in between—the part that's impervious to public whim: the courts and the bureaucracy. From there you thwart whatever legislation you oppose and promote your own agenda. Combine your domination there with your dominion over our country's social institutions, and your effective control extends beyond the government to our entire *culture*. The only two institutions you *haven't* gained control of yet are the religious and military establishments. The first one you'll have to take by force and to do that you'll need the second. When that happens, it will put an end to this charade we call democracy. Only, it will also put and end to me. Even as we speak, your boss is sponsoring legislation which will outlaw my party." Pausing briefly to read his dosimeter, almost as an afterthought, he added, "That's why I decided to act sooner rather than later."

His ardor, single-mindedness and lofty rhetoric made Angela think: *He's got a messiah-complex. Or, worse, he's paranoid. That explains the disconnect between his words and his actions.*

Like children, fools and madmen occasionally give voice to the truth. Sonny's assessment of the Humanist agenda was dead-on, but its high priestess was neither disturbed nor offended. On the contrary, it validated her work. It signaled triumph. If the sole purpose of Collier's rebellion was to reverse the progress she and those like her were making toward building a more perfect union, then final victory was all but assured. To deflect his accusations of subterfuge, however, she responded with false humility, saying "You have a wonderful imagination, Colonel. But your estimate of our power and influence is highly inflated."

"Is it?" he asked. "Then, let me ask you this: Why has our democracy survived this long?"

"Because it is the best system of government man has ever devised to—"

Sonny raised his hand in disgust. "Please! Stop with the platitudes. *It survived because you people allowed it to.* The reason the barbarians never tore down the gates is because the Humanists threw them wide open! Your success depends on the 'great leveling' that the Frenchman, DeToqueville, predicted. It's what allows your shadow government to exist. And not only have you taken advantage of that leveling; you've accelerated it. Dumbing down the education system. Expanding the vote to include even children and criminals. Medicating the herd with porn, dope, and fashion. Now, as we stumble toward oblivion, you sit on the head of the proletariat like an oxpecker on a rhino,

fattening your purses and awarding laurels to each other in antic-
ipation of the day when the whole, rotted mess caves in. When it
does, the ruck and scum will come groveling to you for redemption. On that day, the Theocracy of Humanism will triumph, and
you'll coronate yourselves the conscience of the state."

Angela was unfazed. She'd heard it before. "And your goal is to
stop us?"

"In a nutshell, yes."

"To promote your own interests?"

"That's right," Collier averred, pounding his fist into his palm. "I
want to return this nation to its roots, though. You say my ideology
is racist. But why? Because I would require voters to attain a minimum
of education? Because I'd expect them to display some proficiency
with the English language? Or pass a rudimentary civics exam? Or
meet more stringent citizenship requirements? Jefferson wrote that
'whenever the people are well informed, they can be trusted with their
own government.' Doesn't it follow that if they aren't, they can't?"

Angela was itching to submit the massacre in Newark as proof
of his bigotry, but she was still unsure of how he would react. Instead,
she said coyly, "Well, if your cause is so righteous, Colonel, then why
hasn't it taken root in the marketplace of ideas? Why are you forced
to fire on American troops—to commit treason—to advance it?"

"Because *you* have a monopoly on the marketplace of ideas!
Under the *status quo*, our beliefs have no hope of taking root. We
had no option *but* to fire on American troops. If that's treason, then
so be it. An English lord called it the only refuge from the absolute
will of the majority. But times change. Today it's the only refuge from
the absolute will of the Humanists."

"And where, may I ask, will we take refuge from the absolute will
of Sonny Collier?"

Suddenly, his countenance softened. He looked at her tenderly
and said in a like tone, "Hopefully, in your case, it's at my side."

She let go a laugh more disconcerted than mocking. "That's why you brought me here, isn't it?"

He nodded. But, before he could elaborate, another Omega interrupted them. Reluctantly, Sonny pulled him aside.

"What is it?"

"Sir, Shuler says he can't hold the approaches much longer."

"Okay, I'll be right up."

The man saluted and trotted off.

When Sonny turned around, Angela was standing in the corner of the pavilion overlooking the bluffs. Sullenly, the clouds boiled downward in a race to the channel, intermittently obscuring their view of the ravaged city. Raindrops splattered all around.

"I hate to cut this short," he said, "but I have a few things to attend to. You can wait for me inside."

"You said I could see the journal."

"Certainly. I'll have it brought to you."

As they turned to go, Angela said, "There's something I have to ask."

"What's that?"

Looking down at her hand and in it, the face of Sonya Marynkova, with difficulty, she asked, "You . . . you went to great lengths investigating *her* background." She paused. A troubled look came over her. "Have you had any success locating our father?"

Sonny smiled and took another quick reading of his dosimeter. "As a matter of fact, she made a few references to him in her journal, but they're not really clear. Maybe you can help me decipher them."

With that, they returned to the building.

Fifty-Nine

To the quietly waiting priest, the General said, "All those years of arguing with my friends about the hypocrisy of religion. Of scorning those who praised God for their success. Or laughing inwardly at the prayers of men on the eve of battle." He remembered the President's godsend on the night of the bombing and how he chaffed at those who call out to heaven from the depths of their despair. How drastically his thinking had changed in the span of a week.

The room was quiet. There were so many things the priest wanted to say, but he knew the missionaries of age and adversity were already at work.

When the General resumed, it was with an air of finality. "Honestly, I don't know what's next, but, for me, it's like this: I want to see the people I love again. My father and mother. My wife. When the time comes, my daughter. I can't explain it, but I know one thing. If there *is* life after death, you don't get there on the road I'm traveling."

Peter joked, "Well, maybe, but your final destination may not be all that cool."

"And that's my concern."

Seeing an opening, Peter offered this: "You spoke of hellfire, Jim, but hell has many manifestations. In reality, it's any separation from God. And it can be as agonizing in this life as it is in the next. But, separating from him is *our* decision. He doesn't abandon us;

we abandon him. He holds us to that decision, too, despite his love for us."

"But if he is so loving, why is he so cruel?" Recalling his wife's ordeal, Freeman charged, "How could he allow a good woman to be brutally and repeatedly raped? Must we all wail out in pain to satisfy his lust for—"

Peter interrupted him. "God didn't rape your wife, General. The al Jinn did."

"I said he *allowed* it."

"That's true."

"But why? Why does he allow such suffering to exist?"

Given the past five years, the big Jesuit wondered himself.

"It's a good question," he said. "In fact, it's the question of the ages." Then, rolling up his mental sleeves, he cautioned, "I'll try to answer, but you have to allow that my argument is grounded in faith, not science. Apart from Revelation, no one can fathom the mind of God or the *whys* of the universe, not even a Jesuit."

Predictably, he opened with what he knew best: history. "Let's start with something that every American is taught from an early age—the idea that all men are created *equal*. It might surprise you to hear a black man say this, but I consider that to be of secondary importance. The salient fact of creation is that God made us free— free to reject even him. It's the only right truly guaranteed to all of us. And, since his universe has a *moral* thread to it, how could he do otherwise? How can 'hearts, not free, be tried?'"

"What are you saying? That God prefers our suffering to our slavery?"

"Well . . . yes," Peter answered, surprised by the facile-minded Freeman. "Evil is the price we pay for freedom. Although that wasn't God's wish. Genesis reveals that the Father never intended for us to suffer and die, only to love and serve. We were formed in his image: *timeless, supernatural beings*, with gifts of intellect and free will. From the beginning, he left us free to choose between a life where he is present and a life where he is not—between good and evil. He also made it clear from the start that the cost of choosing the latter would be suffering and death. Sadly, that's what we chose. Instead of using our great gifts to glorify him, we rebelled and used them to glorify ourselves. In so doing, we bought suffering and death into the world."

The big priest drew a breath, saw that Freeman was still listening, and continued. "But, even though we chose the Father's justice over his love, by his infinite mercy, he chose to save us from ourselves. Trumping our pride with his humility, he sent his only Son to reconcile us to him through *his* suffering and death. That restored the supernatural and eternal possibilities of our souls. But our minds and bodies he left subject to the corruptions of time and nature."

"You mean to suffering and death."

It was the priest's turn to wince. "Look, Jim," he said, "I'm not trying to minimize the pain of either, but, without them, who would ever bend a knee? For all their ills, they do burn the dross out of our souls and provide us with greater clarity."

Peter wanted to remind the General of his comment about the sound of the gravedigger's shovel but thought better of it. It might interfere with Freeman's reclamation. Nor was he comfortable with personalizing things too much, since his own reclamation occurred only hours before, and he felt like he was dancing dangerously close to the edge of hypocrisy.

Instead, he observed, "In college, I read a book by a doctor, a psychologist, who survived Auschwitz." Suddenly, he realized, "Until now, I'd forgotten about it." It was a story that might have bolstered his faith on those hopeless, sleepless nights at Ellison when the weight of his troubles seemed to suffocate every prayer he uttered.

"Anyway," he said, "this man learned from his travail that we are all prisoners to the vagaries of *how* we exist until we define *why* we exist. Normally, our work or our relationships provide that definition. But, in times of trial, it comes from how we meet with suffering. If we find a higher purpose in it and embrace that purpose, then no amount of suffering, not even death, can ever hold us bound again."

As if recognizing something, he looked down at the plastic ties on his wrists, saying, "So, it isn't suffering we need to fear. It's suffering *without meaning.* For us Christians, that meaning comes from sharing in the redemptive suffering of Christ, whose salvific mission to all humanity descends to us in the Holy Spirit through the Church. Quite simply, in his name, we 'do good by our suffering and do good to those who suffer.' And, in light of his empty tomb, death has become a passage between temporal sorrow and eternal joy. We all owe God a death, but, as a dying soldier at Gettysburg said: 'It's only the last of earth.'"

"*The last of earth,*" Freeman repeated, admiring the soldier's fortitude. He found Bernard's arguments interesting, even entertaining, although, on another level, he was still dogged by doubt. "I don't know," he said, "I've always thought that if Christ really was the Son of God, he would have eliminated suffering and death forever by his cross."

The priest replied, "But he couldn't! At least, not *physical* suffering and death. That would have negated our freedom."

Scratching the stubble on his head, Peter saw that his appeal to Freeman would require a deeper reading of Scripture—and Dostoevsky. Leaning forward, he asked, "Do you remember the story of the Temptation?"

"The one in the desert?"

"Yes."

"Vaguely."

"Well, the gist of it is that, had Christ turned the stones into bread, Satan would have given him the power to feed all mankind and end material want forever. Throwing himself from the parapet of the temple so the angels could rescue him would have removed any mystery as to his divinity—or the existence of God. By prostrating himself before Satan, he would have gained the power to rule all nations and unite mankind in everlasting peace and harmony. But Jesus resisted the Tempter, ordering him to 'Begone!' Can you guess why?"

"Because he had the power to do those things anyway?"

Although it wasn't the answer Peter was fishing for, it was a keeper. Again, he stopped to applaud Freeman's perceptiveness. "Very good, General. You do honor to the Bishop."

Old Teddy donned the look of a satisfied schoolboy.

As he did, the priest made his point. "Obviously, the Father didn't send the Son to recreate Eden. Why put our salvation at risk to pride and envy a second time? That's why Satan's offer to vanquish all of our suffering, doubts, and divisions—in effect, to recreate Eden— was so tempting. Had Jesus bought into this lie in return for his vassalage, he would have merely repeated the sin of Adam. But he rebuked Satan. In the end, God broke our bondage to sin and evil by sacrificing his freedom instead of nullifying ours. He left intact the essence of our creation—the right to think independently from him—while driving home the point of it—to know, love, and serve him. That is the *meaning* of Jesus Christ's suffering and death, and ours as well. All else is vanity. Or, as the godless contend, pointless."

The General was still skeptical. "Having said all that, how do you square it with the claim that, in order to be saved, we must submit totally to God's will? Isn't that just a euphemism for slavery?"

He equates God with slavery, thought the priest, although, for the time being, he sidestepped that issue, saying, "We can choose not to submit, right?"

"Right—but that's not much of a choice."

Peter's dark eyes lit up. "Hey! Although I'm not one of them, a few billion sinners might disagree with you. But no one would argue that it's still our choice to make. By his own rules, God cannot compel or coerce our submission to him *against our will.* It's unnatural, like a parent exhorting the love of his or her child. It can't happen. It can only be given *freely.*"

"So we must *freely enslave* ourselves? Don't you see the contradiction in that?"

Here we go, mused the priest. He felt like he was swirling down the rapids of a swollen river. It was as though his own reconciliation with the Almighty took place years ago, not hours before; as though he had spoken with Luke Monaghan last year, not last week.

"No. It's not a contradiction," he replied. "It's a paradox. Something that sounds contrary to common sense but is, nonetheless, true. You must understand: true freedom isn't being able to do the things we *want* to do but the things we *ought* to do. It entails responsibility—that is, the ability to respond to God's love. When we speak of 'freely enslaving' ourselves, what we're really talking about is *obedience.* St. Paul taught that we are all slaves to what we obey, either our passions for the things of this world or those of the next. But, make no mistake. It is the passions of this world that enslave us. Those passionate for the world to come—the 'slaves to righteousness' of whom Paul wrote—are liberated from sin and evil. Their ability to love one another frees them from the law. They no longer live under it but above it. *Under grace.*"

The General grunted, "No one is above the law."

To which the priest insisted, "Yes, they most certainly are!" Now the historian in him couldn't keep still. "The true genius of the Founding Fathers, whether they knew it or not, was to establish a nation of laws in a nation where the righteousness of its citizens transcended them anyway. Habituated by their religion to hard choices and self-discipline, it was the descendants of the Puritans who put the heavy horses of democracy and capitalism to the yoke of Christian morality. In the end, it wasn't the patriot leaders who made the American Experiment work. *It was the followers!*" He gulped and tacked on, "And those followers trusted in God's law. They were leery of those advanced by men."

"And how is it different today?"

"Because, just as Christian morality once made our laws almost unnecessary, now, its demise makes them almost unenforceable. Our nation of laws has become an ocean of laws! Today, we sink beneath waves we once soared above, while bemoaning the loss of things like personal responsibility and respect for authority. And, as a result, coercion alone assures our obedience to the state, not a sense of duty to—or love for—God and country."

The priest suddenly pulled up, frustrated by an uncharacteristic loss of words. He knew there was the risk that he was overselling the deal. With his wheels spinning, he offhandedly remarked, "But it couldn't have been otherwise."

"Why?" asked Freeman.

"Because of the Humanists."

And, with that, he regained his traction. "Their goal is to succeed where they think Jesus failed. To feed mankind. To remove any doubt as to the *non*-existence of God. To unite mankind under a single banner. But again, their price for eliminating our suffering is the same as Satan's: we must surrender our freedom."

Waving him off with his one good arm, Freeman countered, "But they don't have any more political power than, say, the Pathfinders."

"That's because their goal isn't *political* power. They want to control the culture from which it flows. That's why they deny God. Their goal isn't to prove or disprove his existence. It is to *dethrone* him because they covet the authority and influence he has over our lives. To pry us away from him, they separate freedom from the truth and encourage our worship at the altars of Pleasure, Profit, and Prestige. But not Power. That's their idol. And once they seize it for good, any moral certainty in the affairs of state, except for that which they impose will disappear." The bear-like priest mopped his brow awkwardly on muscular forearms and concluded, "I tell you, Jim, when they deny God, they deny the very basis of our freedom."

Freeman's response was defensive. "Say what you will—it's pretty clear to me that the Church and the Humanists are battling over the same prize: the soul of humanity. And, at least, the Humanists have reason on their side. All you have is a bunch of primitive superstitions."

Ignoring the slight, Peter responded, "But their dogmas require even greater faith in the unknown than ours do! And, don't forget, when it comes to the whys of the universe, we have the only plausible answers in Revelation." Looking away briefly, when he turned back, Peter said, "Keep in mind, too, that, without faith, reason is a cosmic dead end."

The priest wanted to get up and move around, but he feared it would draw the attention of the hooded guards out in the hall. So, he shifted restlessly in his chair and asked, "Do you remember the day we met, Jim?"

"You mean in Denver?"

"Yes. Do you remember—in the courtroom—the inscription on the frieze above the judge's bench?"

"Of course not!"

"It read: *Reason is the soul of all law.*"

"So?"

"Well, that's because reason is the soul of God's law! But, a Humanist like Angela DeKalb cannot allow that the law of God is as much a product of reason as the laws of the state. It would diminish her power. She insists that, if we follow her creed, we can perfect ourselves on a collective basis. But, I ask you—which is the greater leap of faith? To trust in the power of mankind to perfect itself? Or the power of God's saving grace?"

Sixty

On the floor below, the Humanist in question was sitting at a table in an empty, half-lit cafeteria. She had removed her hood and gloves. With the exception of the men who guarded her, there was no one else in the room. Five minutes passed, during which she agonized over what might happen if Collier's letter and the recording she made of her "negotiations" with General Freeman fell into the wrong hands. There was little doubt the recording would do more damage.

That should light a bonfire under my career, she thought. *The letter will only drive the gas truck into it.*

A short, stocky Omega entered from a door at the far side of the room. He carried a book in his hand. When he reached the place where she was sitting, he dismissed all the men except for three, posting them at the doors. Then, he handed her the book.

"Colonel Collier said he's highlighted the passages that would be of interest to you."

He left. Angela opened the black leather journal. It was about two inches thick. The entries were ordered by date and written legibly but contained, for the most part, scientific data that was barely comprehensible.

Turning the pages slowly, she read with fascination. The first highlighted passage was dated 2/4/14: *Met an interesting prospect at Georgio's last night. Works on the Hill. The consummate Alpha. As they say: tall, dark, and handsome. A veritable king of hearts. Not particularly brilliant, but that will only serve to validate my hypothesis.*

The next entry was dated 2/11: *Bedded JAF. Broached the subject of #66. Said he's game. Smarter than I first thought (for a soldier), but not a problem. Time constraints make action imperative.*

Angela read each of the subsequent postings carefully.

2/15: He's in! Must assure no strings attach. Otherwise, he's in.

2/18: Having second thoughts (the bane of science). Talk has turned to love! I'm undecided, as well. He wants more than just friendship. Enormous sexual energy. Athletic and sensitive. Loves Sinatra, my accent, even—

Angela halted abruptly. W*ait! Sinatra?* She considered the initials: JAF. No way! The thought of it was too grotesque. Rather than hang on it, though, she kept reading. But her concentration was blown— *my cooking! How could I allow #66 to become so personal? Sunday picnic in Rock Creek. Straight out of Studio B. If only I can believe him!*

2/20: Lovemaking till dawn. He's tireless. I'm exhausted! #66 on hold. Can't work. Turns out, he's something of a media darling. What is America's obsession with sports?

No further entries were made until 2/28. This one read simply: *JAF called. It's over.*

Then, 3/1: *Met JAF at The Dupont for lunch. Very cold, even distracted. A side I haven't seen. Apparently, heard stories about the Guardians that concern him. Mentioned father's Communist Party membership, too. Said he needed time to think things over, but Evelyn saw him last weekend at The Dubliner with a secretary from Sen. Trilling's office. No matter. I need time to think things over, too. All that matters is #66. I've recovered enough of JAF from the linen to replicate him a thousand times over. That should get his attention.*

There were no highlights for many pages. These were filled with a lot of chromo-babble relating to the experiment Sonya Marynkova referred to as "#66." Arcane studies in synthetic biology that concerned recipient cells, phenotypes, iPS cells, organelles, chromatids, watermarks, and cross-transcription were detailed. None of these passages were highlighted, but Angela scanned them anyway.

There was a lengthy section detailing the medium that would support the type of acid-hatch being contemplated. Some pages included random, indiscernible sketches of helix designs and others, the required chemical composites and proteins. She noted that to ensure the confidentiality of her research, she had decided to use herself as "the delivery vehicle." This passage was highlighted.

Further on, there was a brief account, also highlighted, of how the two best embryos—one male, one female—were implanted in her womb by a doctor in Miami. Then, on 3/23, the following entry appeared: *Success!*

After 3/1, she never mentioned JAF again. There was no indication that the male chromosomes she used were taken from his DNA. Nor was there any indication they were not. The entries made during her pregnancy reported a normal progression of both fetuses. She continually referred to her male baby as Alpha and the female as Epsilon.

The final entry Collier highlighted was dated 12/7/14. It read: *Stage I complete. Gave birth yesterday at 3:23 A.M. under the name Semynkova. Avoiding contact. Dr. Chen assures me that both babies are exceedingly robust. Stage II, proving heightened capacity, will be difficult but not impossible. Will depend on the adoption process. Anticipate future difficulty isolating the effects of nurture (vs. nature).*

This was the last entry concerning "#66." The balance of the journal was devoted to observations on other research projects she was contemplating.

When Angela was finished, what nettled her most was the identity of the mysterious JAF. She was almost certain that "A" was Jim Freeman's middle initial. He never used it, though, so she couldn't be sure. Although the odds of it being him were impossibly long, there was no minimizing the cruelty of fate.

Sixty-One

James Freeman's admiration for the big Jesuit was growing. He was a capable fighter for his cause. A good soldier. Though the old man's heart was as hard as knotted oak at the start of the day, it had softened considerably. "You know," he said, "I listen to you talk, Bernard, and I have to admit, what you say has merit. But whenever I think of your Church, I'm reminded of Gandhi's line: 'I like their Christ but not their Christians.'"

Instead of mounting a defense, as was his wont, Peter asked incredulously, "You like our Christ?!"

"Always have. Ever since I was a boy."

Peter's incredulity was understandable. When he was president, Freeman attended a gala at an art museum where the infamous *piss christ*—a jar of urine with a crucifix inside—was the featured exhibit. Responding to a reporter's query afterwards, he quipped, "Beauty's in the eye of the beholder."

So, the priest asked, "Do you believe it? I mean, that Jesus was the Son of God?"

"Oh, no. I've always felt he was a wise man and a good teacher but not the Son of God."

"But that's just it, Jim. Jesus was either God, or he was the greatest fraud who ever lived!"

"Ah, c'mon, even I wouldn't go that far."

"But you must! There's no calling him a great philosopher, or a wise teacher, or a good man. It's the old 'Lord, liar, or lunatic' argument. If he wasn't who he said he was—God—then he was either a pathological liar or a raving lunatic!" He grew even more earnest as he said, "Anyone who believes in an eternal God must decide whether or not Jesus of Nazareth was his entry into time itself—*in human form*. If, like me, they believe he was, then all human history pales in significance to the events of his life and death, and, logically, their devotion to his Church and Gospel should supersede all other earthly loyalties."

The Presidential neck stiffened. "And if we remain unconvinced?"

Peter was ready. "General, *you* are a great man. But Jesus Christ— regardless of how much you and Gandhi like him—was not."

Laughing, the General leaned back in his chair, flinched from the pain of moving, then, with his free hand, patted the bump on his head.

Peter saw that he was tired of talking. Or, more accurately, of listening. But there was something else. The priest had some house-keeping of his own to do.

"Jim, can I say one last thing?"

His captive nodded patiently.

"It may sound like I'm telling you to shape up," he confessed, "but, in reality, I'm the one who has to change. For the past five years, I've been at war with God, too. If I *am* guilty of sedition, it's toward him. Ever since my last conviction I've felt angry and abandoned. Believe it or not, I'm still reconciling with him myself. By this talk, you've helped me more than I could have ever helped you."

"You can't be serious!"

"I am. For the first time in years, I'm feeling centered again." He clasped his manacled hands prayerfully, shook them for emphasis, and with his brown eyes gleaming, said, "Don't you see? We're both prodigals who long to eat the swine husks, but still cling to the vanity that by sheer force of will—and without God's grace— we can attain perfection. Or redemption. But a thistle might just as easily turn itself into a fig. Without Christ, there is no perfection or redemption, let alone eternal life, no matter how intelligent or free we are. The bottom line is that we either trust God or ourselves. There's no middle ground. It reminds me of the warning from Scripture: 'A man of two minds is unstable in his ways.'"

This time it was Freeman who got punched in the gut. That was the verse he quoted when, after leaving home, he returned the Bible that the Bishop gave him as a boy.

He found himself standing on the bridge spanning the shores of faith and doubt that he crossed as a young man. And, now, though he yearned for life beyond the grave—to see his loved ones again and, possibly, the face of God—he couldn't cross back.

Not yet.

To do so required that he repent and, although he may have surrendered his sword, his heart remained in its scabbard. He waffled in choosing between love and justice. So, instead of re-crossing the bridge, like the ones over the Delaware, he simply occupied it.

The priest sensed correctly that the thought of surrender was repugnant to Freeman, so he tried softening the blow. Borrowing from Chesty Puller's combative assessment at the Chosin Reservoir, he urged, "Don't look at this as a retreat, Jim. Think of it as attacking in a different direction."

Freeman's bemused expression lasted only a second or two. The door swung open and one of the guards scowled, "Let's go, General. The boss wants to see you."

Sixty-Two

Halfway through Angela DeKalb's second reading of the Marynkova journal, Sonny Collier returned. Like the man who delivered the journal, he entered through the door on the far side of the cafeteria, accompanied by a detachment of ten men from his Omega force. By his graceful bearing, and the deference accorded to him, she recognized him immediately, even with his headgear in place.

"Have you had time to read it?" he asked.

"Yes, twice," she replied. "Most interesting. The initials: J-A-F? You say it's unclear?"

Collier dismissed the three regulars who were guarding her. Then, with his bodyguard standing by, he spoke openly, as if no one else was present. "That's what threw me. It's the only mention Sonya made of him. I researched the newspapers from the period. At the time, there weren't many 'tall, dark, and handsome' soldiers working on Capitol Hill with those initials. In fact, I could only find one." He asked nonchalantly, "Would you like to meet him?"

She was so surprised that before she could respond, Collier gave a signal to his men. There was some commotion at the other end of the room.

Presently, a man with his arm bound up in a sling was led through the door. As the escort made its way across the room, Angela noticed that his headgear was reversed and placed haphazardly atop his head, as if to blindfold him. As a result, he looked quite tall. His gait was wobbly. He wore the same protective armor as everyone else but no green armband. The Omegas guided him over to a chair not fifteen feet away. Then Collier ordered them to cover the exits and moved over to the man's side.

"Let me come straight to the point, Angela." There was a measure of affectation in his tone. "Like I said, once I came into possession of Sonya's journal, I started researching the record to find our father— the so-called *King of Hearts*. Needless to say, his identity came as cruel joke. I don't suppose it will be any less traumatic for you than it was for me, so brace yourself."

As he pulled the hood off, he announced, "I give you the bow that fired the arrow!"

Angela's reaction to seeing Jim Freeman was not immediate. Initially, she was too stunned. But when it came, it was violent. The dam holding her resentment over the train of abuses she had suffered since leaving Washington finally broke. She rose swiftly, quivering with rage, and pounced on the old man like a lioness on a tethered goat.

The force of her attack overturned the chair, knocking the General ass-over-teakettle. She rode him down to the floor, swatting, scratching, and clawing at his face. Freeman tried to defend himself, but with one arm bound tightly in the sling, he could only grab her neck and hold tight. That turned her insensate.

According to the Bard, "the hands obey the blood" and hers grabbed hold of Freeman's head. With bestial instinct, she tried dashing it against the floor. But he arched his back to prevent it. So, instead, she aimed her taloned thumbs at the corners of his eyes and drove them mercilessly downward with all her strength, mindless of the consequences. Freeman screamed, let go of her neck, and swung wildly at her with his free arm and fist.

Collier and the fast-converging Omegas finally pulled her off him. As they did, she kicked at him, landing a glancing shot that, had it connected, might have broken his jaw. The Omegas wrestled her to the floor, pinning her there. The old soldier, his eyes flowing with blood, turned on his side and curled up in a ball, wreathing and groaning in a crimson puddle.

Collier went to his side. Pointing at two of the bigger guards, he barked, "Adams! Miller! Get him upstairs!"

The two troopers rolled Freeman onto his back. Since his legs were still tucked under his chin, it allowed them to slip their arms behind his back and under his thighs in a seat carry.

"Take him to Slocum," ordered Collier, referring to the company doctor.

The two men lifted Freeman and headed slowly toward the back door.

All eyes now turned to the Attorney General, who lay on the floor immobilized by the Omegas. She was panting heavily, her eyes glowing like charcoal.

"Let her up," Collier demanded.

Immediately, the men peeled off. She sat up, legs outstretched, still panting, with her head buried in her chin. She started to run her hands through her hair but, noticing how bloody they were, instead let them fall to her side, palms up. An Omega would later recall: "She looked like a homicidal rag-doll."

Collier pulled a chair over. When she was seated, he looked around and said, "All right, everyone. Out!" Within seconds, brother and sister were alone.

Angela's passion cooled faster than aluminum. She sat there silently for a minute, then spotted the doors leading into the kitchen.

Showing her hands, she asked, "Would you mind?"

"No. By all means," allowed Sonny.

Soon they were both standing over a stainless steel sink where Angela slowly, methodically, scrubbed her hands. The pressure was weak and the water was tepid, but the flow from the building's recycling system was adequate to the task. When she finished with her hands, she patted her face with water.

Sonny grabbed a few dishtowels off a shelf and handed them to her.

It was obvious from her look that she was still very agitated but not distraught. Her breathing slowed. As she tended to her hair, she gradually recovered her gritty demeanor.

Casting a glare at Collier, she hissed, "Let him *smell* his way back to Philadelphia."

Sonny laughed uneasily, saying, "I can't say I didn't expect some reaction, but you sure fooled me. I didn't think you'd maim him!"

Through clenched teeth, she answered, "No, I think you got exactly what you wanted. Otherwise, you wouldn't have orchestrated the whole thing the way you did. You might've had the decency to warn me."

Her brother took a step back, insisting, "I told you to brace yourself! To tell the truth, I really wasn't totally sure that he was the soldier in Sonya's journal." With a snort, he said, "I am now, though."

"Why all the stagecraft then—the bit about the bow and arrow?"

"All right, I admit. That was a little hokey. But your reaction was, shall I say, out of character." Weighing the possible consequences of her actions, he injected, "I just hope he's okay."

"I don't!" she cried defiantly, eyes flashing. "I hope he's dead." Then, contemptuously, she asked, "Are there any *more* surprises?"

The question, together with her poisonous stare, made Sonny uncomfortable.

"As a matter of fact, there is one," he admitted, "but I'm not sure this is either the time or the place."

"What is it?" she demanded, closing with him.

"Angela, it can wait."

"No!" she snapped, scissoring her arms in a gesture of finality. "No more games. I want to know *now*."

Sonny combed nervously through his hair, then folded his hands against his chest to feign composure as he spoke. "Remember this afternoon when I told you that things were going well—that it was an embarrassment of riches?"

She nodded affirmatively, her eyes closing slightly.

"Well, this morning, not long after we captured Freeman, a few of my men were mopping up after a fight near the cathedral in Newark. One of them found a guy hiding in the bushes outside. Any other time, they might have shot him, but he fit the description of someone I told them to look for."

Angela stared at him.

"When questioned, he identified himself as Peter Bernard."

This time, Angela's reaction was entirely different. She stepped back, put her hands atop her head and sighed, "Well, I'll be damned. Where is he?"

"Here. Upstairs."

She stood there smiling for a few seconds, then Sonny said, "I thought you might be pleased. Call it a gift from brother to sister."

As she wrestled with that thought, he revealed, "You know, ever since that day in Denver, I've lived for this moment. That nigger ruined me. Now, like Ahab astride his whale, I have him. It looks like we're both about to see the triumph of justice."

Angela replied, "When can I see him?"

"Whoa!" he protested. "After what you just did? No way. I'll be handling this prosecution."

"How so?"

"I haven't decided, yet. Just keep your hands off him. He's mine. I've waited twenty years for this moment, and I won't be denied my claim because you can't restrain yourself."

He paced a little with his head down, looked up with a philosophical squint, saying, "It's all so poetic, isn't it?"

"What?"

"Jim Freeman. The Carrolite. You and I. Don't you see what an ethereal confluence this is?"

But Angela wanted no part of it. With second thoughts over the mauling she gave the General setting in, she pleaded, "You have things the way you want them, now. What's the point of keeping me here? I'm no use to you. If you really cared about me, you'd let me go."

"In time," her brother said, reassuringly. "But for now, I have work to do. We'll be moving across the river soon. You'll go in advance of me and my men. In the meantime, I wish you'd rethink your decision. I *do* want you to join me. I have big plans for us."

Angela checked him. "I could never be party to this nonsense. I'd as soon join up with the Pope."

"You feel no affinity to me at all? No sense of kinship?"

"None. I wish I'd never met you." Pointing to the leather-bound journal that lay open on the table in the cafeteria, she added, "Or learned of your awful secret." Shaking her head slowly, she said, "It may not bother you that your existence is the result of an acid hatch, but it does me. I have nothing but contempt for you—and for the two reckless fools who gave us life. If my reaction to learning Freeman's identity hasn't convinced you of that, then I don't know what will."

Her brother just shrugged and led her out of the kitchen. As they walked, he said, "Despite what you're feeling, you'd do well to reconsider. It's not like you have a lot of options."

"What do you mean?"

On the floor, near the giant smear of blood, lay his headpiece. He picked it up and said with a grin, "Need I remind you that one of my most trusted agents is dead—a man who worked for you?"

"That can all be explained."

"No matter. Life, as you know it, is over. You'll spend the rest of your days under a cloud of suspicion. There might even be speculation that the kidnapping was staged to cover your involvement in Addison's death."

"But I didn't kill him!"

"What does that matter?" he countered, leaning toward her. "You make unfounded accusations every day. And, what's more, unless you embrace your fate, from this day forward you'll walk the earth a freak of nature."

"What do you mean? A freak of nature? Is that what you think?"

"No. I'm good with it. I'm just telling you what the great unwashed will think."

Angela recoiled. He might just as easily have threatened her with a baseball bat.

"Although I wouldn't spend much time worrying about it," he allowed, brushing off his headpiece. "Once word gets out what you did to Jim Freeman, no one's gonna give a rat what happened to Stew Addison."

* * * * *

About ten feet from where this exchange took place, there was a heating duct that opened to both the cafeteria and the kitchen and connected to vents on the upper floors, one of which was in the conference room directly above them.

An ear was glued to that vent. It belonged to Collier's black whale. And he had heard it all.

The first voice he heard was clearly that of the man who played the starring role in his nightmares, the one who would soon render judgment on him.

It took him a little longer to distinguish the second but only because of the absurdity of hearing it in this setting. It was that of the Attorney General. He never met DeKalb personally, but, during his trial for sedition, he must have listened to her handicapping the proceedings on the news a dozen times. Had his mother been speaking, the sound of her voice would be no less discernable. Nevertheless, when her name was eventually spoken, it burned through him like a shard of hot metal.

He listened as she pummeled the King of Hearts; bristled at the word nigger; frowned at Collier's allusion to an ethereal confluence; and learned of their "awful secret." And, what's more, he knew Jim Freeman's middle initial.

However, when the vent grew quiet, whether it was from dread, fatigue, hunger, thirst, radiation poisoning, or a combination thereof, he blacked out.

Sixty-Three

On the heels of the slaughter in Branch Brook Park, the 301st Infantry was transformed, once again, into an engine of war. Now, the momentum of these sullied and angry men was being impelled by the same lust for vengeance that was consuming the rest of the country. As a consequence, Sonny Collier's "embarrassment of riches" was fast becoming a simple embarrassment. While he and DeKalb were giving James Freeman his comeuppance in the basement of the Baldwin Towers, Travis Hawkins' division had one company of Greenshirts retreating pell-mell through North Bergen and a hundred more trapped at LaGuardia Airport—one of the planned rallying points for the rebels. But neither of these actions compared with the pasting that was being administered to Collier's largest formation in Fort Lee. Hawkins' Third Battalion was in the process of annihilating the unit holding the approaches to the George Washington Bridge. In this action alone, 450 of Collier's men had already been killed or captured.

Collier learned of these reversals when he returned to his nerve center on the third floor. His second-in-command, a former Ranger named Tully, informed him of the situation. "Dickson's men are surrounded, and we're losing badly in Ft. Lee." Then, he said what no one else dared. Turning from the sit board, he looked at Collier intently and declared, "I hope we're done with all the shenanigans, Colonel."

Collier quickly scanned the room. The silent faces of his staff were as reproachful as Tully's. As they say, word travels fast. All of them knew what happened down in the cafeteria. Most were retired military and, although they were true believers in the Pathfinder mission, nothing justified the harrowing of their former Commander-in-Chief. Tully obviously spoke for all of them.

So Collier greatly tempered his response. He leaned down next to his second-in-command and seethed loud enough for all to hear, "And I hope you haven't forgotten the cost of insubordination, Joseph."

His menacing tone may have quelled the mutiny, but it didn't change how the men felt. Most of them honestly considered themselves to be freedom fighters, not the modern equivalent of the Brownshirts, and, as such, they had no more stomach for torture and murder than the men who dumped the tea in Boston Harbor.

Angela had accompanied Sonny upstairs. She was standing off to the side when Tully admonished him. As a result, she saw first-hand the reaction to her deed.

Sonny was right: even these brutes are put off by what I did. How will the rest of the country react? All hope for a return to her former life was fading.

A transmission came in from LaGuardia. *"We can't hold. We're outnumbered and surrounded. Elkins is dead. Fournier wounded. The half the company is gone. We have no course but to surrender."*

"No!" cried Collier. "Shuler will be there within the hour. Just hunker down."

Tully broke in. "Sir, Shuler's headed for Zebra." Zebra was the code word for Grand Central, another rallying point. "As soon as he got across the bridge, he turned south. There's no way he can get to LaGuardia in time."

Sonny hollered, "I'm not asking—" He straightened up, took a quick look at the blinking sit board and concluded: *He's right.* The battle was lost. But then, it was never a battle he thought he could win.

* * * * *

Two days prior to the launch of Collier's insurgency and the morning before his troops ambushed the convoy on the Hutchinson River Parkway, three cargo vans carrying a detachment of fifty-six Greenshirts pulled into a service road leading from Fifth Avenue, through Central Park, to the rear of the Metropolitan Museum of Art. Making no effort to quiet or conceal their movements, these fifty men quickly gained entry to the building using plastic explosives and then proceeded to ransack it.

With nothing and no one to stop them, such masterpieces as Van Gogh's *Starry Night*, Cezanne's *The Bather*, Manet's *Boating*, and *The Death of Socrates* fell to them. So did many priceless antiquities like the ivory *Seated Ganesha* of Hindu and the *Adam and Eve* cylinder seal from Mesopotamia, both on loan from the British Museum. The heist was widely attributed to underworld activity by the police with the loss put at one hundred billion. Within hours, the entire haul was loaded on high-speed surface runners and headed for the Caribbean, where the black market for such rarities in the Dutch Antilles and Venezuela was robust.

Actually, Collier's whole insurgency was a feint, a smokescreen designed to cover his real objective, which had little to do with re-turning America to its former glory. While a portion of his troops kept the government's forces occupied, the rest were stripping New York of all the loot they could plunder.

It was a plan he had developed over the past two years. Originally, Washington was the mark. Specifically, the Library of Congress and the National Archives. With the bombing, however, New York became the logical target. It had a greater store of wealth than the Capitol, and it would avert the visceral backlash that would come from stealing things like Gutenberg Bible or the Declaration of Independence. So the original plan was modified. The looting began well in advance of the fighting, and for the last three days, it never stopped.

It was a wildly successful gambit. In addition to the bounty stolen from the Met, rare editions of books like *Pilgrim's Progress* and *Leaves of Grass* were "checked out" of the New York Public Library. Even a collection of rare coins from the California Gold Rush recovered from the sunken *Central America* were lifted from a display in the visitor's section of the Federal Reserve Bank; the bullion in the vaults below proved unassailable.

So, in truth, it was not Collier's intent to take and hold territory, or win a military victory. As he told his sister, his ultimate goal was to seize power, not territory—and power doesn't come cheap.

It didn't matter that his crime would turn many against him, either. He was not looking to be president. He once said, "I want to own the Oval Office, not occupy it!" And, at the going rate of the average politician, the robbery might buy him a majority stake.

It was crucial, however, that he elude capture, for reasons other than the obvious. The Pathfinder Party's access to funds would dry up overnight if its most generous donors were outed as a result of Collier's arrest or indictment. So, his ultimate destination was the island of Bimini, which had recently repealed its extradition laws. And, if all went well, he would be there by morning.

But, for now, the race was on to Point Zebra. There, Collier's legions would split up into small groups and beat it out of the city through the bullet lines emanating from Grand Central Terminal, melting back into the civilian population.

* * * * *

All along, Collier planned to quit the Cordon after the attack in Branch Brook Park. He dragged his feet, though, distracted by the mountain of spoil and the sound of the guns. But the losses in Ft. Lee finally convinced him to pull back. In the past few hours, he had lost the bulk of his command. Reduced to the contingent in Weehawken—primarily, his Omega force—and another handful of Greenshirts stationed at the Williamsburg Bridge, he came to the same realization as Tully. It was futile to continue fighting.

"It's time," he muttered.

He shook his head and, without looking at anyone directly, said, "Tell the men to fall back. Except for the Omegas. I want them here with me. We'll act as a rearguard."

Turning to Tully, he added, "You take the first group over. If we haven't joined up with you in two hours, disperse the men."

"What about the prisoners?" Other than their own survival, this was the most pressing question to Collier's staff.

After a moment of deliberation, Collier said, "Take the General and Ms. DeKalb with you. Leave the priest to me."

This decision was met by muted stares. Had he used the word *with* instead of *to* the reaction may have been different. As it was, his staff displayed the same revulsion to this decision as they did to Collier's cafeteria court.

Although the average rebel could not care less what happened to Collier's three captives, the same wasn't true of the men closest to him. Responsibility for the robberies, together with the slaughters of the two previous mornings and the blinding of General Freeman, was sure to fall hardest on them. Now Collier was angling for an opportunity to close out his vendetta against the Black Whale, and they were feeling the rope.

However, sensing the discontent, Collier again moved to defuse it. He wanted desperately to settle his score with the priest, but he also knew that the deteriorating situation to the north and east required his full attention.

So he conceded, "On second thought, take the priest with you." Then, pointing to his sister, he warned, "But keep him away him from her."

Everyone in the room glanced scornfully at Angela. The growing hostility toward Sonny was a mere tantrum compared to the disdain they had for her. For this reason, when Tully's advance party took her in tow, she was unusually docile.

Sixty-Four

Sunday, July 10 (6:24 P.M. EDT)
The White House

"So it's just a big smash-and-grab?"

The President scanned his advisors incredulously.

"That's what the prisoners are saying." The respondent was Defense Secretary Elliot Thompson.

Unlike the day after the bombing, at this extemporaneous meeting of the Cabinet, all were present, except for Angela DeKalb. Admiral Towne and Avery Milliken were also there.

"What else are they saying?"

"That Collier won't fight it out. His militia will disband once the pillage is complete."

"What's the latest on Angela?"

Steve Nunn answered. "Nothing new to report, sir. However, given the details surrounding her abduction, it now appears certain that security at the Justice Department and the DPS has been compromised."

Nunn was extremely nervous, this being only the second time he had been asked to join a Cabinet session. Only two hours before Gonzales appointed him acting AG. He cleared his throat.

"The missing agent—a man named Dolan—had extensive communications in the past two days with a known Pathfinder operative."

A few of the President's aides looked bewildered.

He continued, "We became suspicious after the abduction and began tracing his phone calls. At your suggestion, Mr. President, we also traced any he might have made to Mr. Addison. As it turned out, they traded calls yesterday afternoon. So it may be that Addison was on Collier's payroll, too."

The President looked solemnly around the table. "My guess is," he said, "that our problems with security aren't unique to Justice."

His eyes bounced between the Defense Secretary and the Chairman of the Joint Chiefs as he said it.

These two exchanged glances and Thompson replied, "Mr. President, if you're referring to Defense, I can assure you, our clearance procedures are impeccable."

"Is that so? Then why is it that Collier seems to be reading our mail? I can't help but think that he knows about it every time a toilet flushes over in Alexandria."

While Thompson and Towne fumed, the President decided to test an observation by Boomer Holman that Collier's press release was a red herring designed to throw the authorities off his scent. He asked Nunn, "How do you read Collier's allegation that Peter Bernard confessed to his involvement and implicated the Church in the bombing?"

The acting AG replied, "I don't believe it, Mr. President. Collier's indictment of Bernard only makes us more suspicious of Collier."

Sixty-Five

Sunday, July 10 (6:25 P.M. EDT)
The Baldwin Towers, Level B2, Weehawken, N. J.

Peter's slumber lasted only a few minutes. When he awoke, though, it felt like it lasted ten hours. He was strangely refreshed. With his hands still tied in front, he curled up on his side in a jack-knife position and inclined slightly forward with his head planted on the carpet like a stabilizer. Before long, he fixated on the word Collier used to describe him, drinking in every ounce of gall it gives rise to. Like a street fighter passing a switchblade from hand to hand at the outset of a rumble, he turned the word over in his mind. His anger made him think the unthinkable.

What if I get Collier before he gets me? What've I got to lose? Either he'll kill me or his men will.

He followed this vein for a while, but, in the end, it was useless.

I could no more kill a man than raise him from the dead! Not even Collier. No matter how many times he calls me a nigger. Devoted as he was to the precepts of his faith, the big Jesuit was vexed even by the thought of it.

So, closing his eyes, he prayed. *Please, God, help me. I'm afraid. I know if I weaken now, I'll only dishonor you, myself, and the Church. If it's your will that I die today, please send your Spirit to strengthen me. I, alone, am too weak. I know you won't forsake me and I ask only for the courage not to forsake you, as I have so many times before. I beg forgiveness for my sins and place my trust in the only weapon left to me now—your good grace.*

And, with that, his mental preparations were complete. In that instant, had Sonny Collier burst into the room and put a bullet in his head, he would have been grateful. That's because he knew he was destined for trial before he heard the angels sing. He could only imagine the shape of the cross, the length of the nails and the depth of the lance, but he knew for certain his Pilate and Caiaphas.

Then he remembered something else he heard. Collier's bigotry so distracted him that he never stopped to reflect on DeKalb's comment: *It may not bother you that your existence is the product of an acid hatch, but it does me.*

It was a stunning revelation.

Children so born were commonly referred to as *dollies* or *pollies*. These epithets derived from a pair of sheep that were cloned at the end of the previous century. To be the product of an acid hatch was to be cursed. It was the modern equivalent of leprosy. These creations were generally subjected to ridicule and, often, ostracism. To refer to anyone as such was slanderous—the moral equivalent of calling them a nigger.

But DeKalb's admission had implications of a different sort. Ominous implications. Not only for Peter but for all humanity. And that consumed his thinking right up until the guards came to get him.

Sixty-Six

"**O**w!"

"Hold still, General."

Collier's doctor, Slocum, was treating Freeman's injuries. The orb of the left eye was punctured and still oozing a bloody, yellow custard. The right was partially lacerated. And his collarbone, once cracked, was now broken. An orthopedic surgeon in private life, Slocum reset Freeman's shoulder and tightened his sling. But, given the conditions, beyond cleaning them, applying a compress, and shooting him full of Nerveblock, there wasn't much he could do for his eyes. He didn't even have any antibiotics left.

Freeman was anything but stoic while the doctor worked on him, moaning and yelping throughout. When Slocum reset his collarbone, he let out a holler that Peter Bernard heard down the hall.

"Please, doc . . . anything for the pain," the old soldier cried, prostrate on the couch where Adams and Miller had laid him down. When the Nerveblock finally kicked in, he quieted down. Then the soldiers came to take him away.

Presently, he was reunited with the priest. Peter saw the massive bandage across his eyes and became alarmed.

"Are you all right, General?"

Before Freeman could answer though, one of the guards intoned, "That's enough, padre. It ain't a church social. We got a long hike ahead of us and we need to move fast. So keep your mouth shut—both of you."

Immediately, they were separated. Climbing the stairs to the ground floor, they joined up with a larger squad of soldiers in the lobby and exited the building. Tully's main detachment, escorting Attorney General DeKalb had gone ahead.

It was still daylight, but the iron clouds and slanting rain hastened the dusk. The fresh but blustery air, seasoned by the sea, fortified them. But this restorative was short-lived.

They were led down from the Weehawken cliffs along a 360-degree entrance ramp and into the south tube of the Obama Tunnel. There, they proceeded east on the elevated catwalk in single file. The smell was rank and seemed to issue from a crack in the ceiling of the Abyss. As they proceeded, the beams of the flashlights caromed wildly from the roof to the floor, revealing numerous dead and decomposed bodies scattered along the pavement. The going was slow and, halfway across, the General faltered.

"Keep moving!" shouted one of the guards.

"I can't," he mumbled. Not only had his injuries depleted him. The Nerveblock, a combination painkiller and muscle-relaxer, neutralized the benefit of the endorphin battery planted in his neck. The General was having problems standing, let alone walking. By the time Peter came up, he was winded and clinging tightly to the rail. His bandaged head hung limply over the side. Several Greenshirts stood snickering at his infirmities.

Since the priest was the only man among them who was of equal size to Freeman, he was pressed into service as a crutch. With the nylon ties removed from his wrists, he stooped down, wrapped the old man's good arm around his neck, and said, "*C'mon*, General."

On hearing Bernard's voice, Freeman labored to right himself. A grimacing smile passed his lips. "Lead the way, my man," he rejoined firmly but without his usual bravado.

Carefully, the priest shifted the weight of the stumbling icon onto himself and guided him forward. The guards demanded they hurry and prodded them with their weapons. Nonetheless, Peter stubbornly set a pace his charge could handle, which, at the start, was not much faster than a crawl.

It took almost half an hour before they emerged on the Manhattan side. There, though chilled by the rain, the air smelled almost as bad as down in the tunnel. Blackened corpses were scattered everywhere. The bulk of the escort was now far ahead of them, and Peter was virtually carrying the old man.

As they ascended the exit ramp, he tripped on the flap of his disintegrating sneakers and fell. Going down, he let go of the General, but the old man fell on top of him, and, although he landed on his good shoulder, he let out a holler. The weight of his fall knocked the wind out of the priest.

Seeing that both prisoners were drained, the squad leader ordered a halt. He called out, "We'll rest here a minute."

The two prisoners lay down on the pavement in the driving rain, head-to-head. Although both were sick and wounded and cold, they benefitted greatly from the respite. The pain from Freeman's injuries was returning. But he was also less woozy.

On recovering his wind, Peter was the first to speak.

"What happened when they took you downstairs?" he whispered, without looking at his afflicted companion.

"She attacked me—blinded me!" bawled Freeman softly.

"DeKalb?"

"Yeah."

"Why?"

"I don't know!" Freeman groaned. But it was a lie, and after thinking about it, he came clean.

"Oh . . . what the hell," he said. "The other night . . . no, I guess it was last night!" He stopped momentarily to marvel at all that had transpired since. Resuming, he said, "I treated her badly. I mean, we had sex. We did it. No, *I did it*, against her will."

Peter wasn't startled, but neither did he quite grasp the significance of it. Certainly, a woman so scorned would be justified to seek retribution for such an offense. But to put out a man's eyes?

He thought: *DeKalb's no garden flower. If the rumors are true, she's a regular Thais of Athens. So why did she—*

Then it hit him.

He asked, "Jim, are Collier and DeKalb related?"

It surprised the old man that Peter knew some of the details of what happened, but he was still trying to regain his wits. "Until today, I didn't think so," he said, "but before she attacked me, Collier called me their father."

"When you were young, did you ever know a woman named Sonya?"

The old man turned his head toward the priest even though he couldn't see him. He heard the name mentioned, too. Weakly, through a very sore jaw, he replied, "Why do you ask?"

Peter told him about the air duct. "So, when they took you downstairs, I heard everything that happened. Well, most of it, anyway. Just before DeKalb attacked you, Collier spoke of a woman named Sonya. I gathered that she was their mother and that she had a lover, a tall soldier."

And with that, the bow that fired the arrow came unstrung.

"Oh, my God," Freeman bawled. "That's what he's talking about!" Quickly recalling his affair with the Russian, he wailed, "The little wench must have kept a record of our affair." Then he raised his free hand as if to shield his eyes from a bright light.

"Then you *are* the soldier they're referring to?"

The old man shook his head in confusion. "How do I know?"

"Did you know the woman? I mean, did you *know* the woman?"

Freeman was still trying to picture her. He sniffed hard, which led Peter to think he was sobbing.

"I knew *a* woman named Sonya a long time ago. In my sporting days. Her name was Sonya Mar . . . Marynkova. She was a Russian émigré. A geneticist. We had a go. But it was over before it got started.

She really spooked me with all her talk about transhumanism and stuff like that. She asked me to participate in an experiment . . . to combine our DNA. At first, I played along. Hell, I was just trying to get some squack. But once I realized she was serious—and that her father was ex-KGB—I cut it off." Adamantly, he added, "But who's to say that's what they're referring to?"

Then the priest turned the key that unlocked the mystery.

"General," he said, "what's your middle name?"

"My middle name? Why? Americus." Then, he made an attempt to explain, as anyone saddled with an unusual name might. "My mother was from Americus, Georgia. She told me that when she was carrying me she dreamed I was destined for greatness, so she gave me that name." He paused and said, "If she could only see me now."

But, as soon as he said *Americus*, the explanation was lost on Peter. Now the motivation for Collier's theatrics and DeKalb's attack was clear. It didn't matter if it was a coincidence that Freeman's initials were the same as the mysterious JAF, or if he really was one of the two reckless fools who gave them life—*they* thought he was.

Noticing that the leader of the detachment was beginning to muster the men, he leaned into Freeman's ear and whispered, "We're getting ready to go, General, so I need to talk fast. I'm quite certain that we're talking about the same Sonya here. At first, I thought the soldier Collier mentioned was a man named Jeff. But you just solved the riddle. *They were referring to your initials.* Right or wrong, they're convinced that this woman went forward with her experiment and that they were conceived in an acid hatch. What's more, they think you're *their* father. That explains why DeKalb attacked you so—"

That was as far as he got. The hooded squad leader came over and with his weapon leveled at them, said, "Let's get going, you two." Then, he bent over and asked politely, "Or would you rather wait for the Colonel to come up?"

Sixty-Seven

Turning onto Fifth Avenue, Angela DeKalb was heartened to see the venerable stone lions of Patience and Fortitude still guarding the entrance to the library. Here, only weeks before, she was the keynote speaker at a dinner sponsored by the Humanist Guild. It was held to rededicate Room 315 on the upper floor after a two-year restoration project. She recalled the title of her address that evening: *Modern Virtue and the New Hyperboreans.*

The giant bronze doors leading to Astor Hall were blown off. Climbing the steps, she asked one of the men escorting her, "Would you be so kind as to take me upstairs? I'd like to look around."

Nervously, he responded, "Ma'am, I'm not really familiar with the place."

"I know the way," she assured him. "Please? It will only take a minute."

The last thing this trooper wanted to do was waste time gratifying her curiosity when he should have been hightailing it out to Long Island. But since Tully's orders were to stay put until he arrived, the soldier decided to humor her. Together with three other men, they climbed the stairway at the north end of the building and entered a hall spanning almost two city blocks called the Rose Reading Room.

The damage to this great cathedral of learning was severe. Their flashlights were immediately drawn to the lofty ceiling, to the paintings of serene blue skies and scudding red clouds in the coffers.

There, the rain was pouring through a hole at least thirty feet in diameter.

Within seconds, they pieced together what had happened. A steel structure—it looked like a radio tower—had blown through the roof, landed in the aisle running the length of the room, careened into the rows of oak tables running its flanks and stacked a small mountain of them against the shelving that lined the outer wall.

Most of the massive chandeliers that hung so majestically from the wood-paneled ceiling on the evening of the re-dedication now sprawled atop the tables or lay shattered on the ground. A half-dozen of these crystal titans still dangled haphazardly from their chains like tormented Prometheans. Green-shaded bronze lamps, those featured in a hundred movies, were strewn about. The great arches of glass that for a century and a half bathed in sunshine the investigations of so many readers, writers, and scholars were blown out, giving unchecked passage to the wind and rain. Everything was saturated. Puddles abounded, and, as in the street, everything was encrusted with glass and a grey, slimy grit.

The musty smell of wet paper and spine glue permeated the filters of Angela's protective headgear. The vision system in it was faulty, however. So, aggravated by the inability to see clearly, and convinced by the reading on her forearm dosimeter that it was safe to do so, Angela removed it. She sat quietly for a few minutes, intermittently contemplating the damage to the building and to her career.

The events of the past twenty-four hours had turned her life on end. *There'll be no returning to the status quo*, she surmised. Like the glass that glittered in the sweep of the lights, her dreams were shattered. The immediate question was whether to join with Sonny Collier for a few days or try to escape.

But where? To what? Or whom? I'm finished, no matter which option I chose.

Her thoughts turned to Jim Freeman. Since hearing from Sonny that the old bastard would lose an eye, she was seized by regret. But it wasn't for him. With all the new ocular regeneration technologies, she assumed his blindness was temporary. Her lament stemmed from the realization that the one person who might have been willing to protect her from the damage done by Collier would have been Freeman.

Without him, I wouldn't be where I am—literally!

Less than twenty-four hours ago, she was pinned beneath this man whose genes she shared, fighting to ward off his savage thrusts. She cursed the decision to use her body to win his advocacy. The smell of the oil she used to pleasure him still clung to her like the stench of vomit. *What will people say when they find out that their vaunted hero raped his own daughter?* When she remembered how she tried to squeeze a final commitment out of him with the naughty little girl routine, the same anger she felt on seeing him in the cafeteria came rushing back. But this time, she mastered it.

Ever the opportunist, she calculated that Freeman might still be willing to overlook the mauling she gave him. *All I need to do is convince him that, on learning of my paternity, the memory of our incestuous interludes overwhelmed me.* Only her motive in asking for his forgiveness needed to be disguised, not her sincere desire to have it. She mused: *As soon as the truth about our sordid little family becomes known, he'll have no choice but to give it, either. Other than murder, the only taboos left in this world are rape and incest, a double-bogey that's sure to get his attention. The thought of his legacy being tarnished any further will force him to protect me. By virtue of his forbidden love, he'll be under my thumb from this day forward.*

That brought a smile to her face.

Then she remembered the recording.

That's the joker. My only hope is to find it.

Sixty-Eight

Sunday, July 10 (7:44 P.M. EDT)
Near the Port Authority Bus Terminal, New York City

Within minutes of resuming their march, Collier's two other captives turned east onto 42nd Street. Peter was still helping Freeman, who, though regaining strength, was still addled by his blindness. This continued to limit the pace of the detail. So did the mud and wreckage. And the rotting dead. On some blocks, the walkways beneath construction scaffolding provided clear passage, when they were unencumbered by bodies.

Although all the soldiers were angered over their slow pace, no reprisals were taken against the captives. They were even permitted to converse. Between stops and starts and turns, the priest guided the former President down the street while they shared what they knew about the "awful secret."

"You said they were hatched," said Freeman. "That's what that crazy Russian was into—creative eugenics. Like I said, her goal was to create a *transhuman*. I thought she was just goofy. I was too young to see the harm in it. She was a sexual dynamo." With that, he made the inevitable comparison between mother and daughter and set his mind to reeling. He grew silent.

They passed the oldest structure on 42nd Street, the venerable Church of the Holy Cross, then crossed Broadway. Surveying the damage, Peter exclaimed softly, "Holy cow!"

The massive signs on the buildings in Times Square looked as if they had been hit by a meteor shower. Autos were scattered like cordwood. A jumble of charred bodies, strewn wildly about like toys in a child's room, lay before them. But for the downpour, he might have fainted from the smell.

In an attempt to block out the horror, he recalled how his aunt and uncle brought him here when he was in high school to see *The Phantom of the Opera*: the brilliant displays of color and light that thrilled him; the bustle and rhythm of the passing crowds that frightened him; how the car-horns blared and the taxis wove in and out of traffic; and the sweet, alluring carnival smell that cut through the carbon monoxide. But then, inescapably, he thought: *How many of these dead were experiencing the same sensations when their lives were so mercilessly cut short?*

Times Square—the great crossroads that welcomed the start of every year and embodied all the virtues and vices of a great nation—now stood frozen, mute, and lifeless. A foreboding gorge in a tangled forest on a desolate isle. A very dark place.

And it was to a very dark place that the thoughts of General Freeman were headed. He was ridden by guilt. The words rape and incest grew in his head like a pair of newly-sprung tumors. His foul behavior during the past week stunk worse than the charnel house smell that polluted his every breath. So did his bad conduct toward those who loved him most during his life. He knew that his long charade was finally over. Bernard was on to him. Now people would know him for what he really was—a fool.

He was less concerned for himself than he was for his daughter, though. His real daughter. How the news of his indiscretions would impact her he could only guess: *Will she come out fighting? Or lose hope?*

He was about to say a prayer—if only to the ghost of his dead wife—when the priest interrupted him.

"General," he said, "I know it pains you to talk about this, but there's something I need to ask. Back when you had this affair, the technology required to hatch a goat was still in its infancy. Is there any chance that Collier and DeKalb were conceived naturally?"

The term *goat* was derived from the word *zygote*. It was another derogatory term for the genetically-engineered.

The old soldier mulled it over, relieved to be thinking about something else. "I don't know how," he replied. "Back then, they had pills we took and, like most guys, I took them. So the chance of that is awfully slim."

"Were you able to talk to her afterwards—this Sonya?"

"No. When I realized that she was serious, I split. I knew I was in over my head. I never heard from her again. When I was overseas, I heard she was killed by some guy whose kid was born with no arms. Until today, I thought I had dodged a bullet." He concluded with a grunt, "Now, I'm not so sure."

The Jesuit replied, "Neither am I, General." Then he added quickly, "But I'm not sure that you've done anything wrong, either."

This heartened the old man. "What do you mean?" he said.

"I don't know. I haven't thought the whole thing through. Just don't be too hard on yourself. Don't give up."

Normally, Freeman would have taken this badly, but, given the circumstances, he simply replied, "I can't! My real daughter is down in Maryland waiting for me. I'm all she has. I could care less about DeKalb, or what happened between us. I didn't know who she was." He added, "Hell, I didn't even know who *I was!*"

That convinced the priest that Freeman had no prior knowledge of his kinship to DeKalb.

"If what you say is true, General, then your guilt is limited to the liberties you took with her, not incest."

A second later, after recalling DeKalb's characterization of Freeman and Marynkova as "two reckless fools," he added, "And for putting yourself in a position to be used like that in the first place."

They were past Broadway before either man spoke again.

Finally, Freeman said, "There's something I have to ask."

"What's that?"

"You're allowed to hear confessions, right? I mean, can anyone make a confession?"

"Certainly."

"Well, is it true what they say? That you have the power to forgive sin?"

"In God's name, as his intermediary."

"Well, I'm not a Catholic, but I'm haunted by the advice Walt Thomas gave me when I was considering a reconciliation with my father. He said, 'It's never too late to ask forgiveness.' But in my case, it was. My father died before I could say I was sorry. Now, I can't get past the feeling that it's happening again, only this time it's me who's going to die."

Peter replied, "Are you asking me to hear your confession?"

"Can you?"

"I can if you've been baptized."

The old man nodded affirmatively. "Will you, then?"

"I'm quite certain that Heaven is listening, Jim."

So, there on the same ground that once served as an earthly redoubt for the legions of darkness, the General unsheathed his heart. And, to his eternal credit, he gave a thorough enumeration of his sins.

As a guide, he used the Commandments, which he memorized as a kid. He told of false idols, churchless Sundays, and swearing like a naval officer. He lamented the disrespect he showed toward his father and how he returned the Bible gifted to him with the "man of two minds" inscription. Much of his vent concerned the mistreatment—his word was "torture"—that he subjected his wife to after she was raped, how he failed to dignify her courage until it was too late and then adulterated their marriage. He told of abandoning his daughter in search of political redemption and personal glory. He even gave a truncated account of the rape he committed the previous evening.

But it was his shooting of the man in Valley Stream that rattled him most. "I simply can't dismiss that as an act of war. Or even good police work. I only did it to assert my authority." Then, he admitted, "For the first time in my life, I can't blame God. It wasn't him who shot that guy. *It was me!*"

The priest listened quietly. When Freeman was finished, he asked, "Are you truly sorry for your sins, and are you resolved, out of a love for God and not the fear of his just punishment, never to commit them again?"

"I am."

In the Catholic rite, the penitential service is a time for healing as well as forgiveness. And in that spirit, as they stumbled along, the priest offered this: "That must have been quite a burden. It strikes me that, no matter how many times I hear confession, there is one constant—the sorrow that sin brings into our lives. It's a reality we must defend against, and the only weapon we have is God's grace. By it, we know the joy of hope that comes from faith. And that's my wish for you, Jim—that, by your faith, you, too, will someday know the joy of hope."

Then, in the shadow of the Grace Building, the priest made the Sign of the Cross and dispensed the absolution: *"God the Father of mercies, through the death and resurrection of his Son, has reconciled the world to himself and sent the Holy Spirit among us for the forgiveness of sins; through the ministry of the Church may God give you pardon and peace, and I absolve you from your sins in the name of the Father, and of the Son, and of the Holy Spirit. Amen."*

Instinctively, Freeman responded, "Amen."

Nothing more was said until they were past Bryant Park, where the escort detail stopped for a moment. While the guards argued over whether or not they should go directly to Grand Central, while he was out of their earshot, Freeman whispered, "Is that it?"

Bernard smiled and whispered back, "God's love and mercy are infinite, Jim. At least, to those who seek it." After thinking about it a little more, he appended, "But there is one thing."

"What's that?"

"Normally, when I hear confession, I give the person a penance. Something they must do to atone for their sins. Usually it's just a few prayers. You know, 'Say one Our Father and three Hail Marys.' But in the case of major offenses, it helps the healing process if a penitent does something to *demonstrate* their remorse."

"What do you suggest?"

"Two things. First—the man you shot. Even though God's forgiven you, you may not forgive yourself. So try to find his family someday and share your grief with them. They'll respect you for it, and it'll help everyone move on with their lives, including you."

Grimly, Freeman replied, "Do you really think I'll get that chance?"

Realizing his gaff, Peter was crestfallen. Sadly, he lowered his head. "No, I guess not. I'm being overly optimistic, aren't I?"

But Freeman was filled with the elation that attends the remission of sin. "Not to worry, Father. If I ever get the chance, I'll do it."

They started moving again, turning the corner onto Fifth Avenue.

Freeman again whispered, "What was the second thing?"

The priest seemed to have forgotten it. "Oh," he replied, half-heartedly, as they climbed the marble steps to the library, "I was going to make you sing the Notre Dame fight song at your next class reunion."

And that's where the old soldier dug in. "Don't you think that's a bit much?" he protested. "I not only have to watch them thrash us year in and year out, now I have to sing their stupid song? Besides, I should think that lugging your sorry ass all over New York is enough penance for any man. Especially a blind one!"

They laughed so loud that the guards warned them to dummy up or suffer the consequences. But, by then, these two former enemies had forged a bond of friendship that only cured in the silence, a bond that drew them closer than two sides of a coin.

For Freeman, the absolution was water to the thirsty. If there was life beyond death, he couldn't say, but he knew the living death that attends a sinful man and how it felt to be reprieved. If he had averted a suicide of eternal proportions by crossing the bridge of reconciliation, then he was sure to be reunited with those he lost. Including God. And that's what he wanted most.

For the first time in years, he prayed. A heartfelt prayer. The kind his father said drove the heavenly hosts into flights of ecstasy. His only disappointment was that he couldn't drop to his knees in ecstasy with them.

At the same time, Father Bernard finally understood his role in "the ethereal confluence." This truly was his Nineveh and the old soul on his shoulder its repentant king. The nausea he felt only hours before was gone. Gone, as well, was all the confusion, resentment, and fear he had suffered for the past week. Nay, the past five years. In the place of all the suffering was a new sense of power and vitality. Truly, it had proven to be redemptive.

At no point in his convoluted journey did he feel destined for anything but humiliation and disgrace. Over the years, despite his continual pursuit of it, there had been very little in the way of happiness for this man. But now he was truly happy. Now his journey made sense. He felt liberated. If, indeed, God had called him to mediate a rapprochement between this great but flawed man and the Court of Heaven, then he was honored and humbled to have done so. That Deacon Carroll and Rita Scanlon, the Armstrongs and Father Luke, had conspired, albeit unwittingly, to assist in that regard also seemed certain, regardless of how absurd. Nor did he fear anymore the likelihood that his long ordeal, which began in Denver and led him to this bombed-out wasteland, would end in death.

By virtue of his Jesuit formation, he had always imagined himself walking, however unsteadily, in the footsteps of Christ. Now, he was sprinting through them.

Sixty-Nine

When they entered Astor Hall, they met Doctor Slocum.

Seeing Freeman's bloody and rain-soaked bandages, he said, "Those need to be changed, General."

The old soldier was led off. Unaware of Collier's directive to keep the prisoners separated, the remaining guards bound Peter's hands and took him upstairs to the third floor.

Angela DeKalb stood up as the priest entered the room. But for the flashlights, an ultra bright lantern on a nearby table provided the only illumination.

With his gray stubble and prison buff, the priest appeared much larger than the man she prosecuted five years before. He looked downright pathetic in his muddy shoes, tattered clothes, and plastic cuffs—not unlike the bondsman's ghost.

On seeing her there, Peter received a mild jolt. But he quickly composed himself. "Madam General," he said politely

"Father Bernard. I've been looking forward to meeting you after all these years. Please." She made a motion for him to be seated.

But, warily, the priest remained standing.

"I must say, when I heard you were captured with General Freeman, I was surprised. All along, we thought you were in South Jersey. Until yesterday, that is. What possessed you to come in this direction?"

Peter shrugged. "I might ask you the same thing."

She got up to turn the lantern down, and when she did Peter stepped back, hinting that he knew about the mugging she gave Freeman.

"Please, Father, have a seat."

Still, he declined.

Angela sat back and inquired, "Tell me, am I mistaken or have we ever met? I mean, formally?"

A crowd of curious Greenshirts was forming.

"No, but during my trial, you sat in the gallery one day. As I remember, it caused quite a stir."

"Yes. I remember it, too." She coughed discreetly. "It was during the closing arguments. You refused to make eye contact with me."

"That's true. I have never despised anyone more than I do you."

"That sounds odd! I mean, coming from a priest."

Her headgear was lying on the table, and she fingered it nervously for a few seconds. "Do you still feel that way?"

"I loathe everything you stand for."

"Now that's not very Christian-like, either," she objected, surprised by his lack of pretense.

"It's not often that a Christian comes face-to-face with a demon."

"*A demon!* Is that what you think of me?" She let go a laugh. "I've been called a lot of things, but *really!* What gave you that idea? Did you have a visitation in your cell one night?"

"You could say that."

"How flattering!" she exclaimed. Playfully, she leaned toward him and said, "Tell me about it."

"You might not like what you hear."

"Please. I insist."

Peter's brown eyes widened, and he became animated. "Well, it was just like in the Bible stories. I was sleeping when, suddenly, a brilliant light filled the room. Before me appeared a serpent. It spoke to me kindly and begged me to follow it. I remember answering,

'It may not bother you that your existence is the product of an acid hatch, but it does me.'"

These words had the intended effect. Angela clouded over. The Jesuit was gooning her. Her previously condescending mood gave way to a mixture of anger and sullenness, but, at first, she didn't reply.

Each was daring the other to raise, but Angela was out of chips. So she called. "How did you find out?"

Peter told her about the vent.

"Then you know about Freeman?"

"Yes."

She shook her head. "Well, I don't see how it'll do you any good. My so-called brother will be along shortly. He seems determined to square his account with you. This will only heighten his sense of urgency."

"If you're trying to scare me, don't bother. From the moment he killed Mrs. Scanlon, I knew what he was all about. But you? You're not so easy to read. But I can see how you made it to the top of the Humanist illuminati and why you worked so tirelessly to silence people that—"

Before he could finish, the guards led the freshly bandaged Freeman into the room. Peter measured DeKalb's reaction as they walked the General over to where he was standing, prepared to interpose himself if she moved. But she didn't.

Her only reaction was a look of self-consciousness. When Freeman sat down, she said contritely, "I'm sorry, Jim."

At the sound of her voice, the General jumped out of his chair, backed up, and lost his balance. Using only his body and arms, Peter steadied him.

He cried out, "How could you, you little—" But, knowing that, if ever there was a time when he needed to keep his wits about him, this was it. So, Freeman quickly composed himself.

Angela was reluctant to explain herself in the presence of the Greenshirts but finally offered, "Honestly, Jim, I don't know. Call it the culmination of a lot of things." Lowering her eyes, she said, "I *am* sorry, though."

It was obvious to Peter that she was playing to the audience, so he decided to do the same. He bellowed, "Sorry! That's not what you said before. You called it revenge. You said he was your *father!* And Collier's, too."

Angela stood to object, but before she could Peter turned to the assemblage and cried, "That's right. The *father* of your beloved commander—and the Attorney General here—is this man." He extended his pinioned hands toward Freeman. In a very loud voice, he added, "Years ago, without his knowledge, they were manufactured from his DNA in an *acid hatch*." He added some volume to the last two words.

Then, turning back to DeKalb, in the same full-throated manner, he said, "You know, Madam, we Christians have a superstition that goats—or is it more correct to say *pollies?* Anyway, we have a superstition that they cast no shadows. But, clearly, your reflection over there belies that notion." He pointed to her shadow slanting black and ominous against the east wall of the library, obliging all to look. Then, he went all in. There were speculations in both the Church and academia as to the truth of his next statement, but he didn't care. This was *his* chance to frame *her*. He declared, "What *is* certain, though, is that creatures like you and your vile brother never received the Divine spark at birth. So, I ask—if you're *not* of God's creation, who *can* we thank for you?"

Turning again to the guards, he clarified his point. "Understand me well. *These goats have no souls! They're a race of devils.*"

The room fell silent. The only sound was that of the wind rushing through the shattered windows of the great hall.

Then, from the door, came another sound. The sound of applause.

It was the Rottweiler.

"Bravo!" he shouted, removing his headgear. "Bravo!" Entering the room, he snarled, "But now it's time for the big dog to eat."

He walked over to where the priest was standing and said, "I hate to interrupt this minstrel show, but these men have work to do."

To the troopers who heard the priest's stunning disclosure, he said, "Gentlemen, you have rendered an invaluable service to the Party and to the country. Now we must return to our civilian duties until another opportunity presents itself. I'm told our best avenue of escape is north on the Lexington Avenue line, but it's imperative that you cross the river as soon as possible. The Williamsburg Bridge is still open. Again, I thank you for your noble efforts and wish you good luck. *Dismissed!*"

In seconds, the only people left were the three prisoners, Collier, and a detail of ten Omegas who entered with him. They formed a wide ring around the three captives and ordered Peter to sit down.

Collier strutted around the hall for a minute, surveying the damage. Turning back, he said jokingly, "I hope we got all the good stuff out of here."

This breezy reference to his master plan was less intended to entertain his men than to buy him time. Deep down, he was rattled. He had arrived too late. The "awful secret" was now being disseminated to all points. It was certain to spell trouble. So, naturally, he was drawn back to the man who revealed it.

Standing before the big priest, he glowered at him, fuming, "I've waited a long time for this, maggot."

The eyes that glowered back at him, however, were not those he remembered from the stairwell. These had grown teeth of their own.

Before Collier could go on, General Freeman broke in. "You know, Sonny," he said, matter-of-factly, "until today I often regretted not having a son."

Collier moved over to his sightless captive and, in a pained voice, said, "I bet you'd never say that to your daughter." Checking himself, he said, "Oh, not the dancer, mind you. I mean the one you rogered up in your penthouse last night."

Angela's reacted instantly. She came out of her chair, roaring, "How dare you!"

"Oh, sit down, Angela," he shot back in disdain.

His tone was so hostile that she thought it best to obey. Then, just like out on the promenade, his demeanor suddenly changed. Removing his gloves, he looked at her affectionately and sighed, "I had such high hopes for us."

Pointing to the priest, he said, "He may think we haven't any souls, but we know better—don't we? We are the soul of a new humanity. *The Transhuman Race!* Made in man's image. Unfettered by the corruptions of conscience and free to explore the limits of knowledge and power." He shook his head with feigned dejection. "And here I've given you the chance to climb this mountain with me and you reject it. It's so disappointing. Not long ago, you gave a speech in this very room describing 'the new Eve.' Remember?"

Angela nodded.

"You stated she must be *hard.* I believe your word was 'unromantic' and given to a steady diet of apples. I was inspired by it, so much so I decided it was time to act." Making a grand gesture toward the hole in the ceiling, with arms extended, he proudly proclaimed, "You could say I did all this for you."

The gravity of this admission, however cryptic, was lost on no one, including his men. "And, when I saw your reaction to meeting our *father* for the first time, I thought for sure you had what it takes. But now I can see I was wrong. The words you spoke were just that— *words!* You dare speak of the New Hyperboreans. *You're a fraud!* The opiates of prestige and affluence have left you weak. My hope was that *our* progeny would transcend the infirmities of parasites like this." He waved his hand toward Freeman and Bernard. "But you lack the hardness requisite of the new Eve. Now, my only recourse is to find another mate."

Breathlessly, Angela cried, "A *mate*! Are you insane?"

But Sonny replied impassively, "I think not. Unless I'm mistaken, Cain's wife was also his sister. Or his mother. Wasn't she?"

The question hung unanswered. Collier stepped toward the priest.

"Care to weigh in on it, kingfish?"

Peter said nothing.

"I didn't think so."

Returning to Angela, he changed tack, saying, "All my life, I've listened to people blowing hard on the issue of freedom as if it were some treasure to be shared. But freedom is power, and it's never shared for long. If you look at it in the cold light of day, history shows that the acquisition of power is the highest of all human aspirations. Power over nature. Power over men. Power over oneself. Power over God. But man is a creature born to serve. A natural coward. A strutting rabbit."

He stood over his sister, his eyes burning.

"Not all men, mind you, but the exceptions are rare. The Caesars, the Khans, the Stalins. And what set them apart wasn't their love of God and neighbor. No! It was their refusal to kneel, to slip the bonds of conscience and use whatever means necessary to gain and hold power, regardless of how illegal, immoral, or sanguinary."

The Omegas stood listening, hands clasped behind their backs, wondering if they heard their leader correctly when he admitted to the bombing. The three prisoners, all seated, were positive that they did.

Pointing to Bernard, Sonny continued his diatribe. "He condemns us for having no souls. To him, we are the spawn of Satan. But, what would you expect him to say. Souls are his stock-in-trade. His competitive advantage. Without them, he's bankrupt. And though an inferior man might despair at having such a charge leveled against him, I sing: *Alleluia!* In truth, if I had a soul, *I'd sell it*, if only to free myself from the yoke of his spidery God."

He paused momentarily to dwell on his hatred for the priest. Then, he turned back to his sister. "I dream of a new communion of saints, Angela. The technological perfection of the species. A new breed of ultra-humans who refuse to be poisoned by the mythologies of the past, who give rise to a new line of priests that will put an end to the suffering that has stunted human progress since the dawn of creation. I should think a Humanist like you would welcome the change. But then, you have a flaw that keeps you from realizing your dreams."

She said, "And that is?"

"*A conscience.*"

Then, abruptly, he positioned himself in front of Freeman. "As for you *General*, I no more want you for a father than you want me for a son. I can understand why Angela doesn't share my passion for the new order. The old one served her well. She was fortunate to land in a good home where she parlayed her inheritance into a successful career. But not me. I was cast adrift. I became the garbage I was forced to eat. The streets of Miami taught me a lot about charity and compassion—which is to say, *nothing*! Whatever dreams I had for a better life were snuffed out the day you pissed backward on me. I honestly don't know who I despise more, you—or him." He pointed at the priest.

"I never pissed backwards on you," Freeman replied. "You disobeyed a direct order. I tried to mitigate that by my testimony, but the recordings did you in. It was all a matter of record. We both know you were lucky to get off with a reprimand."

"Lucky?" he replied with astonishment. "You call that *luck*? I was all but cashiered. And, no matter what spin you put on it now, it was *you* who brought me down."

"I gave you a direct order, Sonny. I told you *twice* not to let your boots hit the ground. But you went in like Sergeant Rock."

"And how was that different from what you did in Port-au-Prince?

I was only trying to emulate you. Didn't you violate a direct order that day?"

"I did. But it was a different situation. My entire command was shot up in the first hour. We were down to our non-coms."

"And you won the Star."

"But not for that."

"And I got the boot."

"Not because of me! I didn't shoot Rita Scanlon. *You did*! Why don't you just accept that responsibility—like you did the bombing?"

At this, Collier shot a concerned look at his Omegas. He glanced at Angela and the priest, whose accusatory looks gave added potency to the General's words. Only then, did he regret the vanity of alluding to the bombing as his handiwork. He couldn't recall precisely what he said, but rather than draw further attention to it, or risk sounding defensive, he ignored the General's remark. "It was an accident. My weapon discharged as I was coming down the stairs."

"That's a lie."

This time, his accuser was Peter Bernard.

Collier turned and shouted, "Ah, the Black Whale!"

He moved off Freeman and stood over the Jesuit, declaring, "I might have sailed the oceans until the end of my days in search of you, and, instead, you swam straight to my ship! Can it be that your God is as eager to see you die as I am?" He backed away slightly, then with feigned sympathy, said, "But then, the reward for a lifetime of loyalty and service is often betrayal, isn't it?" He looked at Freeman as he said it.

"I serve at his whim," the priest rejoined.

"And I'll make sure you give the last full measure of devotion." Wagging his finger back and forth between the general and the priest, he said, "Both of you."

This thinly-veiled threat disturbed his Omegas. It was beyond their loyalty to think him responsible for the bombing. When, at first, he implied that he was, they thought they mistook him. But when General Freeman confirmed what they heard, they paled as one. Though they were callous and brutal men, it spooked them to think how their allegiance to the man who bombed New York would be judged in the courts of this world and how their hand in the death of a priest might be judged in the next. And, since many in this group were also ex-military, in the case of Freeman, like Collier's staff before them, their misgivings were only magnified. If the Rottweiler's intent was to murder his prisoners, they wanted no part of it.

Unlike the Omegas, James Freeman ignored Collier's threat. Though his perceptions were limited, he listened to the proceedings carefully and sensed that, if he could keep Sonny talking, he might think better of exacting his revenge—especially against Bernard.

Calmly, he asked, "Why did you refer to me as the king of hearts before, Colonel?"

"Those weren't my words. That's how our mother described you in her journal. I thought it appropriate, though, in light of your career."

Freeman thought: *So she was keeping a journal.* He asked, "And is that what the death cards symbolize?"

"Very good, General! It's hard to slip anything past you. Not without lots of B.S. and bootlicking."

Freeman pressed on. "You're right, Sonny. I've been very foolish. But of all the stupid, selfish things I've done in my life, nothing compares to what you're doing." Removing the death card he found in Branch Brook Park from his breast pocket, he remarked, "Like I said this morning, it's fitting you chose the suicide king because that's what your decision to bomb this city was—*suicide.*"

He flipped the card in the direction of Sonny's voice.

"That may be," Collier acknowledged, eschewing any further attempt to shield his guilt. "But there is *one* thing that compares: your decision to provide the clay from which I was formed. And, regardless of whether or not you did it willfully, *I'm your son.* So, really, the only question is—who's *more* suicidal? You or me?"

He flipped the card back at Freeman, hitting his bandaged face.

Noticing that the Omegas began backing away after Freeman's reference to the bombing, Peter attempted to widen the breach between them and their leader. "I wonder how the rest of the Pathfinders will react when they learn that the blood of millions is on their hands?"

The ploy worked. Three of Collier's Omegas bolted.

"Stand fast," Sonny ordered the remaining seven.

Reaching down, he grabbed Peter by the throat. "Say what you will, soon *my* progeny—the free spirits—will rid the world of bloodsuckers like you." Then, releasing his grip, he bent down slightly, staring into his captive's eyes and cackled, "Sorry you won't be around to see it, nigger."

And, with that, the whale spewed.

In his face.

Collier went white. Quivering uncontrollably, he wiped off the spit, turned as if to move away, then suddenly drove his fist into the priest's throat.

Peter fell from the chair to his knees, wheezing for air. His assailant landed a few kicks to his mid-section, shouting emphatically as he did, "Be sure to . . . thank your . . . *brother* . . . for his *boat*."

Peter fought to remain on all fours knowing that if he didn't, the man's boot would soon find his head.

From where she was sitting behind him, the other half of the Marynkova clan jumped up, grabbed Sonny's arms, and attempted to pull him away. Her efforts were futile. He quickly wrestled free, then dropped to one knee and put the priest in a choke hold.

Once again, Angela tried to stop him. "Help me!" she screamed.

At that moment, Tully entered the hall. Together with a pair of Omegas, he quickly subdued Collier, prying his hands off the priest.

"What's going on?" the blinded Freeman kept repeating, his tone more strident with each repetition. But that question and the other entreaties he made went unanswered.

The Omegas continued to restrain Collier for a minute, during which time Peter recovered his breath.

Cognizant of Collier's reference to the stolen Wavejammer, Angela talked soothingly to her brother, as one might try to appease a vicious dog when confronted in the street. "Sonny, this is so beneath you."

Because he was tiring, it worked. Composing himself, Sonny shook off the guards, combed through his hair with both hands and stood bristling over the priest.

"Enough of this," he growled, drawing a TL-25 from his holster. "We're wasting time."

Angela grabbed his arm. "No, *don't.*" Again, the Omegas restrained him.

He faced his sister and replied facetiously, "I thought you were an advocate of capital punishment?"

Imploringly, she looked at him and panted, "Please—don't kill him."

As he calibrated his pulse gun, she argued, "*Think what you're doing.* Think how a bunch of no-count Jews, from a filthy, little backwater turned the execution of a criminal into the greatest fraud in history. And now, *two thousand years later,* a billion of these imbeciles are still drinking his blood like savages and kneeling in adoration of his poisoned tree. *A billion of them!*" Pointing to the priest, she warned, "Don't dignify the life of this scum. Let him live. His death will only bring him sainthood, not disgrace."

In a gesture worthy of Mussolini, Collier folded his arms, stuck out his jaw, and nodded haughtily. "It's a good point," he said. "Why attach any importance to this termite?" He took a step back and announced, "I have a better idea."

When the Omegas released him, he barked at the faltering priest, "Look at me, you coward."

Defiantly, Peter refused.

"I said, *look—at—me!*"

Without hesitating, he fired a downward shot. The charge was set on low, but, nonetheless, it knocked the big priest flat.

Again, Angela tried to restrain her brother, grabbing his arm. "No!"

She had nothing but loathing for him or the Jesuit, but it was outweighed by the fear of being cast as an accessory to murder. She was playing to the audience, again, which was now down to five Omegas and Collier's XO.

"Get up," Collier ordered the priest. "And look at me when I talk to you."

Grimacing, the big priest struggled to rise, his body convulsed with pain. He retched as if to throw up. Gaining his knees, he could go no further.

In a voice that dripped of civility, Collier said, "I'll spare your life on one condition, Bernard: that you renounce your king."

There was a rustling among the Omegas, a sense of relief. Thinking the end of this ill-conceived detour was near, they were anxiously awaiting the order to disperse. Their swaying flashlights lent a surreal quality to the scene.

"Gentlemen, *quiet!*" Collier shouted, raising his arm. "Show some respect. We're about to witness the defining moment of this man's life."

Extending his hand down to the priest, he urged, "Kiss it, Bernard, and you're free to go."

Without looking up, the priest adamantly shook his head.

"Go ahead," Collier urged with mock gentleness, "Kiss it. Renounce your foot-washing God and live."

But the priest didn't move. Neither did anyone else. Except for the wind, the library was still.

In the silence, Collier's frustration mounted.

He shouted, "Look at me, you worm." Then, losing control again, he screamed, "*Look at me!*"

Reaching down, he grabbed the priest by the chin and jerked his head up. "*Don't tempt me*," he seethed. Then, taking a knee and fronting his prisoner with the same fiendish eyes that had instilled such terror in him years before, he added, "*I own you, nigger.*"

But, this time, Peter wasn't cowed. Defiantly, he croaked, "*Begone, Satan!*"

Startled, the Rottweiler dropped his grip and stood up. Simultaneously, he maxed out his TL-25, aimed it at the crown of the priest's head, and fired.

A nimbus of blue and white fingers danced wildly. In that instant, every cell in the Jesuit's body exploded, boiled in a stream of electrons. Before the heinous arc disappeared, before he even hit the floor, the priest was dead.

Like a boy who scorches ants with a glass, Sonny studied the body of his victim, enthralled by his power over life and death. When he finally looked up, he saw that only one of his men, Tully, was still with him.

Probably hasn't got the guts to run, he thought.

Then, without relent, he turned to the blinded Freeman and said, "Now, let's get back to you, Pap. Angela, I think we should—"

But she was gone, too. "What the hell?!"

Before he could get the words out, the General made his move. Knowing from the telltale hum that Collier used a TL-25 on Bernard and that it would take a minute to recharge, he locked onto the voice that commanded the death of millions, leapt from his seat, and with his good arm outstretched and his last ounce of strength, hit him in the side, knocking the pulse gun loose, and driving him to floor.

The younger man quickly rolled his blinded "father" over and hit him several times in the face as hard and as fast as he could. Freeman's collarbone broke again as he hit the floor, so he was virtually defenseless against the rain of blows. Straddling the old man, Collier fumbled for his knife. His intent was to dispatch him in a manner up-close and personal, but he never got the chance.

When General Freeman hit Collier, Tully unsheathed his Ka-Bar and approached the combatants unnoticed. Then, as Collier drew his knife, in a practiced motion, he grabbed the Rottweiler from behind and slit his throat. Just as quickly, he disengaged and assumed a defensive posture.

Collier clutched his neck in astonishment. The gushing blood told him the wound was mortal. Swinging around madly, his blood sprinkling Freeman, he faced his assassin.

"You filthy bas—"

Choking, he rose to his feet, staggered, then dropped his knife. Lurching forward a few steps, his cold, wolfish eyes rolled and, in a half-pirouette, he crashed to the floor.

As he passed into eternity, he muttered softly, "I am—"

Hearing Collier's words and sensing his end, the battered Freeman wiped the man's blood from his face, crying, "Help me! Please, somebody—help me!"

Tully bent down and took him by the arm, raising him to his feet. "It's alright, General. He's dead."

Then, after ensuring that Freeman was fit to travel, he started for the door of the great hall, saying, "Let's get out of here."

After a few steps, Freeman stopped. "What about Bernard?"

"He's dead, too."

The old man stood silently for a moment, then corrected him. "No, he's not dead."

"But sir—"

"No," Freeman insisted, shaking his head. "It's only the last of earth."

Then, he was led by Tully out of the library and into the street where, unseen to him, Patience and Fortitude still stood watch.

Seventy

When she reached the steps of the library, the Attorney General never looked back. She sprinted to the south, dodging both bodies and autos, and covered six blocks before she slowed down. The Fashion District was dark and foreboding, but, mercifully, the rain was letting up, which made it easier to navigate. It miffed her how quickly she got winded, given her daily regimen of swimming and aerobics, although the rank air was overpowering. Spying three suspicious, hulking figures up ahead with flashlights, she stopped short. Needing a minute to catch her breath and plan her next move, she ducked through a shattered, revolving glass door into a once-swanky department store that, mercifully, was clear of bodies because it was closed on the night of the blast.

For a second, she paused, adjusting to the light. The walls were covered with partially-shattered mirrors. Ceiling tiles, broken glass, and papers covered everything. Toppled mannequins were still clothed in their Vera Wang and Lazaro gowns, although much of the jewelry in the showcases had been looted. The metallic smell of ionization loomed menacingly in the air, displacing the fetid smell of human decay. She found a dry spot behind one of the sales counters in the far corner of the store and sat down on the carpet with her back to the wall.

Under her body armor, she was perspiring heavily. It activated the smell of the oil she used to pleasure . . . *her father*? Assuming, by this time, he was dead, she wondered how close she had come to her own demise.

"What difference does it make?" she whimpered, fighting back the tears. "Everything I've worked for is gone. I'll never clear my name. And, even if I do, I'll forever be branded a goat."

There was no way she could resume her duties at Justice. Surely, President Gonzales, on the advice of his nettlesome Chief-of-Staff, would urge her to resign. The risk and embarrassment of retaining her in the cabinet would be too great.

Now, even if Jim Freeman was still alive, her plan to extort another round of patronage from him was moot. More than a dozen Greenshirts heard the priest's disclosure. *The story will be out by morning.* Eventually, their accounts would be corroborated by the recording of her vile congress with the General at the Armitage. And once Collier's letter went public, the scandalmongers would dredge up evidence of Freeman's youthful dalliance with Sonya Marynkova and draw a straight line from there to their one-nighter in Palm Beach. *That should add an element of seaminess to the whole thing—and breathe new life into the rumors of how and why he promoted me.*

"Leading to outright charges of corruption," she muttered aloud. To compound matters, was there any doubt in the minds of Freeman's security detail what they were doing in his suite last night?

Last night!

Like Freeman before her, the Devil's Advocate marveled at all that had transpired in just twenty-four hours. In that short span, it seemed that all of man and nature had turned against her—the wind, the rain, and the stench in league with Freeman, Addison, and Collier.

Then, there was Bernard. Sitting motionless, she flashed on the hideous, blue arc that suspended him in a final tick of agony. In death, the spirit of the man she framed in the Spark Park bombing clawed at her unshakeable belief in the equality of the grave. She asked herself: *If there is a final judgment, how can the oppressed and the oppressor expect the same verdict? Doesn't Justice demand that his tomb be opened?*

She quickly dismissed the thought: What do I care about life after death? Hers was a more immediate concern, and she framed it aloud. "The real question is if there's any life after *Sonny Collier!*"

Sadly, with no hope of redemption on either front, she reeled under the weight of her ponderings. No matter how she tried to shake it off, she couldn't escape the absurdity that her life was the result of a genetic experiment. Learning that her mental capabilities may have been "downloaded" only compounded the trauma. *If cattle are engineered to produce more meat and wheat to yield more grain, why was I created? And what of my achievements? Were they predestined? Or did I squander my destiny?* It never occurred to her that these questions must be answered by the children of God, too.

Her dearest beliefs also became suspect. *Were they formed by a free conscience? Or the deft arrangement of proteins?* And, as a product of advanced chemistry, to whom should she seek redress if she was so inclined? The laboratory in which she was hatched? It led her, inevitably, to ask: *Am I really even human?*

And with that came the greatest irony of all: *How will America react when it learns that the humanity of its most distinguished Humanist is, at best, questionable?*

Into the slough of despond, she slid even deeper. As she did, she tried to ascribe some meaning to her plight. But there was nothing to impute. The law and science, the reasoned tenets of her creed, were useless to her now. All was for naught.

Her fleeting glimpse, moments before, into the Court of Final Equity made her doubt herself. Had anyone told her yesterday that she had no prospects for salvation, she would have agreed whole-heartedly! Like most materialists, she thought of death as an eternal sleep. Now, for the first time in her life, she knew the poverty of spirit required for passage into the Kingdom, but, at the same time, no passage was imminent. According to the priest, even if she got on her knees at that moment and begged for the mercy of God, it would be futile.

I'm not one of his children.

After a few moments of contemplation, she cried softly but defiantly, "Nor would I want to be!"

Reaching into one of the cargo pockets on her protective armor, she pulled out the rain-stained photograph of her mother that Sonny gave her, but it was difficult to see by the blue light of her forearm dosimeter. Under the register at the sales counter were several drawers. It occurred to her that there might be a flashlight in one of them.

Rising to her knees, she opened the top one. As she poked through it, the base of her palm slid across the blade of an unshielded box-cutter, leaving a two-inch gash. She gave a yelp and quickly examined her spurting wound, thinking, *I must have hit an artery.* Then, feeling around in the drawer, she found the razor, and taking it out she sat back down without making any effort to stop the profusion of blood.

It rekindled memories of cutting herself as a child—at the time, to release the hurt of being treated like a Pomeranian. But her troubled past seemed so trivial compared to her current affliction. "If only I *was* the child of Evan and Joanne DeKalb," she cried.

Then, impulsively, but with certitude, she unzipped the sleeve of her armored left wrist, took up the razor, and cut again.

"Not a humbled life but a proud death," she concluded, albeit, in her heart, she knew that by her godless faith she had stripped herself of the hope she needed to weather this private midnight.

Not all hope, though. She still aspired to an eternal sleep as the spurious blood of the Freeman-Marynkova union gushed from her arm.

Seventy-One

Sunday, July 10 (9:23 P.M. EDT)
Bryant Park, New York City

On leaving the library, instead of following the other Omegas over to Grand Central Station, Joseph Tully led General Freeman around the south side of building into Bryant Park. Over the slippery flagstones and through the charred and denuded plane trees, they proceeded slowly.

It wasn't long before the pain from his re-broken collarbone caused Freeman to falter, so Tully sat him down on a bench across from the old carousel, saying, "We'll follow our previous route, back down 42nd Street."

"Who are you?" Freeman asked.

A pigeon landed at Tully's feet as he replied, "You don't know me, sir, but I know you. My uncle was with you during the Haitian Campaign. I believe you knew him as *Irish.*"

Ten minutes later, an advance unit from the 24th Armored intercepted them as they crossed Sixth Avenue. That ended the old man's ordeal. He was so overcome that he broke down. His bandage concealed only the tears that flowed from his darkened eyes but not the pain and sorrow etched on his face over the death of his friend.

An MT-51 med-evac was standing by in West Orange to airlift him out of the city in the event he was found. It was summoned.

While they waited in the dark for it to arrive, the General told the captain of the armored unit, "Go back to the library, and recover the body of Father Bernard. Collier, too. Tully will show you the way.

Bring them back to Philadelphia." Then, pointing to where he thought Tully was standing, he added, "And make sure this man gets back there, too. *Safely!*"

The chopper landed in the park's quadrangle while they were gone. As Freeman boarded, he issued the final directive of his military career. "Hahnemann Medical Center, Philadelphia."

The pilot offered no resistance. He wasn't about to question an order from a former president; not even the governor of the Atlantic Cordon.

As for the Lion of Jaffa, he had but one priority: to see his daughter.

Or, at least, to hear her voice.

Seventy-Two

"Have any copies of these been made?"

"No. Both items were delivered straight from the airport," replied Avery Milliken.

The questioner was the President of the United States. Sitting atop the *H.M.S. Resolute* desk in the Oval Office was Sonny Collier's letter to Stewart Addison and the tiny recorder found in Angela DeKalb's shoulder bag. Katie Holman, Steve Nunn, and Michel Paggiano, the President's senior counsel, were present. They had all read the letter and listened to the recording of Angela's penthouse interlude with General Freeman.

The President addressed Paggiano. "Is there anything that leads you to believe a crime was committed?"

He replied, "It's hard to say, Mr. President. With regard to the recording, it doesn't sound like much more than a spirited romp—unless you have a problem with this shipment of prisoners the two of them talked about. In my estimate, it all sounds quite innocuous." With a pained expression, he said, "But the letter's another thing. In light of Collier's insurgency, his allegation of common parentage is problematic, even if it does imply that DeKalb wasn't aware of it. If it's made known, it will have major repercussions."

"Is there any requirement or precedent that demands we make *either* known?"

"Offhand, I'd say no. In fact, doing so may violate Angela's privacy rights."

Everyone knew how damaging the letter and recording would be to the reputations of both Freeman and DeKalb and none of them, not even Boomer Holman, wanted to see that happen.

The content of both was so sensitive that, on learning of it, Milliken, who counted the AG as one of his only friends, demanded his agents route it immediately to him in Washington. He, in turn, brought it directly to Nunn, who requested an audience with the President. Now the question was what to do with them.

Gonzales' first reaction was to destroy both items on the spot. *But that wouldn't do*, he thought. *Too many witnesses.* So he did the next best thing.

He told Paggiano, "Hold these in your safe until the Attorney General returns."

Nothing ever survived entry into the senior counsel's safe.

Seventy-Three

Sunday, July 10 (9:59 P.M. EDT)
Hahnemann Medical Center, Philadelphia

Lena Walker was about to make her direct appeal to Sonny Collier via the press corps gathered in the Armitage ballroom when General Hawkins called personally with the news of her father. At first, she swooned. But, within minutes, she was bouncing off the walls. Then, in front of everyone, she fell to her knees in tearful gratitude.

Thirty minutes later, when she and Jack Clancey arrived at Hahnemann, they found out that "Teddy" was already in surgery. It took three hours. On hearing of his capture earlier that day, his neurologist from Charleston had contacted the regimental surgeon of the 301st Infantry and told him of Freeman's brain tumor. Both doctors then conferred with the chief of neurosurgery at Hahnemann, who implanted the tumites that night.

It was past two o'clock in the morning before Freeman was situated in his room. Shortly thereafter, Lena and Jack were permitted to see him.

"Daddy?" Lena said, entering the room.

The General stirred. "Lena," he muttered groggily, reaching for her with his free hand. Although his eyes were heavily bandaged, he imagined her sweet smile. After a bout of coughing, and though it hurt to talk through his swollen jaw, he added, weakly, "Can you forgive me?"

She grabbed his hand and kissed it. "Have I got a choice?" she blubbered.

With mock disgust, her father replied softly and slowly, "Answering a question with a question. You've been hanging around Clancey too long!"

His former press secretary piped in. "She's a natural, General."

Freeman smiled on hearing his voice. "Jackpot!"

Then, squeezing Lena's hand, he added, "I'm so happy you're here."

"I am, too, Daddy."

Clancey said, "You gave us quite a scare, General."

"I gave myself one!" With another hard cough, he wheezed, "But it'll all be in the book—right, Jack?"

Clancey, never at a loss, replied, "If Lena would just get out of here, we could get started right away."

Amidst the laughter, the General asked, "Do you think a book about a blind old fool will sell?"

Before Clancey could crack wise, Lena interjected, "But, Daddy, you only lost one eye. The right one has a lacerated cornea. The doctor said it should heal in a few days. He said whoever treated you during your capture prevented any infection from setting in. In the morning, they're going take the bandage off and test your vision, but the prognosis is good."

She omitted the fact that the nerves in his left eye were damaged beyond repair.

Freeman got excited. "That's great news! I . . . I can't believe . . . why—"

He was, again, overcome. Silently he offered a prayer of thanks. It felt good. After a minute or so, he said, "It's comforting to know that all I *really* am is an old fool. Maybe I'll see things better with one eye than I ever did with two."

Then, excitedly, he said, "I must tell you about Peter Bernard." He proceeded with a rather disjointed account of their capture, pausing occasionally, but it heartened Lena and Jack to hear that the surgery hadn't impaired his memory or ability to think.

When he came to Angela DeKalb's attack, Lena interrupted him to ask, "What made her do it?"

He simply replied, "She had her reasons."

Freeman didn't know how long it would take for the world to learn of Sonya Marynkova's hatch, but he didn't suppose it would be that night. He would have time to discuss DeKalb's "reasons" with his daughter in the morning, before it hit the wires. No matter. When the time came, he intended to confront the problem honestly and with humility.

His description of what took place in the library was limited to what he had heard and what little he had gotten from Tully as they waited for the med-evac in Bryant Park. Although he passed right over it, Collier's admission that he was responsible for the bombing amazed Lena and Jack. Instead of dwelling on that, though, the General continued talking about the priest and the friendship that blossomed between them over the course of a few long hours. He even quoted his final, ominous statement.

"I'll never forget it," he said. "Never."

A doctor entered with two nurses, who administered the sedatives that age and injury failed to supply.

As they said their goodbyes, he began to doze off but, ever the General, he asked sleepily as they departed, "Before you go—anything to report?"

"It stopped raining," said Clancey.

Epilogue

Monday, July 11, 2061
St. Francis of Assisi Parish, Philadelphia

L uke Monaghan exploded in tears as he finished the letter.

When Peter Bernard's body was recovered from the library, the missive he wrote to the press in the event of his capture was found in his pocket. General Freeman had Jack Clancey pass it on to Turk Findlay at the *Los Humanos Examiner*, and after some editorial squabbling they published it the next day. Within hours, it appeared on virtually every news-related website in the world. It read as follows:

July 7, 2061

My dear countrymen and women,

My name is Peter Bernard. I'm an African American. I'm also a Professed Priest of the Society of Jesus, with a doctorate in American history. You may be aware that, over the years, I've been involved with numerable protests against commercial eugenics. I have been twice convicted of crimes. The first time I was guilty; the second time I was not. Between them, I spent almost seven years in prison. Now, I'm wanted for questioning in the bombing of New York. That I am innocent of this horrible crime will someday be proven. On that day, I pray you will also begin to see me for what I really am: a loyal dissident, not a traitorous subversive.

For the most part, the letter was a protest of his innocence. But, toward the end, almost out of habit, he fired off what would prove to be his final volley at the Humanists, saying:

> *Whereas the Christian looks to the past for the source of his salvation—specifically, 33 A.D.—the Humanist looks to the future. He imagines a day when he will be delivered **from himself by himself** through advances in law and science. But, such deliverance never comes. And it never will.*

Again, he assailed the "dictatorship of relativism" and the "anything goes" mentality it produces, especially with regard to the sciences:

> *Together with their wards, the eugenic engineers, the Humanists are herding humanity into a technological blind alley with no prospect of escape. Just as the physicist destroyed New York, the geneticist will destroy the rest of us. The cumulative effect of his unbridled and amoral experiments will be the same as bombarding a nucleus with electrons. When it splits, it will set off an irreversible chain reaction. In my opinion, that reaction, regardless of whether it is biological, chemical, or otherwise, will be cataclysmic. It will signal the end of the human race.*

Ultimately, the questions he raised at the end of the letter concerning transhumanism caused the greatest controversy:

> *As we enter the dawn of it-story, I often wonder how long God will abide the threat posed to His creative monopoly by the geneticist? Where will He draw the line on prideful follies of man? When will His long-tested mercy and grace be exhausted?*
> *No one can answer.*
> *So, in the hope that our world grows wise before it grows old, I'll close by repeating Gabriel's warning in* Paradise Lost. *After*

relating the story of how Lucifer's minions were driven from Heaven like a herd of goats, and about the threat he now posed to humanity, the affable angel tells Adam:

'Remember, and fear to transgress.'

Yours in Christ,
Fr. Peter Bernard, S.J.

THE END

About the Author

Ken Schultz is the president of a Colorado company which oversees investments in distribution, finance, and real estate development for a group of Greeley-area investors. A few years ago, alarmed by the secular movement's progress in undermining the Judeo-Christian foundations of our culture, he decided to write a novel that would explore what might happen to our country if they succeed. **A Race of Devils** is the result.

One of seven children from a Catholic family who grew up in New Jersey and survived such dislocations as the Baby Boom, the Death of God, and disco, Mr. Schultz is optimistic about the future of the United States—but only to the extent that it returns to its spiritual roots. Married to his wife of twenty-eight years, Pat, and blessed by two children, Harry and Lynn, he dedicates this book to *their* children, who will, no doubt, come of age in an America wholly unrecognizable from that of his youth.

www.ingramcontent.com/pod-product-compliance
Lightning Source LLC
Chambersburg PA
CBHW032139010726
47494CB00002B/273